Love Finds You

in

Lonesome Prairie

MONTANA

Love Finds You
in
Lonesome Prairie
MONTANA

BY TRICIA GOYER
& OCIEANNA FLEISS

**Doubleday Large Print
Home Library Edition**

summerside
PRESS

This Large Print Edition, prepared especially for
Doubleday Large Print Home Library, contains
the complete, unabridged text of the original
Publisher's Edition.

Summerside Press, Inc.
Minneapolis 55438

Love Finds You in Lonesome Prairie, Montana
© 2009 by Tricia Goyer and Ocieanna Fleiss

ISBN 978-1-61664-670-7

All scripture quotations, unless otherwise noted,
are taken from the The Holy Bible, King James
Version (KJV). Scripture quotations marked ESV
are taken from The Holy Bible, English Standard
Version® (ESV), copyright © 2001 by Crossway
Bibles, a publishing ministry of Good News
Publishers. Used by permission.

The town depicted in this book is a real place, but
all characters are fictional. Any resemblances to
actual people or events are purely coincidental.

Cover design by Müllerhaus Publishing Group.

Back cover photo of Bear's Paw Mountains taken by
John Wickland, www.johnwickland.blogspot.com.

Printed in USA.

Dedication

....

For John, whose love for God first caught my
eye and touched my heart.
Tricia Goyer

For my Michael, who shows me the love of
Christ every day.
Ocieanna Fleiss

Acknowledgments

....

Many thanks to Keith Edwards from Big Sandy, Montana, who opened up his home to us and shared his stories. To Hank in Fort Benton, who cracked open the historical archives for our research. What wonderful help we received! Also thanks to Amy Lathrop for all the reading, input, and help, as well as Annette Irby, Dawn Kinzer, and Veronica McCann, who saved us from several blunders and challenged us to strive for excellence.

Thanks to our wonderful agent, Janet Grant, and the awesome Summerside staff: Carlton Garborg, Rachel Meisel, Jason Rovenstine, and Connie Troyer.
Tricia Goyer and Ocieanna Fleiss

Acknowledgments

Thank you to my amazing family: John, Cory, Leslie, Nathan, Andrea. And Grandma too. Thanks for loving me and supporting me on this journey.

Tricia Goyer

I want to add an extra thanks to my old friend Carlton Garborg, who contacted me on Facebook and set this dream in motion. I'd like to thank my mother-in-law, librarian Nellie Fleiss, who made herself available to seek out my toughest research questions. And to our church intern, Matt Barker, for his help with Isaac's sermon— substitutionary atonement's a good thing to remember! I don't know if I could've finished this book if it weren't for Rosalyn Kay introducing me to Kangen water, which annihilated my migraines. Also I'm incredibly grateful for my friends at

ACKNOWLEDGMENTS

Emmanuel Orthodox Presbyterian Church and HIS Co-op (especially Lorena) as well as others who supported, encouraged, and prayed unceasingly for me. Thanks to my mom, who would've been so proud of me. For my sweet kids, Benjamin, Gabrielle, Christian, and Abigail, who put up with Mama being busy, and especially to my husband, who sacrificed more than seemed humanly possible for me to finish this book. Finally, to my faithful savior Jesus Christ, who fully paid for all my sins with His precious blood.

Ocieanna Fleiss

**Not to us, O Lord, not to us,
but to your name give glory.**

PSALM 115:1 ESV

At one point in Lonesome Prairie's history, a debate arose between locals about changing the name of the vast cattle and sheep land to Paradise Prairie. The country grass spreading out limitlessly toward the horizon and the glassy lake may have seemed paradise-like to some. And it was certainly a more pleasant name. But an old homesteader named Hard Scrabble Ole wrote to the *Bear Paw Mountaineer* saying anyone who wanted to change the name to Paradise was foolish. "I find it purty lonesome out har," he wrote, "twenty mile from any place in a 10 X14 shack that just got tar paper on outside and an ol' cook stov. It Lonesome Prairie alright." His argument won, and the name Lonesome Prairie stuck. Although Lonesome Prairie no longer exists as a town, we found a wealth of information from the enthusiastic locals, proud of their area's homesteading and ranching history. If you trek to north central Montana today, you'll find it much as Hard Scrabble Ole described it, "purty lonesome."

Tricia Goyer and Ocieanna Fleiss

Chapter One

"Feels like I'm sleeping in a covered wagon with all this shaking." Nineteen-year-old Julia Cavanaugh forced her eyes open. "At least that's what I think it would feel like." She spied one of the orphans under her charge—twelve-year-old Shelby—shaking her flimsy mattress. Her iron-framed bed squawked as it shook.

"Wake up, Miss Cavanaugh. Mrs. Hamlin just left with Mr. Gaffin, and we all think he's gonna ask her to marry him. Do you think so?"

The sun streaming through the tall,

second-story window of the Open Door
Home for Destitute Girls, a privately
owned orphanage on upper Manhattan,
told Julia the day had started without her.
An orphan herself, now running the place
for the owner, she brushed a strand of
dark hair from her eyes.

"Oh, Shelby." Julia wiped the sleep
from her eyes and smiled into the freckled
face staring eagerly at her. "Give me a
moment to wake before you go asking
such things." Julia stroked the girl's
cheek, her heart seeming to double
within her chest with love for the
youngster.

The embroidery sampler she'd fallen
asleep working on still lay at the end of
her bed. She picked it up and eyed the
image of a small house she'd copied from
Godey's Lady's Book. Above the house,
she'd stitched the words *Home Sweet
Home* in fancy script. Gazing around the
broad room lined with small metal cots
and bustling with little-girl chatter, Julia
noted the embroidered pillowslips,
carefully pressed—albeit dingy—curtains,
and dandelions smiling from scavenged
jam-jar vases. She'd done her best to make

the room pleasant for the girls—and herself. She glanced at their faces and smiled, gladly embracing her role as caretaker.

A less-than-subtle "ahem" from Shelby reminded Julia she'd been asked a question. She glanced at her young charge, still perched on the end of her bed. "What did you ask?"

"Finally." Shelby eyed her with mock frustration. "I said, do you think they will get *married*—Mrs. Hamlin and Mr. Gaffin? Haven't you noticed the way they look at each other?" Shelby's cheeks hinted of red. Her golden hair was already fixed in a proper bun, her hands and face washed, and her simple dress clean and pressed despite its patches and stray threads.

"Shelby Bruce." Julia shook her head, as Shelby's two-year-old sister Beatrice wiggled onto Julia's lap with a squeal. She planted a firm kiss on the top of Bea's head.

"Married? I don't think so," Julia continued. "Mrs. Hamlin would've told us—told me—if she was being courted. Mr. Gaffin's just an old family friend." Julia wondered where on earth the girl got the notion that their headmistress wished to marry.

Although they have *been spending a lot of time together.* Julia pushed the thought out of her mind as little Bea shuffled to a stand, planting her pint-sized feet on Julia's thighs. "Fammy fend!" She pointed a chubby finger at her older sister, Shelby.

"All right, Bea." Julia plopped the toddler on the floor and swiveled her toward the small bed she shared with Shelby. "Time to straighten your bed." Then Julia eyed the twins. "Charity, Grace, would you two virtuous girls fetch fresh water for the basin?"

Shelby pushed away from the bed, wrinkled her brow, and thrust her hand behind her as if to support her back—a perfect imitation of their middle-aged headmistress. "Now where did I put my spectacles?" Shelby clucked her tongue as she waddled forward.

Laughter spilled from the lips of the girls around the room.

Encouraged, Shelby scratched her head. She plopped down on her bed then hopped up again as if surprised, pulling imaginary spectacles from under her rump. "Oh!" she squealed. "There they are."

The laughter grew louder, and Julia pursed her lips together to smother the impulse to laugh along with them. She planted her fists on her hips. "That's enough. All of you know what must be done before breakfast." The girls' laughter quieted to soft giggles hidden behind cupped palms as they scattered to do their chores.

Shelby lingered behind, her form now straight and her eyes pensive. "Maybe she forgot to tell you, Miss Cavanaugh." The young girl gazed up at her. "The way they look at each other—it's like my ma and pa used to, that's all."

Julia folded a stray yellow-blond curl behind the girl's ear. "Don't worry, my sweet. If Mrs. Hamlin was getting married, we'd be the first to know."

Julia hoped her own gaze didn't reflect the sinking disquiet that draped her. Mr. Gaffin was a rich world traveler. If there was any truth to Shelby's suspicion, Julia couldn't imagine he'd let Mrs. Hamlin continue to work with orphans. Perhaps they'd get a new headmistress.

Or maybe the girls would be separated, moved to new homes. . .

If Mrs. Hamlin got married, all their lives would be radically changed. And if Julia had to leave the orphanage, she had no idea what she would do. She swept that painful thought away and steadied her gaze at Shelby. She couldn't hide her true feelings from this girl. Julia took Shelby's hand and answered as honestly as she could.

"I don't think she'll get married, but if she does, God will take care of us, like He always has." Julia lifted her chin in a smile. "And really, Mrs. Hamlin may be forgetful, but no one could forget that. I sure wouldn't."

Ardy, a shy Swedish girl, removed her dirty sheets from a small bed and then approached, taking Julia's hand. "Don't ya think you'll ever be gettin' married?"

"Actually, there is something I've been wanting to tell you all. . . ." Julia leaned forward, resting her hands on her knees.

The two girls eyed each other in surprise, and Shelby's brow furrowed.

"Come closer." Julia curled a finger, bidding them.

"What is it?" Shelby asked, her eyes glued to Julia.

The girls leaned in. "I'd like to tell you. . .that there's a wonderful man who's asked me to marry him!"

The squeals of two girls erupted, followed by the cheers of nearly three dozen others who'd been quietly listening from the stairwell.

"There is?" Shelby reached forward and squeezed Julia's hand.

Julia let out a hefty sigh and giggled. "No, you sillies. Well, at least not yet. Someday. Maybe."

Shelby pouted "But you said. . . "

"I said I'd *like* to tell you I had a man. I'd sure like to, but of course since I don't, I'm happy to stay here with all of you."

The girls moaned.

The squeak of the front door down on the first floor of the Revolutionary War–era home-turned-orphanage drew their attention. They waited as Mrs. Hamlin's familiar chortle filled the air, along with a bash and clang of items—hopefully food and supplies that she'd picked up.

"Julia!" Mrs. Hamlin yelped. "Julia, dear, where are you?"

"Coming." Julia hurried down the stairs to help the older woman.

Julia neared the bottom of the steps and paused, trying to stifle a laugh at the sight of the twinkly eyed woman sprawled flat on her back. Scattered boxes and bags covered the donated rug.

"Mrs. Hamlin! What on earth? Why didn't you get a steward to help you?"

"Oh, I didn't want to be a bother." She cheerfully picked herself up. "I was in such a hurry to show you all what I'd bought. And to tell you my surprise. Such a wonderful surprise." Julia eyed the boxes and noted they were from R.H. Macy & Co. More than a dozen boxes waited to be opened, and she couldn't imagine the cost.

"I found just what the girls need, and on sale!" the headmistress exclaimed.

What they need is more food—vitamin drops, too—and maybe a few new schoolbooks. But Julia didn't dare say it. And somehow God's hand of providence always provided.

"New clothes, I gather. That *is* a surprise."

"But only half of it, dear." Mrs. Hamlin

rubbed her palms expectantly. "I also must tell you my news. The best news an old widow could hope for."

Julia followed Mrs. Hamlin's gaze toward the idle youngsters who'd gathered on the staircase to watch. Her eyes locked with Shelby's, then she quickly looked away. "News?" The muscles in Julia's stomach tightened.

"Girls," Julia shooed them away with a wave of her hand, "you know better than to eavesdrop. Off to chores with you. We'll have breakfast soon."

The girls started to scurry off, but Mrs. Hamlin halted them with her words.

"No, no," her high-pitched voice hailed. "Come back. This news is for all of you." They circled around her, and she tenderly patted their bobbing heads.

"What is it?" Julia wasn't sure she'd ever seen Mrs. Hamlin's cheeks so rosy or her eyes so bright.

"I'm getting married!"

Chapter Two

It wasn't the first time a rowdy frontiersman had brandished a gun during his worship service. Parson Isaac Shepherd tried not to take it personally. His jaw tensed, and he laid the black, frayed ribbon across the page he was reading from the Psalms. He shook his head as he placed his leather Bible on the bar behind him. *Not another interruption.* It seemed he never made it through a whole sermon. *Next time, I'm gonna start with the call to repentance. Switch things around. . .all they ever hear is the setup.*

Preaching in livery stables, ferry docks,

open fields, as well as saloons—like this afternoon—brought complications. But the exhilaration of seeing these rough folk growing in their faith made him even prouder than the time he rode ol' Sven Flatness's bronco for ten seconds. It's why he'd come. Why he'd chosen the lifestyle of an unmarried circuit preacher.

Then there were days like today.

"I swar, Parson Ike." Forty-year-old Horace Whitbaum, who looked as though he'd never bathed in his adult life, raised a toothless plea. "I never done jumped his claim. I don't even know whar 'tis." The desperate prospector's hands, rough from years of mining the hills of the Montana plains, reached for the rafters, unleashing a pungent odor from his armpits.

"You did take my claim. I seen ya." Another scruffy man with patched shirt and trousers, Giant Jim Newman, directed his Colt Peacemaker at Horace's heart.

Isaac gazed at the nervous faces of the dozen faithful parishioners sitting along two lone benches on the mud-splattered, ash-sprinkled, beer-splashed floor. Young Jed Robertson and his mail-order bride

huddled their new baby in their arms.
Beside the Robertsons, Mr. Milo
Godfrey, Isaac's only ordained elder in
the seventy-mile circuit, sat with his
Indian wife and seven daughters. Isaac
wondered which girl Mrs. Godfrey would
try to marry off to him this week. Didn't
seem to matter to her that the oldest
wasn't even seventeen yet. Though the
girls were nice enough, everyone should
have known by now that Isaac wasn't the
marrying type.

The man sitting in the corner, Milo's
stepson, Mr. Warren Boyle, was the only
one not seemingly troubled by the episode.
Years earlier, Milo had married a young
widow and adopted her son, Warren.
After his young bride died, he'd raised the
strong-willed boy as his own, but Warren
had never embraced the Christian faith.
Still, Milo loved the young man and even
made him partner in his business. Not a
church-going man, Warren laid low at the
far table nursing a whiskey. Even with the
shouting, he didn't look up to see what
the commotion was about.

Giant Jim's black mustache waggled
over his lip as if he were winding up for a

spit. "I swore to kill that villain dead as a can of corned beef, and I aim to do it!"

"Jim." Isaac spoke firmly as he approached the towering man. "Go ahead and shoot him if you want to be strung up at sunrise. The vigilantes will be on you faster than a hungry hawk on a lame jackrabbit. You know for yourself they'd hunt down anyone, guilty or not, in hopes of a bounty. And from what I hear, that new circuit judge doesn't take too kindly to bar fights. So if you don't want the so-called law to take you away on the next train, you better put the gun down." Isaac positioned himself between Jim and Horace.

Giant Jim ignored Isaac's warning. Instead, his black eyebrows scrunched into an arrow as he glared at the preacher. Though Isaac tried not to show his fear, his chest squeezed tight like a lariat around a steer. *Lord, protect us. Protect Your flock.*

"Listen to Parson Ike," Horace sputtered, cowering behind Isaac, his grimy hand on the parson's shoulder. "I swar. I don't even know whar yer claim be."

Isaac broadened his stance and patted Horace's hand, attempting to calm him.

At first Horace had been one of the "drinkin' saints." Those were the folks already planted on barstools when the preaching started, who hung around out of laziness. Then, after a few months, the grungy forty-niner had meandered up after the sermon with a question.

"If yer Jesus died on the cross fer my sins, why can't I jest do wat I want?"

From then on, Isaac had enjoyed surprisingly deep discussions with the hard-edged man. Horace's growth was just another reason Isaac marveled at the far-reaching, saving power of God. It also affirmed his decision to decline the assistant parson's position offered to him when he was fresh out of seminary in St. Louis.

"I swar it, Parson, I ain't done him no wrong. I've been minin' my own land. . .I swar!"

"Please don't swear, Horace," Isaac whispered then glanced to his elder Milo, whose hand clasped the ivory handle of his parlor gun. A seasoned rancher, adept at dealing with hot-headed prairie folk, Milo would be quick to help settle the situation.

Giant Jim shook his head. "Not *that* claim—"

"Wait!" A woman's voice screeched from the doorway behind them. "It's me he wants, Horace. I'm the claim Jim's talking about."

Isaac glanced back, seeing the woman's large frame silhouetted by the sunlight streaming in through the door. Mabelina Tigard, a woman of easy virtue and a sometimes visitor to church, stepped through the door. Strands of red hair escaped from a shabbily pinned-up bun. She straightened her tattered, faded emerald dress as she glanced around the room. Her jutting chin hinted of pride for creating the commotion, yet the timid look in Mabelina's eyes as she stepped through the door told Isaac she wasn't nearly as proud of her reputation.

"Mabelina," Giant Jim yelled, "git outside!"

"Horace." Mabelina threw her hand to her hip. "He knows about us! I told him everything. Just last night I told Jim I didn't know if I could continue seeing him because you wanted to marry me." She winked at Horace and bobbed her head, her gaze pleading.

Horace glanced up, his eyes wide as wells. "What're you talkin' 'bout, woman?"

"I told you he stole my claim." Giant Jim pointed his thumbs at Horace and Mabelina. "Those two been fraternizin' behind my back. I was gonna make an honest woman outta her. And he done asked her to marry him." Jim spit on the floor. "That's what I call jumpin' my claim."

Mabelina slipped her hand behind her back, and Isaac noticed a streak of silver.

A gun? Why does she have a gun? Isaac's shoulders tightened as he remembered the rumors. Mabelina's temper, it seemed, was often as fiery as her hair, and though she'd never shot a person, her bullets had shattered shot glasses, busted windows, and drilled into wooden ceilings in her effort to make sure she got her point across.

"Can you repeat that?" Mabelina tilted her head flirtatiously. "You were gonna do what, Jimbo?"

"You heard me. I was gonna ask you

ta marry me, my little marmot, but then Horace—"

Horace squeezed Isaac's shoulder tighter. "She's as crazy as a loon!"

Isaac ignored Horace and focused on the two lovers. And the two guns. It was obvious Mabelina was making the whole thing up to unleash Giant Jim's jealousy. And, Isaac guessed, to spark a fire under him that might spur him to a real commitment. Well, it had worked.

Isaac cleared his throat. He'd had enough of Mabelina's drama. She may have merely been seeking attention from her man, but those were real guns and real bullets. If it didn't settle down soon, someone would get hurt. "Jim, will you please put the gun down? Miss Mabelina still loves you, and Horace has made it clear he doesn't want your claim. I'm sure you can work this out."

Mabelina batted her eyelashes at Jim, a coy smile curving her lips.

Horace didn't notice. His gaze was narrowed on Giant Jim's barrels pointed at his chest. "I wouldn't hitch up to that used-up ol' cow in a million years. I'd rather marry my mule!"

31

Mabelina's jaw dropped and her eyes bore down on Horace.

The saloon patrons hooted with laughter.

"Bet you would, Horace," Jed Robertson called out. "You do love that ol' mule of yours."

Horace turned on them, a fierce glare shooting from his eyes. "Don't be disrespectin' my Ladygirl. Besides, I got me a wife comin'."

"You been sayin' that for ten years!" From his table, Warren Boyle smirked, apparently interested now. He finished his whiskey in one swallow.

"How dare you talk about me like that!" Mabelina's face reddened to a shade just slightly lighter than her hair color. She stamped her foot and raised her gun above her head.

A burst of movement caught Isaac's eye. Moving with the quickness of a man half his age, Milo jumped from his place on the bench and knocked the gun from Giant Jim's hand.

Seeing his chance, Isaac lunged forward in an attempt to disarm Mabelina. Before he made it two steps, a gunshot split the air. As Isaac spun around, the Indian women screamed, a baby's cry followed, and from outside a dog—Isaac's black-and-white sheepdog, Calamity—yapped.

Isaac's gaze jerked to the screaming women, and his heart clamped into a tight panic as he watched Elder Milo slump off his seat to the dirty floor.

"Mabelina!" Giant Jim dropped to his knees. His eyes drilled the redhead. "Why'd you do that?"

The woman gripped the pistol in her hand with two fingers, as if she were holding up a dead rattler, her face etched with fear. "I aimed at the ceiling. I just wanted to get your attention. I didn't like y'all besmirchin' my good name." Her shoulders slouched. "It must've ricocheted."

Isaac hurried forward and took the gun from her limp hand.

Chapter Three

Julia stepped into the backyard, sprawling compared to other gardens of New York City. The afternoon's humid heat bombarded her like the worries in her heart. Since Mrs. Hamlin's announcement this morning, Julia's mind had swirled with questions. How soon was the wedding? What would happen to the orphanage? To her?

And especially, what was the purpose of those white dresses from R.H. Macy's? They looked like traveling garments. Where were the girls going? To another orphanage? Mrs. Hamlin wouldn't send them to a state-run facility in the horrid Five Points District, would she? Julia shuddered. Many of those poor children were abused and forced to work in the sweatshops. Some lost their lives.

And where was Julia's dress? Not that she particularly cared if she received a new gown, but it was strange. There had been no package for her. Mrs. Hamlin wouldn't give all the girls presents and exclude Julia. Not unless she had a reason. *Oh, Mrs. Hamlin, what are you doing?*

But the headmistress had swept out the door as quickly as she'd arrived, leaving her queries unanswered.

Julia peeked behind her at the handful of girls who followed in a staggered line, like ducklings following their mother. Julia loved her role as stand-in parent, and she knew her bright-eyed girls found stability and reassurance in her care of them, even if her efforts were far from perfect.

She wiped a drip of perspiration from her forehead with the back of her hand.

"Miss Cav'naw." Beatrice tugged on her apron. "What I do? I help, too."

Book lessons done for the day, garden

duties now commenced. They'd weed and hopefully harvest carrots, radishes, and lettuce for tonight's dinner. Although it was still early for the growing season, this crew of future gardeners could always uncover a good supply of ready-to-eat vegetables.

"Absolutely, Bea." Julia tweaked her chin. "Why don't you put the weeds that Shelby pulls into the wheelbarrow? Does that sound good?"

Bea nodded.

After making sure each child labored a proportion more than she played in the dirt, Julia strode to the small flower garden closer to the old stone house. As she dug her hands into the soft, moist soil, a thousand alternatives about their future worked through her mind. The headmistress's plans mystified Julia, as her well-intentioned—though sometimes disastrous—plots often did.

Chuckling softly, she remembered the plentiful ways the woman's love had bungled Julia's life. Like the time she gifted Julia with music lessons from a woman who fell asleep in her chair as soon as the piano started plunking. One, two. . .*snore.* Or the time she trimmed eleven-year-old Julia's hair so short that most people thought she was a boy. Yet, at least Mrs. Hamlin had a loving heart. At least she tried.

"Julia! Julia, dear!" Mrs. Hamlin's musical voice summoned her.

Julia bolted upright, her eyes shooting toward the door. Finally, she'd get some answers. She quickly brushed dirt from her hands and turned to the girls. "I'm going inside, my sweets," she said. "Keep working. You're doing a fine job."

"We will, Miss Cavanaugh," Shelby called.

Julia sent her a reassuring smile, knowing Shelby's mind most likely spun with questions, too.

"Julia!" Mrs. Hamlin sang again.

"Coming, Mrs. Hamlin." Julia scuttled up the steps to the back door. "I'm coming."

Entering through the kitchen where two girls scrubbed the breakfast dishes, Julia crossed over the white and black tile into the lobby. The room was once a fine parlor in the home of a wealthy doctor. Mrs. Hamlin sat on the burgundy floral settee. The tall, arched window behind her seemed to protect those inside and welcome the lonely. Next to Mrs. Hamlin's feet sat a large box wrapped in brown paper.

"Come here, my darling." She opened her arms, beseeching her for an embrace.

Julia gladly accepted, cherishing the love of this woman who was not her mother but was the nearest semblance she'd known for the past eight years. She took in Mrs. Hamlin's sweet smell of rosewater and relished the feel of her cotton shirtwaist.

Mrs. Hamlin gently rocked Julia as if she were holding a baby. "I know this is hard for you." Her voice quivered as emotion burbled toward the surface. "I love you, my dear, dear girl." Then she gripped her even tighter, squeezing Julia's breath away.

Mrs. Hamlin finally let go, and Julia sucked in air.

"I love you, too." Julia smiled. "Even if you do choke me with those mighty hugs."

"Now, my dear." Mrs. Hamlin jiggled as she sat up straighter. "We have a lot to talk about."

The scent of freshly planted roses outside the window, mingling with the faint waft of smoke from factories and trash barrel fires, reminded Julia of how glad she'd been to live and work here—distant from the bleak life faced by many orphans housed in the downtown asylums.

Julia tucked a stray hair behind her ear. "I'm glad. I have so many questions."

Mrs. Hamlin tilted her head and sandwiched Julia's hand between hers. "Of course, you poor dear. You're probably wondering how it came about that I got engaged."

Fear of having to listen to one of Mrs. Hamlin's long and shifting stories gripped Julia. "Mrs. Hamlin—"

The headmistress smoothed her dress and adjusted in her seat. "Our story beats all—how we fell in love. How hard it was to keep it a secret. But Mr. Gaffin insisted, saying it would worry you if you knew about the two of us. Isn't he the kindest of men?"

In unison, Julia's right foot patted the hardwood floor and her fingers drummed on her lap. "Yes, I'm sure he's very kind, but—"

"And ours is the loveliest romance in all creation. It would make a wonderful novel—like those dime novels you read. Hmm. . . Maybe you could write it down. Wouldn't that be amazing?"

Julia's tapping amplified. If she had to listen to the whole story of how they met. . . "I can't wait to hear it, really." Julia produced a smile. "But perhaps first you could tell me what those dresses were for. They look like travel dresses for the girls. Are they going somewhere?"

"Oh!" the blissful woman squeaked as if she were a train forced to come to a screeching stop. A silent moment followed, as the wheels churned in a different direction. "You mean I didn't tell you what's going to happen?" Her forehead crinkled and her eyes squinted.

"No, you just told us you were getting married. Then you left."

"Strange. I thought I did." She grasped Julia's hands. "I'm so excited to tell you, Julia. It's the perfect thing. Just perfect."

Julia wanted to yell *Just tell me!* but clenched her teeth, fighting the outburst.

"Well, Julia, the girls are taking a great adventure. Mr. Gaffin, you know how rich he is. He doesn't want me to work anymore, the dear man. So we're selling the orphanage, and all the girls are going—oh, I'm too excited to even tell you!"

"Please, Mrs. Hamlin." Julia pressed a hand to her stomach, sure she was going to be sick.

"They're going out West on the orphan train!"

Julia gasped in surprise. "The orphan train?" Varied feelings barraged her, and she slumped under their weight. She reviewed everything she'd ever heard about the trains. The Children's Aid Society—a Christian organization her own father had worked for—persuaded the big rail companies to transport destitute children away from the evils of the city. They believed the best place for an orphan was at the table of a farmer. Why hadn't she thought of that? It's just the sort of thing the headmistress would do.

Mrs. Hamlin tilted her head. "It's for the best, I think. They'll get out of this deplorable town for good. It's no place for the poor, you know."

Grateful her biggest fear—that the girls would be sent to another orphanage—was averted, other emotions rushed in, filling that fear's place. She stared out the window.

Julia appreciated the rationale behind this choice. Sending the girls west to live in the vast countryside—where they could breathe fresh air, learn good, honest work, and be embraced by a family—was the best decision for everyone. She knew it was.

It was good the girls would have homes, families, yet a deep ache took root as she considered mornings without waking up to the sound of their laughter or heading to bed at night without the many whispered prayers.

More than that, she'd no longer be their caretaker. Julia placed a hand over her chest as if attempting to protect her heart. Yet she knew it would do little good.

The girls' voices floated in and with each one—so familiar, so much a part of her life—Julia's mind struggled to believe she would have to give the responsibility of their care to others. Her glance moved over the room as she took in the comfortable, happy home she'd resigned herself to living in for. . .well, forever. This place, the girls, Mrs. Hamlin—they were home to her. The only home she'd known since her parents' deaths. How would she ever find a new one?

She kissed the headmistress's hand. "You've done the right thing."

Relief softened Mrs. Hamlin's face. "I didn't want you to be disappointed in me, Julia. I hope you don't think me too selfish."

Julia regarded the dear woman's eyes, bordered with lines of laughter and love. "Of course not. I'm happy for you. For the girls."

Plans and details for the coming days flooded Julia's mind. She'd have to pack their things. What would they need? And who would see them safely to their new homes? Suddenly, nothing in her world seemed more important than traveling with the girls on the train, being their guardian one last time. She'd never have peace until she scrutinized the families for herself, made sure each girl was put into the care of upright, stable, and kind parents.

"Now." Mrs. Hamlin lifted the heavy package, handing it to her. "Your gift." The woman's double chin bulged as an excited grin filled her round face. "You didn't think I forgot you, did you?"

Julia received and opened the box. A beautiful blue wool flannel skirt, a new white silk blouse, and a light wool tan jacket—perfectly suited for travel—were arranged inside a sturdy leather valise. Also in the box was a fancy tan and blue parasol. Julia's heart skipped. "Does this mean. . . ?"

"You're going with them!" Mrs. Hamlin handed her a ticket.

Julia embraced her again. "Thank you. Thank you so much. I couldn't imagine letting them board the train without me."

"You're welcome, dear." She clapped her hands. "I know how much you've wanted to go out West."

Julia smiled. "I only wish my father could take the trip with me. He always wanted to, you know."

"He'd be so proud of you, Julia." Mrs. Hamlin touched Julia's cheek. "You go, my dear, and experience all the things he never had the chance to."

"I will. . .and then I'll come back to New York City, and you." An idea emerged in Julia's mind. "Mrs. Hamlin, when I come back, may I work in your new house? I could do whatever you wanted. Cook, clean, wait on you."

Mrs. Hamlin's eyes sparkled. "Of course. Of course you may stay with us. You know how I love you."

"Thank you. I don't know what I'd do if I couldn't return to you." As long as Julia could cling to that assurance, she'd be able to face what was to come.

"But," Mrs. Hamlin clutched Julia's arm and tugged her closer, "I think you may not want to come back. You may find something even better on the prairie. Something involving romance, adventure—even love may surprise you." Mrs. Hamlin let out a loud laugh, and Julia giggled along, unsure why.

Julia shook her head. "No, all I want is to see the girls safely to their new homes and then come back here. . .to *my* home."

A clang sounded from the kitchen, and their cook emerged. "Soup! Soup!"

"Oh my," Mrs. Hamlin said. "You'd

45

better get those girls fed. We'll talk some more later."

"But. . .I have more questions." Julia touched Mrs. Hamlin's arm. "When is your wedding?"

Mrs. Hamlin folded up the brown papers. "Uh, let's see, what's today? Monday? Oh! It's tomorrow! Yes, I love Tuesday weddings, don't you? So much to do! Actually everything's done, thanks to my dear Mr. Gaffin."

A knock pounded on the door, interrupting them.

Julia eyed Mrs. Hamlin then stood and opened the door. A middle-aged couple appeared before her, their chins tilted upward and their eyes fixed beyond her as if she didn't exist. The man wore a fine black suit with tails, and the woman's dress rivaled anything Julia had ever seen, even in the Montgomery Ward catalog.

"We're here for a Mrs. Hamlin," the man announced. "Looking at the house."

Julia showed them in and then motioned to the headmistress. "She's right here."

"Oh! You're the folks thinking of buying

the place." Mrs. Hamlin shook their hands, then turned to Julia. "They want to make it into a dog and cat hospital. Isn't that lovely?"

* * * *

A week had passed since her conversation with Mrs. Hamlin, now Gaffin. The moon's dreamlike beams cast faint shadows on the street as Julia sat on the cool stone steps outside the orphanage.

The church bells chimed midnight. Though her own cobblestone street was quiet, the rumble of hooves and wagons and the shouts of impatient hansom cab drivers blended in a comforting dissonance from a few blocks away. Sounds she'd fallen asleep to for the last eleven years.

A crisp breeze swept through, and Julia rubbed her arms to fight off the chill. An old newspaper fluttered and caught on the breeze. It landed against the boardinghouse across the street, leaving *The New York Times* plastered on the stone wall.

Julia remembered an article she'd once read in the *Times* about a woman who had traveled from Albania to the United States with her five young children, all under the age of eight. She'd longed to escape her abusive husband, a leader in her home city's government. When she arrived on Ellis Island, the authorities arrested her for kidnapping and wrenched her children from her. The article said they had to pry the woman's fingers from her baby, who was screaming from the pain of his mother's grasp. The picture in the paper showed the woman crouched on the ground, her hand reaching out as if to reclaim her children by sheer will.

Heaving sobs shook her shoulders. Each night since Julia had learned that the orphanage would be closing, she'd sat on these steps in the humid May air and wept. Tonight she wiped tears from her cheeks and shuddered, struggling to calm herself. In a few hours she'd march her thirty-two girls to Grand Central Depot. At nine o'clock they'd board the train, and in the weeks to come at each stop along the way, it would be her duty to hand her girls—whom she loved as sisters, daughters—into the care of unknown families.

I don't know how I can do this. She

longed for her father's strength—his sturdy build, his warm smile, the safety she so clearly remembered feeling in his arms—and her mother's wisdom and sound advice.

"Trust the Lord." Julia twisted a strand of her long dark hair around her finger as she repeated her mother's words. "You may not always understand His ways, but He will never leave you."

Julia pulled in a shaky breath. *God, please don't leave me.*

This was the last night she'd spend in New York for a long time. She stood and gazed at the brick buildings lining the cobblestone streets. So familiar. In her mind's eye she traveled one last time through her weekly routine. She imagined the vendors who knew her by name when she shopped down by the waterfront. Her Saturday afternoons with the girls at Central Park. And church on Sundays. She glanced at the tall steeple of their church looming above the city buildings like a shepherd watching its sheep. She'd miss it.

This was also the last night she'd be able to weep over losing the girls. Once on the train, she'd smile, laugh, sing, and play. She'd be strong and brave and never let her dear children see a hint of her concern. She'd be their mother.

One last time.

Chapter Four

"Oh, Lord, no!" Isaac flew to his friend's side.

Milo's wife, Aponi, dashed to her husband. No tears flowed. Only quick determination showed on the woman's face. Her hands, skilled from years of caring for wounded and ill neighbors and travelers, tore through Milo's several layers of shirts. A bullet wound, ripped and ragged, trickled blood onto his chest. Aponi gasped despite her obvious attempts to remain controlled. From Milo's strained breaths, it was clear the bullet had punctured his lungs. Isaac just hoped it had missed his heart. Blood pooled on the floor.

"Move chairs, girls." Aponi pressed the skirt of her fashionable Sunday dress into the wound in the left side of his chest as she directed her daughters. "Ruth, watch little ones. Alice, boil water. Dusty!" she hollered at the bartender. "Whiskey!"

Isaac knelt next to her, silently awaiting her instruction.

"Need bandages," she said in a deep, focused voice, without shifting her eyes from her husband. "And your shirt."

Isaac took off his only preaching shirt and handed it to her, smoothing his undershirt. Yet he knew Aponi's attempts to stop the bleeding wouldn't be much help if Milo's internal organs were damaged. It was the bleeding in Milo's insides—if there was any—that would take his life.

Pressing his shirt on top of her dress, Aponi tilted her face toward Isaac. Her gaze pierced his. "Pray, Parson Ike. Pray."

"I am praying." He glanced up to see Horace, Giant Jim, and Mabelina sitting at one of the poker tables holding hands. Their eyes were closed and Giant Jim's mouth moved. "And so are they." He pointed to the table. "We're all praying."

He gazed into his friend's pale face and panic gripped him. He couldn't lose Milo. *Please, Lord.*

Years before, Milo had attended the same seminary as Isaac, but the Lord had called the successful sheep rancher to support the church rather than to lead it. How would Isaac survive without his mentor's advice, love, and support? *Please, Lord. I need him.* Need his wisdom, sound judgment, friendship.

And Milo was also the only person who respected Isaac's decision to stay single. What a relief to have one person in Montana Territory who didn't badger him about finding a wife.

Mary, one of the near-grown daughters, rushed to her father's side with a water bucket and washrag in her bronze hands. She mopped his forehead. "You will be fine, Papa. You will be fine." A strand of long black hair slipped from her braid to her moist cheek. She pushed it behind her ear, wiping the tears as she struggled to speak words of comfort.

Isaac longed with every impulse to

comfort Mary and the other girls. *O Lord, please don't let these children lose their father.* He knew the years of loneliness that losing a parent would bring—knew the missing never went away.

Isaac laid a hand on Mary's arm. "You're doing well, Mary. You are a good nurse."

After a moment, Milo's eyes pried open and he uttered a name. "Warren."

Milo's stepson rose from his place at the corner table. All color had drained from Warren's face. "Dear God." It was an exclamation rather than a prayer. Milo motioned with his hand and the stocky, young upstart approached and knelt next to the wounded man.

"I'm here." Warren awkwardly patted his arm. "What do you need, Father?"

"We never finished my will." Milo's voice was hoarse. "Promise me you'll take care of Aponi and my girls. Make sure they have enough." A rasping cough seized him, before he finally added, "And the school. I promised to pay for the supplies. Take care of that."

"I promise." Sweat dripped from Warren's forehead onto Milo's neck. "Don't worry."

"Isaac," Milo called next, dismissing Warren.

Isaac leaned in. "Don't give up, my friend." His throat felt thick. "We have too many plans. I can't do it without you." He grasped the sheep rancher's hand—a hand rugged from years of laboring with sheep in the fields, a hand gentle from shepherding God's people with kindness and love.

His and Milo's plans emanated from their passion to redeem this land. Both men knew the only way to "civilize" the West was for God's sanctifying work to change men's and women's hearts. They'd spent many prayerful hours laying out a plan. First, Isaac would preach the Word at every opportunity—something he craved to do.

Second, the orphan train. Isaac had persuaded the Children's Aid Society to send a crop of destitute city children right here to Big Sandy via the train depot, and the first group would arrive in less than a month. He'd hoped many families would take in the children, and many here and in the surrounding townships had promised they would. Caring for orphans had been Milo's dream. *Let him live to see the children arrive. . .please, Lord.*

Their final dream was the school. How many hours had they spent planning it? The school that would be a refuge for prairie children and Indians alike. The school that would keep children with their families rather than away in boarding institutions. The school that provided another step toward spreading the gospel to the western territories.

"Isaac. . .finish all we started. . . ." Milo struggled for breath.

"I won't give up, my friend," he said, but doubt gripped him. Without Milo Godfrey, could there be a school? Would everything else crumble as well?

Now wasn't the time to worry about that. Isaac needed to exemplify strength for his parishioners—to help and comfort his sheep.

Milo turned to his daughters. As Isaac stepped back to give them a moment together, a woman's jovial voice called from the swinging door of the saloon, an awkward interruption to the somber setting. "Where's my brother?"

Isaac looked up and saw his two

sisters and their families standing in the doorway. Milo's daughters crouched around their father as Isaac slowly rose and walked toward the door.

Isaac herded his family onto the porch, and their countenances fell when they noticed the pain on his face. The blood on his hands.

Miriam, his oldest sister, peered past him. Her belly bulged with child, and Isaac's nephew Josh hung on her leg. Seeing Milo on the floor, her hand flew to her mouth as if blocking a shriek. "Is that Elder Godfrey? Oh, Isaac, what happened?"

Isaac explained.

"We came to hear your sermon," his sister Elizabeth added, "but one of the wagon wheels got stuck in a rut. All the mud . . ."

"In a week it'll be dry," Isaac commented absently.

"Go to him," Elizabeth whispered, patting his hand. "We'll pray."

His family joined those at the table in prayer, and Isaac returned to Milo.

His friend's face had faded to a pale, greenish hue. His breathing faltered.

Aponi's eyes fixed on Isaac, her face stoic, but her brown eyes brimmed with fear and disbelief. "He will not live."

"I know." Isaac wrapped an arm around her.

"Isaac," Milo mumbled, his blue eyes opening. "You need a wife. A good one like Aponi."

He's delirious. Isaac nodded. "She is a wonderful woman," he said, avoiding Milo's point. "God has blessed you."

"That vow you made is stupid. 'It is not good that the man should be alone.' Remember." The dying man grumbled and lifted his head slightly.

"Stupid? I thought you understood why I—"

"I was trying to let you figure it out yourself." Milo coughed, and a trickle of blood seeped from his lips. "But you need a good woman. Find one. Promise you'll try."

"I'm sorry, my friend, but I can't." Isaac patted Milo's hand. "Don't worry about that now."

"Promise."

Isaac shook his head.

"Stubborn!" Milo's head sank back, his eyes closing again.

After what seemed like a long time, Milo's eyes opened and searched for his wife. "Aponi, I love you."

"Your eternity. It has come." Her voice faltered. "God is with you."

Isaac opened his Bible to Psalm 23. "'The Lord is my shepherd. . . .'"

And by the end of the psalm, as Aponi rested her head against her husband's chest, it had stilled.

Chapter Five

"I'm bored," Liza, one of the five remaining girls, whined in her Italian accent. She twisted around in the bench in front of Julia and rested her chin on the tall seat back. "Three weeks is too long to sit on this rumble-tumble train. My *sedere* hurts."

Julia rubbed her forehead and threw the girl a cynical glance. "I know. We've heard you at least a dozen times. . .today." Julia patted Liza's dark hair. "And it's so much harder on you than the rest of us." Julia winked.

Liza stuck out her lower lip. "It is, Miss

Cavanaugh. It really is. I'm more *miserabile* than anyone."

"Oh brother." Shelby, sitting next to Julia, rolled her eyes.

Julia tucked a bookmark into the last Wild West novel she'd brought with her, *The Prairie Knight*, and returned it to her valise. She was eager to find out what happened but knew she'd have to wait.

Soon I'll have lots of time to read. She needed to focus on the five girls who remained. The twenty-seven others had already gone to new homes at stops along the way.

At first Julia had been uncertain of the system. Who were these men and women who would be taking her girls into their homes? Thankfully, the nun from the Children's Aid Society had explained everything to her. Local clergy recommended the families, who promised to provide the girls with the same food, clothing, education, and spiritual training as they would any biological children. Yet Julia had wondered if her girls would receive the same love.

Julia's worries had eased when she'd met the mothers and fathers along the way. Their tender gazes, open arms, and kind words assured her the girls would be cared for.

At the next town, the five sitting in the seats around her would also be handed over to new parents. And though she was grateful the girls would have new families and hopeful futures, she realized that for the first time in her life, she'd be alone. The wrench tightened in her stomach, but Julia chose to focus on the present—not her fearful future. *I should enjoy my girls while I still have the chance.*

"Did you finish your stitching, Liza? Do you need help?"

"I'm sick of stitching!" Liza pinched her lips together. Standing, she announced, "I'm going to ask the conductor how much longer. He's sitting in the dining car. I saw him."

"That's fine. A walk'll do you good." Julia blew out another breath and focused on the never-ending Montana prairie that passed by the window like a blurred Monet painting.

"Maybe you should go, too, Miss Cavanaugh," Shelby said. "That conductor's so handsome."

Julia's cheeks warmed, thinking of the tall young man who'd "conducted" them on their journey. "He does have really nice eyes, doesn't he? So dark and mysterious."

"I think he likes you."

Julia shook her head. "Oh, he's just a friendly sort. Besides, who'd want a husband always gone on another train trip? Not me." She adjusted in her seat. The trip *had* been long, and if Julia was honest, her *sedere* hurt, too.

Over the miles, the landscape had transformed from bustling cities of the East to small townships to miles of uninhabited wilderness. Small depots and water towers located at regular intervals provided brief respites from the smoky, chugging train ride. For the first few days, the girls had awoken every time the train stopped to have its water tanks refilled for the steam engines. After the first week they learned to sleep through it all.

At many depots farther west—out past Nebraska and into the Dakotas—the sound of new construction filled the air. Town plans were a common topic among land scouts, who frequently joined Julia and the girls on the train while surveying the prospective new communities. They talked about the six-mile-square townships and showed one another their sketches of roads and buildings.

Peering out the window in the evenings, Julia caught glimpses of the first residents' flickering campfires in these sprouting gardens of America. She wondered what dreams and hopes these late-century pioneers had carried with them—and what they had discarded along the way.

Julia fumbled through her bag for the letter she'd started writing to Mrs. Gaffin in Bismarck, North Dakota. She remembered that remarkable territory and how, at one of the depots, she'd seen a mighty elk, antlers stretching against the sky, chest puffed proudly. She ran a finger over her penciled descriptions.

Dear Mrs. Gaffin,

    First, as we passed the Mississippi River (I can hardly believe I was finally able to see the "Mighty Mississippi"), I saw loons and eagles swirling for

prey over the waters. As we traveled farther west, you wouldn't believe the prairie critters! Meadowlarks, coyotes, prairie dogs—their diminutive forms propped up like little street beggars. I even saw a herd of bison. How huge they were! Pictures in books do not portray their strength and power. I am eager to see more.

The girls have been good. I'll write again soon.

Yours,
Julia

Intending to post the letter at the next depot, Julia placed it on the top of her new valise.

The wind outside picked up, and the prairie grass swayed gently. So far the West had been all she'd dreamed. Looming buttes, acres of lush sage, wild prairie roses and foxgloves, vast skies, and rambling streams. And how she loved the people she'd met at the depots. Such peculiar characters, just like out of her books.

Just this morning they'd met a woman, Mabelina, in Fort Benton. The stocky, cherry-haired woman lavished warm greetings on them. When she learned their last stop would be Big Sandy, Mabelina grasped Julia in a full hug.

"We need good womenfolk in my town." A twinkle lit her brown eyes. "Our parson needs a wife!"

Julia had chuckled and explained she was only dropping off the remaining girls and would immediately return to New York. The woman's whole face frowned, and then, as quick as a city rat could scamper off with a dropped morsel, her face depicted sweet joy once again.

"Oh well, the Good Lord's sure to bring someone, someday."

"Miss Cavanaugh." A voice jolted Julia from her thoughts, and Liza rushed in. "The conductor said Big Sandy is five miles away. Fifteen minutes. We're almost there! I can't wait to meet my new parents. I just know they're good people."

"I good people!" Bea, who'd been snoozing in the seat behind Julia, wobbled to her and clambered onto her lap. Julia lifted a ledger from her bag. The nun at Grand Central Depot had given it to her before they'd left New York. It listed where each girl would be living.

Bea sat up on Julia's lap. "I go Wonesome Pwaiwee."

Julia viewed her list. "That's right. I suppose it must be a town close to Big Sandy. Sounds wonderful, doesn't it?"

Shelby scooted next to Julia and leaned her head against Julia's shoulder. "It doesn't sound good to me. Sounds lonely."

"Maybe not. Let's hope not." Julia smoothed Shelby's straight, yellow-blond hair.

Even though the girls had been with Julia since Bea was a newborn, Shelby hadn't been easy to win over. Too many years of disappointment and neglect had built a fortress of feisty, stubborn anger around the girl. It was only recently that Julia had broken through. She'd gained Shelby's trust. *And now?*

Shelby glanced up, and Julia took the moment to memorize the girl's blue eyes. Her cheeks. Her smile. *Such a beautiful face. Such a beautiful heart.*

"I don't want to leave you, Miss

Cavanaugh." Shelby's voice quivered like a leaf on a windy day. "I've been thinking." She sat straighter in the seat next to Julia. "Why can't you adopt us? You can be our mother. Wherever you go, we'll go. I can work in the factories to help pay, and Bea will be a good girl."

Please, no. Didn't Shelby think Julia had already considered this?

More than once Julia had imagined returning to New York with Shelby and Bea. Surely Mrs. Gaffin wouldn't put them out on the street. Maybe they all could live in her big, new house. . .at least until Julia could find work. Then she and the girls could rent a small room somewhere. It wouldn't be much, but they'd at least have each other.

An ache pounded at her temples, but its source was the throbbing in her heart. When she considered these things, reality always took over. Mrs. Gaffin was starting a new life. She'd done her duty by providing for the girls to go on the orphan train. Julia couldn't ask her to do more. And Julia simply couldn't provide for them herself, not as a new family could.

"Sweetie." Julia touched Shelby's cheek. "I want to be your mother. . .with all my heart, but—"

Shelby cut her off, her eyes pleading. "We need each other. What will Bea do without you?"

Julia struggled to keep her voice calm. "We have to trust that this is the right thing to do. That God has chosen these folks as your parents." She reached for the girl's hand.

Shelby jerked it away, pulling back as if stung by a wasp. "I knew you'd say no. I thought you loved us, but you're just like everyone else—happy to be rid of us."

Shelby stood and stomped to the next car.

"Please, Shelby," Julia called after her, but she was already gone.

The train's whistle blared as it approached the depot.

Julia focused on the four girls anxiously staring out the window. "Girls," she said, organizing her things and watching for Shelby, "make sure you have everything ready."

"We're here?" Liza frowned. "But I don't see any town. Not even a building."

Only a stark and waterless prairie stretched in all directions. "I see what you mean," Julia said. "But don't worry. Big Sandy must be nearby. Now come on, girls; are you ready to meet your new parents?"

Before any of the girls could answer, the train jerked to a stop. Shelby entered and, without looking at Julia, grabbed her carpetbag.

"All right, girls." Julia somehow found the strength to sound cheerful. "Quickly, gather around."

Julia reached into her valise and pulled out the pillowslips she'd embroidered for each one during their journey. Creating these personal mementos had eased Julia's ache and distracted her thoughts. She would not send them off empty-handed; she'd send them with a memory of her love. And when lonely or scary moments came, maybe these simple pillowslips would remind them of that.

She handed a pillowslip to each girl with a simple hug. "Fold them up and tuck them inside your carpetbags."

They did as she asked. All except Shelby.

Shelby glared at Julia, her eyes red from crying. "I don't want it!" She grabbed the intricately sewn fabric, tossed it to the floor, and stomped on it.

Julia winced as if it were her heart on the floor feeling the strike of Shelby's black patent leather shoe.

"That naughty!" Bea pointed accusingly at the smudged pillowslip.

Julia swallowed hard and then focused on Shelby, reaching a trembling hand to her shoulder. "I'll put it in my bag. Maybe you'll change your mind later."

"I don't want anything reminding me of you!"

Julia felt a wave of relief when the conductor chose that moment to enter. "This way," he called, his cheerful voice helping to dissipate the gloom that had settled over the train car.

"Is the train leaving from here right away?" Julia asked him. "I need to see my girls to their new homes." She straightened her shoulders, regaining control—of herself, the girls, her emotions.

The conductor offered a reassuring smile. "We just have to scoot up to the water tower over yonder. Once we get filled up, we'll come back. You have one hour, but don't be late. We need to get to Cascade on time, and we won't be waitin'."

"I'll be here." Quickly wiping her eyes, Julia led the girls out the door and down the steps to a dusty road. Yet there was no town, and no parents waited as in the other stops—just an old rail car used as the depot and one lone wagon with a sign.

RIDE TO TOWN. 2 BITS.

"Howdy, miss." A short, scruffy man, the driver of the wagon, approached. "I'm Horace." A big toothless smile filled his face. "These the orphans from a Mrs. Hamlin's school?"

"Yes," Julia answered.

"You Julia Cavanaw-guh?"

"Yes. . ." Odd, none of the other folks who met them at the depots knew her name.

The man did a happy little jig, and Julia laughed. Must just be one of the quirky characters in these parts—like that Mabelina.

"Thank you, sir," she said and then

turned to the girls. "Go ahead and climb in that wagon." Julia reached in her pocket for the two bits the sign indicated, but Horace shook his hands, stopping her.

"This one's on me."

Chapter Six

Situated on the buckboard next to the odd man, Julia settled Bea onto her lap. The other girls sat on the dirty wagon bed. Their simple traveling dresses—far from the bright white they'd been—gathered yet another layer of dirt. *Well,* Julia thought, *perhaps I'll have a moment to brush them off before the parents see them.*

"Gitup," Horace called to the large black stallion as he lifted the reins.

"Pe-ew!" Bea pinched her nose. "That man stinky."

Julia struggled to hold back a laugh.

Then she snuggled Beatrice closer to her side, hoping the man hadn't heard. "No, Bea. Not nice."

The wagon lunged forward, and Julia and Bea were nearly jolted off their seat. She used her free hand to steady them as she took in the barren scenery and frosted mountains that formed a border to the vast, reaching sky. But the wagon joggled and jerked so much that the only thing she could focus on was keeping herself and Bea from bouncing clear off and onto the dusty road.

Bea giggled, liking the ride. "Ah-h-h-h. . ." Her voice wobbled along with the wagon.

As they approached the town, the music of a single hand organ joined in with hoofbeats, whinnies, and the jingle of bridles. Julia viewed the dirt- and weed-covered road and the half-a-dozen or so buildings alongside, which she assumed made up Big Sandy. Some of the buildings looked newer, with fresh paint announcing their goods. Most had porches, and on them men—exclusively men—talked with each other and watched the wagon rolling in.

Large white tents also lined the main street, and they looked more suitable for a wilderness expedition than a town. *What are those tents for?* She counted nine. Were they family dwellings? Why couldn't they have built houses?

The wagon pulled up in front of a whitewashed building with a single gable gazing down.

"Is this my new house?" Liza stood and leaned over Julia's shoulder to see. "It's so big. I hope it is."

"No." The hot wind slapped strands of Julia's hair against her cheek. "See, it says The Spokane House. That means it's a hotel."

Julia began directing the girls off the wagon, and a beautiful brunette woman, with a pregnant belly bulging beneath her flowing prairie skirt, approached with a smile.

"Hello, I'm Miriam Lafuze." She held the rough planks of the cart and glanced at Julia and the girls. "We're so happy you're here. You can't imagine how blessed our families feel to take in their new daughters."

"Thank you." Julia liked the woman's

face and her gentle tone. Just being near her put Julia at ease.

Miriam walked to the back and offered the girls a hand as they jumped off. Julia was last, but before she could take Miriam's hand, Horace shouldered Miriam, sending her wobbling out of the way.

"May I halp you, miss?" He offered his hand like a prairie gentleman.

Julia took it and jumped down, noticing Miriam's frown.

"Horace, you'd better be getting my wagon back to the stable. Parson Ike and I will want it later, and the horses need to be fed and watered."

Horace's forehead folded into a frown. "Fine." His gaze shifted toward Julia. "But I'll be seein' you later, as sure as a possum comes out at night."

Seeing me later? He must think I'll be staying. Julia didn't have time to explain. "Fine, sure."

Horace tipped his hat and moseyed off.

Julia glanced at the porch where men outfitted in Stetson hats and boots and women in bonnets and aprons gathered. They were paired as couples, a few with children tagging along.

The girls' families.

Julia said a silent prayer to help her make it through the next hour, as she'd release the last of her girls to strangers.

Miriam laid a hand on Julia's back, seeming to sense her anxiety. Then Bea, still at Julia's side, tugged on her arm. Julia picked her up. "This is our youngest."

"I'm Bea! Buzz, buzz, buzz."

Miriam tickled the toddler. "You are a little bee, aren't you? So adorable."

Bea wiggled and grinned, and suddenly the thought of never watching the girl's curly hair bouncing, sweet blue eyes twinkling, or squeaky voice laughing sent a jolt of pain through her heart. She pressed Bea tighter to her, not wanting to let go and straining to squelch her emotions.

Julia's chin quivered, and she covered her mouth with her free hand. Her eyes began to sting as tears struggled to the surface. Although she'd nearly shed tears in front of the handsome conductor on several occasions, she hadn't allowed herself to truly weep since that night before they'd left New York. Couldn't she hold it back one more hour?

"Yes. . .she is adorable." Julia's voice wedged in her throat. Her knees weakened, and she scooted toward the porch and leaned against a pole for extra support.

"Buzz, buzz, buzz," Bea said again, now delighted with the attention. But as Julia glanced up, she realized that the men and women no longer watched Bea. Instead they focused on her, and the compassion she read in their gazes only made her feel worse. Two lines of hot tears betrayed her and ran down her cheeks.

Her throat ached as she swallowed a sob. In the midst of a long, sniffling gulp, Julia saw a man walk off the dusty road onto the porch's planks. He was a muscular man in a rough shirt and vest, and he had the most handsome face she'd ever seen—both strong and kindly. As he approached, he removed his hat, which was black and not exactly like the cowboys', and for a quick moment his concerned midnight eyes locked with hers.

"Isaac, you're here," Miriam said.

"I couldn't miss this, now could I?" He

turned to Julia. "Miss." His voice was deep yet gentle. "Is everything all right? Can I help you?"

Julia lifted her gaze, again attempting to wipe away the rebel tears with her hand. She opened her mouth to speak, but no words came.

The man called Isaac held a red bandanna handkerchief out to her. "It's clean." He offered a shy grin. "I promise."

"I'll be fine. . .thank you." She accepted the gesture and wiped her face and nose, nearly soaking it. Wishing he'd look away, she held the handkerchief awkwardly, not knowing how to give it back in such a state.

Thankfully, Miriam spoke. "This is the wonderful woman who brought the girls to us. She, understandably, is a little saddened by saying good-bye—as I would be as well."

Thank you. Julia wished she could say the words but was sure more tears would come with them.

Miriam held Isaac's arms. "Are *you* doing all right? I know the funeral was difficult."

Julia watched the couple. *Miriam must*

be Isaac's wife. She shoved the handkerchief into her valise, planning to mail it back after washing and pressing it.

"I'm fine. Glad to be here. I consider this the sunshine after the storm."

Miriam's forehead creased. "Are you sure?"

"Y'know, I think Milo—" The man's voice snapped off, and his bottom lip tightened. "He would've wanted me to be here. . .to meet these girls."

Miriam took him into an embrace, and another young woman approached, joining them.

Julia averted her eyes and looked to the girls. Their weary eyes pleaded with her to get this over with—all but Shelby's. She stood to the side, leaning against the wall.

Isaac stepped away from Miriam and gazed at Julia. "No need to make things harder for Miss Cavanaugh here," he said. "We should get started."

Miriam straightened her shoulders, apparently ready to work. "You're right." She turned to Julia. "I'll go into the hotel office and prepare the paperwork. You can bring the girls in, and then we'll match them up. My brother can help you with their bags." Miriam squeezed Julia's hand.

Brother? Julia felt a smidge of hope bubble up, and then she chided herself. She'd be gone in an hour. What was she thinking?

Julia held Miriam's hand for a moment longer. "Thank you."

Miriam's eyes crinkled as she smiled. "You're welcome." And before she ambled to the office, she winked at her brother and nodded her head toward Julia. A rush of warmth touched Julia's face at Miriam's obvious hint.

Isaac frowned, immediately dismissing his sister's glance with a quick shake of his head. Was that disgust in his glare? Pride?

Who's he to dismiss me like that? It's not as if I was mooning over him.

Isaac grabbed up as much of the luggage as his hands could seemingly hold. When he reached for Julia's valise, she grasped it. "I can carry my own, thank you."

She pivoted to the girls. "Come. It's time." The girls gathered together, and

Julia hurried them inside, refusing to feel hurt over Isaac's dismissal.

* * * *

The sun beat down through The Spokane House lobby's paned window, casting crisscrossed shadows over the rug on the wood-planked floor. Isaac eyed the children's caretaker. Miss Cavanaugh, Miriam had called her. He watched as she settled onto a long bench, straightened the girls' dresses, and told them to sit like ladies. Her brown eyes squinted and her lower lip rose in a slight frown, yet she was still quite lovely. As much as he tried to aim his glance elsewhere, it kept returning to Miss Cavanaugh.

Isaac chewed his thumbnail. His mind slowed for some reason, and he wasn't sure what to do next.

"Isaac, what's wrong with you?" Elizabeth knocked his hand from his mouth. "You haven't bitten your nails for years, not since Miriam put the camphor solution on them when you were, what, eight?"

Isaac wiped his hands on his trousers and chuckled nervously. "Yeah, and I

83

couldn't pump enough water from the well to get that nasty taste out of my mouth."

Elizabeth, her husband Abe, and the other soon-to-be parents filed into the few chairs or stood against the walls.

Isaac struggled to focus on the task before him, matching the parents with the children, yet his thoughts kept returning to that Miss Cavanaugh like a wagon stuck in a rut.

Abe's grin turned up the corner of his mouth. "Uh, Parson Ike, you sure have a strange look on your face—and you keep starin' at that caregiver. Don't you think you should get started with these girls here? Plenty of time to talk to her later."

Isaac's gaze swept the room, and he found the same smirk on the other adults' faces—all except Miss Cavanaugh's. She seemed clueless about their matchmaking ideas. Isaac clenched his jaw, frustrated with his own thoughts as well as theirs. Would they never give it up? *How many times have I told them I'm never getting married?*

Isaac wiped the cold sweat, which kept returning, from his hands. He picked up the ledger Miriam had left him from the front desk and faced the crowd.

"Well, this is a rare occasion for all of us," he began. "A day Elder Milo and I planned for quite a few years now." Isaac winced as he mentioned Milo's name. The three weeks since his friend's death had passed in a sleepless blur. He'd dug the grave, performed the funeral, and helped Aponi care for the girls. He'd also tended his little band of churchgoers with the only true comfort for those who mourn: the hope of heaven and God's intimate presence with His people. A comfort he himself thirsted for each day.

It surprised Isaac how, even in the short three weeks, he'd felt so alone without Milo. Perhaps he hadn't realized how much he'd relied on the man's companionship, godly wisdom, and fatherly love. He'd known grief before, when as a child he'd lost his mother—and at other times—but Isaac had forgotten the stabbing, physical pain of a fresh wound. He took in a breath and once again eyed the orphans and parents. Uniting these families was their dream—his and

Milo's. He'd put aside his grief and rejoice in God's goodness and mercy. Milo would want him to.

He searched each of the sweet orphan girls' faces. "What a new life each of you will have. You have no reason to fear, for we've picked good, godly families for you."

He was pleased to see that Miss Cavanaugh seemed to take comfort from his words. "I can tell you," he continued, addressing the girls, "I and all the folks in this room have been praying for you, not even knowing your names. God heard our prayers, and His providence has led you here."

The littlest one hopped off Miss Cavanaugh's lap and jumped up and down on the rough-hewn floor. "I here?"

A dozen smiles warmed the faces of the people gathered as the caretaker hoisted the child back to her lap.

"Yes, sweetheart," Isaac answered. "You stay here."

A small smile emerged from Miss Cavanaugh's lips as she met his gaze. Isaac quickly looked away and began to read through the list connecting the girls with the waiting, exuberant families.

Within minutes, three families were matched.

After introductions, Miriam hustled them off to the office to fill out paperwork stating they'd provide stable homes, good education, and Christian training, including church and Sabbath school if possible.

Reaching the bottom of the list, just one child's name remained. And one family. Isaac paused at the names, *Abe and Elizabeth Falcon*, written in his own handwriting.

He'd grieved with his sister and brother-in-law through the heartache of three miscarriages. Each time, his sister had mourned her loss with grace and faith, comforting those around her more than herself. But the last loss nearly took Elizabeth's life, and it rendered her barren. "Barren, like a dry field," she'd said that hot, summer afternoon she'd delivered the tiny infant, gone before it could take breath.

Elizabeth's heart had always overflowed with love toward those around her, yet Isaac knew she longed to lavish that love on a child. He'd spent many hours pleading with God to give her a baby and had longed for some way to help her. It seemed the whole community of Lonesome Prairie prayed for a child to join the Falcon family.

The Children's Aid Society had provided Isaac a way to help, and if truth be told, he'd requested the orphan train to come as much for Elizabeth and Abe as for Milo and his plans.

Isaac read the name of the child on the ledger. *Beatrice Bruce.* Little Bea. A perfect match for his sister. "We have one child remaining," he said. "You, Abe and Elizabeth, are to take Beatrice Bruce."

Even as the words left his lips, Isaac, who'd been pondering the name on the ledger, looked up and noticed the other girl sitting next to Julia. How could he have not realized she was still there? The girl's young face, full of confusion and fear, gaped at him. Compassion for her stung him, and he checked the list again. Only one name and one family.

What could've happened?

Then he saw Miss Cavanaugh, eyes like a mother lion. "You mean two children, right?"

Chapter Seven

Julia struggled to remain calm as she pulled both girls next to her. "There must be some mistake."

Isaac stared at her with an unreadable expression. "Well, the paperwork says just one, but I'm sure we can find a—"

"There's two. See." Worries of children being ripped from their siblings by adoptive parents had plagued Julia's thoughts, yet she'd been assured this wouldn't happen. *And it can't happen, not to Bea and Shelby.*

"All I have here is Beatrice Bruce, but—"

"That me! You my new mama and papa?" Bea stretched her arms toward the only remaining couple, Elizabeth and Abe, but Julia snatched her back to her lap.

Shelby gripped Julia's arm.

"The sisters must be together." Julia's chin twitched upward, and her eyes zeroed in on the parson.

"I'm sorry," Isaac continued, eyeing her right back, starting to appear annoyed. "The paperwork shows no record of another child. I'm not sure how this is handled. The older child may have to go back. . . ."

His voice sounded stiff, unswerving. Julia's foot tapped in nervous frustration. Shelby couldn't be separated from Bea. Julia wouldn't let it happen. Losing Bea would make Shelby as lonely as Julia. That was a reality Julia could never accept—she'd do anything to protect those girls.

Suddenly her plan to keep the two didn't seem so farfetched. What if she took Shelby's and Bea's hands and walked out of that room, back to the train? She could take them to New York with her. It'd be hard to find a place to stay and work, but at least they'd be together. Julia examined Shelby's face. Fear and rejection marked her eyes. Would she be abandoned again? Were there parents for everyone but her? Julia couldn't let this happen to Shelby. She wouldn't.

"Isaac," Julia heard Elizabeth say.

Seemingly oblivious to his sister, Isaac shook his head. "I know siblings are sometimes separated—"

Julia stood, stomping her boot. "These girls *cannot* be separated." She didn't care who was in the room or what they thought of her. What mattered was that Shelby understood she *was* wanted, loved.

She shifted her gaze to Shelby. "I've been your mother for two years." She gently touched the girl's face. "What if we became a real family? It's what we both want, isn't it?"

Shelby's face shone.

"Miss Cavanaugh," Isaac said. "I don't know what you have in mind, but . . ."

Julia set a pleasant expression on her face. She tilted her head as she glanced at him, no longer needing to be angry.

"There is no problem now, sir. I will simply take them with me back to New York. *Both* of them."

He glanced at his sister Elizabeth, and Julia followed his gaze. Her brow creased, and she lowered her head.

"No," he said firmly. "You can't."

"Isaac," Elizabeth said again, louder.

"I was told the girls didn't have to go to anyone they didn't want to." Julia stepped toward him, anger swishing back. He smelled of sweet prairie grass, and the pleasantness of it made Julia even more frustrated.

"From what I can tell, Bea wants to go with my sister." The man's face reddened, and his eyes looked frantic. "Just a moment ago she was reaching for Abe and Elizabeth—her new parents."

Julia clutched Bea to her, and the two-year-old snuggled against her chest. "No, she wants to stay with me. Can't you see that? And if Shelby can't go with them—"

"We'll figure something out about Shelby, but I'm sorry, Bea needs to go with Abe and Elizabeth."

Julia felt her gaze narrow. "You are one

rude parson." She wondered how she'd ever been attracted to him.

Isaac's head jerked back as if he'd been hit. He exhaled. "Look, Miss Cavanaugh. I just can't let you steal my sister's only hope of having a child. She's been waiting forever to be a mother." Julia saw compassion in his eyes but chose to ignore it. Her love for the girls mattered more.

"Isaac!" Elizabeth's shout echoed off the walls, the ceiling. "Listen to me."

Julia winced and looked to the woman. Elizabeth's cheeks were flushed.

Two steps and Isaac was at her side. "What is it?"

"We'll take both girls, Isaac," Elizabeth said, her shoulders slumping in what looked like relief to finally be heard. "We can't separate them. We'd be happy to take both." She held her husband's hand.

"Be happy to." Abe tugged his wife to him and rubbed her arm. "Not right to separate them girls. 'Sides, Shelby can help Elizabeth. Keep 'er company." He smiled at Shelby.

Isaac's face relaxed. "Thank you. That's the perfect solution. I'm sorry; I should have asked you that first."

Julia sank back onto the bench. She didn't know what to do. What was best for the girls? One minute ago she'd decided to take Shelby and Bea—as her own—with her to New York, to be their mother as she'd longed for all these weeks. Her hopes had rushed her forward in time to their happy home together—laughing at the breakfast table, teaching and guiding them throughout the day, seeing their faces every night before bed. How could she just shut off those hopes again despite the woman's offer to take both? She kissed Shelby's head and squeezed Bea tightly, breathing in the scent of their skin.

"Do you want to go back with me? You can still go if you want to, but . . ."

Moments of silent embraces passed. Then Shelby pulled back, wiping her tears on her pinafore. "Miss Cavanaugh," she said softly.

Julia thumbed a straggling tear from her chin. "Yes?"

"You were right. We have to trust—" Shelby forced a smile. "We have to trust that God picked my parents."

Julia bowed her head and clasped

Shelby's hands in hers, gently rubbing the lines in her fingers. She knew she couldn't be their mother. The idea faded as quickly as it arrived.

Shelby sniffed and weaved her fingers through Julia's. "These folks seem like really nice people. They'll make good parents for Bea. Maybe it'd be better for her to grow up here than in New York like I did. She could run around. It might be good for me, too."

Bea's wide blue eyes peered up at Julia and then shifted to her new parents, confused.

"Of course you're right." Julia caressed Shelby's soft hair. "You're so brave."

"Bea brave, too." Bea smiled.

Julia kissed her cheek and then stood, lifting Bea in her arms. *Lord, take care of Your children.* She walked to Elizabeth and handed Bea to the kind young woman.

Elizabeth's eyes brightened and tears rimmed her lids. She touched Julia's arm. "Thank you."

"They're both yours." Julia placed a hand on Shelby's back, urging her forward.

Shelby stood tall before her new mother,

yet her eyes fell, nervous. "We'd be happy to come with you. I promise I'll help take care of Bea."

Elizabeth lifted Shelby's chin. "We'd be honored to be your parents. You're an unexpected gift, Shelby. Because of you, this day is even more wonderful than we first imagined."

Julia glanced at a clock above the doorway. She had fifteen minutes to say good-bye and race to the depot. With determined yet shaky strength, Julia strode to the girls huddled next to Elizabeth and Abe. Kneeling down, she swooped Bea into her arms. "Be good for your new mama and papa." Tears forced their way out, yet Julia fought to smile as she released her little charge. "Good-bye, Bea."

Turning to Shelby, she took the girl's face in her hands. She wanted to give her something, to somehow show her love. Then she remembered the pillowslip. She pulled it out of her bag and brushed off the dust from the train floor. A butterfly fluttering over a colorful rainbow decorated the slip. That's what Shelby had been to her—an arch of color after the rain. Julia handed it to her.

"Thank you, Miss Cavanaugh." Shelby flung herself against her in a tight hug.

"You're welcome, my sweet girl." Julia pulled herself away. "Never forget—" She pressed steepled hands to her mouth, like a child at prayer, then lowered them. "Never forget how much you mean to me."

As if on cue, the train whistle sounded its fifteen-minute warning, and Julia ambled out the door and down the street, her heart breaking with each step.

She didn't look back.

* * * *

Guilt stabbed Isaac's gut as he grabbed the saddle horn and swung onto his mare, Virginia. How could he have been so harsh to that woman who'd showed such strength and grace? In his mind's eye, he saw the two girls wrapping their arms around her slim form after she'd offered to adopt them. Then, when she chose to place them in Abe and Elizabeth's care, she'd put on a brave smile. Even though pain obviously boiled under the surface, her smile radiated comfort to those girls. How blessed they were to have her all those years.

How could I have been so callous? What had she called him? *One rude parson.* She was right. Part of him longed to apologize, to view that lovely face once more. . .but no. Isaac forced the idea aside. He'd only confuse matters. Best to just let her go in peace.

Besides, his poor parishioners over in Lodge Pole had been expecting him for two weeks now. After Milo's death, his circuit had been cut short. But now, with the funeral behind him and the orphans safe in their homes, he could get back to his normal pace. Preaching seven days a week, sleeping under the stars or in the loving homes of his congregants, visiting the sick—the familiarity of this routine would bring rest, peace.

Thoughts of the school returned. In a couple of months, a load of supplies would be coming by train. He and Milo had ordered the precise supplies they'd need for a small yet suitable schoolhouse.

Of course, the most important element hadn't been located yet. A schoolmarm.

Calamity's tongue hung from her mouth as the old dog trotted alongside, keeping her good eye fixed on him. Isaac reached the edge of town. He rode by Milo's house, the only building with an upstairs, and paused. Wooden crates lay stacked on the front porch, and a wagon—was it Warren's?—waited in the grassy side yard. Perhaps Aponi was cleaning out Milo's things. The widow, with her six girls, had exuded enormous strength over the last weeks. But to Isaac, her trusted pastor, she'd confided that inside she felt alone, abandoned on this prairie without the man she loved.

As Isaac considered stopping in to pray with her before heading out, he heard footsteps behind him. He glanced over his shoulder to see his sister Elizabeth racing toward him. Her family's wagon waited on the street. Isaac grinned at the two girls—his sister's future—nestled in the back.

"Aren't you anxious to get your new family home?" he asked from his mount on the horse.

"Of course." Elizabeth beamed. "But I wanted to check on you before you left, since Miriam shooed you out like a bad-tempered ewe."

Isaac chuckled. "I know. You'd think after five years on the prairie, she'd let me grow up."

"She'll always want to mother us." Elizabeth smiled. "Listen, my dear brother, are you sure you don't want to stay out at the ranch tonight? Sometimes parsons need caring for, too."

His horse whinnied and tossed her head, eager to get going. Perhaps she'd grown anxious about staying in one place too long, as he had. Isaac reached down and touched his sister's shoulder. An evening filled with the love of family—a good meal, as much talking as he needed but not more, and a steady night's sleep in a soft bed. The images tempted him. Still, he couldn't shake his obligation to the folks over east. Or his need to sleep under a sky full of stars.

"Thank you kindly, but tonight me and the prairie have an appointment."

"You and God, you mean."

Isaac nodded, grateful his sister understood. "You go. Enjoy your first night with my nieces."

"Yes, I will." Elizabeth paused, glancing at the road. "I just can't stop thinking about that young woman. I feel so bad for her." She lingered, like she had something she wanted to say.

Shame covering him, he tilted his head. "I was really horrible, wasn't I?"

"Mmm-hmm." Elizabeth raised her eyebrows. "Just go apologize."

"You think I should? I mean, you don't think I'll make it worse?"

"No, dear, you can be downright sweet when you put your mind to it." She patted his knee. "But, truly, a kind word from a parson might, I don't know, comfort her." She threw him a cheeky grin. "Even a rude one. Especially if he's repentant."

Isaac chuckled. "You're right. I will."

"You better hurry. She's walkin' back to the depot." Elizabeth squeezed his hand then spun around and hurried to her wagon.

Isaac watched as it rumbled down the street. Shelby and Bea's heads tipped back as if looking ahead to their new lives awaiting them. *Dear Lord, gather them in Your arms. Guide their footsteps. Teach them Your ways.*

"Go on!" Elizabeth hollered back at him.

Isaac leaned forward, but just before he thrust his horse into a gallop, he saw Horace sashay out of the Log Cabin Saloon all gussied up in a black coat and bolo tie. He even wore a new hat. In his left hand, he grasped papers. Horace in a suit? Something wasn't right.

"Hey, Horace," Isaac called. "What're you doing?"

"I done gone bought me a wife. And I'm headin' to cash in." He stamped toward his wagon. Not the nicer wagon he'd borrowed from Miriam to pick up the ladies from the train, but his smaller unit that looked ready to fall apart, pulled by one tired mule. "Ho there, looks like she already hightailed it back to the train. Sorry, Parson Ike, I gotta go fetch that Miss Julia Cavanaw-guh."

Isaac urged his horse next to Horace's wagon. "What? You *paid* for Miss Cavanaugh to marry you?"

"Yup." Horace held up the papers. "Got the receipts right here. But that Mrs. Hamlin, or Gaffin, or whatever it was, she said she wanted ta surprise the little lady."

He snapped his fingers in an arc in front of him. "Now's the time."

Isaac, baffled at the prospector's logic, raced his horse next to him. "But you can't buy a wife."

Horace shook his head, surprised. "Why, o' course you can. Haven't you never heard of them mail-order brides? I could never get my nerve up with the ladies 'round these parts, so I done ordered one." Horace reached the wagon and jumped onto the buckboard, grabbing the reins. "And if you wanna know a secret, I'm not gonna tell her until she gets on my wagon thinkin' she's headin' back to the train." His belly jiggled as he hooted. "Can't wait to see the look on her face."

The prospector whipped his mule, and the wagon jolted ahead.

Chapter Eight

The wind blew in hot and dusty, drying Julia's tears. She tried to swallow, but her throat felt raw, parched. She focused her eyes on the railroad depot, just a lonely rail car, and the train parked at the water tower. She knew it wouldn't be there long.

Soon she'd be climbing its metal steps and sliding into her spot next to the window. She'd make the connections until she boarded an eastbound engine in Helena. Then she'd finish *The Prairie Knight* without interruption. She'd be given a quiet she hadn't known—ever. Yet rather than cherish the prospect, she felt grief like a dark storm grip her heart despite the bright Montana sunshine.

Her feet plodded forward, and she shielded her eyes as she stared into the vast sky, alive with endless white, rolling clouds. "Are You taking care of me like my mama said?" The wind carried away her whispered words along with the dust.

Up ahead the train rumbled and chugged a half mile from the water tower to the depot. As she quickened her steps, the sound of hoofbeats rumbled behind her. In a blink, a horse sprinted across her path and stopped. The parson tugged off his hat.

His dark eyes unsettling her, Julia sucked in a breath.

The parson fixed his eyes on her and seemed to shift uncomfortably in his saddle. "Miss Cavanaugh, uh, I need to tell you"—the man sucked in a slow breath—"I'm sorry . . ."

Perceiving his purpose, she nodded quickly and looked around him toward the train. "There's no need to apologize. Thank you, but," she pointed ahead, "the train will be leaving. I have just a few minutes." She walked around the horse, moving forward again. So he wanted to make things right. Maybe he wasn't so rude after all.

Isaac jumped down and hurried toward her, leading his horse.

Julia curved stray strands of her hair behind her ear. "It's really all right, Parson," she called over her shoulder. "My behavior also left much to be desired."

He reached her. "No—you were—fine." His eyebrows slanted as he gazed at her, and Julia couldn't help but notice his strong jaw line.

Her knees softened. Her hands trembled. A new nervousness came over her that had nothing to do with the train. *What's wrong with me?*

He kept pace beside her. "You're an admirable woman to take care of those children as you have. I'm sorry for the way I treated you. It was inexcusable."

She looked to him again.

His lips formed a crooked grin. "I *am* a rude parson."

Julia halted her steps and shifted her gaze to him. "No, you're not." She shook her head. "It was awful of me to say. I'm sorry."

A surge of wind tugged at Julia's skirt. Out of the corner of her eye she noticed it also tipped Isaac's hat. He moved his hand to settle it.

"I also wanted to tell you," Isaac continued, as they set off again, "that I'll be praying for you." After a quiet moment, he continued. "Do you have a Bible?"

"Yes, in my valise." The bag weighed heavy on her arm. Isaac took it from her, his fingers grazing her sleeve.

"I don't mean to assume anything," he continued. "I don't know if you're a Bible-reading person, but if you think of it, you may want to read Psalm 63:1. It brings me a lot of comfort."

Julia tilted her face toward his. A soft smile, genuine as if springing from a soul at peace, graced his features. Julia understood why his parishioners would turn to him in times of trouble. She knew his kindness stemmed from his occupation, but she appreciated it nonetheless.

"Thank you, I'll do that." She viewed the train and gave an apologetic smile. "I really have to go. The train won't wait."

The sound of creaky wheels and a

slow shuffle as from an animal broke the moment.

Isaac turned. "Oh no, I almost forgot. Horace?"

"Did I hear my name?" Horace pulled up in his wagon.

Horace eyed the parson. "Why'd you take off so fast, Parson Ike?"

"I needed to talk to Miss Cavanaugh here, and I wanted to catch her before she got on the train."

The old character grinned and winked at the parson, then he turned his full attention to Julia. "So, little missy, can I give ya a ride the rest of the way?"

Julia glanced at Isaac. He frowned and shook his head.

"Thank you, but I, uh, think I can make it on foot," she said, taking his unspoken advice. She moved forward. "I'm almost there now."

Horace nudged his mule, and it pulled the wagon beside her. Isaac kept pace on the other side, leading his horse. Julia fanned her face with her hand. She needed air.

"I thought we could go somewhere to talk for a bit, miss."

Julia's gut wrenched. Her day had been troubled enough; she didn't need another distraction. She forced herself to send the man a smile. "I'm sure I'd be happy to, but. . .the train." It was at least the tenth time she'd said that. Why didn't these men seem to grasp the urgency?

Horace halted the wagon and hopped off. He marched to her side, papers clutched in his hand. Stepping back, she nearly bumped into the parson. His hand caught her, resting in the small of her back. An embarrassed rush of warmth rose to her neck, and she moved herself forward.

"The thing is," Horace grinned, "I'm gonna be talkin' to ya. If ya wanna do it right here, that's downright fine. Whatever suits ya."

Julia's gaze focused on the train waiting at the depot. Her heart pounded. They'd be boarding soon. If she hurried, she still had time to find her seat and get situated. "I'm sorry, sir. I don't quite know what you want." Julia pulled her valise from the parson's hand and took a step toward the train. "I really need to go."

Horace jounced in her way, his portly

body continuing its movement after he stopped. "Now hold on, thar, miss. I got somethin' to show ya." He handed her a photograph. "That's you, ain't it?"

Figuring the only way to get past was to humor him, Julia glanced at the photo. Her jaw dropped. *How'd he get that?*

It was her. About two months ago, long before Julia knew of the orphan train, Mrs. Hamlin had insisted she go to a photographer. Mrs. Hamlin said she wanted a photograph, for a keepsake. Julia had thought it strange. "Yes, that's me."

Horace took off his hat. Sparse hair bobbed wildly in the wind. "Then I'm the man you came fer. Horace Whitbaum. Your new husband." He stuck out his hand. "Nice to make yer acquaintance."

Isaac swayed to Horace. "I don't think you understand," he stated calmly—much more calmly than Julia felt. "Miss Cavanaugh isn't planning on staying here. She needs to get to the depot."

Julia tossed Isaac a grateful smile, still unable to imagine that this gray-haired man thought she would become his wife. "I'm not sure what's going on, but I'm not intending to marry anyone." She spoke as sympathetically, yet firmly, as she could. "So please. My train will be leaving in a few minutes."

"Horace, you've got to let her go." Isaac's voice took on a parental tone. "Now stand aside."

Horace pushed his lips in and out, as if he was trying to find the right words. His eyelids lowered, his nostrils flared, and he swallowed hard. For a moment Julia thought he was going to cry.

There was something sad about the grungy man; he reminded her of the abandoned puppy Ardy had brought to the orphanage. She'd had to turn that poor little creature away, too. Julia dared to touch the man's filthy arm, telling herself she could wash later. "I'm sorry."

"C'mon, my friend." Isaac gazed at him. "Let's go talk. I'll buy you a sarsaparilla."

But Horace didn't stand aside. Instead, he held up the papers. "Says right here on this letter from a Mrs. Hamlin that yer my wife. Look." He shoved the papers, flapping in the blustery breeze, toward Julia.

At the sound of Mrs. Hamlin's name Julia felt short of breath, as if an invisible force had cinched a corset tight around her waist.

I have a surprise for you, dear, the headmistress had said. Could this. . .could *he* be the surprise?

Julia's knees quivered, and she hoped she didn't faint like the ladies in the dime novels. Even if Isaac caught her, the embarrassment wouldn't be worth it. Reluctantly she set her valise at her feet and took the letter. It was dated months ago.

March 13, 1889

Dear Mr. Whitbaum,

What luck! I just so happen to have a young woman under my care who is in desperate need of a husband. There's a good chance she's coming to your area soon. If you send the required funds, I'll make sure she's on the train.

Sincerely,

Mrs. Edith Hamlin

Julia blanched. *Oh, Mrs. Gaffin, you didn't. I'm a grown woman, and you—a hopeless romantic with no common sense!*

A sick dread grabbed her stomach. The man was serious. He really thought he had a right to her. And clearly Mrs. Gaffin knew about the orphan train long ago. How long had she been planning this? Julia's foot tapped the ground, stirring up the wisping dirt. She looked at the next paper. It was a promissory note.

I, Edith Hamlin, promise to use the money you wire to send Julia Cavanaugh on the train leaving May 15, 1889, to be your wife.

A notary stamp and Mrs. Hamlin's signature were on the bottom of the page.

"Oh dear," Julia whispered.

"I done good, didn't I?" Horace said, grinning at the parson. "Gotta make sure them big-city folk don't swindle ya." He pulled a crumpled envelope from his pocket. "Almost fergot. This one's fer ya. I sware I didn't open it."

He held out a letter addressed to her. With limp fingers, Julia opened the envelope.

Dearest Julia,

    I can barely contain my giggles. How surprised you must be right now. You knew I would take care of you, didn't you? When I saw Mr. Whitbaum's ad in the Times, I couldn't believe he lived near the same place the orphan train was going. I knew all along you'd be staying out there! With your new husband, no less. A prospector! Imagine the luck! I can only hope you'll be as happy with your Prince Charming as I am with mine. I know this world can be a lonely place sometimes. A husband will care for you even when I can't. Thinking of that does my old heart good.

    Please don't thank me, dear Julia. It's the least I could do for all your years of faithful service to me.

    Love,
    Your Mrs. Hamlin
    (which will be Mrs. Gaffin by the time you read this)

Julia slowly looked up, avoiding Horace and sending a silent, pleading cry for help to Isaac. "It says she promised me to him."

"Don't worry." His dark eyes displayed compassion. "It can't be valid."

Horace cleared his throat and growled at Isaac.

Hesitantly, Julia turned her focus toward the wide, gap-toothed smile that shone from Horace's face.

"I done got you this." Before anyone could stop him, Horace knelt down and held up a silver ring. "'Tain't much, but it's fer you." He grabbed her hand. "Will you marry me, Miss, uh, hold up." He glanced at the paper. "Oh yeah, Miss Cavaunaw-guh?"

Julia shook her head. "Mr. Whitbaum, please stand up," she begged.

Horace frowned as he creaked to a stand.

The train whistled, and the engine's rumble vibrated the ground. Julia clutched her valise. Every muscle in her body wanted to fly to that depot and let the train take her far away.

Horace's eyes peered at her. "Well? Will ya?"

"No!" Julia said. "I don't care what papers you have. I'm not going to marry you."

115

Horace's eyes squinted, and his forehead scrunched. Then he clamped onto her arm and yanked, making her fall into him. "But you got to." His voice sounded desperate.

Isaac grasped Julia away from Horace. He settled her, making sure she was steady on her feet before pulling Horace aside, their backs to the depot.

Julia saw her chance. She grabbed up the valise and darted to the train with quickened steps. One hand held up her skirt, the other swung with the motion of her valise. She knew ladies should not run, but she didn't have a choice.

"Parson Ike," Julia heard Horace's loud voice say as she scampered away. "It's real lonesome out here bein' by myself. None of the fine ladies out here'll have me, I don't think. Plus, I done paid good money."

Any pity she might have felt for the poor man was overcome by her desperation to reach the depot in time.

Yet after a few strides, she knew the train was no use. The long chain of railway cars began to slowly chug away from the station, and as it gained speed, its black smoke streaked across the cloud-dappled sky. Julia slowed her pace. Her steps stilled. And as the wind whipped her hair again, she watched her future fade into the dust.

* * * *

Isaac spied Julia's shoulders slump when the steam engine departed, and compassion for the woman filled his chest. He couldn't imagine the pain she'd endured earlier in the day, and now, to be left here. Isaac knew the prairie he loved seemed desolate and uncivilized to city folk—even foreboding, frightening. It had for him when he first arrived from St. Louis. And she'd come from the biggest city of all.

He glanced at her still form as she watched the train disappear and knew he should comfort her. Of course, the first way to help was to handle Horace.

Isaac returned his attention to his distressed companion. "I'm sorry, my friend. You just can't force someone to marry you—or love you, for that matter."

Horace shook his head like an unbroken horse. "That's where you're wrong. I told you. I done paid fer her."

"Why, you're about as stubborn as I am," Isaac said, realizing the simple-minded settler might not be easily moved. And, looking at Julia, he couldn't really blame the man. Were he the type to marry—which he wasn't—he'd hope to find a wife like Miss Julia Cavanaugh. Beautiful, definitely. Brave. Kind and loving. And a hard worker—she must be—taking care of all those children. Gracious to forgive him. And when he'd touched her back. . . Isaac shook his head, brushing off his straying thoughts.

But what to do about Horace? He glanced at the Bear's Paw Mountains outside of town, where the man lived. "Why don't you take my sister's wagon back to her and then head home? On your way, do some talkin' with God. Miss Cavanaugh just missed her train, so there's no rush."

The slouching man suddenly perked up. "That's right. I can be a real gentleman suitor." He wiggled his fingers together in excitement and then hopped on the wagon. "I'll be back fer ya!" he called to Julia, whose back still faced them. "You'll see. I'll make you love me yet."

Julia rotated toward Isaac from her spot. The evening sun created a candle-like glow on her pretty features, and the wind sent her hair and skirt dancing softly about her. He removed his parson's hat and palmed his hair, then stepped toward her.

She shook her head. A slight, sad smile arched her lips. She looked disappointed, but there seemed to be something else in her gaze, too. Gratitude?

Julia stepped forward and met him halfway. "Guess I'm stuck here for a bit."

Isaac nodded, trying to exude as much compassion as he felt. "Yes, miss, you are."

Chapter Nine

A grasshopper landed on Julia's leather traveling boot as she inched her way toward the parson. She possessed no mental energy to plan. No tears to cry. Not enough strength to fear. The only emotion that rolled through her was a bizarre urge to laugh at the absurdity of her situation. When she awoke this morning in the sleeper car, she knew this day would be one of the most difficult of her life. Yet she'd never imagined quite this much turmoil.

She glanced at the parson. "The next train is. . .when?"

The parson's brown hair caught in the wind as he tilted his head toward her. "Well, it's supposed to come once a week, but," he raised his eyebrows apologetically, "it's hardly ever on time."

Julia took in a breath. "Maybe I can send a telegram to Mrs. Gaffin to wire some money."

Isaac shook his head. "Let me take you back to the hotel." His lips formed a compassionate frown. "I think you should talk to my sister Miriam. She'll come up with a plan." Isaac picked up his horse's reins from the dust, clutched her valise, and guided Julia beside him.

Julia trudged along in silence.

After a few moments, the parson turned to her, a hint of a smile on his lips "So," he said, surveying the landscape, "not much different from New York, eh?"

Julia eyed him, not sure if he was serious. "Excuse me?"

His playful grin broadened. A twinkle lit his eyes. "I mean, I've never been there, only read about it in books, but it's pretty much like our Big Sandy, right?"

Like Big Sandy? "Oh!" she blurted, catching his joke. How did he know she needed a distraction? She could play this. "Well, there are many similarities, but I suppose it's a *little* different."

"That's what I thought." Isaac grinned, spurred on by her comment. "See over there?" He pointed to the rickety wooden water tower. Loose planks stuck out and the wood appeared old and worn. Julia wondered how it managed to stay standing with all the wind. "It's almost as tall as the Statue of Liberty. Don't you think?"

"Definitely," Julia said. "Maybe taller. And so regal, just like the Lady."

A rustling sound emerged from the tall grass, and three antelope hopped across their path.

"It's the New York Easter parade. I feel like I'm at home."

Isaac chuckled softly then placed his finger over his lips and stopped walking. "Look." He pointed toward the small mountain range to the east, where Julia's loving new fiancé, Horace, apparently lived.

She eyed a beat-up shack tucked into the hillside. "Where do you want me to look? At my future home with my husband-to-be?"

Isaac angled his head. "Don't worry about Horace. I'll talk to him. He's actually a good man, but once he gets his mind stuck on something—"

"Such as marrying a mail-order bride who didn't know she was even up for ordering?"

"Really, you shouldn't worry. Now look." More antelope galloped through the field, shifting and turning as one body. Their shadows danced across the yellow grass at odd angles. "They were headed back to their herd, probably searching for water up yonder at Gold Creek."

"Beautiful. Like a ballet."

Isaac bent and picked a sprig of sage from a skinny bush. "Smell," he said, holding it to her nose.

"Sage. I like it."

"See? Old, primitive Montana's not as bad as you thought, is it?"

The horse whinnied, and Julia reached up and rubbed behind its ears. She glanced at the never-ending prairie grass and the tiny group of shacks that made up the town. She shook her head. "No, it's not." She peeked up at him with a smile. "It's worse. Much, much worse."

"What?" Isaac gasped, a teasing glint in his eye. "How could you say that?" He nodded to her, and they continued walking.

"I never thought it'd be so empty. It's not like this in books. Authors make it seem like the West buzzes with folks living in real towns, with sheriffs, banks, and storekeepers. Dancing girls. Like an adventure."

"Well, it's like that in states like Nebraska and, where I came from, Missouri. They call it the Eastern West. Those communities have had a lot more years to establish themselves. You've got second-generation settlers there. But the railroad just got to these parts two years ago. Not many folks have ventured this far west."

"You mean a cowboy rodeo doesn't happen every day?" Julia gave a mock frown. "I was really looking forward to that."

"Sorry, but hey, maybe sometime I can show you. I'm the best wild bronco rider in Montana." He held his hands like a cowboy—one in the air, one down as if holding the saddle horn.

"Really? I'd love to see that." She rubbed her eyes, still dry from the dusty breeze.

"Yeah, it'd be something to see all right."

"I love watching bona fide bronco riders. Ever since Mrs. Gaffin took me to the Wild West Show, I've been awed. Oh, the sight of those horses—even the smell of them—didn't bother me that day. You're that good, are you?"

Isaac laughed. "No. I'm actually awful."

"What?" Julia pressed a hand over her heart and gave a mock gasp. "You lied to me?"

"Aw, I was only hoodwinking you a little bit."

"Well, sir, I'd say you've got 'more wind than a bull in green-corn time.'" As soon as she said the phrase, she flung her hand over her mouth, surprised at herself. Her face warmed.

Isaac stopped in his tracks. He bent over and laughter shook his shoulders. "Where did you hear that?"

"In one of my books." She couldn't help but giggle. "I've always wanted to try it out. Maybe it wasn't such a good idea."

"I've never heard that one." He straightened. "I haven't had such a good laugh in a long time."

Julia sucked in a breath, realizing they were approaching town. *How did we get here so fast?* It felt good to laugh, even if it was at her own expense. "Thanks for taking my mind off everything."

Isaac blinked and for a moment gazed into her eyes. "You're welcome. I hope I was of some help."

"You were. More than you know." She brushed her hair from her eyes. "I sure didn't expect to laugh today."

They reached the hotel, and Isaac held the door for her as they sauntered in. Miriam stood at the front desk talking to a sturdy young woman with black hair, whom Julia assumed was the hotel proprietor.

"Isaac? Julia? What are you doing here?" She stepped to them and grasped Julia's hands. Her forehead crinkled. "You missed your train, didn't you, dear?"

"She sure did." Isaac explained the Horace situation as well. "I was hoping she could stay with you. If she stays in town, Horace'll be bothering her."

Miriam smiled at Julia. "Of course. I'm so sorry you missed your train." She turned back to Isaac but continued speaking to Julia. "I hope my brother was gentlemanly to you on your walk back." Miriam smiled, her gaze full of implication as it had been earlier in the day, and Julia knew the hints had something to do with her.

Julia noticed Isaac's frown and wished Miriam would keep the hints to herself.

"So you're off to Lodge Pole?" Miriam asked, smiling as if unperturbed by his glare.

"Won't make it today." Isaac's voice was curt, so different from what it had been minutes ago. "I'll stop and make camp on the prairie tonight and get there by tomorrow. Then I'll head to the other towns I've neglected of late."

"But you'll be home soon, won't you?"

He paced toward the door. "I'll definitely be back in two months for the delivery of school supplies from the train."

127

"Don't forget about your birthday party next month, dear."

Isaac didn't look back. "I'll be there."

"Good. Do you want to wash up before you go?"

"No, I need to get on." He threw a quick glance at Julia. "Good-bye, miss. And don't worry about Horace, all right?"

"I won't."

Thirty minutes later Julia sat next to Miriam on the buckboard of the pregnant woman's wagon.

Miriam rattled the reins, and the horses, as if shocked out of a stupor, jerked ahead. Pressing her hands against the seat's rough wood to steady herself, Julia lifted her eyes to peruse the town. As soon as she did, she quickly returned her gaze to the road ahead. Cowboys, infantry men, and every other representative of the male persuasion gawked at her. They were lined up outside the Log Cabin Saloon and the nine white tents—which she now realized were makeshift taverns. Some of the men appeared young, probably making a life for themselves out West, and some were older, perhaps veterans from the War.

But all of them ogled her as if she was the only single woman they'd seen in months. The disquieting feeling made her want to take a bath to wash their stares away.

The wagon moved past The Spokane House on her left, and just beyond it they rumbled by a small cabin that touched the edge of the prairie. Small plants outlined the path toward the cabin's planked front door. Julia craned her neck to get a better look, unsure of what she saw. "Is that house surrounded by—cactus?"

Miriam chuckled. "That's the home of the lady I was talkin' to at the hotel—the cook, front desk gal, and maid all in one. She's the only unmarried woman of any virtue in town. We had to do something to keep the drunks away."

"I don't understand."

"Well, let me put it this way. There's a very narrow path to the door, and a cowboy has to be steady on his feet to make it to the entrance without bein' jabbed all over. If a man has any liquor in him he won't make it."

"And if he doesn't have liquor in him?"

"He's not tempted to try."

"Oh my." *What a strange place.* Julia struggled to settle into the rhythm of the bumpy ride. Miriam, who appeared to be in her thirties, seemed content riding along. She hummed a tune Julia didn't recognize.

"Is it far to your place?" Julia asked after they passed the train depot and headed up a small hill.

"Thankfully we're one of the nearest settlements to town, about two miles—right close to Lonesome Lake."

"There's a lake?" It seemed impossible that any water existed in this dry place.

"Yes, it's not much to speak of, but we're grateful to the Lord for it. Couldn't survive out here without water close by."

The wind calmed, and the sun, dipping slightly into the western horizon, heated Julia's head. Remembering her parasol, she opened it and rested it on her shoulder, thankful for the shade.

Miriam's lips pursed together in an obvious effort to stifle a fit of laughter.

"What?" Julia asked, gaping at Miriam's shaking shoulders.

"You are a prissy thing, aren't you?

That outfit and parasol. They're lovely, but not things I've seen much of out here."

"They were gifts from the headmistress at the orphanage, Mrs. Gaffin." Julia lifted her chin and focused her gaze ahead. Then she relaxed and smiled. "I guess they do seem a bit out of place." She placed it over Miriam's head. "But see how nice the shade feels?"

"It does at that."

Julia closed her parasol and placed it next to her valise in the back. It was too bumpy to hold it still anyway. "This place. It's just so different from what I'm used to."

"Well, dear, it is," Miriam said with a slight chuckle. "I've known city folk who come out here with everything they own to get cheap land from the Homestead Act. After a week, they're discouraged. After two, disappointed. After a month, they pack up and go home. I'm not sure if you noticed a family by the train today, but they were there—jumping on as you jumped off."

"A month?"

"Sometimes more. Sometimes less."

Julia's heart felt as if it had been trampled by the horses' hooves. If it only took a month for most folks—those who'd risked everything to come out here—to turn back, how would she survive? Who knew how long it would take the train to arrive? "It must be horrible here," she mumbled.

"The problem's not the hard life so much," Miriam continued, her voice softer as if discerning Julia's thoughts. "It's the loneliness."

"I can imagine."

Miriam shifted her gaze to Julia, who studied the woman's hands loosely gripping the reins. It was as if the horses had clopped down this road so many times, they knew their way by heart. Julia couldn't imagine settling into a place like this. It didn't feel like home.

Miriam patted Julia's knee. "I know you're terrified. I was. When we came from St. Louis, my husband, Jefferson, and I had only Isaac's tales of good-hearted people, crazy characters, and starry skies. We wanted to come, felt called to support my brother's ministry, but it was much more difficult than we anticipated. And, just like it did to those folks who turned back, the isolation got to me. Isaac was gone a lot, and Jefferson had to work from sunup to sundown just to get our cabin built. I was alone with the kids, day after day. That was before my sister Elizabeth showed up, of course. Things got easier when she came, but it still tends to be quiet out here. Lonesome Prairie is an appropriate name."

A sparrow darted over the wagon, and Julia watched it flutter and fly away. "Did it get easier? I mean, before your sister came."

Miriam nodded. "I learned to love it, actually, but I had to teach myself to handle the seclusion." Her head slanted upward and her eyes focused on the path ahead. "First, I forced myself to keep busy. Now I know what you're thinkin', how can a body not be as busy as a one-armed gold miner out here? But you'd be surprised. When you start feelin' depressed, you want to do the bare minimum to get by. And that only makes it worse."

"I know that to be true," Julia said. "When I first came to the orphanage after my parents died, all I wanted to do was hide under my blanket and sleep, but Mrs. Gaffin encouraged me to do a little bit every day. And when I did, I felt better."

"The same'll work out here. The other thing is that if you can, try to be around people as much as possible. God made us for human companionship. A body can spend weeks talkin' to a goat, but that won't do." Miriam patted her hand. "You shouldn't have much trouble with that. We'll keep you company."

Julia rubbed the tight muscles of her neck. A torrent of thankfulness washed over her. She might have been stranded out here alone, sad, and at a loss about how to survive, but Miriam—and Isaac and their whole family—seemed to have adopted her just as they had her wards. It was a temporary adoption, but full of a generosity she'd never forget.

"Have I mentioned how grateful I am for you?"

Miriam's fingers lifted off the reins. "Believe me, we'll be glad to have the extra hands." She gripped Julia's shoulder. "And your company."

Julia gazed ahead and saw that the

ruts in the road split and another lane branched off north. Miriam stopped the wagon and stood, pointing to the north. "If you stand, you can see our place."

Julia rose and shielded her face from the sun. In the distance two small houses joined together, and a large barn-like structure behind them nestled into the landscape. A cluster of trees and a small lake sat beyond that.

"That's our house to the right and Abe and Elizabeth's to the left. We have a framed-in walkway between."

Julia nodded. Then Miriam's words replayed in her mind. She plunked down on the seat. "Did you say you live with Abe and Elizabeth?"

"Not *with* them. We have two homes, but we do share the kitchen and privy." Miriam pressed a hand to her forehead. "But yes, we're together. It's pretty snug."

"So, Shelby and Bea are there?" Julia whispered. Delight at seeing them again fought with dread. A reunion meant another parting, and the last one had been hard enough. "I didn't realize."

As much as she longed to stay in the safety of Miriam's home—to experience a real family life that she'd missed for so long and to uncover the closeness they all seemed to have with God—Julia couldn't. It wouldn't be fair to Shelby and Bea; how could they settle in to a new life with their old guardian hovering close by? It would only confuse them. Nor would it be fair to Abe and Elizabeth. They needed a chance to earn the girls' undivided loyalty and affection.

Julia's hand settled on Miriam's. "I'm sorry to inconvenience you." She searched Miriam's eyes, finding empathy there. "Is there anywhere else I can stay?"

Miriam's eyebrows angled. "I'm so sorry I didn't think of that. You can't be with Shelby and Bea. Not so soon."

"No, I can't. Or rather, *they* can't be with me."

A lone rider drew near from the direction of Miriam's house. Julia recognized Abe, Elizabeth's husband. No longer wearing the black slacks and vest, he was dressed in work pants and a simple white cotton shirt rolled to his elbows.

"Yer sister just sent me out to look for you," he said. "She was worried." He stopped his horse alongside the wagon, and his eyes fixed on Julia. "Where you headed with Miss Cavanaugh?"

"I was taking her home. She missed the train and had a bit of an incident in town with Horace, but—"

"Oh, well. . ." Abe leaned forward in his saddle. His eyes looked concerned but determined. "I'm sorry you missed yer train. It's jest that the girls, well, they are finally getting settled with 'Lizbeth. She was reading them a story when I left. Don't want to see tears like that again all my live-long day."

"Tears?" Julia's hand flew to her chest as she gazed at Abe. "I understand. I was already hoping to stay somewhere else."

Miriam wrapped an arm around her and held her tightly. "Do you want me to take you back to town?"

The sight of those men gawking at her played in her mind. She'd rather risk sleeping on the prairie with the threat of Indians and outlaws. She shook her head. "That's not possible. I have only a little money left, and I was hoping to send a telegram to Mrs. Gaffin."

"That's more bad news. The closest place to send a telegram is Cascade, a day's journey by horseback. Two days by wagon." Her voice trailed off, and then in a burst of energy she once more took hold of the reins. "I have an idea." She steered the horses to the left and urged them forward. "Julia can stay at Isaac's place. He'll be gone for a month at least."

"That'll do." Abe nodded once. "I better head back. Yer husband's up to his neck trying to get dinner on the table for your young'uns. Can I tell him you'll be home soon?"

"Yes!" Miriam's voice was followed by the whinny of one of the horses. "I'll just get Julia settled in and be right back."

Julia's head jerked toward the pregnant woman sitting next to her, who was determined to have her stay. . .where? *The parson's place?* "Wait a minute." Julia reached for the reins and tugged. The horses stopped short. "I don't think that's a good idea. Your brother, the parson, well. . .I don't think he'd want me there. In fact, I'm positive he won't."

"Of course he won't mind. Isaac likes you—just as he likes everyone," she quickly added. "And besides, he won't be back for a month, remember?"

Chapter Ten

"Calamity, c'mon girl." Isaac's half-blind sheepdog, who'd been faithfully waiting by the door of the hotel, scurried toward him, bumping into his leg as she reached him. The pleased dog let out a low bark, and Isaac knelt as she nudged against him. "Wanna sleep on the prairie tonight, girl? We're riding out east." He scratched her ears as she panted. "First, I need to check on Aponi."

Isaac strode toward the opposite edge of town to his late friend's house, thinking over the day's events. Calamity kept up with his long strides.

Isaac shook his head as he thought about the scene at the hotel. Miriam's hints had annoyed him more than anything on the good earth. Had Julia not been standing there, Isaac would've rebuked his sister. That's what she needed. A good old-fashioned rebuke. She knew Isaac had promised God he'd stay single. Plus, like him, Miriam knew very well the danger of leaving a woman alone night after night while her husband was gone. They'd both seen what had happened to their mother while their father was away fighting in the Indian wars.

No, he'd not risk a wife getting hurt or killed during his absence. He'd never marry. Isaac had accepted the fact years ago.

Reaching Milo's home, Isaac sighed. *Not Milo's house anymore, Aponi's.* He hesitated briefly as he took in the only two-story in town, and then walked up the porch steps and knocked. Warren, Milo's stepson, opened the door. His eyes widened, and his jaw dropped. He reminded Isaac of an eight-year-old caught taking a pinch from his pa's tobacco pouch.

Isaac had hoped for a chance to see Warren. He'd prayed that Milo's death would jostle the young man's earthly focus, making him think about things eternal. God often used the soul's darkest hours to draw folks into close communion with Himself—like a shepherd who holds a wounded lamb in his arms. He hoped this would happen with Warren.

"It's good to see you." Isaac shook the stout man's hand. "How you holding up?"

Warren stepped onto the porch, closing the door behind him. He bowed his head, the corner of thick lips turned down. "Well, it's hard, you know. We miss him."

Isaac patted the man's back as a pang of grief hit him. "I do, too." He paused, waiting to see if Warren wanted to talk, but the man fidgeted, shifting his weight.

"So, can I help you with something, Parson?"

Isaac let his hand drop. "I'd like to talk to Aponi and the girls before I head out of town. Maybe we can all share a pot of coffee?"

"Sounds good, but I'm sorry. I don't think the womenfolk are up to it."

The thought of Aponi not inclined

141

toward a cup of coffee with any soul who knocked on her door unbalanced Isaac's sense of stability. If Aponi's hospitality couldn't withstand Milo's loss, Isaac wondered what else in his world now rested on unstable ground. He dreaded leaving town without at least praying with her.

Isaac glanced at the wooden crate he'd noticed earlier in the day. More crates were lined up against the house. Lifting one of the lids, he discovered a tanned leather jacket Aponi had made for Milo atop a stack of books. Milo had worn the jacket for years. In fact, Isaac couldn't remember many times—aside from worship and sweltering hot days—when he *hadn't* seen his friend wearing it. Seeing it now sparked fresh mourning, as hard and sharp as the northeastern wind.

Isaac eyed Milo's stepson, unsure how to read him. *Lord, help me minister to Warren.* "Well, if the ladies aren't game, why don't you and I sit down? I'd love to talk to you about the school. The train with supplies'll be here in a couple months."

A slight grin appeared on the young

man's face. "My father told me. The lumber."

"Yes, and schoolbooks, slates, even a chalkboard. The children will love it. . . .Your father would've loved it. It was very generous of him to offer to pay for it all."

"That it was."

Isaac edged toward the door. If he could get inside, perhaps he'd have a chance to talk to Aponi and the girls. "Well, how 'bout that coffee. Got some for a parson heading out of town?"

"Maybe we should go over to the Log Cabin. Get a table."

"Nah, we can use your kitchen. If I head over there we'll have lots of interruptions from folks wanting to talk."

Warren reluctantly moved aside.

Isaac's gaze adjusted to the dim parlor, and he immediately realized why Warren had wanted to take the conversation elsewhere. The walls, normally bedecked with paintings, a cuckoo clock, and peg lamps, now stood empty. Most of the crates were nailed closed, but inside some half-full crates, Isaac spied not only Milo's things but also his family's belongings—children's winter boots and wool coats, a supply of medicines, a chamber set, girls' clothing.

But worse, six small cardboard valises with dolls perched on top rested next to the door. Another satchel held books and a photographic portrait of Milo and Aponi. A tightness, like a lariat around a steer's neck, constricted Isaac's chest.

Warren hurriedly moved to the kitchen, and Isaac followed. The scent of biscuits baking in the woodstove filled the room. A brown broth simmered in a pot on the cookstove. "Why are the girls' things packed up? What are the satchels for?"

Warren leaned against the table. "Well, I know this may be hard for you to hear, Parson. I didn't want to tell you. . . ."

Isaac reached for the back of a tall wooden chair. "What is it?"

"I'm sending the girls to boarding school and Aponi to the reservation."

Isaac released a heavy breath, unable to believe Warren's words.

He visited the Assiniboine reservation often. He'd prayed for the tribes' sick children and performed funerals for those who'd embraced Christ. And each time he went, he left with a heavy ache in his

heart for these once mighty people,
so stripped by the broken promises of the
white man. The reservation was too small
to provide enough game. And the U.S.
government had forced warring tribes—
the Assiniboine and Blackfoot—to live on
the same land. The rivalries persevered,
and skirmishes often broke out.

The poor condition of the reservation
was one of the reasons he and Milo had
wanted to start a school—for both white
and Indian children.

But as bad as the reservation was
for Indians, boarding schools were worse.
Indian children slept on the floor, many
in one small room, without enough heat.
Forced to do chores for the white children,
they endured severe punishments for
even a slight misstep. Isaac pictured
Milo's beautiful girls, so happy and
secure. How could Warren do this?

A low wind whistled through the
maples in the back yard. Next to Aponi's
herb garden a row of white dresses,
descending in sizes, flapped in the
breeze on a clothesline.

"Why, Warren?" It was all he could ask.
Warren's eyes darted out the window,

145

refusing to meet Isaac's gaze. "I'm the executor of a will that was never finished. It's my responsibility to take care of them."

"And you think this—these decisions are fulfilling your responsibility?"

"I don't know how to care for a woman and six girls. I figure they need a good place to live, food, and an education. It's all I know to do."

Isaac trudged to the cookstove. Out of habit he picked up the wooden spoon from a peg on the wall and stirred, more like a family member than a guest. "But why make them leave their home?"

"Gotta sell it—at least the goods—to pay for the school."

"But Aponi teaches them. The girls are smart, more cultured than any others in town."

Warren shook his head. "No, Aponi can't teach them all in the same way a school would. And after what has happened—I don't think she can shoulder the responsibility alone. I promised my father I'd give them the best." He pulled a hunk of jerky from a jar in the cupboard and stuck it in his mouth.

"But they treat Indians horribly. You

know that." None of Warren's reasons made sense. Isaac pivoted toward him. "We'll have a school in a few months. Wait. Let them attend there."

"You think so?" Warren's voice raised, impatience tingeing his tone. "You and my father had all these great plans for a school, but do you have a teacher? A building's not much use without a schoolmarm."

Isaac clenched his fist. He'd said the same thing to Milo.

God provides for the sparrows, doesn't He? Milo had said. *He'll bring a teacher at the right time.*

The back door opened, and Aponi entered. The wind swept in with her tired steps. Strands of her raven black hair flew from her braids, and then they stilled as she closed the door behind her. Aponi's head was bowed, her shoulders wilted.

She strode in and then glanced up, for the first time noticing Isaac. "Parson." The word released in a shaky breath as she rushed to him and grabbed his arm. "My girls. Warren say they leave."

Isaac rested his large palm over the woman's small hand. Her hand felt dry, rough from years of scrubbing laundry, cleaning floors, digging the garden, teaching her girls to tan hides. Dedication Isaac witnessed every time he saw her.

As quickly as Aponi gripped his arm, she released it. Embarrassment replaced the anxious look in her eyes, and it was obvious she wasn't accustomed to showing such emotion. Once again setting a brave face, she took a rag and wiped crumbs from the table, dented and stained from countless meals with toddlers and children.

The table clean, Aponi retrieved the biscuits from the oven and stirred the stew. Then she stood before the two men. Her eyes, aimed toward Warren, brimmed with determination. "I get them back. I not let my girls stay at white man's school."

With a quick shake of his head, Warren blinked, then turned and faced the window again.

"Aponi, I'm not giving up on our school—the one we planned—and neither is Warren." Isaac hoped this was true. "In a couple months the supplies will be here. Then your girls can go to school there. They could be back by Christmas."

Aponi's eyes shifted toward Warren. "Christmas?"

Isaac wished he could stand up to Warren, chase him out of town, and let Aponi and her daughters remain in their home. But he hadn't the right to intervene. And neither did Aponi. An Indian woman, even when married to an American citizen, held no legal standing. Isaac knew of several Indian wives who'd been abandoned when their husbands found more "suitable" white women to marry. The men didn't even have to file for divorce. Most just unloaded their wives and children, who'd served and cared for them, at a reservation, never to see them again.

"Christmas," Isaac repeated, hopeful.

Aponi nodded, yet she didn't look convinced.

Isaac silently walked to the crate on the porch and took out Milo's jacket. Returning, he displayed it to Aponi. "Your hands made this." He pointed to the fine stitching, the soft, perfectly stained leather. "You served your husband well, every day of his life—even on the last day. . . ." He handed the coat to Aponi.

"When you hold this, remember how he loved you. How proud he was of you. And, Mrs. Godfrey, continue to be his good wife, no matter where this life may lead you."

A single trail of tears lined Aponi's high cheekbones. "I serve my true husband, Christ. I always served Christ." She closed her eyes, took in a breath, and then opened them. "I go to reservation. Let Warren have Milo's house." Her voice was strong, almost fierce. "My God take care of me and my girls, wherever we go." And a faint hint of hope, a hope of a home eternal, settled in her eyes.

* * * *

"Hold on, Julia!" Miriam warned. She guided the horses out of the ravine called Lonesome Lake Coulee. Straining forward, Julia's backside still hung off the buckboard. With all her strength, she gripped the rough plank—slivers digging into her fingers—and slid back on.

The horses surged forward, and soon they were back on level ground.

"Oh," Julia muttered. "What more will this day bring?" Though the sun hid behind looming clouds, she knew by her hunger that it must be around dinnertime. The day felt like it would never end, and assured Isaac wouldn't return, she looked forward to settling into the parsonage.

In her neighborhood church in Manhattan, the parishioners maintained their minister's house. Though not large, it was clean and painted, even boasting an indoor bathroom with a bathtub. *How I'd love a bath.* Julia longed to clean the dust off her body and soak for a while. She'd even take the time to heat the water.

Miriam released a breath. "We're almost there. See that?" She pointed up ahead. "That's Isaac's house."

Julia looked ahead, noting a small shed made of dirt and hay rising up from the land around it.

"All I see is that shed and the barn-structure behind it." She surveyed the surrounding area.

The corners of Miriam's mouth raised in an apologetic smile. "That's Isaac's place. It's call a soddy. Doesn't look like much, I suppose."

"*That's* the parson's house?" Tucked into a small hillside, the "house" wasn't even made of wood. It was just a big dirt clod that could be the residence of an oversized groundhog. Only a door and window gave evidence that it was a dwelling. Behind it stood a small barn that she supposed could shelter a horse.

It's not even as big as the kitchen in the orphanage. Julia wanted to cry, but she'd already wept enough that day. Instead, she laughed. "It'll be fine. I've read about sod houses in books."

"Probably saw a few on your train ride, too."

Julia nodded.

"One of Isaac's parishioners, Mr. Robertson, thought the parson should have his own place. Isaac had been staying with us whenever he was in the area. So he let Isaac use his land, and the two of them, with Jefferson and Abe, built the house and barn in an afternoon."

"That was kind of them."

Miriam glanced at Julia and laughed. "You poor dear. Look at you."

Julia glanced at her clothes. Singe holes from the sparks flying through the train's windows, a wet hem from the coulee, and a whole lot of dust. She could only imagine the state of her hair. She reached in the back for her parasol and popped it open.

"What?" she said, mockingly blinking her eyes. "Don't I look like a fine New York lady?"

They both laughed as Miriam parked the wagon near the soddy. Julia hopped down, grateful to be on the hard earth, and hurried over to help Miriam. The pregnant woman clutched her belly as she gingerly climbed down.

"It's getting close to the time to have this little one." She cupped her hands under her round belly. "I'm getting sore."

"I'm so sorry. It must be very uncomfortable." Julia gazed at the one-windowed shelter and tilted her head. "Is it leaning?"

Miriam placed an arm around her shoulders and slanted her head as well. "Hmm. . .sort of is, isn't it?" She wiped her hands on her apron as they approached the soddy.

Sprigs grew from the dirt roof, which was topped by a chimney. Miriam palmed a rocking chair of sticks and branches that stood outside next to the black door.

"Mrs. Wells made this chair for Isaac. She's a member of the circuit in Lodge Pole, where he's headed tonight."

Julia touched it, surprised by the smooth surface and complex design. "It's lovely."

"See that?" Miriam pointed to a small wool welcome rug. The words, *As for me and my house, we will serve the* Lord, were woven into it. "The ladies from Fort Benton made that for him." She opened the door and walked inside.

The cave-like room smelled of mud, sweat, and gunpowder.

"Let me get you some light." Miriam fumbled for the lantern. Within a minute, a golden glow filled the dank room. A table, a bookshelf with a dozen or so books, and a woodstove filled the rest of the space. A small wooden bed sat on one side. Above the door was a set of deer horns, and a shotgun of some sort hung from them. Julia shivered at the sight.

Miriam rubbed her hands on her apron. "You must need to be fed and watered. Let me see if I can get a fire going."

She's talking about me like I'm her horse. . .or maybe one of her children. Julia tried to hide her smile as she stepped to her side. "Here's the wood and tinder." She touched Miriam's arm. "And actually, I know how to light a woodstove. My parents used to have one just like this. Go ahead and head for home. It's been a long day for you, too."

Miriam exhaled and her shoulders drooped. "I am getting pretty tuckered."

A gust of wind blew, slamming the door shut.

Julia peered out the small, dingy window. The few white, willowy clouds had transformed into looming gray. "It's getting stormy out there. You'd better go."

"All right then. But before I go, I want to tell you another thing that helped me when we first came." Miriam placed a hand on Julia's back as they turned toward the door.

"I'd love any advice you can give."

Miriam stopped and held Julia's hands, and the deep brown eyes that had comforted her so much earlier today again enveloped Julia with a sense of peace, safety. "More than anything else, the one thing that helped this place feel like home was remembering that it's *not* my home."

Julia paused, unfolding the woman's words. "I don't understand."

"I know you don't understand yet, but you will. Pray about it. And . . ." Miriam touched Julia's hair. "Did my brother give you a verse?"

Julia lifted her eyes. "Actually, he did. It was Psalm 63:1."

Miriam pointed to a large family Bible sitting on the shelf. "You're welcome to use that Bible. It was our great-great-grandfather's from Scotland. Start by reading Psalm 63. Isaac's got a knack for picking just the right verse."

Julia opened her valise and displayed her own family Bible. "I will read it," she said. "Thank you for everything."

Miriam embraced her tightly. "I'll be back in the morning to check on you."

Julia nodded. "I appreciate that."

Julia watched Miriam go and then perched on the edge of the bed. She thought about the changes in her life. There had been a few, and this was just one more.

She sniffed the air and didn't understand how someone could live in a dirt cave. *It's just not civilized.* Then again, she didn't have to worry about living here forever. It was just a temporary fix. Whether two days or even two months, she knew she'd be moving on—heading back to the land of paved streets, stone and brick buildings, and streetlamps. *I can do anything for a short amount of time.*

It's not forever.

"Miriam will be back tomorrow," she spoke out loud, but there was no one to comment. No one who heard her. In fact, she knew if she were to yell at the top of her lungs, there would be no one to hear.

She looked through the small window and then glanced around the space, taking it all in. And for the first time in her life Julia Cavanaugh realized she was completely and utterly alone.

Chapter Eleven

Isaac pressed his body tightly against his mare, Virginia, as he rode at a gallop, hunkering under the stone-sized hail that pounded against his arms, neck, and back.

"Calamity!" Sidelong torrents hurled the icy orbs against his dog's ribs. She yowled in pain. "Stay by me, girl."

They'd left Aponi's house two hours ago, the sky blue with a slight wind. After three miles, threatening clouds chased away the blue, changing the wide Montana expanse to closed-in, suffocating gloom. Thunder roared. Lightning, like claws, scratched the sky. Then came the inevitable hail. They were small beads at first, so Isaac had decided to forge ahead. Soon the balls grew to cherry-size, and now. . . Now his horse trod on dead jackrabbits, their bodies battered by the large hail.

It'd taken them the last hour to make it barely a half mile. Streaks of white ice marring his vision, Isaac attempted to veer his horse westward—or what he hoped was westward. Back to his soddy where they would be safe and dry.

"Lord, get us there before nightfall," he cried out loud. With each stride, more hail pummeled his weakening body.

* * * *

The sound of hoofbeats and jangling bridles gone, all the world seemed silent. Yet, as Julia listened, she became aware of softer, subtler sounds. The growing wind's consistent drone. Crows cawing as they searched for shelter from the coming storm. She even sensed her own footsteps as she shifted from the red gingham curtains and stepped toward her valise next to the table. The same red-checkered material formed a tablecloth, and Julia wondered which parish ladies had given them to Parson Ike.

She plopped onto the bench, pulled out her Bible, and rested it on the table. She let her fingers glide over the ornate cover. Her father's voice reading to her and her mother each night after supper echoed in her ears. She slipped the thin pages open to the verse Isaac had suggested, Psalm 63:1, but her weary eyes struggled to focus. *In the morning*. She'd read it then.

Leaving the Bible on the table, Julia slouched to the bed and slipped off her shoes. The bed creaked as Julia's body sank into the soft padding. Her arms felt heavy. Her legs felt heavy. Her mind felt heavy, as if she'd been dipped in molten iron and left to harden.

Hunger gnawed at her stomach, but the strength to get up and fix herself a meal eluded her. Without bath or dinner, she slid her head against the pillow, drew the patchwork quilt over herself, and escaped into a deep sleep.

After what seemed like minutes, but must've been hours judging by the night sky, Julia was awakened by a loud hammering. At first groggy, she couldn't imagine who'd be pounding on the orphanage door. Once her eyes adjusted to the dim light, she realized where she was and bolted upright in bed. Her heart thrashed against her ribs.

Who was pounding on the soddy? Her mind foggy, she imagined Jesse James and his band of outlaws. Or Indians. Julia knew exactly what those Indians did to prairie women—sliced their scalps right off their heads. What if it was a bear? Julia sat frozen, fear paralyzing her. *O God, help me.*

Sucking in a quick breath, she peeked out the window. *Oh.* She exhaled. Pounding hail was barely visible in the pale moonlight. *How silly of me.* She'd known a storm was coming. She was just surprised she'd slept through any of it. Realizing she wouldn't get any more sleep till the weather calmed, she decided to get up and find something to eat. She peeked outside again at her first prairie storm. By the sound of it, it was a big one.

Reaching for the lantern, she paused as she felt something land on her head. "Oh my, the roof is leaking!" She touched her head, expecting to feel a wet spot, but instead some*thing* wriggled under her hand and tried to crawl up her arm.

She brushed against her hair frantically, squealed, and scampered to the other side of the bed. She groped in the dark for the lantern, found it, and lit it. Light filled the room, and she set the lantern on the small chair. Her eyes searched the blankets for the insect so she could shake it off. But before she could spot the disgusting creature something else tumbled from the earth above. *A spider.* Another squeal.

Julia shot a glance upward and realized the storm was forcing the critters to fall from the dirt roof. She guessed it was because they scurried through the sod above, trying to get away from the storm.

Returning to the bed, she threw herself on her back and grabbed for the blanket to cover her face. She wasn't quick enough. A large, squirmy creature with scaly skin landed on her forehead with a thud. *A snake.*

A snake! Julia screamed and flung it off her, not knowing where it landed or even what kind of snake it was.

A rattler, she guessed. *I know it is!*

Julia bounced from the bed onto the dirt floor. Her chest heaved. Her skin crawled. But she knew her only safe place was under that blanket. She ripped it from the bed, and moving the lantern to the table, she slouched on the bench. Not willing to touch her stockinged feet to the dirt, she lifted them up and hugged her knees. With trembling hands, she draped the blanket over her head. *Why am I here? I want to go back to New York.*

I'm going back. I'll walk if I have to.

As she caught her breath, she heard another noise. With the hail beating down, she couldn't be sure, but it sounded like footsteps. She waited, listening. The sound got louder. *Definitely footsteps.* She cautiously stood up and grabbed the shotgun from above the door. Unsure how to make it fire, she held it like a club.

Julia stood behind the door, waiting.

The door pushed open.

* * * *

Isaac secured poor, wet Virginia in the barn. Ice-covered and shivering uncontrollably, he hurried to his soddy,

Calamity plodding alongside him. He pushed the door open, and the dog let out a quick bark. Isaac looked at the dog, confused. "What's wrong, girl?"

Then, as he stepped his foot inside, a woman's scream split the air. Before he could respond, a hard object slammed against his left ear. Pain blurred his vision.

"What in the—" Isaac's hand shot to his head as he tumbled forward, tripping over Calamity. More pain surged as a second blow struck his back. He slumped to his knees then reached forward and scrambled toward his bed, turning and lifting his arms to block any additional blows. A liquid warmed his hand, and in the dim lantern light he saw that it was blood. Before he could look up, he heard a woman's voice.

"Oh no! Parson!"

The woman dropped the gun on the dirt floor, hurried to him, and gently lowered his arms. He flinched, and then the woman's face became clear before him. *Julia Cavanaugh.* Anger tightened the muscles in his neck. Pain shot through his temples.

Calamity moseyed next to the woman

and sniffed her hand. Then the dog's tail wagged, and she pranced like she always did when they had special visitors.

"Calamity, no. Sit." His voice was sharp.

"I'm so sorry. I didn't know it was you." Her voice blabbered on. "Miriam said I could stay here. You weren't supposed to be back, and I thought you were . . ." Her chin quivered. "Oh, I don't know what I thought. Look at you. You're bleeding."

The young woman, lamplight flickering in her brown eyes, moved toward the empty water basin. "Don't you have a clean rag around here?" Long hair, probably let down for sleep, fell over her shoulders in soft, dark waves. He'd thought her pretty the first time he'd seen her, but now she looked more than pretty—beautiful—like a princess from the book of stories Miriam read to her girls.

Isaac quickly looked away. He took off his soaked coat and slung it over the bedpost. Shivers shook his body, and he struggled to pull the blanket around him. "I d–d–don't know." His teeth chattered as he attempted to answer her question. "Maybe in—"

She glanced at him. "It's fine. Never

mind." She crouched and rummaged through her things, finally displaying a thick piece of white fabric. "This'll work perfectly. It's made to soak up liquid." She walked toward him.

"Uh, is that a diaper?" Isaac asked, his anger fading to confusion. *Why did she say she was here?*

Julia chuckled. "Don't worry. It's been boiled, so it's perfectly clean. I always keep some with me to use for. . .whatever I may need."

"Like cleaning the wound of a poor parson who's been walloped in his own home?"

"I'm so sorry." Julia's lower lip pushed out in a pout. Her eyes glistened as she gazed at him. "I was afraid. I've never spent the night alone before, much less in a house made of earth. But Mr. Falcon and I agreed it would be easier on the girls if I didn't stay at their place, and then the storm came and"—she tentatively glanced up—"and the critters fell on me. I suppose I just panicked, like a silly schoolgirl."

Isaac tilted his head, taking in the sight of her sincere eyes. First leaving the girls, then Horace trying to wed her, then missing the train. He couldn't imagine a worse first day on the prairie. "You're not a silly schoolgirl."

Julia's lips turned up in a half smile, and she curved a strand of hair behind her ear.

"You poor thing. You're freezing." She lifted the quilt from the bed, shook it off, and then wrapped it around his shoulders, folding it snug under his chin like a mother bundling a child after he'd played in the snow. "Does it hurt?"

"Only a little." He turned his head and realized he hadn't told the whole truth. It hurt more than a little.

She held the lantern and examined his head. A strand of her hair came loose and brushed Isaac's cheek. Her fingers gingerly rubbed over his wound. He winced, but only slightly.

"It's not a big gash, and not deep." Her shoulders relaxed. "There's a pretty big knot behind your ear, but it should be gone in a few days." She dabbed the blood with the diaper, then positioned it over the wound. "Hold this here. Tight." She placed his hand over it. Then her soft palm covered his. "So, uh, leave it there until the bleeding stops." Pink tinged her cheeks as she pulled her hand away.

She patted his pillow. "Lie down here. Get comfortable."

He did as he was told and rolled to his side.

Satisfied, she turned toward the stove. "Now to get you and Calamity warm."

Julia opened the gate of the stove and moved to the basket of coal. She hesitated and sucked in a deep breath.

"What is it?" He lifted his head.

She kicked the wooden coal box toward him. He peered inside and saw a snake shift from the movement.

"It's not a rattler, is it?"

Isaac eyed the critter's brown markings. "It's a gopher snake." He pressed his lips together, forcing his laughter to stay inside.

With quick movements, she reached down and stood back up, holding the snake as it quivered and squirmed in her hand. She stood tall, trying to be brave, but Isaac saw the fear and revulsion in her eyes.

"I thought not. No rattle." She marched

to the door, held it open against the wind, and hurled the creature into the storm. "Sorry, snake. You can't find refuge in this house."

As she closed the door behind her, the brave demeanor vanished, and she shuddered. "That was awful."

Isaac chuckled. "You were made for the prairie."

Julia pulled her hair behind her and tied it into a knot, which utterly baffled him. *How did she get it to stay up like that?*

"Not hardly." She shook her head. "I'm a city girl. I always wanted to come out West—to visit, but never to stay." She threw coal into the stove. "When the train comes, I'll be heading back—as long as they'll still take my round-trip ticket. It says no exchanges on it, but surely they wouldn't leave me stranded out here."

Isaac had never known the railroad folks to be compassionate, but he didn't want to burden her with that now. "You never know. You might decide you like it out here."

She skillfully lit the coal, fanning the flames into a strong fire. "I doubt it."

Julia lifted Isaac's folded Indian

blanket from a peg on the wall and laid it on the ground near the fire. She walked to him. "I think you should sit in front of the heat. The sooner you get warm, the better."

Isaac attempted to pull his legs around, but pain shot through them as well as through the rest of his body. He tried to sit up, but his head felt fuzzy. He lay back down and let out a low moan. "Guess the hail battered me a bit."

Julia approached and kneeled before him. Her face, only inches from his, displayed compassion. "And you're probably stinging from the numbness, too." She reached for his hand. "Let me help you."

Isaac shook his head. "No, it's fine. I can do it." He struggled to his feet, but his knees gave out beneath him and he nearly toppled onto her. He felt like a weak fool crumpling into her like that and did his best to get his footing. It did little good, and she reached her arm under his, propping him up.

"Just think of me as your nurse," she said as she walked him to the blanket and eased him to the floor. Isaac's heart raced, and he knew it had nothing to do with the hail or the blow to his head.

He crouched before the black stove, taking in its warmth. Calamity curled up beside him. "Just like that lady I read about. What was her name? Oh yes, Florence Nightingale."

She took the quilt from the bed, laying it over him and tucking it around his shoulders. Then he watched as she set to work, making a stew from the canned goods and dried meat she found. He was awed by this woman—the way she cared for him so selflessly. She moved about her work without complaint. He almost thought he spotted a hint of joy. And despite her own suffering, she served him, helped him. Milo's quote of Scripture drifted to his consciousness. *It is not good that the man should be alone.*

Isaac stroked Calamity, noticing her tail wag. He wouldn't have blamed her if she let him care for his own wounds, make his own fire, prepare his own meal. Especially after the way he'd treated her earlier.

Deeply sighing, Isaac breathed in the stew's rich, inviting scent and somehow also breathed in her presence, realizing how right it felt.

"Thank you," he said.

Julia poured the stew into a bowl and placed some in front of Calamity, who slurped it up. Then she filled two mugs, grabbed a couple squares of hard tack, and sat down in the chair next to him. Despite his pounding head, he righted himself, leaning back against the wall.

"You better try it first before thanking me." She smiled. "It might be the worst 'vittles' you ever 'done ate'—or at least I think that's what they call dinner in 'these here parts.'"

"I didn't mean that. Or rather only that." He balanced the mug on his knee. "Thank you for taking care of me tonight."

"Well." She glanced over at him, and for the first time Isaac noticed small freckles on the bridge of her nose. "I hurt you, so I had to help you." She paused for a moment. "Actually, that's not the complete truth. I'm glad to do it. I feel better being busy. Besides . . ." She smiled simply. "I'm starting to like you." She winked. "Just a little."

I like you, too, Isaac wanted to say, but

the words caught. He'd longed for a night alone on the prairie, but somehow this time with Miss Cavanaugh felt like an unexpected blessing—a comfort he hadn't realized he needed. He felt grateful not just for her help, but for her company.

They sat silent for a moment as each one ate. Isaac found himself distracted by her nearness.

After a few moments, Isaac saw Julia's gaze sweep the room. "This sure isn't where I thought I'd be tonight."

A tinge of embarrassment touched Isaac for his rough surroundings. "It's pretty primitive—not like New York, I'd imagine." He angled his head toward the curtains. "Except for those—and all the other kind gifts my flock bestows on me." The thought of his ministry relaxed him, gave him joy. "And after I get back from my circuit, Abe and Jefferson are gonna help put up some planks to keep the critters out." He grinned.

Julia's shoulders scrunched up. "Oh, it's not that. I was just thinking this is the first night in a long time that I haven't slept to the sound of a clacking train—or surrounded by little girls."

"That must be a strange feeling."

Julia's lips arched downward. She took in a breath and then shook her head, as if pushing the sad thoughts away. "Tell me about your sweet dog here." She buried her finger in Calamity's fur behind her ears, causing the sheepdog to moan in bliss. "Did I hear you call her Calamity? That's an unusual name."

Isaac chuckled. "Yes, well, I'm not sure if you noticed, but she's blind in one eye. Was born that way. I came upon a farmer who was going to put her down." He stroked the dog's back.

"And you call her Calamity because . . ."

"Well, because half the time she's bumping into stuff. And also because she reminds me of Calamity Jane, who was my friend William Hickok's woman. Jane is a whirlwind on the outside but is sweet and faithful as anyone you've ever seen."

"William Hickok, as in Wild Bill Hickok?"

Isaac nodded. "You know of him?"

"I read about him fighting the Indians. It made me want to see the West—like my

174

father. He always dreamed of coming out West."

The coal crackled, its dry smell filling the room.

"Your father passed away?"

"Yes, and my mother, when I was eight."

"My ma died when I was five."

"I'm sorry." Her eyes linked with his, and then she swept her hand around the room. "Of course, nothing could have prepared me for this version of the Wild West—snakes falling on my head . . ."

Isaac shook his head and grinned compassionately. "Sorry 'bout that." He sat up straighter, realizing his muscles ached less and his head no longer throbbed. "But I do love this old soddy. It's safe and it's snug. And it's perfect for one . . ." He paused, and she looked at him.

And even more perfect for two. The thought came unbidden, and for the first time in many years, Isaac realized he longed for a companion. The strong emotions surprised him, stirring up longings he thought he'd buried long ago—for a wife, a family. And worse, these desires centered at this moment around Miss Cavanaugh, a woman he barely knew, but someone he unexpectedly craved to know better. He forced himself to push those thoughts away and think of her as nothing more than someone he could minister to in his official role as a parson. *She's just another sheep, a member of the flock.* Still, he knew he couldn't stay.

"I've got to go," he said, abruptly grabbing the hard tack. "I'm sorry, Miss Cavanaugh. The storm seems to have settled down and I really can't—" He paused, anxiety hammering his heart. "I can't stay here."

And without waiting for her reply, Isaac stepped into the cold night air, Calamity trailing behind.

Chapter Twelve

A cry filtered through Julia's grogginess, stirring her awake.

In her sleepy haze, she believed Bea had again wedged her leg between the rods of her bed frame.

"I'll be right there, sweetie." She attempted to open her eyes, but the room was bright—the sunlight streamed onto her face. Julia sat up, reaching. Reaching for Bea. . .

Yet something was wrong. The room was quiet. Too quiet and still. There were no clomping footsteps or little girl giggles. Then, like dust stirred by wagon wheels over the prairie, truth descended upon Julia's confused thoughts. *Isaac's soddy.*

She closed her eyes tight once more and tucked her head back under blankets that smelled of the parson and the prairie.

The realization the girls were gone, combined with the loneliness of this place, threatened to engulf her. Yet other thoughts emerged—such as the memory of her conversation last night with Isaac. The way he looked in the lantern light. His smile. His thankfulness for a simple meal, even though *she* was the one taking over *his* space. And even though she'd nearly knocked him out went he'd entered his own home.

The cry wailed again, louder than before, interrupting her reverie.

"What on earth?" Julia slid her feet to the floor and froze when she felt the dirt.

"Don't these people know about wooden floors?" she mumbled, reaching under her petticoats to peel off her stockings. The last thing she needed was to get them even dirtier than they already were.

She tossed the stockings onto the bed and tiptoed to the window. The crisp morning's prickly fingers contrasted with the sun's rays reaching through the glass. She shivered and pulled her arms tight to her.

"Maah!" it sounded again.

Julia directed her gaze to the spot from where she believed the cry had come. *There.* Fifty feet away, she spied a lamb, lolling on its side and caught in the branches of a short, jagged tree.

After Isaac had left last night with a slam of the door, Julia had listened as he and his dog joined the horse in the barn. She assumed that's where he'd stayed. Was he sleeping in? Why wasn't he rushing out to save the scared creature? When she spied no movement in the barn—heard no sound of Isaac or Calamity rustling—Julia's stomach clenched. She was the lamb's only hope.

"Hold on, little one. I'm coming."

She plopped back onto the bed, brushed the dirt from her feet, and put her stockings back on. Picking up her traveling boots, she shook them—checking for critters—then put them on and went outside.

Julia hurried through the tall prairie

grass, finally reaching the lamb, and spotted one of its front hooves wedged in the tree's twisted trunk.

"Oh, sweetie." She knelt down. "Let me help you."

Her heart pounded as she stared into the lamb's sweet face. So scared, alone, trapped. *I understand, little one.*

"Maah!" The animal's eyes darted, and its hind legs kicked as Julia reached out toward the embedded front hoof.

"Shh. It's all right." She caressed its head, as if she were comforting Bea. The lamb relaxed, and Julia cautiously wiggled the hoof free.

The lamb scrambled to stand and then paused, looking at her.

Julia rubbed its head. "Where's your mama?"

The lamb let out a low "maah."

"Well, you can stay here for now, I suppose. C'mon." She knew the lamb couldn't understand her words, but maybe he'd realize she would do what she could to keep him safe. She took a few steps and felt pleased when the little lamb followed her.

Julia meandered back to the soddy

then walked the lamb around back in search of a shady spot. Finding one behind the house, she showed the creature a spot of greenish grass.

"I'll come back in a little bit." She patted the lamb's woolly back. "I have to admit. It's kind of nice having you for company."

Back inside, Julia rummanged in her valise for clean clothes. For now, a bath would have to wait, but it was far beyond time to get out of the filthy traveling dress.

Stuffed inside the valise was the parson's red bandanna. She hoped today she'd have a chance to wash it. She'd return to the clear water of the coulee if she had to.

Then, if I see him again, I can return it. The thought made her smile.

She undressed, leaving her clothes in a pile to be washed later, then slipped a simple light blue dress over her head.

Julia straightened the bodice and palmed the skirt. "Now, there's a woman who can survive on the prairie." She arranged her hair into a bun without the benefit of a mirror. "If I can just avoid being forced to marry an old prospector." She chuckled at her own contrariness.

Looking toward the small shelf of food, Julia spotted something on the table and clasped her hands together. A basket, covered with a yellow cloth, and a jar of inky purple jam waited on the table next to her Bible. A fresh bucket of water rested on the floor.

Julia lifted the cloth and breathed in the doughy scent. "Buckwheat cakes!" She'd tasted the baked snacks at one of the depot stops along the way. With the jam—which Julia guessed to be made from wild Montana huckleberries—it'd be a feast.

As she folded the cloth back over the bread, she found a small scrap of paper under the basket.

Came by this morning but didn't want to wake you. Glad you could catch up on your sleep. Be back on the morrow. Miriam.

"Did I sleep all day?" She did feel well rested.

She placed a buckwheat cake on the plate and slathered it with the sweet-smelling huckleberry jam, her stomach growling in expectation. So that's why Isaac was gone. Long gone. Heading out to meet his parishioners, and she was alone on the prairie.

The lamb's cry echoed to her again. *Well, alone except for you, little one.* "I'll be there in a minute," she called. "I'll bring you water."

As she consumed the satisfying meal, her thoughts returned to the handsome parson. His black eyes held such kindness. And something else. *Admiration?* Julia's heartbeat kicked up its tempo. Couldn't be. What was there to admire about a poor, stranded, pampered city girl with no family?

But she definitely admired *him*. His wit, compassion, strength. Isaac felt like a friend—a friend she craved to learn more about. Yet, since he was determined to head out on his preaching circuit, she doubted she'd have any time with him before she returned to New York.

She supposed she'd have to settle for spending time with his soddy. Julia's gaze traveled around the room, lingering over

the parson's few belongings before they
rested on the family Bible Miriam had
pointed out. She stepped to the bookshelf
and tugged it from its spot.

She hoisted the heavy book to the
table. It landed front-down with a *thud*,
and the flimsy back cover flopped open.
The back page was filled with notes in
a man's handwriting, made in thick,
broad strokes. A tinge of guilt nudged
her. She closed it and folded her hands,
considering whether she was prying.
Would Isaac want her to read it? Was
she being nosy?

Of course, it might not be Isaac's
handwriting at all. If this Bible was as
old as her family's, there could be
generations' worth of notes in here. Julia
placed her hand on the leather casing.
And if there was anything she wasn't
supposed to read, Miriam wouldn't have
offered it to her.

She reopened it to the back page. Just
as she thought—notes dating back to
before the War filled the white parchment.
Julia was amazed by the prayers and
songs of praise, the cries of various

men's hearts. Near the bottom, she read one prayer written in the form of a letter.

December 29, 1882

Dear God,

You know I promised to not marry and instead dedicate my life to ministry. I broke that vow, God, by marrying Bethany. And now she's dead, because I left her alone. God, I promise to never break my vow again. Please forgive me. Help me to serve You all my days.

Isaac Shepherd

Julia closed the Bible. Her throat tightened, and her chest ached for Isaac's loss, for his latent sense of guilt that leaked through. Rising tears burned her eyes.

"I shouldn't have read that. I'm so sorry," she muttered in prayer.

She lifted the Bible from the table and shoved the thick book back into its place. Her arms slunk to her sides, and her head roiled with a mixture of guilt, compassion, and curiosity. What had the letter meant? Was it even from the parson? Perhaps he had a great-grandfather Isaac. But the ink wasn't faded as it was in the other notes, and it was dated not seven years ago.

Julia propped her hands on the table for support. And who was Bethany? How did she die?

Why did I read those notes? What was I thinking?

* * * *

The next morning, Julia's eyes drooped as she swallowed her second breakfast in a row of buckwheat cakes and huckleberry jam. She failed to savor the sweet tastes as she had yesterday morning—not because the morsels had grown stale, but because the Herculean effort of the day before to keep her mounting loneliness at bay had left her exhausted. She'd striven to stay positive and busy, but by nightfall the effort seemed useless. Plus, try as she might, she couldn't squelch her curiosity about Isaac's past heartbreak. Her guilt about prying gnawed at her.

There was something else that

bothered her. If she was honest, she'd have to admit that she was beginning to care for the parson—at least in the sense that his opinion of her mattered.

Julia sighed and wiped a crumb from her lip. Her thoughts had spun around this way for the last twenty-four hours. A knock sounded at the door. She froze.

A second knock, then the door creaked open and she heard a soft footfall.

"Julia? Are you in here?" Miriam hurried in, hands swinging as if to balance her heavy middle.

Julia turned, and a strand of hair fell to her eyes. She brushed it back. "Yes, I'm sorry. You—you scared me."

But she felt more than fear. The sight of Isaac's sister had sent a rush of guilt into Julia's stomach.

"You had me worried when you didn't come to the door."

Avoiding the woman's eyes, Julia glanced down and watched a beetle scurry across her boot.

"Are you all right?" Miriam opened her arms, and Julia stepped into the embrace. "Did you have a difficult couple of nights out here?"

"No, that's not it." Julia pulled back. "Well, they *were* difficult, but . . ." Julia explored the woman's strong features, her square forehead, her compassionate eyes. "I must admit something." She took a deep breath, relieved to be able to talk to someone about what had been troubling her, yet nervous to see the kind woman's reaction. "I was looking around yesterday, and I saw Isaac's Bible. I didn't mean to pry, but there were handwritten notes in back." The words spilled from her. "And now I feel just awful. I think I read something I shouldn't have. . . ." She swallowed. "Among Isaac's notes."

A faint frown crept over Miriam's face, and Julia's heart sank. She didn't know why this woman's good regard mattered so much, but she didn't want to disappoint her—not after all the kindness she'd shown. Miriam's eyes searched hers.

"I'm sorry." Julia crossed her arms over her chest.

Miriam gently grasped Julia's shoulders. "I don't know what my brother wrote, but I can guess, and I don't want you to fret. My family doesn't have any secrets, nothing most folks around here don't already know. The best solution is for you to talk to Isaac. He shares his story and his heart with many. And I can fill you in, too. I'm good at keeping abreast of the matters in my little brother's life and heart."

Julia pinched a bit of her skirt's fabric and leaned a hand on one of the two chairs around the table. "Oh no, I couldn't ask. It's not my business. I'll be gone with the next train anyway. I probably won't even see your brother again." That thought sent with it a mild streak of regret. *Why do I so crave to see him?* Julia questioned herself. *I barely know the man, yet my thoughts keep drifting to him.* She returned her attention to Miriam. "If I talk to Isaac about it, it will only be to apologize for prying—and to offer my condolensces. He must have been devastated."

Miriam pointed to the chairs then walked past Julia to the other side of the table and sat down. "My back aches when I stand for too long—and this way we can talk."

Julia slid into the chair across from her.

"As for my brother," Miriam wiped perspiration with the back of her tanned hand, "I don't think you need to apologize, but if you feel you want to, I'm sure he will understand."

A hint of relief filtered through Julia's mind. If Miriam didn't think her intrusion in the parson's business was worrisome, she'd also try to let it go. And with the guilt gone, perhaps the curiosity would fly away as well. But Miriam didn't seem finished with the conversation. She folded her hands and tilted her head. A beat of silence passed before she spoke.

"I, uh, wanted to talk to you, well, about the train. . . ." A sympathetic crease formed in the prairie woman's forehead, and she twisted her lips as if trying to think of a way to say something.

"What?" Julia leaned closer. "Don't tell me it comes once a year."

"No, no." She shook her head. "It's just that Isaac, well, he's up at the ranch resting for a day or two. I guess that storm left him with some aching muscles as well as a bad cold."

A dash of warmth rushed to Julia's neck

at the thought of his being just a couple miles away. "I did my best to help him the other night. Poor man." She leaned back in her chair, remembering their conversation and the comfort of being near him. "But he sure was a sight when he arrived. I'm not surprised he's ill."

Miriam's eyes glinted briefly and the look of pity returned. Julia's chest tightened. What was Miriam trying to tell her?

"I know you thought your ticket would still be good for the next train, but it doesn't work that way. Isaac said he saw your ticket when he was here, and. . .oh dear." She tipped her head to the side. "It's one-way. You'll have to buy a ticket home."

"That can't be right." Julia's mind churned. "I was to return the same day I arrived. Mrs. Gaffin, my headmistress, she knew that. She took care of everything." Julia stood and moved to the valise next to the bed. She pulled the ticket out and handed it to Miriam.

Miriam glanced at it and handed it back. "I'm so sorry. I know you want to return as soon as you can, but this is not a round-trip ticket. It says the destination is Big Sandy."

"But—but that's just the final stop before I return home." Julia's stomach felt as if the train had chugged over it, leaving her in pieces. "Isn't that what that means?"

Miriam slowly shook her head.

Julia slumped back into the chair. The ramifications swirled in her mind like smoke from the steam engine. "I don't have the fare for a ticket home. I barely have enough money to pay for meager meals along the way." She glanced around the primitive room, remembering the insects and the snake, the storm. How lonely she'd felt the last two days. It seemed the ache of losing the girls would never mend until she got on with her life—and that meant returning to New York. She'd figured the train would return in about a week. Perhaps she could handle that, but longer? "I need to get back to New York."

Miriam reached over and grabbed her hands. "We'd help you out if we could, but we just don't have that kind of money."

"No, of course not." Julia's mind swam,

searching for a solution. "I'll write Mrs. Gaffin. That's all I can do. I'm sure she'll send money." Her voice trailed off as realization dawned. *Oh, Mrs. Gaffin, what have you done?*

Julia fingered the tablecloth. "She thought I'd be getting married here." She glanced up at Miriam and shrugged. "That's why she didn't give me a round-trip ticket. She thought I'd be swept into married bliss with"—she covered her mouth as a desperate laugh emerged—"with Horace the goldminer."

Miriam's eyes exuded sympathy as she flung her big belly across the table and threw her arms around Julia. "I'm so sorry, dear. But try to think of the good things about this." She smirked at Julia. "First and foremost, you'll get to spend more time with my brother."

Julia pulled her body back and sent Miriam a mock glare. "You're terrible." But she had to admit that the thought did make the sentence of staying there a bit less harsh.

Chapter Thirteen

....

Grateful to be feeling better and to be out on the trail again, Isaac had spent the day headed eastward toward Lodge Pole. Yet on his way, he took off on a jackrabbit trail in search of Horace.

When he finally found him in Gold Creek, the obstinate prospector was up to his armpits in the clear mountain water with a white cake of soap clutched in his surprisingly clean hand.

"Horace? Didn't you take a bath just last month?" Isaac climbed down from his horse and led her to the water. Calamity trotted to the stream for a long drink and then jumped in. The dog's lips seemed to curl up in a smile as she dog paddled in a large circle around Horace.

Offended by Isaac's words, Horace refused to talk to the minister for a good five minutes as he slogged out of the creek, dried off next to an old downed tree, and tugged on his grimy clothes.

"Don't you think you should wash those britches before you put them back on?" Isaac ventured.

Horace shoved his foot in his trousers and glanced up, scratching his wet hair. "Huh?"

Isaac figured the man was at least trying.

Horace finished getting dressed, then smoothed his hair back and donned his hat.

"You look very nice," Isaac said.

The middle-aged miner licked his lips and grinned. "Why thank ya," he said, the silent punishment apparently over. "But don't be going on with that small talk. I know why yer here." He squatted on the old log, elbows on knees.

Isaac joined him, grateful to have an opening to start the conversation.

"Horace, I know you want a wife. I can see how you'd be lonely up here, but—"

Horace smiled. "Yup. Real lonely, but I got me a wife now. A real New York lady I can love, and who'll fix me up some good vittles," he pointed to a gash in his pants, "and mend my duds." He beamed. "I hafta tell ya, Parson Ike. This morning I thanked the Good Lord for sendin' her to me."

Calamity ran up the bank to Isaac's side and shook, spraying droplets of water all over him.

Isaac moaned—not because of the dog, but rather the man. Leave it to Horace to try his patience. What would it take to convince him Julia Cavanaugh was not going to become his wife?

After a couple hours of eddying around the same subjects—"She doesn't want to marry," "You can't buy a wife," and "She's going back East"—without so much as budging Horace's mindset, Isaac finally gave up. As he cinched his saddle around the butterscotch mare's girth, he tried one last tactic. "Why not trust the Lord to bring the right woman along?"

Horace moseyed next to Isaac and

placed a hand on his shoulder. His lips puckered, and his eyes squinted. "With all yer advice ta me 'bout trustin' the Lord, a soul's gotta wonder," he gulped a loud swallow, "why don't *you* trust the Good Lord, Parson Ike? Why don't you got no wife?"

Isaac released a low growl. He thought he'd escaped the constant push toward matrimony when he'd left Miriam behind in Lonesome Prairie.

"Horace." His voice came close to a bark. Then he softened his tone. "We are not talking about me." He mounted his mare. "Just leave the poor woman alone. At least wait till I get back before you pursue her."

With the late-afternoon sun on Isaac's back, he headed east again. He'd intended to reach Lodge Pole by morning to preach, but with nightfall came fatigue. When he spied Giant Jim crouching beside a campfire alongside the road, Isaac gratefully laid out his bedroll. And it seemed he'd barely closed his eyes when he opened them to dawn, the smell of meat over a spit, and Giant Jim's smiling face. Fifteen minutes later he was finishing up breakfast around the small campfire.

"You cook up a good bite of gopher, Jim. My compliments." He gnawed one last bite of the tender meat, tossed the carcass into the fire, and then swabbed his greasy fingers on his trousers. "I thank you for the company."

Giant Jim stoked the campfire with a stick. "Glad to meet up with you here. Heading over to Lodge Pole?"

Isaac leaned back on his hands. "Yup, my parishioners over in Lodge Pole probably think they'll never hear a sermon again." He pushed to a stand, but Giant Jim leaned in close, halting him.

"Before you go, Parson." Jim's forehead folded into a frown. "I gotta tell ya somethin'."

Isaac sat back down. "Of course."

"Well, I didn't wanna ruin yer breakfast or nothin', but . . ." His normally bold voice wavered. "Mabelina's run off. I been searchin' fer days, but I can't find 'er. I love 'er, Parson Ike. I don't know what to do."

A spark flew from the fire, and Isaac snuffed it with his boot. "What happened?"

"A man in town told her if she don't go back to. . .well, you know. . .what she was doin' before, he'll turn the vigilantes on 'er for killin' Elder Milo." Jim clasped his brow in his Goliath hand as he shook his head. "It's my fault. If I hadn't been so plum jealous and pulled my gun that day, Milo'd still be here, an' my Mabelina and me'd be together."

Isaac's mind swirled for answers like a hawk seeking prey. Who told Mabelina she had to go back to the brothel? Could it be old Dusty? From what Isaac knew, Dusty—though not a principled man—had never forced any of the girls into prostitution. Isaac didn't think there was anyone of such base character in Big Sandy. Maybe in Great Falls, but not in Big Sandy. *Poor Mabelina. Poor Jim.* Compassion gripped his parson's heart.

"Now you look me in the eye." Isaac angled his head to grab the man's gaze. "You were wrong to pull that gun. I'm not gonna lie to you. But I can tell by the way you're actin' that you're sorry. Am I right?"

Giant Jim's eyelids dropped as he nodded. "I am sorry, Parson. I been thinkin' 'bout it all the time. Tellin' God I'm sorry, over and over. And not jest fer that. My ma and pa were good, God-fearin' folk. They raised me in the Bible teachings. I left 'em years ago, an' when I did, I forsook the Bible, too. Done far too many things I regret. But when Elder Milo died, an' it was all my fault . . ." His lips tightened. "It made me wonder." He suddenly rose, stalked to his sturdy bay, and lifted a black Bible out of the saddlebag. "Been readin', too," he said as he sauntered back. "Funny how the learnin' my folks taught me as a youngster came back."

Isaac nodded.

Jim hunched down next to Isaac and held the Bible in front of himself. "So what I figured out was that this here book says that I'm some kinda dead man. Like that Lazarus." Jim's thick black eyebrows sloped upward as he observed Isaac expectantly. "Dead by all the bad things I done. I wanna be alive." The Bible quaked in Jim's trembling grasp.

Isaac steadied Jim's hands and faced him. "When we were dead in our trespasses and sins, He made us alive in Christ Jesus. I love that passage."

"It says that?"

"Yes." Isaac spoke softly, overwhelmed with gratitude to be the vessel God chose. "Do you trust in the Savior?"

Tears pooled in Jim's eyes. "I do," he said. "More than any other."

The man's simple faith sent a surge of joy through Isaac. He knew the Good Shepherd also rejoiced at the return of one of His sheep. "Then you belong to Him, my friend." A breeze bustled over the camp, bringing with it a shower of white petals shaken loose from a blossoming tree.

"I'm His." The burly Montanan's mustache curved up as his mouth opened in a wide smile. "I know'd it." He stood and raised his fists. "I know'd it!"

"May I pray with you?" Isaac asked, when Jim settled back down.

"O' course." Jim folded his hands and bowed his head like a child.

As the slight breeze washed over them, Isaac lifted a prayer of gratitude to the Father for breathing new life into this man. Finishing, he stood. "I'm proud to call you brother." He patted Jim's arm.

"Thank you, Parson."

Isaac watched as Jim quietly packed up, thinking. Maybe he should go with Jim, help him find Mabelina. Lord knows Mabelina needed the help, too. As a circuit preacher Isaac chose where he went and when. Even though he'd promised to get to Lodge Pole as soon as possible, no one was expecting him on a certain day. He'd be welcomed whenever he arrived. If some time passed between visits, so be it.

As he finished loading the horses, Isaac shot a glance to his new brother in Christ.

"Jim, you ready to go find Mabelina?" He glanced at the sky. "Looks like it will be a good day for a ride."

"You mean you'll help me find 'er?"

"I'd be glad to." Isaac swung a foot over the mare's back and gripped the reins. "And maybe I can help with the vigilantes, too. From what Warren told me, the new judge—Judge Booker—wants to have Mabelina come before him when he comes around to town. But I want both of you to know that there's a lot of folks who will be standing up for Mabelina—making sure it's clear the judge and jury know that the shooting was just an accident."

"My thanks to ya, Parson Ike," Jim said, stomping out the campfire. "I'd sure 'preciate yer help."

Isaac grinned. The folks in Lodge Pole had waited this long. He supposed they'd get by a bit longer.

Chapter Fourteen

"Ready for the surprise?" Miriam's hand on Julia's arm pulled her to the door. Miriam had arrived at Julia's provisional home—Isaac's soddy—after breakfast as she had each of the six days Julia had stayed there. After another twenty-four hours of biding her time alone, Julia was as excited as a child to see Miriam's plump form.

Even before she stepped outside, Julia could tell it was going to be a warm day. She pushed the door open, and a child's voice, along with scampering footsteps, floated to Julia's ears. She stepped into

the hot sunshine, shielding her eyes
and letting them adjust to the brightness.

Then she saw her. Bea scampered
toward the sod house wearing a new
yellow dress. Her arms flopped at her
sides. Her hair bounced.

"Miss Cav'naw!" she shouted as she
sprinted closer. "I coming!"

"Bea," Julia whispered. The girl's image
blurred, and Julia blinked away the tears
that threatened to spill. She covered her
mouth with a trembling hand and then
raced outside and crouched down. She
opened her arms, and the toddler
slammed against her body, nearly
toppling her over. "Oh, little Bea, how
pretty you look. Like a ray of bright
sunshine. What in the world are you
doing here, my sweet?"

Shelby strolled up behind Bea, her
blond hair gleaming in the sun. She'd also
traded Mrs. Gaffin's white travel dress for
a more appropriate blue frock and apron.
She grinned as she planted two fists on
her hips.

"We overheard Ma and Pa—that's what
they want us to call them—talking about
you being here, and we begged to see

you. We promised not to cry when we leave." She ruffled her sister's hair. "Didn't we, Bea?"

"Yep. No cry."

Julia scooped up Bea and stood. Then with the toddler clinging to her neck, she pulled Shelby into a tight hug.

Julia closed her eyes and soaked them in—their smell, their touch.

"You like our dwesses?" Bea asked.

Julia nodded without releasing them, reveling in the sound of their voices. She knew this small morsel of closeness would sustain her for days—until the loneliness came knocking again.

Still holding the girls, Julia glanced up and saw Elizabeth and two other women approaching. They sported frilly aprons and carried dishes of food and baskets. Following them, a throng of children—both boys and girls of varying ages—hiked up from the coulee.

"Good morning!" Elizabeth paced closer, her long light green skirt flowing against the gently swaying grass. Even though there was a smile on her face, her gaze hinted at worry—and maybe even a little pain at witnessing the joyful reunion.

"Good morning, Elizabeth." Julia released her arm from around Shelby and set Bea down, pausing until Bea was steady on her feet. Then she stepped back awkwardly.

Glancing at the beautiful pioneer woman, Julia realized for the first time that Elizabeth didn't seem to be much older than she—twenty-one, perhaps? And slim, gracious, youthful. Yet she was already married and now raising the family she'd been longing for.

Julia opened her mouth to ask Elizabeth how the girls were faring when an older boy scuttled up and tagged Shelby's arm. "You're it!"

Shelby jerked toward the blond boy of about twelve, who tore off running behind the house. "That's Christopher. He's Aunt Miriam's oldest. He's such a *boy*." Then she tugged on Julia's arm. "Play with us, Miss Cavanaugh. Please. Like you used to."

Julia glanced at Elizabeth, still a few steps away, and the other two women. Their kind faces seemed to urge her to go ahead. Julia smiled at Shelby. "I'll be right there. Just a minute."

The children scampered off, and Elizabeth strode to Julia's side then pointed to the plate she carried. A pie, its crust carefully woven, rested on it.

"I hope you like cherries." Her kindhearted gaze met Julia's and paused as if to say it was all right that she'd been embracing the girls.

Julia returned the smile, thankful for the woman's unspoken thoughtfulness.

The other two ladies shuffled up. Another young bride, by her appearance, held a baby slung in an Indian basket on her back. And an older, rounder woman stood next to a pale, red-haired boy about ten years old.

"Well, what I'd like to know is where'd that Miriam dash off to?" the older woman asked in a strong British accent. Her eyes flitted about, and evidently not seeing Miriam, she moved to Julia. "I'm Sarah Mack, dearie. And this is my son William. We are pleased to make your acquaintance." Her tall and robust form dipped in a quick curtsy.

"Nice to meet you." Julia nodded.

"I'm Ellen Robertson. I live just down the road," the young mother with the baby said. "We're the welcoming committee." She straightened her dress. "They call us the Pretty Apron Brigade." The ladies giggled as they bustled about, preparing for whatever had brought them here.

"Can I help with anything?" Julia asked.

"No, I think we have everything. You're our guest," Ellen commented. "Just enjoy yourself."

Sarah pulled a dainty handkerchief from her bodice and patted her forehead. "Oh, this heat. I'm quite spent." She glanced at Julia. "I simply must sit down."

"From the smell of the fire starting up in the cookstove, I think Miriam's inside. You're welcome to go in and rest." Then Julia chuckled. "Listen to me. I'm talking as if it's my own place. Still, it's much cooler inside. . . ."

"Oh, what a sweet little duck you are. Thank you. I don't mind if I do."

Elizabeth patted Julia's shoulder. "Why don't you play with the children? We can handle the preparations."

Julia agreed, still unsure what the preparations were for, and then headed out to the grassy field behind the soddy.

Under the shady tree, Julia noticed the lamb was still there, munching grass. She paused and rubbed its coarse wool back, reminding herself to ask the womenfolk whom she belonged to.

A few yards away, more trees circled what looked to be a small spring. Under the trees stood a picnic table made of rough wood, and she wondered if Isaac had made it.

Where did those children disappear to?

Movement caught her attention, and Julia spotted bodies under the table. At first she thought they were playing a game of hide-and-seek—with her being the seeker. But as she got closer, she spied Miriam's oldest boy Christopher scurrying from the soddy with something in his hand. When Christopher returned to the group, the other children circled around him, completely entranced.

Julia sneaked over, stifling the urge to startle them with a "Boo!"

Instead, she inched close and watched as Christopher and Shelby—her very own Shelby—each held a mouse in one of their hands. In his other hand,

Christopher clutched a tiny wire. He'd formed the end into the letter *C*.

Another boy used a flint to start a small fire under the table, and he heated up the end of the wire.

"Do it!" one of the other youths encouraged.

"I will," Christopher snapped. "It's wiggling."

Then, in a quick movement, Christopher branded the mouse's rump with the wire, leaving the letter *C* in its thin gray fur.

Julia gasped as her stomach turned. To see them holding those disgusting creatures was bad enough, but this. . .

"Children, no!"

Her words were drowned out by an eruption of screams as the mouse squeaked and chomped down on Christopher's hand. "Ouch!" he cried as he dropped it.

Shelby screeched, unleashing her mouse, too. The other children scrambled to their feet, squealing as they hurried out from under the table—all except Bea, who remained where she was, crying.

When they saw Julia standing in front of them, the children came to a quick halt.

"All of you, stay right here," she commanded in an authoritative tone. Then she squatted down to fetch Bea, who scrambled out and tumbled into her arms. Julia patted the little girl's back, calming her, and then stood with Bea still clinging to her leg.

"Hmm." She perused each of their faces. "Seems to me you all have too much time on your hands."

Shelby's eyes widened, and she frowned. "Well, not really."

"Sure you do, but don't worry. We can fix that." Julia pointed to the table. "Sit down, all of you. We will have lunch soon, but first, let's make sure that each of you knows the ABCs, and after that—mathematics. Let's start with you, Christopher."

He opened his mouth and then closed it again.

"Don't be shy," she urged. "I can tell you are a bright boy. I would have never thought of branding a mouse."

Christopher grinned then started, "A, B, C . . ."

By the time the Pretty Apron Brigade wandered out of the house bringing the meal, Julia had assessed each student's abilities and learned all of their names.

"Mama, Miss Cavanaugh taught me how to spell my name," Miriam's youngest boy declared with a toothless grin. "J-o-s-h-u-a."

"Very good. I'm impressed." Miriam opened what appeared to be a bedsheet and spread it over the table. "My, my, Miss Cavanaugh," Miriam said as she smoothed the tablecloth. She eyed the other women with a smile. "You *are* a good teacher."

"Thank you." Julia took the stack of plates from Elizabeth's hands and began setting them at each woman's spot. "But I'm not a real teacher. I only worked with the girls at the orphanage, helping them to read and figure sums. And I read books to them that I liked, too."

"That sounds like a ducky teacher to me." Sarah poured tea for the adults in lovely English Rose teacups she'd brought.

"I told you she would be." Elizabeth opened a basket of buckwheat cakes and placed one on each plate. Then she spread out a blanket for the children. "Wash your hands in the spring, children. Then come back for lunch."

"A combination of tea and luncheon," Sarah commented. "It's teatime in some part of the world. The pastry and berries are just lovely with the fried chicken, pancakes, and boiled eggs, don't you think?"

The warm breeze ruffled the tablecloth slightly as everyone settled.

"Christopher, will you give thanks?" Miriam asked once the children had returned.

"O Bread of Life, from day to day be Thou our Comfort, food, and stay. Amen."

"Thank you, Christopher." Miriam leaned over and patted his head.

Julia gazed at the scene around her, appreciating the women's easy companionship. She imagined their friendship had been formed by shared labor, victories, heartache. And secretly she wondered what it would be like to live in a community like this.

Julia used her fork to cut off a bite of buckwheat pancake. Yet as she lifted it to her mouth, she realized that the others weren't eating. Instead, their eyes were focused on her.

Miriam cleared her throat. "Miss Cavanaugh, we have something we want to ask you."

Julia set down her fork to listen, but Miriam waved a hand her direction. "No need to stop on account of us."

"We know you're hungry, dearie," Sarah interjected.

Miriam rubbed the top of her large stomach and leaned forward. "Welcoming you was not the only reason we've come. Nor was the main purpose of this visit the treats."

Julia tilted her head, feeling the sun warm upon it, taking in the scent of prairie grass on the breeze. "What do you mean?" Julia grinned. "These treats are lovely. I've never seen such wonderful pies, cakes, tea, and—" She held up a triangular pastry.

"That's a scone, dearie." Sarah snapped open a Chinese fan and began cooling herself.

"You mean you don't bring these to all the newcomers?"

Ellen, who'd sat quietly observing while she nursed her baby, furrowed her brow. "Y'all didn't do it for me."

"Yes, we did, dear." Elizabeth patted her hand. "Didn't I bring you a pie?"

Ellen's eyes lifted upward as if trying to remember. "I s'pose so." She gazed at Elizabeth's masterful cherry pie. "But not like that."

Julia clutched Miriam's hand. "So, tell me—why *did* you bring such a feast?"

The women exchanged smiling glances as if waiting for the other to speak.

"We want you to teach our children their lessons," Sarah finally blurted out, her bushy brown eyebrows raised. "Now I must eat, or I'm sure to faint."

"That's right." Miriam fingered her hair back from her brow. "We know you're staying for only a while, but we'd sure appreciate it if you'd teach while you're here. Just the basics: reading, writing, arithmetic."

Julia's heart warmed at the thought. She gazed at the children around the table in their prairie clothes, so different from her New York girls—yet probably much the same.

"I'd love to, of course. But I didn't bring any schoolbooks. Do you have slates?"

"Don't worry about that." Miriam's voice bubbled with excitement. "We have a few, enough for our families. We can pool our books together. It'll work just fine."

The thought of once again spending the day with children seemed almost too good to be true. *To witness their curiosity. To hear their laughter.* She didn't even mind their pranks much.

"As long as you know I have no certification—that I'm not a real teacher—then I'd love to teach your children while I'm waiting to go back."

"Certification?" Sarah waved a hand in the air. "This isn't the city, dearie. Far from it. Who do you think will come around and ask for your teaching papers? Isaac? I think not."

Happy cackles erupted from the ladies, and even the children nodded and smiled—especially Shelby.

"Miss Cav'naw teach?" Bea approached and snuggled up onto Julia's lap.

"Well, you're a little young to go to

school, but I'm sure your new mama will teach you your letters."

Bea hopped off and climbed up on Elizabeth's lap. "Letters, Mama?"

"Yes, Bea." Elizabeth lifted the small girl closer and kissed her cheek. "Mama would love to teach you letters." She turned back to Julia. "We figured you could hold class right up at our place," Elizabeth added. "There's no reason you have to stay at my brother's dirty old soddy when you can be with us. Miriam already talked to Johannah about sharing her bed. We'll fix you up a corner of a room for yourself."

"Really?" Julia glanced at Miriam.

Miriam nodded, a huge smile on her face. "Really. We all talked up at the house, and we think you should come stay with us until you hear from your headmistress."

Julia looked back at Elizabeth. "Are you sure it's all right with Mr. Falcon?"

Elizabeth bit her lip and then nodded. "Yes—it is. Why don't you come in a couple of days? That'll give the girls time to clean their room."

Miriam pulled Julia into an embrace and then patted her back. "And you know. . .we'll be looking for a permanent teacher once Isaac builds the school."

Julia pulled back, shaking her head. It was all so much to take in.

Her smile faded slightly when she met Miriam's gaze and saw the *look*—the one that had clearly frustrated Isaac. The one that said, *Our school needs a teacher, but my brother needs a wife even more.*

Chapter Fifteen

The other women had left nearly an hour prior, but Sarah Mack still sat at the picnic table behind the house. Julia lingered beside her, and together they watched William playing with the lamb. A hint of curls played in the boy's red hair. His skin was nearly as white as the lamb's wool. And as mother watched son, Julia spied the love in her eyes.

"William, love," Sarah called. "Why don't you walk the lamb back to Mrs. Lafuze's house. Although," she added in a lower voice, "he might just run away again and come back." Sarah glanced around. "It is lovely here," she said to Julia. "A beautiful spot."

"Yes." Julia gazed at the tiny spring, the flowing prairie grass, the big sky. "Even though the soddy is small, the parson seems to take good care of his land—when he's around, that is."

"He's a hard worker, that one. He's even stopped by our house once or twice to split wood. And once to clean the stovepipe. It was smoking quite terribly."

Sarah had gray at the temples and was round like Mrs. Gaffin. As they chatted, Julia discovered that the British woman had fallen in love with an American diplomat's son. Her father hadn't approved the match, but the two married anyway, moved from England to the United States, and headed out West. Sarah had become a mother and a settler before she was twenty. Now a widow, she'd sent her three older sons to England for schooling, so it was just her and ten-year-old William.

"I'm sure it's wonderful to get all the help you can, especially with Mr. Mack being gone."

"Yes." Sarah let out a heavy sigh. "Did I

tell you, dearie, that we originally moved here to study the wildlife? Edwin was an ornithologist, you know. They found him at the bottom of a cliff in the Bear's Paw Mountains. I've no doubt he was watching some new bird in some dodgy spot with his field glasses, not paying attention to what he was doing." She placed a hand over her heart. "My only comfort is knowing that in heaven, my dear Edwin can talk to the Creator Himself about all the birds. He loved the feathered creatures—second only to the lads and me, you know."

Julia's gut ached at the thought of losing a husband in this place—of living off this land alone, without protection, and caring for a child on top of that.

In the distance William hurried down the road to Miriam's house. He laughed as he jogged along, the small lamb bleating and following behind.

Julia felt Sarah's hand on hers. "Don't have a sad mug there, dearie. I know mine's not a jolly story, but it's through my heartache I've found my hiding place in God. Before then I believed in Him, but now I depend on Him, day by day."

Sarah removed her hand and played with the cuff of her sleeve, a content look settling on her face. Almost instinctively, the lines of a hymn sang from her lips: "When sorrows like sea billows roll; whatever my lot, Thou hast taught me to say, it is well, it is well, with my soul. . . ."

The breeze carried her song, and the two sat in silence a moment.

"Did you ever think about going back? To England." Julia reached up, plucked a leaf off the tree hanging over the table, and twirled it between her fingers.

"I put my mind to it a couple times, but Edwin was mad for this place. My dear man would recline on the front step for hours just watching the clouds roll in. I think he counted them, trying to calculate how many it would take to fill the vast sky." She chuckled at the memory. "Make tracks to England, you ask? I'd leave all he loved behind." She rose and shook out her apron, apparently finished with the conversation.

She began to wipe the lingering crumbs from the table. "Besides, others come around to help, too. Jefferson Lafuze and Abe Falcon. Milo Godfrey stocked my shelves for the first winter after Edwin died. And then," she paused, "Horace Whitbaum has been the biggest help. He lives the closest to me. Over the past year he's let William tag along with him as he hunts and traps. It has kept us fed."

"That's kind of him. It's wonderful how everyone helps his neighbor in these parts. In New York, there's too much suspicion for that. I've heard stories of good Samaritans being robbed when they stopped to help someone."

"Such a shame. You know, Horace truly has been a good neighbor," she said, blatantly returning to the topic. "Once, during a blizzard, he stopped by to bring in wood for us. He's a little unrefined perhaps, but underneath all that dirt you'll find a heart as golden as the treasure he seeks."

Julia stood and wiped the table with her apron. "Yes, well, I'm sure he's nice—but I have no desire to marry him." Julia couldn't understand why else Sarah would expound on Horace's finer qualities. "I'm sure you've heard of what's happened? Our supposed marriage is a misunderstanding. It'll be cleared up soon. Ellen Robertson took the letter I wrote for the headmistress Mrs. Gaffin. Mr. Robertson is heading to Fort Benton tomorrow, and he'll post it for me. I'm sure Mrs. Gaffin will respond right away to clear this up—and send my return fare."

Sarah blinked and her lips puckered in a frown. "Yes, of course, that situation must get mended up as soon as possible." She opened her fan and began waving it again, as if trying to wave away the discussion about Horace.

Julia was relieved to end the conversation but hoped her words hadn't been too harsh. "I'm so glad you all came to visit today."

"Yes, lovely, dearie. Now, don't you think we should head in and make up supper? My belly is rumbling. And while we're at it, we should lay out some blankets for William in the barn." Sarah hustled toward the house.

"In the barn?" Julia dropped her leaf and followed.

"There isn't enough room for three in the bed. It will be cozy enough for you and me. It's too late for me to head back now, you know. Besides, I thought it would give us more time to make our acquaintance. I'm sure you're eager to hear about all your new neighbors. Such fine folks."

Julia paused as she watched Sarah hustle into the house, her wide hips swaying.

"More time for you to extol for me all the good deeds and hidden virtues of Horace Whitbaum, you mean," Julia muttered under her breath. Was that the main objective of all the women around here—to get any new female in these parts hitched up? At least Miriam's hints weren't so repugnant to Julia. Isaac was closer to her age—and her preference. But Horace Whitbaum? Did Sarah honestly believe that Julia would be drawn to him?

Julia followed Sarah into the soddy and was surprised to see the woman already whipping up something in a small bowl. "I hope you like crepes, dearie. I scrounged up all the ingredients in the parson's cupboards and decided they would be delightful."

"Crepes?" Julia shook her head. "I'm sorry. I've never had the pleasure."

226

Sarah turned, her apple cheeks red from the exertion of whipping the batter. "Oh my, I thought you were more sophisticated than that, having lived in New York. Our former maid, Suzette, made exquisite pastries, and she taught me." Sarah handed the bowl and spoon to Julia. "Here, keep whipping until you get out all the lumps whilst I light the stove."

Twenty minutes later William had returned with a note and a jar of apple butter from Miriam.

Dear Julia,

If Sarah is staying the night with you, I assume you'll have crepes. I thought you'd enjoy this on top. Get plenty of rest, for the children can speak of nothing but school starting.

Love,
Miriam

Julia chuckled as she read the note. "How did she know?"

"Lonesome Prairie isn't just a place where people live, dearie, it's a community of friends. I know you'll be heading back soon, but you're here now, and you'll always be a part of our story."

Julia placed a hand over her chest and then reached her other hand to Sarah's, squeezing it. "You're right. Even when I'm settled back in the city, I'll never forget the sincere friendship all of you have offered me even in the short time I've been here."

"But we'll not speak of you leaving just yet. Besides, we need to eat. Horace Whitbaum likes my crepes best straight from the pan."

Chapter Sixteen

Gripping her treasured copy of *Shakespeare's Comedies* in her hands, Julia watched as the children in her "school" practiced the wedding scene from *Much Ado about Nothing*. Christopher, playing Claudio, returned his rejected betrothed to her father with Elizabethan drama—or at least what he imagined it to be.

"There, Leonato, take her back again. Give not this rotten orange to your friend."

Christopher waved a claw-like hand in the air. Then, refusing to marry Shelby—playing Hero—he shoved her toward Maradon, an Indian boy who was playing Hero's father, Leonato.

The brook behind the actors glistened like diamonds as it ambled along the border of Isaac's property. The coolness of morning had long melted into the usual beating heat, and Julia wiped her forehead. She glanced up to the soddy, grateful the past night had been her last to sleep in the earthen dwelling.

"Is my lord well, that he doth speak so wide?" Shelby portrayed the innocent Hero with pleading desperation as the wedding attendees—the other pupils—gasped and huffed in shock. Even Bea cried, "Oh no!"

The five days since Sarah Mack stayed overnight in the soddy had crept by like a lazy caterpillar. Even with Miriam's daily visits and school time in the mornings, the days presented a striking contrast to Julia's normal, purposeful life—crammed full from morning till night—and ignited moments of fretfulness.

When Julia felt most useless and lonely, she opened the Word—her own family Bible—and read. Yet, although the words created a hankering for more, she still struggled to fully comprehend them. And she wished she could understand more deeply what they meant.

She flicked a fly from her dress sleeve as Maradon belted out his defense of his daughter with broken English. "Hath no man's dagger here a point for me?" Then, breaking character, he twisted toward Julia. "What's a dagger?"

"It's a small knife with a sharp blade," Julia answered.

"Oh, like this?" He reached for his belt, pulled out a leather-bound knife, and pointed it at Christopher.

Julia stepped forward. "Put that away." She sighed, knowing he didn't mean to hurt anyone. "That's exactly right, but in plays, we don't use real knives or swords. Maybe you can find a stick that would work."

Maradon nodded and shoved the blade back into his belt. "Yes, teacher."

"Please continue."

Despite the mild—and sometimes not so mild—incidents involved in educating children of such cultural differences, Julia was thankful for the hours she spent teaching every day. Not only did the

231

precious moments with Shelby and Bea bless her, but she also delighted in getting to know the other children. She appreciated their unique personalities, and she was proud of their scholarly progress. These prairie youngsters knew how to work hard, and that ability transferred to their schoolwork. Julia restored her attention to the play. The children had learned this scene so quickly.

"O, God defend me! how am I beset!" Shelby flung her hand to her forehead and collapsed in Maradon's arms, the sting of Claudio's rejection overcoming her. Then she eyed Julia.

"All right, children." Julia stood and clapped. "That was wonderful! You are definitely ready to show your parents tonight."

"Can we go?" Young Josh tugged on Julia's arm.

Julia rubbed his shoulder. "Yes, go eat your lunches. I'll see you tonight at the Lafuze-Falcon Ranch. And remember, tomorrow we'll have lessons there instead. All right?"

The children didn't answer. Obviously

too fixed on filling their stomachs, they raced to the brook and pulled their lunch pails from a spot beneath the small cluster of box elder trees.

With the children scattered about munching their food, Julia, too wound up to eat, rushed inside and gathered up the few items left to put in her valise. Miriam would be here with the wagon any moment. Stepping back, she gave the room one last glance, knowing she'd probably never see it again.

She was glad to be moving in with Miriam and Elizabeth, but she couldn't help but remember with fondness the few perfect hours she'd spent with the parson on her first stormy night. He'd listened to her intently, gazing into her eyes. And when he'd spoken, he'd projected sincerity and wit. How many times had he made her laugh since she'd arrived? His welcoming friendliness had made her stay here a touch easier. She wondered if she'd have a chance to thank him. She assumed not, since he'd probably not return from his circuit before she left for New York. Surely Mrs. Gaffin wouldn't leave her marooned out here too long.

She sighed and felt her chest rise and fall. She'd never been in love, but the startling sensations that arose as she pondered the parson's handsome smile, dark eyes, and strong build made her wonder if this could be how it felt at the start of a romance.

"Silly girl," she scolded herself aloud for lingering on these thoughts. In truth, she was relieved that she'd probably not see Isaac Shepherd again. She didn't know much about romance, but her simmering feelings surely didn't seem safe.

"Miss Cavanaugh?"

A man's voice.

Julia's heart beat even more quickly. Twirling around to face the door, she saw the owner of the handsome smile, dark eyes, and strong build that she'd been daydreaming about standing before her.

* * * *

"Miriam sent me to fetch you." Isaac gazed at Miss Cavanaugh, whose face was more tanned than the last time he saw her, her hair dappled with blond. She seemed to grow more beautiful with each sunrise.

"Oh! It's you!" Surprise reflected from her eyes, and pink tinged her neck. She dropped the hairbrush she held and gawked at him. Her look made Isaac wonder if he'd done something to offend her.

"I thought Miriam was coming," she said, biting a thumbnail.

A twinge of pain—sensing her apparent disapproval—pinched Isaac. He shrugged. "I'd be happy, Miss Cavanaugh, to go back and get her, if you like."

"No, no, no," she spoke quickly. "I'm sorry." A smile replaced Miss Cavanaugh's shock, her shoulders relaxing. "Parson Shepherd. Of course not." She stepped toward him, wiping her hands on her skirt. "You just surprised me. And please call me Julia. Forgive me for that odd reception. I was just deep. . . in thought." She took another step toward him, and her gaze locked with his. "I'm glad it's you. . .," she said softly.

"You are?" A rush of uninvited emotion pushed his heart against his chest. *What did she mean by that?*

The pink in her neck deepened to red and wandered to her cheeks. "I mean. . .I have questions about the Bible," she said quickly. "If you don't mind."

Isaac let out a breath, relieved. Yet, at the same time, fear crept to his heart—fear of the strength of his attraction to her. *Lord, I need Your help to keep this vow. Help me to serve her as a member of my church.* He gave her a reassuring smile. "Of course. I'd love to talk about the Scriptures." He paced next to her and picked up the valise. "Is this all you have?"

Julia scurried to the table and grabbed the parasol from the back of a chair. "That. . .and this. Oh—" She snatched a book from under the flat pillow. "Can't forget my novel, although I finished it three days ago. I must say, the evenings were quite lonely out here, and when I'd finished the book, they felt even lonelier."

Isaac tilted his head, spying the title. *"The Prairie Knight*, eh?"

"Yes." Julia raised her chin pertly. "And it was quite realistic. The hero rescued the 'prairie princess' from no less than three Indian raids, two rushing rivers, and one rabid dog." She laughed. "I've been out West just a few weeks, but I can't believe anyone takes such stories seriously."

Isaac clamped his lips together, smothering a chuckle.

"Well, if I'm honest," she said with a wry smile, "I suppose I also believed such tales not that long ago. But tell me, don't you ever have Indian raids?"

Isaac led the way outside. "Not in these parts anymore." He paused, letting her catch up to him. "I hope you don't mind, but Jefferson is using the wagon. It's not too long of a walk, and I figured you wouldn't have very much luggage."

"That's fine. I'd love to walk," Julia said as the children ran up to them.

"Uncle Ike!" Bea wrapped an arm around his leg then moved to cuddle Calamity.

Shelby and Johannah strolled up arm-in-arm.

"We want to go for a walk," Shelby said. "All I keep hearing about are the buffalo tunnels. Can we go see them?"

Julia shook her head. "If you two go, everyone will want to, and we can't leave all the children in your care."

Shelby and Johannah twisted their heads to Isaac.

"Please, Uncle Ike, why don't we all

237

go?" Johannah lowered her chin and blinked up at him. Isaac had given in to this look since the blond-haired girl was Bea's age, and apparently Johannah knew her power.

Isaac had planned on making a quick stop at his sisters' ranch for supplies before rejoining Jim on the search for Mabelina. The two had traversed through Big Sandy and the surrounding townships for a week, with no sign of her. Yet the giant man possessed a giant faith, and he was determined to keep searching till they found her.

When Isaac had arrived at Miriam and Elizabeth's place, they'd immediately asked him to stay the night, hoping he'd watch the first Shakespearean production in Chouteau county—performed by his own nieces.

How could Isaac refuse?

His sisters hadn't mentioned that Miss Cavanaugh would also be there, but Isaac figured she would. And the thought of seeing her had propelled a surge of joy through him.

He eyed his nieces, gazing with all earnestness. "All right." He gripped each one's shoulders. "If Miss Cavanaugh doesn't mind."

She nodded. "I've been hearing a lot about those buffalo tunnels myself."

* * * *

"I'll lead the way!" Christopher raced up and dashed ahead.

"Wait! I know where it is. Why do you always have to go first?" Johannah hollered as she and Shelby ran after him.

The others scampered along after them as Julia and Isaac sauntered behind. Julia breathed in the sweet scent of the prairie. The sun overhead warmed her shoulders, and the man walking next to her warmed her thoughts.

He led her toward the coulee Miriam had taken her to once before.

"In the spring these coulees fill with melting snow," he said. Passing through, they reached the other side, which opened up to an ocean of tall, waving grass.

Julia's skirt brushed against the dust as more dirt accumulated on her boots. *So much for the prim and proper city girl.* She glanced up ahead at the herd of children racing through the grasses.

"Do you see Bea?" She surveyed the field.

"I just did. She's so little the grass hides her." He pointed toward the right. "There she is."

Julia could barely make out Bea's head as it bobbed along a few yards behind the others.

"This tall grass . . ." Isaac pushed a clump of it to the side. "They call it buffalo grass. Probably because the first settlers saw the buffalo lazing in it."

Julia grazed the grass with her hands, letting it tickle her palms. "Buffalo?" Her footsteps paused. "I saw some from my window on the train. Do many herds pass through here?"

"Not too many. Like cattle, they don't like drinking from the same waterholes as the sheep. But once in a while, a herd rumbles through. What you have to watch out for are the stragglers and wounded."

"So I've read. In my dime novels, it's the weak animals that are the most frightening. Are they really dangerous?"

"Yes, you wouldn't want to face a live one. But don't worry." He puffed his chest out. "I've stared down more than one in my day."

Julia eyed him, unsure.

He chuckled under his breath, telling Julia he was joking again.

"If I ever have need of a mighty buffalo hunter," she said, "I'll most certainly call on you."

With an impish nod, Isaac winked and started walking again. They tramped over a grassy knoll, and reaching the other side, he pointed. "It's right up there. This way."

She followed him until they came to a low-lying spot where a cluster of trees had sprung up, and behind them the land seemed to fold in on itself. Instead of standing straight up, the tall prairie grass arched, forming what looked like tunnels.

"What *is* this place?"

"It's a buffalo trail." Isaac stomped the ground under the arch. "See, the herds have taken this path for so long, it's packed solid. It's almost like a wagon rut, only wider, and the grass only grows up the sides. Then it curves over, you see, and makes a tunnel."

Julia palmed the top of the curved tunnel. "It's amazing."

"C'mon." Isaac hurried down the tunnel's filtered light, her valise swinging in his hand, and Julia followed.

The scent of the grass was strong, and every so often she noticed brown patches of hair poking out, evidence of the beasts. She giggled as she raced after Isaac and wondered when she'd ever had such a happy day.

Coming out the other side, she stood beside Isaac, who reached out his hands toward the limpid depths of a large pond. "And now, you finally get to see our lake."

Julia thought he was teasing again. "This is it?" she questioned. "I saw lakes on the train ride out here—the Great Lakes, all those quaint Minnesota ones. Is this really considered a lake?"

Isaac frowned. His forehead scrunched. "It's called Lonesome Lake."

Julia covered her lips with her hand. He wasn't fooling. This really was the lake. "I'm sorry. I guess I just expected. . . something bigger."

"You don't like our lake?" His voice sounded disappointed. "I thought you'd like it."

Julia touched his arm, concerned. "Of course I do. It's lovely."

Isaac laughed as he patted her hand. "I suppose it does look pretty meager compared to what you've seen." He shifted his stance to face her and then threw her another wink.

"Oh! You weren't upset." She stomped her foot. "You were teasing me again."

"Forgive me." His voice lowered. "It's so fun." His eyes shone with a smile and then softened to convey compassion. "I'll bet it's not only our lakes that are different from the world you're used to."

A breeze picked up off the water, loosening a strand of Julia's hair. She tucked it behind her ear. "It's very different—in so many ways—and the past couple of weeks haven't been easy, but . . ." She plucked a piece of grass from his sleeve. "I'm glad I came—and even that I've had to stay awhile." Her gaze fell to her hands. "I've been able to learn much more about God." She angled her head up and peered into his eyes. "Thanks to you."

Isaac's gaze joined hers. Julia sensed

tenderness as well as esteem in his eyes, and she was loath to let the moment pass.

Then abruptly, Isaac's eyes shifted to the side, and the tender look was replaced by a cool, awkward glance.

Julia reproved herself for reading something into his actions that wasn't there. *He's only trying to comfort me, behaving like a minister,* she thought. *I've got to stop letting myself think there's anything more.*

As if to affirm her thoughts, Isaac began walking toward his sisters' ranch atop a nearby hill. "We'd better get back," he said pleasantly, swinging the valise again. The intimacy of the previous hour was gone.

Julia gathered up the children, and they plodded home.

Chapter Seventeen

....

After their quick trip back to Lonesome Prairie for supplies, Isaac and Jim had chosen to travel to Great Falls in search of Mabelina. On the way Isaac couldn't help pondering the sincere and profound questions Julia had asked as the two sat on the porch after the others retired for the night—at a strangely early hour.

Isaac knew his family's feigned drowsiness was part of Miriam and Elizabeth's scheme to give him and Julia a chance to get to know each other. Isaac rolled his eyes at his sisters' plotting, even though they weren't there to receive the gesture.

The lantern light had accentuated Julia's smooth cheeks and sparkling eyes. But, of course, he'd overlooked these details. The only reason he'd allowed himself to linger with her was because he'd done so in the capacity of a parson. One question after another seemed to flow from the young woman's heart. *Really*, he told himself, *if a soul has such a hunger to learn about the truths of the Bible, how could I, a minister, refuse?*

He didn't deny he enjoyed the moments with her, but he always relished digging into passages, uncovering the depth of meaning layered in the Word.

But now he had a more pressing issue before him—finding Mabelina. Great Falls was his first stop mostly because it was the biggest town in the area—brimming with stores, Chinese laundries, and new family homes—and would be the perfect place for Mabelina to hide. Also, he knew that Milo's daughters were nearby at boarding school just south of Great Falls. Even though he hadn't told Aponi his plan, he knew she'd be overjoyed to know he'd checked in on her girls.

"You ask around the businesses on Main Street," Isaac told Jim.

"And you?" Jim asked, although Isaac could tell from his understanding gaze that he already guessed where the parson would be.

"I'm going to check on some of the little lambs from my flock. Just because they're far from the fold doesn't mean they don't need tending toward."

Jim nodded and turned his horse to town. Isaac kicked his heels against Virginia, motioning for her to move down one of the dusty roads to the small church and school south of Great Falls.

As he rode up to the school, he noticed a group of children working in the garden. They lifted their faces to him and smiled. Isaac waved. He didn't spot any of Milo and Aponi's daughters.

He dismounted from Virginia and tied her to the hitching post out front—more to keep the children from running away with her than to prevent his horse from wandering off. A short nun in a spotless habit approached, striding toward him.

Isaac didn't remember seeing this nun before, but he knew that nuns often moved in and out of the boarding schools, following the call of the greatest need.

"Hello there." The sister greeted him with a quick smile. "I can see from your hat you're a parson. What can I do for you today?"

Isaac removed his hat and brushed back his hair with his fingers.

"I was looking for the daughters of a dear friend. They are Indian girls. Well, half-Indian. Their last name is Godfrey."

The nun mouthed the name and then the color drained from her face. "Oh yes, the Godfrey girls. They are busy at the moment. Perhaps you can come back in an hour or so? They can be ready for a visitor then." The woman turned and hurried back toward the residential quarters.

Isaac didn't like the look on the woman's face or appreciate her tone. She'd spoken to him as if he were one of her disobedient students and had dismissed him without waiting for his response. Isaac replaced his hat and then followed the woman. He quickened his steps to catch up, but she didn't know he was behind her until she stepped through the door to the building and he caught the door, holding it open for her.

"Actually, I hope to be heading out in an hour. It would be best for me to see them now." Through the doorway to the kitchen, he spotted a black-haired girl carrying a big pot to the stove. He recognized her right away. *Mary.*

Isaac hurried forward, not caring what the nun thought. He entered the kitchen and spotted all six girls.

Mary lifted her head after setting the pot down, and her jaw dropped open as she spotted him. "Parson Ike?"

At hearing his name, the other girls spun around toward the door. Even little Genevieve dropped the brush she'd been using to scrub the floor. "Parson!" She rose from where she'd been kneeling and ran to him, arms outstretched.

"Parson!" The other girls joined her, circling him. He placed a soft kiss on each forehead. "Girls, it's so good to see you." He forced a smile, attempting to hide his anger at seeing them doing hard labor in the heat of the day while the other children enjoyed fresh air.

"Girls, you are working so hard. Is today your day in the kitchen?" he asked, giving the nuns the benefit of the doubt.

"Oh no, Parson, we work in here every day." Little Genevieve stared up at him with large brown eyes.

"Yes, we must work for our tuition, isn't that right, Sister?" Alice eyed the nun.

"Well, unfortunately, yes, that is the truth. Perhaps the parson and I can talk about this elsewhere?" She clapped her hands together. "And I have an idea. After we talk, I'll get some of the other girls to take your places—just for this afternoon. It would be lovely for you to visit with the parson, don't you think?"

Isaac stepped back from the girls' embraces. His heart ached as if it had been set upon a chopping block and split for kindling. "I'll be right back, girls. Do as the good sister has said."

The girls nodded and obeyed, setting to work with determination. They reminded him so much of Aponi. She always thought of others, never complaining of her own plight. Even at Milo's funeral she'd greeted everyone, wishing them safe travels home, extending her appreciation for making the trip.

The girls reminded him of Milo, too. Even though they greatly resembled their mother, like their father, their eyes seemed to gaze beyond the dark tasks of the present toward a brighter future.

The nun scurried back out the door, and Isaac followed her. He held his tongue, waiting for the explanation, hoping it was a good one.

"The Godfrey girls, they are some of the best in our class. They are far more educated than most of the other Indians. They—"

Isaac held up a hand, stopping her words. "They don't need to be compared to the other Indians. They are children. They should be schooled like all the other children. With no distinction."

"Yes, of course," the woman answered, even though Isaac could see she didn't agree.

"Is that why they are in the hot kitchen, cooking and cleaning? Because they're Indians, half-breeds?"

"No, of course not. All the children, no

matter their race and heritage, have chores to perform here. We believe children must gain a good work ethic in addition to book learning. The Godfrey girls work extra in the kitchen in order to pay for their tuition. It was an agreement I made with their brother, Mr. Boyle. He said he had only enough money for a quarter of their tuition. We agreed the girls could work off the rest. They have shown themselves to be excellent workers—and I think we're being more than fair, given the circumstances."

The heat of anger charged across Isaac's chest. Yet his anger was no longer directed at the nun or the school, but at Warren Boyle. Isaac knew Milo would've put away enough money for their unforeseen future. Warren had enough money to properly pay for the girls' schooling—no doubt. Unless. . .

Unless there was trouble with Milo's estate. Troubles no one knew about. The anger cooled.

"So how much will it be?"

"Excuse me?" The woman peered up at him from under her habit.

"The cost—for their schooling. If I were

to pay for the next couple of months, how much would it be?" He pulled out his money pouch from under his shirt.

The nun mentioned a price.

"Is that for all the girls?"

The nun nodded.

"And does that mean they will be treated like the other children—not have to work in the kitchen?"

"They'll still have to work, but no, not in the kitchen."

Isaac pulled the money out—most of what he had left—and placed it in the woman's hands. "Thank you for housing and schooling them, Sister. I know this will ensure you care for them just as I would—or better yet, as their mother would." He replaced his money pouch. *Thank You, Lord, for providing for these girls. I know You will provide for my additional needs.*

He turned back to the building, ready to spend time with the girls. He'd have a talk with Warren when he returned, but for now he was grateful the girls would be taken care of.

"I think I'll go see them now. Maybe we'll take a walk." He strode toward the building.

The nun hurried beside him. "Yes, Parson, that is fine, but I only have one question."

Isaac paused and forced a smile, reminding himself it wasn't this nun's fault. In fact, if anything, he should thank her for finding a way to allow the girls to stay here. "Yes, Sister, what is the question?"

"This money cares for their schooling and boarding for a few months. . .but who will take care of the bill after that?"

Isaac gazed at the woman as they walked. "Don't worry, Sister. By that time the girls will be returning home." Isaac spoke with more confidence than he felt. "We will have a school in Lonesome Prairie they can attend."

Chapter Eighteen

A steamboat whistle accompanied Isaac's final "amen" as he finished his closing prayer outside the depot in Fort Benton two weeks later. Around him, the crowd spread out, and Isaac eyed the boat casting a short shadow across the soft blue Missouri River as it cruised to its final stop. On deck, a banjo player picked "Oh! Susanna."

Isaac and Jim had searched Great Falls and the surrounding townships for two weeks, but they'd paused their hunt for yet another jaunt home to Lonesome Prairie. Isaac wasn't sure why, but on this trip he seemed to forget vital supplies like a flighty squirrel losing its acorns.

On his latest return home, Miriam and Elizabeth were less than subtle—far less—about their attempts to give Isaac and Julia time to talk. They'd pushed them to fetch water from the coulee, no doubt so they could take a romantic sunset stroll. But Isaac didn't mind anymore. In fact, he'd hoped to have another chance to speak with her—about the Bible, of course.

Isaac glanced out at the finely attired Eastern passengers debarking the steamship and strolling toward the Grand Central Hotel. After that, they'd spend their days seeking adventure in the "wild frontier" and most likely be surprised—like the pretty Julia Cavanaugh had been—that the world of Indians, soldiers, and homesteaders wasn't as exhilarating as it was in those dime novels. While it was true that there were moments of excitement on the frontier, most of the people he knew didn't have time for adventure. They worked hard and led quiet lives.

Isaac took in a breath as the breeze

caused his shirtsleeves to flutter, and his mind traced its way back to Julia. He'd grown fond of her over the last weeks, not only during the hours they'd conversed over biblical issues—which inevitably led to candid personal revelations as well—but even as she occupied his thoughts. And he did seem to mull over her more than his other parishioners. He knew it was because he was attracted to her; he couldn't deny that. But as a minister, he'd learned to rein in his personal feelings for the sake of the flock.

Isaac glanced at a dandelion seedling tossed in the wind. A touch of contentment surged through him as he indulged himself in a moment of pondering Julia's character.

When he'd first met her, she'd seemed to possess a real faith even though she knew so little. But like a thirsty lamb, she'd drunk up the bits of the living water he'd shared, and gone further still. She studied and read in his absence and was even prepared with questions when he returned. The opportunity to feed a hungry soul soaked Isaac in the joy of fulfilling one's purpose in life. And if he was truthful, she'd encouraged his own faith more than once. That was a blessing he hadn't expected.

Isaac squelched the thoughts of Julia, knowing too much could lead him to dangerous territory. He instead remembered the morning he first arrived at this very dock, six years ago. He'd ambled off the boat and, with trembling hands and voice, preached his first sermon on the front porch of the town's general store to just two listeners—Milo being one of them. God had grown the church mightily since then, though not with steeples or parsonages. Isaac's eyes moved over the two dozen folks milling about. He'd known many since those early days, having baptized a good lot of them.

The Lord had built the church—Isaac would take no credit for that—with living stones, a people He called His own. Those saints He grew, refined, blessed, and molded each day. Yet sometimes Isaac just wished the refining happened a little quicker.

"Welp, Parson Ike," Giant Jim said, coming alongside. "'Twas another good sermon. Don't know how you do it day after day."

Isaac joined him, and they moseyed under the trees along the riverfront. Up ahead, a row of tables had been set up for a picnic. Isaac sniffed the air, smiling at the scent of buffalo meat roasting on the two large firepits. His stomach rumbled. "Well, I'll tell you, I read the Bible a lot," he answered Jim. "And do a lot of praying."

One of the church ladies approached, touching Isaac's sleeve. "Now Parson Ike, that was a wonderful sermon. Do you ever grow weary of remembering. . .and saying all those words?"

Giant Jim laughed. "You think this here's a lot of talkin', try spendin' a couple weeks straight on the trail with this feller."

"All right, now." Isaac cast a mocking glare to Jim and then jumped up onto a nearby tree stump.

"Let us pray, shall we? O Bread of Life, from day to day be Thou our comfort, food, and stay. Amen." As he recited his nephew Christopher's favorite prayer, a wave of family hankering came over him, and he was thankful he'd be seeing them in just a few days. It was his birthday, and even though he needed no celebration, his sisters would throw a fit if he wasn't there. Another reason to find Mabelina as quickly as possible.

Giant Jim grabbed a biscuit and bit a chunk out of it. "Wonder if I could ever do that preachin' thing like you do?"

Isaac hopped down and joined his friend at the food table. "Why Jim, I think you'd make a fine preacher." He grabbed a plate. "The way I've seen the Lord work in you these last weeks. . . Keep learning and studying and seeking Him first—He'll let you know if that's what He wants."

Joy dawned on Jim's face. "Just think, Parson. A few weeks ago I was a foul ol' varmint. Still am, I s'pose, but I do want to change. And if the Good Lord would let me be a parson like you—" He halted as if snared by his own words. His thick mustache twitched.

"It's a good aspiration, my friend."

Jim squinted. His countenance, all smiles a moment ago, fell as if draped with worry, and he paused filling his plate with potato salad. "There's one problem.

I love that woman of mine sore much. I don't know if I can give 'er up."

Isaac set down the serving spoon he was about to dip into the baked beans and returned the gravity of Jim's look. "Why would you have to give up Mabelina to be a preacher?"

"Well, you ain't got no wife, do you? An' I heard ya say you don't want one because you wanna be a better preacher."

Isaac loved this man's heart. His childlike longing to do right by his lady and his Lord inspired Isaac, but Jim's assumption also sent a stark reminder of the weight of Isaac's example. He'd never preached a sermon promoting an unmarried life, hadn't even talked about it much—except when asked by everyone and his brother seeking to pawn him off on their daughters. Yet Jim had formed a supposition based on Isaac's lifestyle.

Isaac was grateful for the opportunity to clear it up. "You don't need to worry about that. My decision to stay single. . . well, that's just something I decided a long time ago. Not every preacher must do the same." He watched the thin valleys in the man's face curve upward again. "Lots of us get married."

Jim smiled and dug his teeth into a chicken leg. "Well, now that's what I thought, but you got me mixed up by that peculiar vow o' yers." He chewed as he talked. "Seems to me that the preacher I knew growin' up, Brother Keith—he had hisself a good wife. Even said she helped him be a better minister."

Isaac tilted his head back, enjoying his friend's speech. "Well, that's what Mabelina'll be for you. A good wife and helper."

The lofty man frowned. "If we could only find 'er. She shouldn't be that hard to find, what with her flamin' red hair."

In the distance children played tag, laughing and chasing one another while the cool wind from the river whipped their hair around their faces. Beyond that a young man and woman walked hand-in-hand upon the riverbank. Seeing it caused a blanket of loneliness to settle over Isaac.

"You say woman you look for? With hair of flame?" An old, battle-worn Indian man, who'd joined the congregation just a month before, had addressed them.

"Yes." Giant Jim's face brightened.

"Woman hair color of fireweed here last dawn."

"My Mabelina." Jim patted the top of his hat then removed it and stroked his hair.

"Sad eyes." The Indian lowered his gaze.

"Who was she with?" Isaac spoke slow and clearly. "Where were they going?"

"She leave yesterday with Assiniboine woman. Go to reservation."

Isaac glanced at Jim, whose mouth hung open. "Why would she go with Aponi?"

"You don't think those Injuns'd wanna make Mabelina pay for shootin' one of their women's husbands, do ya?" Jim asked.

Isaac's gut tightened. Aponi would never seek vengeance, but then why would she take Mabelina to her people? Unless Mabelina needed a quick hiding place, which could mean the vigilantes were on her trail. Either way, he and Jim needed to go.

Jim pushed his plate to the side. Judging from the look in his eye, he was no longer interested in food.

"Thank you for the information." Isaac patted the old man's shoulder. Within him, hope sparred with fear. Now they knew where they needed to go. The question was, would they get there soon enough?

Within ten minutes they were back on the horses, their gazes fixed north toward the Assiniboine Reservation.

It took them a day and a night to get there. Arriving at the arid plains, Isaac led Jim beyond the boundaries, downward through the broken land. A vulture spiraled overhead, searching for carcasses. Isaac wondered how even a vulture could survive in this desolation. Soon they approached the Indian settlements, and the scent of tanning hides and campfires wafted through the air.

Next to Isaac, Jim's gaze searched each teepee, his knuckles pale as he gripped his reins.

"We'll find her." Isaac kept his voice low, knowing the Indians valued quiet tones. "I come here every so often. I know Aponi's teepee is up ahead."

Men's and women's faces—strong, emotionless—peered at the two riders. Isaac offered smiles, knowing if they didn't recognize him personally, his parson's hat provided a passport.

Reaching Aponi's family group, Isaac motioned for Jim to dismount.

Calamity trotted to the nearest shady spot and lay down, watching the men as if waiting to see how this was going to turn out.

"Which one is it, Parson Ike?" Jim asked. "Mabelina! You here?"

"Not so loud." Isaac led Jim and his horses through the corridor between the clusters of teepees, and as they approached the second to last, Isaac pointed. "That's Aponi's."

"Mabelina, you in there? C'mon out. It's me." Jim scrambled forward.

A moment later, the bleached hide stirred and a red head peered out like a rose pushing through a late spring blanket of frost.

"Jimbo?" Mabelina, wearing a deerskin dress, knee-high leggings, and moccasins, cautiously stepped out, followed by Aponi.

Jim hesitated, apparently nervous now that the moment of seeing her had finally arrived.

Jim and Mabelina walked to each other. Isaac couldn't help but smile at their display, but then his heart fell as he noticed the sorrowful, lonesome look on Aponi's face. Isaac dismounted and moved toward her.

Jim clutched Mabelina's hand. "You look mighty fine," he said, touching her hair.

"I don't even got a real dress on, or any rouge. My hair's not done. . . ." Mabelina's face flushed, and she glanced away.

"Shh." The simple giant covered her mouth with two fingers. "Yer talkin' 'bout my lady."

"Yer lady?"

"If you'll have me."

A simple smile, shy like a schoolgirl's, stole over Mabelina's face.

"Now before you go answerin'," Jim continued, "there's somethin' I gotta tell ya." He took off his hat and held it to his chest. "You know I ain't been much of a saint. Shoulda made that right a long time past, but, Mabelina my girl, I'm a God-fearin' man now. The Good Lord done changed my heart and ain't no way I'm ever goin' back."

Mabelina's cheeks perked up. "That's just fine, Jim. Fine." Her lips pursed. "I don't know if I'm there yet with the Good Lord, but Aponi's been teachin' me all kinds of things 'bout the Bible and ya know what?" She lifted her chin. "I believe it."

Isaac gave Aponi a quick grin. "Guess the Lord had us both working on opposite sides of this match."

"Seems so." Aponi consented with a nod.

"Well, there's jest one more thing to do then, Parson." Jim glanced at Isaac.

"What's that?"

Jim squeezed Mabelina close and kissed her forehead. "Why, get us hitched o' course."

A few snickers and grins emerged from the heads peeking out of their teepees.

"He forgot something." Aponi eyed Mabelina. "Yes?"

Jim's face scrunched up. "What?"

Isaac moseyed over and patted the

groom-to-be's back. "First, you have to propose."

A big smile filled the old prospector's face as he dropped to one knee. "Miss Mabelina Tigard, will ya marry me?"

Chapter Nineteen

"Miss Cavanaugh." Shelby opened the door to the barn, and shafts of sunlight, speckled with motes of hay and dust, angled in beside her.

Julia peered up from where she knelt milking Jesse James, the goat. "Good morning, sweetie. What are you doing?"

"It's Uncle Ike's birthday. My ma is running around the house getting everything ready. I've never seen her in such a state."

"Yes, I know. It seems everyone's excited to see him again." *Especially me.* A kiss of warmth brushed Julia's cheeks, even though she hadn't spoken her thoughts aloud.

Shelby set to work mucking out one of the stalls as if she'd done it every day of her life, and Julia turned her attention back to the goat.

It'd taken her a barrelful of tries, but Julia had finally mastered the rhythm. She continued pumping, relishing the accomplishment of seeing white foamy milk fill the bucket. The idea of offering the work of her hands to the group gathering today for Isaac's birthday—and not just the milk, but a pie, a plate of corn fritters, and a basket of fresh huckleberries—filled her with satisfaction.

Just a month ago she'd been a fumbling city girl. How much she'd learned in that span! And although two trains came and went, no letter had arrived from Mrs. Gaffin with them. More importantly, no money to buy a return ticket or to pay back Horace. She couldn't leave until she heard from her headmistress, so she decided to keep busy, as Miriam had suggested.

When the invitation came to move in with the Lafuze and Falcon families, Julia at first wondered whether she'd feel like she didn't belong. Quite the opposite had occurred, actually. Julia was amazed at how they embraced her. Sharing a bed with Johanna had been an unexpected blessing. They often talked—and giggled—late into the night. Julia loved sharing the stories she'd told to her orphan girls over the years. Abe had even crafted an extra chair so she could have a place at the table for meals.

One of her favorite times was joining the family for evening Bible readings and prayers—especially on the occasions when Isaac had come to visit. He seemed to understand the Word so well, as if it were a treasure trove of life-giving nuggets he lived to unearth. Julia couldn't seem to get enough of the nurturing Word. She laughed to herself. Who would've thought she'd learn so much about the Bible way out here on the prairie? Who would've guessed that the more she dug into the truths of Scripture, the more her love for her Savior would grow? It seemed obvious to her now, but she'd never been taught these things before.

If Julia had only one challenge, it was

getting used to boys. They were louder, more active, and stinkier than the girls she'd cared for!

Perhaps the thing that surprised Julia the most was her enjoyment of the simple tasks of running the ranch. She squirted more milk into the bucket, remembering Miriam's patience as she'd taught her. The first time Julia had tried, they'd laughed when the goat's milk squirted the cat in the eye, sending the proud feline scurrying out of the barn with an indignant yowl.

Julia smiled at the memory, but then a stitch of nervousness tightened her chest as she thought of the birthday gift she made Isaac—a leather cover for his Bible. Miriam and Elizabeth gave her the hide, and the two Indian children who joined their "school" taught her how to tan and tenderize it. At first she thought it the perfect gift for a minister—practical, applicable. She'd made it in the size of the Bible that Miriam told her Isaac carried with him—smaller by far than the large family heirloom.

But now she worried that it was presumptuous of her to get him anything at all, especially something for his personal Bible. She assumed the book meant more to him than anything. He used it every day. Would he want to look at some long-forgotten girl's cover every time he opened it?

She had to quit fretting about it. Miriam and Elizabeth said it was a thoughtful gift, and she'd leave it at that. Anyway, she'd know tonight if he liked it.

"I have something for you." Shelby traipsed to her, holding a rough scrap of paper, folded and sealed with candle wax. "It's from 'yer *husband*.'"

"Not another one." Julia sent Shelby a frown, and then she nodded at the twelve-year-old. "Go ahead and read it."

Shelby giggled then ripped open the letter.

" 'My dear wife,' " she read aloud, mimicking Horace to near perfection. " 'This is the fifth letter I done sent. I want to be yer husband. I done paid good money. I won't wait much longer. Yer husband, Horace.' " Shelby folded it and grinned.

"Where'd you find it this time?" Julia scanned the yard and sheep stalls beyond the barn. "He's not here, is he?"

"I didn't see him. This was under the new welcome mat Ma put out yesterday."

A hollow feeling grew in Julia's stomach, as if she'd swallowed the Montana sky all at once. "At least he didn't come 'callin' again. Remember last time?"

"Yeah, drank enough lemonade for the whole lot of us."

"Poor man. I wouldn't mind him so much if he—well, if he weren't trying to marry me."

Shelby strolled to a bench next to Julia and sat down. "I'm sorry for you, Miss Cavanaugh. I can't believe he thinks you're gonna be his wife."

Julia finished milking Jesse James and then moved on to Wild Bill. "I know."

"He's so dirty and old."

"But he is really sweet. I think he's just lonely. I wish there were someone for him." She scrunched her forehead. "Just not me."

Shelby stood up. She mussed her hair, stuck out her belly, and marched around, mocking him. " 'I done paid fer a wife.' "

Julia attempted to hold in a chuckle. "Oh Shelby, that's not kind."

"Shore ain't!" Out of nowhere, Horace marched into the barn and stood blocking the doorway.

Shelby let out a startled scream and then scurried next to Julia, who stopped milking and stood.

"Horace." She tried to smile. "I'm so sorry. Shelby didn't mean anything by it."

Horace pursed his lower lip in and out like he had that first day on the way to the depot. "I don't much care what that young'un thinks. But yer my wife. You shouldn't be hootin' along with 'er."

"I'm sorry," she repeated. "It wasn't kind of me. Now let's go back to the house and get some lemonade. Parson Ike's coming today. You'll want to see him."

Horace hiked up his britches. "No, I'm not stayin'. I jes wanted to git a quick peep at you and give you that thar note, but when I heard ya mockin', now that hurt, so I 'cided to say somethin'."

"You were right to," she conceded with a smile.

"But thar's some kinda rush on some

gold up over east, so I'll be headin' that way fer a few weeks." He stepped up to her and peered directly into her eyes. "When I come back, I'll be a ready fer our weddin'."

She shook her head. "Horace, I told you—"

"Don't matter." He fished the folded "official" papers—the letters from Mrs. Gaffin and the photograph—from his pocket. "I got it all worked out." He paused, making sure she saw the papers again, then lumbered around and left.

She slumped on the stool.

"I hope you hear from Mrs. Gaffin soon," Shelby said.

"Me too. I sent her that letter with Ellen a month ago. I don't know how much longer I can hold Horace off. I just wish Mrs. Gaffin would send the money for the train ticket. I'd be happy to work it off when I return to New York." She stood and gave Wild Bill a pat on the back. "Well, let's go inside." She handed one of the buckets of milk to Shelby.

As they crossed the yard to the house, Julia spotted two horses approaching. A large black horse carried a man and a woman, and it was followed by a butterscotch mare. And on the mare's back sat a tall, handsome parson.

* * * *

Hot wind brought no relief from the sun's rays. Isaac dabbed his brow with his sleeve. Up ahead his family's place grew in size with each step of Virginia's hooves, and Isaac couldn't help but smile. After a month on the prairie, the expectation of a tall mug of Miriam's lemonade, a home-cooked meal—which he hoped included his favorite, corn fritters—and an evening spent with family filled Isaac from boots to hat with a sense of contentment.

"Say, Parson, who's that li'l filly up at yer sister's ranch?" Mabelina's head rested on Jim's back as they rode. "She looks sorta familiar, but I don't remember her from 'round here."

Despite the heat, a cold sweat moistened Isaac's hands. He watched Julia stroll alongside his new niece, Shelby, carrying a milk bucket. She looked up and spotted him, and a smile filled her face. His stomach flipped once, then twice, as if a prairie dog rolled around inside.

"That's Julia. Julia Cavanaugh." The hairs on the back of his neck rose as he said her name. Or maybe that reaction was due to the sight of her. "She came with the orphans, and she sort of got stuck here. She'll be leaving on the next train. I think. Unless things have changed."

"Mighty purdy." Mabelina adjusted on her seat.

Isaac took in the sight of her slim frame, her long hair all tucked up in a bun. . . and the feelings he tried to suppress scampered to the surface. He'd forgotten just how pleasing she was.

"Well, she may be purdy," Jim angled his scruffy head toward Mabelina's, "but she's not as purdy as you."

A smile plumped up Mabelina's cheeks.

As their pastor, Isaac appreciated their happiness, especially since both took wobbly, yet determined, steps toward a faithful walk with God. Yet if someone had told him a few months ago that such a thing would happen, he would have laughed. Isaac shook his head. Though painful, it was Milo's death that had brought them to a saving faith in Christ. And Aponi's forgiveness and refuge had also contributed to their growth. God's ways were above Isaac's understanding, but he rejoiced in them just the same.

Virginia whinnied and Calamity barked, the animals sensing their closeness to home—and food. Isaac's gaze again lingered on Julia Cavanaugh, who giggled with Shelby. He couldn't help but notice Julia eyeing him as she hurried inside.

Within a few minutes, the horses were tended to, and the three travelers turned from the barn toward Miriam's front door. Calamity trotted ahead of them, most likely smelling whatever Miriam was cooking up inside.

Isaac took only two steps, and then he paused. Jim and Mabelina also slowed as they saw it—a new grave next to the path in front of the ranch house.

It can't be. What happened? Who?

Horrible possibilities slammed his thoughts. Did Indians attack? Was someone struck with cholera or scarlet fever while he was gone? Was there an accident? He sprinted to the dirt mound to make out the sign's wording. Then

Isaac's heart slowed its frantic pace as he realized what it was.

Two old boots poked out of the ground, and the words *Isaac Shepherd RIP* were scraped onto an old board.

"Those sisters of mine," he muttered. "My good working boots, too." He walked up the steps and onto the front porch bedecked with clay Indian pots brimming with orange, purple, and yellow flowers.

Glancing to the window, he grinned to himself, pretending not to see two sets of eyes peeking out from behind the white curtains. Muffled laughter carried out to him.

"What are they up to, girl?" he asked Calamity. The dog expectantly wagged her tail as Isaac knocked on the door. "Let me in," he said in a gravelly voice. "I've returned from the grave, and I'm hungry."

He could hear the children shrieking with laughter. "Come on in!" Miriam called over the din. "You know you don't need to knock."

Isaac cautiously opened the door, and before he could step a mule-eared boot inside, a loud "Happy Birthday!" rang out from his sisters and their families.

Two of Miriam's boys barreled into his legs with embraces, and Isaac inspected the room. He nodded to his brothers-in-law, his sisters, and the rest of the children, and finally, his gaze landed on Julia. Her red dress with tiny beige flowers accentuated her slender waist. Her eyes shifted shyly from his, but a kind smile formed on her lips.

"Uncle Isaac, what're you starin' at our teacher for?" Josh, Miriam's youngest, asked as he shot Isaac with imaginary guns.

Isaac grinned, embarrassed. "I'm sorry." He "shot" Josh back and then winked at Julia. "It's been a long ride."

Julia's cheeks tinted pink as a prairie rose. "It's quite all right."

"Don't mind Josh." Elizabeth walked up, Bea in her arms. "He's quite fond of his teacher and is easily jealous." She winked at the young boy.

Isaac stroked little Bea's cheek, noting the sparkle in Elizabeth's gaze. "How *is* our new teacher doing?"

"Julia's been teaching the children every day after chores." Miriam approached and braced her arched back with her hands.

"Even little Josh can read a few words now."

"I'm just helping out," Julia interjected. "I'm not certified or anything."

"But we've been talkin' about that," Miriam said. "It's not like one really needs certification around here. At least not at the start."

Isaac gazed at Julia. "Have you decided to stay in Lonesome Prairie?"

She hesitated and then shook her head. "Oh no, I'm still planning to head back to New York. Mrs. Gaffin is expecting me. . . ."

Isaac took off his parson's hat and hung it on a peg near the door, trying to hide his disappointment. "It's real kind of you to teach my nieces and nephews while you're here." He scrutinized her face, wanting to ask if she'd be all right when she had to say good-bye again, but deciding not to.

"It's no problem." She sent him a reassuring glance. There was something else in her gaze. Sadness? *Why?* "I like teaching them. It helps pass the time, and it makes me feel useful. The children are wonderful."

"Well, I'm thankful just the same."

"Uncle Isaac, how'd you like yer grave?" Christopher piped up from his spot under the table where he and the other youths were playing marbles.

Isaac glared around the room. "That grave had me more worried than a chicken in a fox hole. Whose idea was that?" Isaac pointed a finger at Christopher. "It was my ornery nephew, wasn't it?"

Christopher shook his blond head. "Wasn't me." His gaze, along with everyone else's, turned to Julia.

"You?" Isaac asked. "And here I thought you were a sweet girl."

Julia's lips pursed in a tight smile. "We–ll." She stretched the word out. "I read it in a book once." Her face and neck flushed to a brighter shade of pink. "I'm sorry if it spooked you."

Miriam squeezed an arm around Julia's shoulders. "Don't worry, dear. We were all in on it. Besides, my brother deserves a good spookin' every once in a while." She glanced toward the kitchen. "C'mon, ladies, time to get dinner on the table."

"Hold up a minute." Isaac focused his

gaze on the crowd. "Before we eat, I want to tell you something." He swept a hand toward Jim and Mabelina, who were still standing at the threshold. "We have something much more important to celebrate." He crept between the two newlyweds and put his arms around them. "Let me introduce you to Mr. and Mrs. James Newman. They were hitched today."

A gasp arose from the womenfolk, and the men took turns shaking Jim's hand. As Isaac's sisters towed Mabelina to the kitchen to crow and giggle, Isaac watched Julia fluttering along with them. She rejoiced with Mabelina—a woman she'd just met. The impulse to serve others seemed to flow from Julia's heart. He'd seen it each time he'd been around her.

An hour later, dinner eaten and dishes cleared, Miriam corralled the children back around the table. The sun hung low in the sky, and a welcome evening breeze wafted through the house.

"Johannah, time for family worship." Miriam called her oldest daughter, who was nine years old and meandering outside.

"I know. I know." She dashed back inside. "I was just usin' the privy, Mama," Johannah whispered as she plopped onto her chair next to Shelby at the long table.

"Johannah, please." Miriam narrowed her gaze at her daughter. "One does not speak of such things in public."

"Isn't Uncle Ike gonna open his presents?" Christopher asked.

"Later. God's Word comes first." Miriam smiled.

"I thought we'd continue reading from St. John," Jefferson announced from the head of the table. He opened the Bible. "That all right with you, Parson?"

Isaac nodded as he took his seat across from Elizabeth, grateful to his brother-in-law for letting him receive the Word rather than dispense it this time. It was a respite he savored.

Jefferson began to read, "'Now Jacob's well was there. Jesus therefore, being wearied with his journey, sat thus on the well: and it was about the sixth hour.'"

Jefferson continued on, sharing the story of the woman from Samaria from John 4, and as he spoke, Isaac tried to picture it in his mind's eye. Her pain. Her shame. What it must have felt like to see the compassion on Jesus' face.

"'But whosoever drinketh of the water that I shall give him shall never thirst; but the water that I shall give him shall be in him a well of water springing up into everlasting life.'" Jefferson finished and gazed around the table, waiting for comments.

"There seems to be a lot of wells in the Bible," Julia observed from where she sat in the chair next to Jefferson.

Jefferson nodded. "That's true. They lived in a dry spot, like us."

"I know where there's another well." Josh perched on his knees on his chair. "I learned it from Mama's Bible story times. That man, Isaac, done got his woman at a well. Sent his servant to fetch 'er."

Miriam scuffed his head playfully. "He 'done got his woman'? Is that how a man finds a wife?"

"Ain't that right, Pa?" He climbed onto his father's lap. "That's how you got Ma?"

The sun-wrinkled lines in Jefferson's face creased as he smiled. He rubbed the little boy's back. "Well," he started.

"No, Josh, that's not how you git a wife." Christopher rolled his eyes, obviously exasperated by his little brother's ignorance. "The Good Lord brings one when the time is right, just like He did for that Isaac in the Bible."

"And just like He'll do for our Isaac." Miriam's face shifted, and her eyes peered at her brother.

"Who can tell me the main point of the passage in John?" Jefferson asked, rescuing Isaac from his wife's meddling.

"I think it means that Christ is the well that never runs dry." Julia, who seemed oblivious to the bantering, leaned over the Bible, her eyes skimming the passage. "He gives us what we need. He gave Isaac in the Bible what he needed, a wife. And He gives all of those who trust in Him living water, eternal life." She lifted her head.

"Well, I think Miss Cavanaugh got it jest 'bout right." Jefferson placed his hands on the table.

Isaac leaned back in his chair, watching her.

Miriam patted Julia's hand. "God opens the eyes of His people to His Word." She squinted at Isaac. "I think I heard that somewhere before."

Jefferson closed their Bible time in prayer, and as they cleaned up and prepared for the party, Isaac watched Jim and Mabelina exchanging glances and sneaking kisses. Something in him longed for the trust, friendship, and love they shared.

It is not good that the man should be alone. Milo had quoted this verse before he died. Those words had gnawed at Isaac, replaying in his head ever since. Now they came back.

He stole another glance at Julia Cavanaugh, joining so seamlessly with his family, and for the first time Isaac allowed himself to wonder if perhaps Milo and Miriam and Elizabeth were right. Could a wife be something God intended for him?

Chapter Twenty

Julia tucked her present for Isaac under the gifts piled on the padded wooden sofa. Then she sat down next to the pile. Her stomach churned with nervous excitement as Isaac sank into the spot on the other side of the gifts.

"Open mine first, Uncle Ike." Twelve-year-old Christopher thumbed his overalls and licked his lips as he handed Isaac a red bandanna-wrapped gift then plopped down on the bearskin rug next to the other children.

"Hey, is that my bandanna? I've been

missing it." He glanced at Julia, with a playful grin.

A tinge of warmth spread to Julia's neck remembering her emotional outburst that caused him to let her borrow his kerchief. "Yes, and don't worry, it's clean."

Inside the bandanna was a hand-carved slingshot. "Oh, that's perfect." Isaac held up his gift for those sitting around the room to admire.

Julia had watched Christopher carve it over the last few days, finally attaching the leather strap. She patted his shoulder.

Isaac eyed it again. "You've done a fine job. I think it's your best work."

Christopher's face beamed at his uncle's approval. "I found the old stick over in the coulee, then I carved it."

"It's just right for fetching a quick gopher dinner on the prairie. Thank you."

As the afternoon sun's rays sloped through the window, Julia's foot tapped on the wood-planked floor. She waited as Isaac received each present—painted rocks she'd helped Josh and Bea make, a new hand-sewn shirt from Abe and Elizabeth, and an old dusty commentary on the book of Genesis Miriam and Jefferson gave.

Only her gift remained, and the tension in her stomach made her wish she'd never put the leather Bible cover with the others. She chided herself. *Why am I so nervous? It's only a gift.*

"There's one more." Miriam pushed the heap of treasures to the side and uncovered Julia's package. The gift waited inside a simple bag Julia had sewn from potato sack scraps. She'd embroidered "Happy Birthday" on it with thick thread.

Isaac picked it up, his hands smoothing the bag as he examined the stitchery. "That's some nice-looking needlework. Who's this from?"

Elizabeth, who sat on Abe's lap in a wide, high-backed chair, threw Julia a smile. "Julia made it. That girl's a harvest of talent."

Bea hopped down and clambered over to Julia, resting an elbow on her knees. "Miss Cav'naw tawented."

Julia patted Bea's head and then thrummed her fingers on her leg. "It's not much, just something I threw together."

Isaac locked eyes with her then

loosened the cinch to open the sack. He lifted out the Bible cover and moved it between his hands, as though trying to make out what it was. Julia's heart felt as if it would break through her ribs, until a slight grin finally crept over his mouth and into his eyes. He ran his fingers over his stitched name.

"You made this for me?" The grin changed into a full-faced smile. "It's perfect."

"That's real nice, Miss Cavanaugh," Johannah said. "Maybe you could teach us to embroider in school."

"I'd love to." Julia bit a nail and then glanced at Isaac. "You should try it on your Bible. We had to guess at the measurements. I used one of Miriam's books as a model."

Isaac reached into his pack beside the sofa and retrieved his Bible. He fumbled as he tried to fit the cover over its limp sleeves, and Julia slid next to him to help.

"You put it on like this." She laid the cover on the bench then scooped Isaac's Bible from his lap, her finger lightly brushing his thigh. Ignoring the flood of warmth shooting to her face, she slipped the sleeves in and folded the Bible closed.

She smiled and handed it to him, relieved to have the task complete. "I'm so glad it fits."

Isaac turned the covered Bible over, opened it, and closed it. Then he tilted his chin toward Julia and smiled. "This is one of the most thoughtful gifts anyone has ever given me."

She swept her hand through the air, as if brushing his comment aside. "I just thought with all your traveling, you might need it. The children helped me. And—and after everything you've taught me about the Scriptures, I figured it was the least I could do."

"Well, you didn't have to go to all the trouble." He leaned closer to her and lowered his voice. "Especially for someone as rude as I am."

Julia laughed at his reference to their first meeting.

Bea suddenly bolted upright and then raced to the window. "Horsies!" her voice squeaked. "Someone home!"

Miriam lumbered to her feet. "Oh, the

guests are here." She and Elizabeth, along with the girls, scrambled to the kitchen to fetch tablecloths and lanterns.

"Doggie!" Bea wrapped her fist in Calamity's fur and they hurried outside to the back yard together.

"At least the dog doesn't seem to mind," Julia mumbled as she grabbed a bowl of apple dumplings she'd made and wandered out back. Bea'd grown more attached to the sheepdog every time Isaac brought her around.

Within thirty minutes, with the sun sagging low on the horizon, a vigorous fire burned. The back table boasted more delights than the group could eat, and at least three dozen folks milled about talking and laughing.

The ever-present wind grew cold, and Julia warmed her hands and arms over the fire. Sage branches released their musky scent as they burned. Julia took in a breath as Bea toddled over and held up a cookie she'd been nibbling on, showing Julia.

"Mmm, that looks good."

Then Julia laughed as Bea took another bite, spotted Calamity, and toddled over to the dog, offering the rest of the cookie. Calamity accepted the treat from Bea's hand with a wag of her tail. "Hun-gy dog-gie."

Glancing at the faces around her, gilded by the sunset and fire's glow, Julia sensed a feeling she'd not acknowledged since she arrived. One she was still reluctant to admit. This place felt like home.

Home.

Isaac's family had so easily accepted her. She'd fallen into the pattern of life here: chores, teaching, more chores—with an occasional hoedown or dip in the lake to break up the repetitiveness. She'd worked harder than she ever had at the orphanage, but her fellowship with Miriam, Elizabeth, and the other Lonesome Prairie ladies, along with her time spent with children, added a deep joy that far outweighed the difficulty of the work.

The long talks with Isaac when he breezed into town every couple of weeks also anchored her heart here. How Miriam and Elizabeth managed to maneuver them to the porch and then create excuses to leave them alone amused both Julia and

Isaac. It had become a guessing game, each boasting they knew what the excuse would be—Miriam saying she needed to shuck the corn at that moment, Elizabeth wanting to give Bea a bath. . . .

But Julia was secretly grateful to Isaac's sisters. Not only because time alone with him gave her the opportunity to uncover Isaac's admirable character and easy laugh, but also because their conversations often turned to the Bible. He seemed more than willing to discuss her questions for hours. And as they talked, the foundational truths she'd learned as a child became woven together, forming a beautiful pattern she never knew was in the Bible. And she hungered for more.

She also savored each meal she shared with these folks—for the company as well as for the food, which seemed richer, heartier than anything she'd eaten in the city. *Probably because we work so hard for it.* She fingered a pleat in her cotton skirt. With each day that passed, her city-girl shell slipped away, and a stronger, more secure woman emerged. A woman who might discover she actually felt at home on the prairie. In fact, truth be told, there were some days Julia didn't mind so much that Mrs. Gaffin hadn't responded with the funds needed to reimburse Horace and to purchase a return ticket to New York.

Branches snapped in the fire, causing a series of pops, and she tried to push out the thoughts that stirred in her mind. She knew if she let herself continue down this trail, dreaming of a life for herself here, she'd never see Mrs. Gaffin again. And she felt guilty for being willing to trade in her old life for a new one so quickly. Plus, was staying here realistic?

She'd known Isaac's family a month. True, they welcomed and seemed to accept her, but how could she exchange the long years she'd spent with her loving headmistress for a life with people she barely knew? Her heartbeat quickened as she realized the longer she stayed here, the more her heart would become attached to these folks who'd already grown so dear. And the more difficult it would be to leave.

But she'd made up her mind. She'd return to New York as soon as she received the money for a ticket. She couldn't just abandon Mrs. Gaffin and her life there. After all, Mrs. Gaffin had done so much for her. . . .

Julia meandered back into the kitchen to fetch another dish, her mind rolling along the same paths it had for the last few days. Returning merely because of Mrs. Gaffin was a poor excuse, she knew. Certainly the headmistress could take care of herself, especially with her wealthy new husband.

The whole truth was, Julia didn't know how she could live here and not completely fall in love with Isaac. *There, I finally admitted it.* Acknowledging the truth to herself washed a sense of relief over her. Now that she accepted it, she could stifle her feelings—just until she could go home. She set down the plate of chicken on the table.

Isaac walked up just then, driving her thoughts back to the present. His handsome, strong build sent a quiver up her arms. He tipped his hat as he sidled up next to her. "I just wanted to tell you—"

Her heart raced, expecting a word of encouragement or another thank-you for the gift.

298

Instead, his forehead furrowed, his eyes narrowed. "I don't let things like that sit for long."

She twisted her head toward him, confused and sensing his disapproval.

"That grave joke you put them up to? I'll get you back." He threw her a sober glance then winked and walked off.

Her jaw dropped as she watched him. "Wait a minute . . ." But before she could think of a retort, Miriam stepped in and tugged him away. She called for everyone to gather, and soon benches formed a wide circle around the fire with Isaac situated closest to the house. Before Julia could navigate herself toward a seat, Elizabeth shuffled her to the spot next to Isaac.

One after another, the folks gathered paid tribute to Parson Ike. Julia hadn't realized, but folks from all over Isaac's circuit had come out to celebrate their parson's birthday.

The children—now comfortable with performing for adults, thanks to Miss Cavanaugh and Shakespeare—initiated the festivities with a series of short skits. In one, they acted out a time when Isaac apparently showed up at the meeting room in Cascade in the cold of winter wearing only his long johns. Apparently a bandit along the way had stolen his coat, and Isaac offered him his clothes, too, if he'd only come to the meeting.

Julia laughed and watched as the parson dipped his head.

Then a woman stood and shared a story about how she hadn't seen her father since she was a little girl—until Parson Ike rode down to the mines in Butte and found him, urging him to make it home for his daughter's birthday. And when the man claimed he'd never be able to get there in time on foot, Isaac lent him Virginia and caught a ride back on the stage.

The night stole on as Isaac's parishioners told their stories. Widows shared about how he helped repair their homes. Ranchers injured by one accident or another explained how Isaac had tended their livestock until they could heal. A young man stood up and told how he believed God used Isaac's faith to "make an honest man" out of him.

The tales now finished, a blanket of quiet settled on the group as folks leaned back and gazed at the crackling fire. Julia took in the night sky, the Milky Way strewn across it, and the bright moon adding a majestic mist over the fields and lake. Most of the children snuggled into a parent's lap, and husbands and wives rested against each other.

Amid the quiet, Sarah Mack stood up, her puffed white sleeves and frilly lace flowing over her tall frame. With a simple smile at Isaac, she opened her mouth and sang a glorious rendition of Isaac's favorite hymn, "Rock of Ages."

From the first note, Julia was swept away by the woman's skill. Not a noise stirred in the crowd. It seemed even the wind stilled to listen to Sarah's voice blending the words and melody in praise to heaven.

Enveloped by the fire's warmth, a desire to share the splendor of the moment with another person kindled in Julia's heart. She glanced at Isaac sitting beside her, flashes of firelight dancing on his face. For a moment, his eyes caught hers. The beating of her heart seemed to stop, and everything melted into a haze. She never wanted to cease feeling his eyes' embrace. What would it be like to live each day knowing he sought her, cared for her, needed her?

The edges of his mouth inched up, and Julia thought he was going to say something, but Sarah finished singing and the bond between them released. As Julia clapped for the singer, she realized she'd never admired another man as much as she did Isaac. Hearing the stories about him—some funny, but so many revealing his parson's heart, his bravery, and his kindness—Julia felt she knew him even more.

A blast of wind slapped Julia's cheek, and she shivered. Of course, these thoughts were frivolous and perhaps dangerous for her emotions. She'd be leaving soon to travel hundreds of miles away from Montana and Isaac Shepherd, but still, her heart wouldn't obey.

She smiled at him as he stood. She knew whoever would someday have the privilege of becoming his wife, if anyone, would be a very blessed woman.

* * * *

Isaac gazed into the faces around the campfire, wondering what he'd done to deserve such love and caring. When he'd set off for Montana, barely nineteen years old, he'd left everyone he knew behind. At the time he had no idea his sisters would move out and start families of their own. He'd hoped to build a community of believers, but now they were more than community—they were family.

He moseyed up to Miriam after all the guests had ambled out to make their camps on the property for the night. "This was a wonderful evening. I'm grateful to you."

Miriam received the embrace her brother offered. "I suppose we must love you," she said with a teasing gleam in her eye.

"I figured that out." He smiled as he stepped out of the embrace. "All those embarrassing plays and stories made me feel real loved." He threw her a sarcastic wink.

She sauntered toward the kitchen, her mid-section leading the way. "All right, let's get this place cleaned up so we can go to bed."

As Isaac returned the chairs to their places around the table, Shelby ran in.

"Anyone seen Bea?"

"No. I haven't." Isaac scooted in a chair then leaned on its back. "I haven't seen her since she was sitting on your lap at the fire." He shot a glance toward Miriam, who was returning from the kitchen. "We can't find Bea."

Miriam reached for the table and steadied herself. "Have you asked Elizabeth?"

Shelby's forehead scrunched as she bent low to search under the sofa. "She and Miss Cavanaugh are checking outside. She's got to be here." Her voice rose. "She was sitting on my lap when that British lady sang, but then she ran off. I thought she was going to Ma, but Ma thought she was still with me. . . ."

Isaac's heartbeat quickened, but he clothed himself with calmness. It wouldn't do for anyone to panic. "You stay here," he instructed Shelby, "in case she comes back. We'll go looking for her."

Then those inside the house—Isaac, Miriam, Sarah Mack, her son William, and a few other guests—scattered, searching every section of the ranch inside and out. When Isaac strode back inside about ten minutes later, he saw that everyone had returned. He glanced around the room and discovered the same look on everyone's faces: worry, fear. They hadn't found her.

Isaac glanced at Shelby, whose eyes bore into him, desperately seeking his help. He bent to meet her gaze. "Don't worry, we'll find your sister. There are a lot of people around. Someone must've seen her."

The twelve-year-old swallowed and nodded. "Ma and Miss Cavanaugh haven't come back. They must still be looking. Where could she be? Please find her, Uncle Isaac."

He held her face in his hands. "We'll do our best. Will you do me a favor?"

She nodded.

"Pray."

"I already have been, but I won't stop."

He squeezed her shoulder and then faced Miriam. "Why don't you stay here and keep looking around the house. The men are outside."

Isaac rushed out the front door, and in the yard he came upon Abe and Jefferson already mounted on their horses.

"Whoa." Abe steadied his mount. The horse's front legs pranced with excitement, sensing the tension in the air.

"I'm going to check by the coulee," Jefferson called from his palomino. "And Abe'll ask around at the campsites."

Isaac threw his saddle blanket on Virginia. "I'll check down by the lake."

"Fine." Abe spun his horse around. "Let out a whistle if you find her."

With that, the two men galloped off into the silvery prairie.

Isaac finished saddling his horse then mounted. *O God, please let us find her,* he prayed as he spurred Virginia to a gallop. The thought of that sweet little girl out on the prairie by herself sent a frigid jolt up Isaac's spine. Even though she was little, Isaac knew toddlers could travel fast as jackrabbits when they got something set in their minds. With the miles of tall grass, she could be hidden anywhere, and it'd be nearly impossible to spot her. And if she got stuck in the coulee or the muddy lake. . .it could already be too late.

With a quick kick, Isaac urged Virginia

onward. Within minutes he spotted the lake. The low-hanging moon's light was doubled by the reflection on the motionless surface. His eyes surveyed the area as he galloped, but he saw no sign of the girl.

Then over the sound of his horse's hoofbeats, he heard something.

"Bea!" The shrill voice carried on the wind.

He slowed Virginia to a trot and scrutinized the prairie before him, his eyes adjusting to the gray light.

"Bea!" the voice called out again.

Ahead of him, silhouetted in black against the moonlit horizon, a figure paced, searching. A woman.

"Bea! Where are you?" the woman called again.

Isaac's gut clenched as he drove Virginia toward the figure. The woman turned when she heard him approach and Isaac saw that it was Julia.

"Isaac, thank God," she called, her voice shrill with worry. Her eyes flared with determination. "Please. We've got to find her."

Chapter Twenty-One

Julia's face, etched with fear and sadness, reminded Isaac of his first memory of her as she self-sacrificially handed Bea to Elizabeth. The devotion she felt for the girls had pained his heart. What fear must be gripping her now?

Isaac situated himself in his saddle and then drew back on the reins. Virginia stopped, and he dismounted. Dropping the reins, he hurried to Julia's side. "It's all right. We'll find her."

She turned to him, and her hands clutched his arm, desperate. He felt

308

needed, and he was glad he could be here for her as they searched for Bea.

Julia let go of his arm and pointed to the small, oval lake. "We went swimming last week, and she never stopped talking about it. What if she's in the water?" Her voice rose in panic. Her hands formed tight fists.

"Julia—"

"Bea tried to swim but then slipped under and couldn't get back up," Julia interrupted. "If Shelby hadn't been right next to her . . ."

"Julia, listen—"

"What will Elizabeth and Abe do if . . ." She shook her head, unwilling to speak the words. "They love her so much. She's as much a part of the family now as any of Miriam's children."

Isaac took her chin with his hand, softly turning her face to his. "Julia, listen to me." He caught her eyes with his gaze. "We'll find her."

She nodded but didn't speak. Even in the dim light he could see her fear.

As he stared into her face, the clouds drifted past the moon, revealing a large flawless orb. The prairie brightened under the moonlight. *Thank You, Lord. Thank You for the light.*

"Let's search together." He dropped his hand and stepped toward the lake. "With both of us looking, we have a better chance."

"But don't you think we should split up? Cover more ground?"

Isaac stroked her shoulder. Her muscles relaxed under his touch. "Listen. This lake's not very big. If she were in the water, we'd hear splashing. Besides, there are all kinds of dips and snags. I don't want you falling in."

Isaac led his horse with one hand. He placed his other hand on the small of Julia's back and hurriedly guided her over the prairie toward the lake. He knew it would be quicker if he went alone. He also knew she would never allow it.

They approached the shore, and his eyes swept over the water. It was perfectly still, except for the slightest ripple caused by the breeze warping and shifting the moon's reflection.

Julia's head tilted as she listened. "I don't hear anything, but what if she's already—"

"We're not thinking that. She's fine. Maybe she's not even here." Suddenly he was struck by an idea. "Let's search here then make our way to the other side. The buffalo tunnels are there."

Julia nodded. "Yes—she loved those tunnels." She took a breath. "Thank you."

"Bea!" Isaac called, scanning the water and shore.

"Bea!" Julia echoed.

Isaac led her along the bank. As they walked in silence, he scanned the gently lapping water for any disturbance. He knew Julia did the same. Many dangers waited for a tiny child on the prairie alone at night, but if he could rule out the lake, they might have time to free the girl from any other predicament.

They followed the curve to the other side. Gazing back across the lake toward the ranch, Isaac spotted the campfires and tents set up by his birthday guests.

"Do you see that?" He pointed to forms carrying lanterns, moving across the prairie. "Someone's bound to find her."

"It's amazing. All these people, searching, praying."

"They're good folks. They'd do anything for their own."

Isaac surveyed the ground ahead, and as his eyes focused on a patch of trees near the buffalo tunnels, he perceived a faint noise.

Julia jerked toward him. "Did you hear that? It sounds like a dog barking."

"I did."

They trudged toward the sound. The bark grew louder as they got closer, and Isaac's mind pricked in recognition. "That's Calamity. We'll get there faster if we ride."

He took Julia's hand and helped her step into the stirrup and onto Virginia—an awkward undertaking, since she wasn't wearing a split skirt. Once she was settled, he climbed onto the saddle behind her.

Ahead, toward the far end of the lake, he spied a cluster of sagebrush and low-lying box elder trees. He could barely make out the white splotches of Calamity's coat. Virginia galloped toward the trees. Julia's hair brushed his face; it smelled of soap and smoke from the fire.

"Do you think that's them?" Julia's voice quivered.

"Yeah, Bea played with the dog all day. Calamity probably followed her when she wandered off." *Good girl, Calamity.*

Isaac spotted the girl, her arm resting on Calamity's back, her blond curls almost white in the moonlight. Relief loosened the squeezing of his chest and the knots in his stomach. "Thank You, Lord."

But when they came within twenty feet of the girl and the dog, Virginia spooked. Isaac pulled back on the reins. Something was wrong.

Calamity was hunched down in a protective position, facing the prairie beyond. The dog's barking grew more ferocious, interspersed with growls.

"Bea!" Julia screamed, but a wind stirred, whipping her words behind them. "She's there, Isaac. Do you see her? Why'd you stop?" Julia shifted her weight to dismount.

Isaac braced his arms around her, not wanting her to rashly jump down. "Shh. . . quiet, Julia." He knew Calamity saw something. Hurrying upon them would spook whatever was out there.

"But I need to get her." Julia struggled in his arms.

He gripped her shoulder. "I need you to be still, for Bea's sake."

At the foot of the dark clump of trees, a large white sliver, like a fist-sized crescent moon, appeared in a sea of black. At first, Isaac couldn't make out what it was, but then it disappeared and returned—blinked. Now it slowly shifted, looking at him. He was staring into the eye of a buffalo.

Isaac's vision focused, and he perceived the buffalo's hulking form lying on its side. Its massive face was almost as large as Bea herself. As he watched, it twitched as if in pain. His guess was that one of the new settlers had shot it—trying to bring it down—but had wounded it instead. He knew an injured buffalo was deadly; he'd heard more than one story of full-grown men losing their lives. And Bea was so little. . . .

Isaac felt Julia's body tense.

"Do you see that? There under the trees. What—what is that thing?" Julia's voice shuttered.

Isaac placed his hands on her shoulders protectively. "It's a wounded buffalo."

Julia struggled again, trying to get down. "Bea!"

Bea, who was facing the buffalo, heard her name, looked back then stood.

That a girl. Slowly.

But instead of heading their direction, Bea toddled toward the large beast. "Wook, horsey!"

The closer Bea got, the more agitated the animal became, and it thrashed back and forth as if struggling to stand.

Julia gasped. "I've got to get her."

Isaac held her arms against her struggle. He would protect her—he *had* to protect her.

Virginia pawed the ground. Calamity barked again.

"If you spook it, it'll charge. Or thrash even harder." His mind raced, searching for what to do. *Lord, help me think. Guide us.*

Bea took another step toward the animal. "Hi, horsey."

If I run to the right, by the trees, hopefully it won't see me coming. He shifted his weight, preparing to put his foot in the stirrup and swing off, routing the path toward rescuing the girl in this mind.

Bea stretched out her hand, and the

buffalo let out a deep, throaty groan that echoed over the open prairie. Bea screamed at the sound and scampered to Calamity.

"No!" Julia squirmed and pulled from Isaac's grasp. In an instant, she was off the saddle, on the ground, and darting toward Bea.

"Julia, no!" Isaac jumped down.

The little girl whirled around and saw Julia approach. The buffalo also spotted her. It struggled even harder, attempting to stand, scraping the ground with its hooves. Calamity barked and growled, poised to attack.

"Julia, stop!" Isaac hissed, not wanting to yell and panic the buffalo even further.

He stretched for his rifle and aimed to shoot, but Julia blocked his shot.

Julia reached Bea and scooped the little girl up in her arms. She turned and dashed back toward Isaac, but then she cried out as her foot caught on a rock and the two tumbled to the ground.

Isaac jumped back on Virginia, certain of his next course of action.

The buffalo, fueled by fear, finally

righted itself and began its charge just as Julia was reclaiming her footing.

Isaac galloped toward them. "Julia!" He stretched out his hands, guiding the horse with just his thighs. She handed up Bea. He plunked her in front of him on the saddle, facing him.

The buffalo stumbled, favoring its right front leg, then righted itself.

"Now you." He gripped her wrist and then pulled his foot out of the stirrup.

She placed her own foot in the stirrup and Isaac pulled. Julia flew up, swinging her leg over. She landed behind him with a gasp, the wind jarred out of her. The buffalo neared.

Isaac kicked Virginia with both heels and took off at a gallop, leaving the injured beast behind.

He felt Julia's head against his back and Bea curled in front of him. The toddler was quiet now, but her body shook as quick sobs escaped.

Julia's arms wrapped around him, clasping in front, as they jolted and bumped on the loping mare.

Isaac heard a dog bark and released a

breath, knowing Calamity followed right behind.

Arriving at a safe distance, Isaac again pulled out his rifle and pointed it at the animal that was now laboring along the shore of Lonesome Lake.

"What are you doing?" Julia asked, her voice still out of breath.

"It's not safe to have a wounded animal about." He raised his sights on the buffalo. "Cover Bea's ears."

Julia's hands moved to the little girl's head as she pressed one of her ears hard against his back. Isaac squeezed the trigger. A loud shot reverberated across the plains, and the buffalo toppled to the ground.

Isaac let out a breath as he replaced his rifle in its scabbard.

From behind him in the saddle, he heard soft sobs and felt Julia's body quaking. His chest tightened with a thick dose of empathy. The rush of danger gone, he could imagine what circled through Julia's mind. If they hadn't heard Calamity's barks. If they hadn't reached her in time. . .

He kissed the top of Bea's head. "We found you."

"Find me."

Isaac stuck his thumb and forefinger in his mouth and whistled a message to the others. After a few seconds, a whistle was returned, letting Isaac know they understood.

"What do you think, Bea?" he said. "You've had quite an adventure. What say we get you to bed?"

"Bed. No! I not tired."

Isaac shifted a little more in his seat and patted Julia on the knee—his awkward attempt at comforting her.

Gratitude filled his heart as they approached the house, where Elizabeth stood with her arms outstretched. Isaac handed Bea to her.

"You sweet girl. I'm so glad you're back safe. Never go away without Mama or Papa again." Laughter bubbled through Elizabeth's tears, and she placed a dozen kisses on the small girl's forehead. "We need to get you inside and warm you up. You scared Mama."

"Mama scare?" Bea clung to her.

The rest of the group dispersed to their camps as Julia and Isaac dismounted.

As the voices faded, Julia meandered back to the smoldering fire. Isaac followed. Standing before the dimming firelight, Isaac took her hand. When she gazed up at him, Isaac saw tears dampening her face, the dancing flames creating a gleam.

"I'm sorry," she said as more tears flowed. "I don't know why I'm crying." She leaned toward him, her forehead almost touching his chest.

"Julia." Isaac's hesitation flew away, and in its place came an overwhelming desire to comfort this woman whose bravery had saved his niece. Whose strong, yet content, character had intrigued him since the first time he'd met her. Without worrying or questioning, he wrapped his arms around her. Warmth rushed through him as she collapsed into his embrace, her arms slipping to his back. She released her sobs, and he savored that he was here to help her carry her pain. Nothing else mattered in that moment.

His hands caressed her back as she leaned into the refuge he longed to provide. He wondered why he'd fought his feelings for so long. All those talks on the porch, the walks to the coulee, even the playful bantering—and yet he'd rationalized that he was simply ministering to her as a parson. He chuckled to himself as he stroked her hair. The rationalizations didn't make much sense, even to him. Yes, he cared about her spiritual condition, but as the weeks passed, the admiration he felt for her had taken root deep in his heart—and he no longer desired to deny it. To himself or her.

Finally, her sobs turned to soft cries, and her breathing calmed. Her hands slipped to his waist as she pulled back and gazed up at him. Her eyes exuded gratitude, trust, and, perhaps, longing. *Longing for me.*

"I'm glad you're all right," Isaac said, his hand gently stroking a strand of hair from her face.

"I wouldn't be if not for you." Her lips curved up in a quivering smile. "And neither would Bea."

"You're the brave one." He gazed at her, soaking in the beautiful face of the woman who stood before him. "You acted while I was still trying to figure out what to do." His finger followed the curve of her jaw. Could he continue to deny his feelings? Why? *Why should I?*

"Julia." His fingers moved to her lips, outlining them, and then shifted to weave themselves between the runaway strands of her hair. He lowered his head, longing to feel her lips against his. His gaze caught her eyes, and she tipped her head up. . . .

The sound of footsteps moved toward them, and they abruptly stepped apart. Isaac breathed in to calm his racing heart. He hadn't been this close to a woman for a long time.

Am I a fool?

Abe approached. When he saw the two of them together, he awkwardly pivoted the other way. "Oh, sorry."

Isaac threw an embarrassed grin to Abe. "It's all right. What do you need?"

Abe inched closer, a grin bending his lips. "Really it's nothing. We just heard a shot, and I wondered what it was."

Julia's face shed its vulnerability as her chin lifted and her lips assumed a small smile. She touched Isaac's arm. "I'll let you tell your story. I'd better check to see if they need any help inside." Before she turned to go, she paused, still gripping his arm. Her tender gaze, brimming with emotion, lingered on him—just for a fleeting instant. And in that moment, a sapling of hope blossomed in Isaac's heart.

Chapter Twenty-Two

Deep purple, the darkness before the dawn, stretched over the prairie, and it was hard for Julia to believe the drama of last night had really happened. It seemed like a bad dream.

Except for Isaac's touch. The feel of his embrace. The memory of it had made it hard for her to sleep. So while the children, partygoers, and family members settled in to rest, she'd gone to the pump for fresh water—something to get her mind off the look in Isaac's eyes.

Julia stepped across the yard toward the house with a lantern and a pitcher of water. She thought of more chores she could do while the others slept—milking the goats, weeding the garden. These plans didn't hold her attention for long, and her swirling thoughts circled back to Isaac.

Even if she tried, she couldn't banish the parson from her mind. Every moment he was near brought them closer—from the fiasco with Horace when she'd first arrived, to the evening spent in Isaac's soddy, their first walk to the buffalo tunnels, the hours of talks on the porch, the birthday party, and finally, the search for Bea. It was as if someone had designed their steps, leading them inch by inch, until that final moment when the parson had enfolded her in his arms. Isaac would probably call it God's providence.

Julia paused on the porch, relishing the memory of his embrace. His scent, hinting of smoke from the fire. His gentle caress of her hair and face. She closed her eyes. The reality of such contentment was almost beyond belief.

Yet, as she opened the door, one worry nibbled at her joy. That letter in Isaac's

Bible. Who was Bethany, and what had happened? Julia's curiosity tapped at her, yet it wasn't the mystery that bothered her, rather the guilt she felt for knowing something private about him. What would he think, or say, if he knew she'd read it? She didn't want to hide anything from him. *I should mention it the next chance I get. Maybe at breakfast—or lunch—whenever he comes around again.*

She set the bucket of water on the back porch and then quietly entered, closing the door behind her. It was dim inside, and she felt a yawn coming on. She hung the lantern on the peg and turned the wick until it barely glimmered. *I should try to rest.*

Crossing through the parlor toward her room, she heard a noise and jumped, startled. Someone was there, watching her. She expected it to be one of the children but instead turned to see Isaac sitting on the sofa, reading by candlelight. He smiled a casual, comfortable smile, and Julia quietly stepped toward him.

"What are you doing here?" she whispered. "I thought you were going back to your soddy."

He fingered the hat that sat on his knee. "Well, I plan on it, but I'm so beat. I just can't bring myself to get up and head down there."

"I'm sure Miriam wouldn't mind if you slept right there." She sat down beside him. "At least put your feet up for a while."

Isaac palmed his hair. "That's what I was thinking. It wouldn't be the first time."

"Do you want me to get you a blanket?" Julia didn't wait for an answer. The room was still dim despite the lantern, so she gingerly felt her way to the storage basket beneath the front window and retrieved one.

Returning, she handed it to him and knew if there was ever a moment designed to talk to him, now was that moment.

She clasped her hands together and then sank into the chair next to the sofa. His eyes gazed into hers, and when he smiled, she detected a bit of nervousness, shyness even. A side of the self-assured parson she'd not seen before.

"Isaac?" she finally ventured.

He must've detected the question in

her tone, because a look of concern replaced the smile. "What is it?" His voice was so soft, gentle. He leaned forward.

A tautness clamped Julia's throat, but she pushed ahead. "I read something. . . in your Bible."

The lines in Isaac's forehead relaxed. "Oh, you had me worried. Do you have a question about a passage? I love talking with you about the Scriptures."

"No, no, not that." Julia gripped the arms of the chair. "I mean in your notes in the back. That first day I stayed in your soddy, I was reading the notes written by your grandfather—at least I think that's who it was. He seemed like such a godly man, and his words encouraged me." Her words spilled out, and she glanced up to see Isaac leaning back again. She couldn't read his gaze.

"What did you find?" He asked the question as if he already knew.

A heaviness fell on Julia's chest. "I didn't think I would find anything. . .well, personal. And Miriam said I could read your Bible." She paused, waiting for his response.

"Please." His voice sounded tired, weak.

His eyes were intent on hers. "Tell me what you found."

"I found a letter you wrote to God. It said something about a vow to never get married, and it mentioned someone named Bethany. . . ."

Isaac rose from the sofa and pushed his hand toward her, stopping her words.

"I didn't mean to read it." Julia started to rise and then sat down again. "I don't want to know about it—I just thought I should tell you that I read it."

Gathering her courage, she stood and approached him. She wanted him to hold her as he had last night. Instead, she stood there, feeling helpless. "I'm sorry," she whispered, moving her gaze to his eyes.

Isaac's face did not hold the tenderness she longed to see, yet no bitterness resided there either—just a pained stare. "It's not your fault." He stepped back. "You don't have to apologize." He moved to the table. Pulling out a chair, he sat down. Then he motioned to the chair next to him.

She sat down and waited, relieved to be getting an explanation even as her foot tapped nervously. Bethany had obviously been a significant part of his past to inspire such a vow. Her heart sank even thinking the words. If he still held to his promise, it would mean the end of her newly sprouting dreams—of a happy life with the man she was falling in love with.

Yet, she had to know. And—her thoughts moved a different direction—why would he have spent so much time with her if he had no intention of courting? *Why did he almost kiss me?* He was surely a more honorable man than that.

A few moments passed, and he turned to the window, gazing out at the blank darkness as if finding his story.

"When I was no older than little Bea, my father was off fighting in the Indian wars." He glanced at her briefly, and then his gaze turned to his hands—the strong, working hands that had caressed Julia's face just hours before. "He'd left my mother alone with us children. There was no man there to protect her when a band of Apaches came through looking for revenge. Those Indians—they killed her."

Julia longed to reach for his hand.

Instead she rubbed the back of her neck, squeezing it, trying to ease the tension. "I'm so sorry."

"I love my father, make no mistake. He's a good, godly man, and he raised us the best he could, but I always promised myself I'd never leave a wife alone." His deep brown eyes gazed at hers. "So when I felt God's call on my life to be a circuit preacher at the age of sixteen, I knew the transient life—always moving from town to town, sleeping on the prairie, never having a permanent home—would not provide the safety a wife would need. I couldn't let what happened to my mother happen to a wife. So I promised God I'd never marry."

Julia's gaze stayed on his face, and she waited for him to continue.

"I knew Milo back then, and he encouraged me to go to seminary—to prepare for ministry—back in my hometown of St. Louis, so I did. And while I was there I met a young woman."

"Bethany?"

Isaac closed his eyes then opened them. "Yes. We were young and full of dreams and ideas, and we got swept away by a romantic idea of love. The week after I graduated, I asked her to marry me, laying aside my promise to stay single. She said yes, and we made plans to wed in the fall.

"The next month, I journeyed here, to Montana, where Milo had hoped I'd start my circuit-riding ministry. Just as he'd foretold, I soon felt the inward call to minister to the flock here." A slim smile formed on Isaac's lips, and he glanced upward, as if traversing back to that time. "When the small group of believers asked me to become their pastor, I longed for nothing more than to fetch Bethany and start our life here. But when I returned to St. Louis, where she was waiting for me. . ."

Julia sensed the pain in his voice. She silently leaned closer, praying to be a comfort to him, whatever words came next.

"She'd been killed."

"Oh, Isaac." Julia ached to take his pain away—as he'd done for her. "What happened?"

"While I was gone, a group of drunken cowboys, returning from a round-up, came through town. She was out walking alone." His voice dropped to a harsher tone. "We caught one of them—Buck Wiley. He told us when she refused them, they put their hands on her and scuffled. A gun went off—accidentally, according to Wiley—and before any of them knew what happened, she lay on the ground in a pool of blood. She died that night. Alone in the streets. If I'd been there. . ." Isaac's gaze pierced into Julia's.

"But you can't think it was your fault."

Such pain filled the parson's face—and something she thought she'd never see in his eyes. Fear. An anxiety that seemed to grip him tighter than his words could express.

"I know God wasn't punishing me for breaking my promise. I believe that now. But losing her, after I'd known the danger. . ." He shook his head. "I don't think I could suffer that kind of loss—or guilt—again." He stood and paced to the sofa.

A sick pain lodged in Julia's throat. Even though she didn't want to admit it, she knew what he was implying. He was no longer talking about Bethany. He was talking about her—about *them*.

333

Retrieving his hat, Isaac stepped back and faced her. "I'm sorry, Julia. I never meant for any of this to happen. I shouldn't have . . ." His eyes met hers, and he squeezed them shut. "I shouldn't have offered you anything more than spiritual guidance." He stepped closer and softened his voice. "After last night I thought maybe I could change. . .to be with you." He lifted his hand, and Julia thought he might touch her cheek, but he lowered it again. "But talking about Bethany brings back all the reasons I made the promise in the first place. It's not safe for a wife to be alone on the prairie. I couldn't risk your safety."

Julia saw Isaac's chest rise and fall. She knew he ached inside, but pain throbbed in her heart, too. "You—you led me to believe. . ."

Isaac's eyes pleaded with her. "I've done wrong by you, and I don't blame you if you never forgive me."

Julia swallowed, stifling the tears, refusing to let them rise. "You never expressed any intentions." Disappointment filled her like a flash flood, but anger did, too. Anger at herself.

Why did I let myself hope? I had no right to expect a happy future—not for me, a poor orphan with no family but a flighty headmistress. She waved her hand. "I wasn't planning on staying around anyway, so you don't have to worry." She stood and turned her back to him, knowing if her eyes snagged his, she'd no longer be able to tame her tears.

Behind her, she heard his boot step closer, then pause.

She continued. "Abe says the train comes through every year on the Fourth of July—hasn't missed that arrival for years." The idea of getting on that steam engine, going back to New York as she'd planned, now left a raw ache in her heart. When Isaac's arms had wrapped around her, the strength of his embrace—the comfort of his closeness—had settled over her, resolving her mind with an almost unconscious decision to stay. . .

Yet it wasn't to be, and allowing him to witness her disappointment would only prolong her suffering. She pushed away the pang of rejection and stood straighter. Her foolish dreams were all over now. Her choice was clear.

335

She whirled around, facing him with renewed intensity. "So, even if I don't hear from Mrs. Gaffin by then, I'll find a way to be on that train. I've heard of women working on the trains to pay their way. Or perhaps I could borrow the money from. . .someone. . .and get a job in New York to pay it back. However I do it, I will find a way to go back to New York on or before July fourth." Julia waited for Isaac to respond, but he said nothing. A sparrow chirping outside the window was the only sound that met her ears.

Finally Isaac nodded, as if coming to a decision. "It's probably best for you to go back—best for *you*, I mean." His voice faltered, and Julia wondered if the regret she felt pounded through him as well. "But to go by yourself? It's not safe."

Julia shook her head. What did he think she'd been planning to do this whole time? She'd never even considered a chaperone. Didn't need one. Plenty of women traveled alone these days. She'd even heard of women homesteading by themselves. They'd need a man's name on the deed, but after that, they were able to manage it alone.

"I'll be fine." She turned her head to catch his gaze, which eyed the floorboards. "It's not your concern."

"Julia. . ."

"You better go on home and get some rest," she finally said. "And I think I'll do the same." She crossed her arms, pain coursing from her chest to her stomach.

She'd been abandoned before. First her parents, then Mrs. Gaffin, Bea and Shelby, and now Isaac. The love of a family wasn't to be hers after all—never would be. Her hands trembled, despite her resolve to be strong. Her knees felt weak. She closed her eyes and an image rushed before her—of him placing his hands on her shoulders once again, telling her he'd changed his mind.

But he didn't speak. Instead he tipped his hat, his eyes sending an unspoken apology.

And he left.

Chapter Twenty-Three

Isaac told himself he needed to eat, smile, spend time with the people he'd dedicated his life to—even if it was the last thing he felt like doing.

The Captain Matthew Jay family, one of his favorites, and other parishioners sat around the long table at the Jay home. Everything about this afternoon should've created joy and contentment in Isaac. He dearly loved the faithful Lodge Pole church family. Mrs. Jay's cooking was the best for twenty miles—and Isaac had eaten at most every dinner table in the surrounding townships. He always relished the one day set aside for worship and fellowship. Yet Isaac sighed as he swathed butter atop Mrs. Jay's honey cornbread. *Why can't I enjoy myself?*

He couldn't shake the loneliness gnawing at him. His mind had been distracted by one thing, or rather one person, all day. He just hoped no one from Lodge Pole noticed.

The Jays came from a wealthy family back East. Isaac glanced around the house. Not only did they boast a separate kitchen—a luxury in these parts—but a large parlor, too, where both children and adults were now gathered. The air from the open window blew in, swirling the scents of the fresh-baked bread, leg of lamb, and fried potatoes. Tommy Jay, seven-year-old son of Captain Matthew Jay of the cavalry, gnawed a bite from his ear of corn. "Boy howdy, Parson," he spouted, kernels stuck between his teeth, "that sermon went on for a coon's age."

Isaac, slowly emerging from his thoughts, set his fork next to the fine china plate, which he knew was reserved for visits from the parson. "I suppose it *was* a mite long." The boy's comment rattled his already gloomy mood, but he searched to find something agreeable to say. "You did a fine job sitting still."

"My pa said if I didn't embarrass him during the sermon, he'd give me a penny." Tommy furtively peeked at his father manning the head of the table and then plunged his hand into his pocket and pulled up a bright copper piece. His smile spread. "I did pretty good considerin' that dull sermon. I like it better when you're all fired up."

"Tommy." His mother, who'd been dishing up the dessert in the kitchen, entered just in time to hear her son's indiscreet remark. Her brunette eyebrows scrunched in warning. "Mind your manners. Parson Ike preached a fine sermon." She smiled sympathetically, which made Isaac feel worse.

Isaac had reached Lodge Pole early that morning, pleased for the opportunity to preach the Good News. But a few hours ago as he'd stood in their parlor—with the dining table pushed to the side—expounding on the awe-inspiring symbolism of the temple garments in Exodus, he sensed the churchgoers' lack of interest. The drooping eyelids, yawns, and even a sustained snore from Grandpa Pete had been hard to miss.

He didn't blame them. His sermons this past week had lost their spark. He'd attempted to remedy his sagging preaching by spending hours in prayer and meditating on the Word. Yet, perhaps because every time he grabbed his Bible the beautiful new leather cover roused memories of the person whose skilled hands had sewn it—or perhaps simply because of his own unruly emotions—his mind remained preoccupied. The peace that usually cloaked him like a garment had been lost somewhere on the trail as he headed east—away from Lonesome Prairie—leaving him feeling exposed and alone.

He took a bite of the pound cake drenched in marmalade. Gazing out the window at the gloomy sky overlooking Main Street, his thoughts churned as the conversation carried on around him.

Since walking out of his sister's house that night, leaving Julia in his wake, he'd struggled to regain his normal routine.

Maybe it was the memory of the heartbroken look on her face that made him cringe. Everything about her—her tears, smile, laugh, curiosity about the Bible—was etched in his mind. And the indescribable light in her eyes. How it felt to hold her. . .

Little Tommy finished his corn then reached for the piece of cake his mom offered. "Mmm."

Isaac knew how to discipline his thoughts, and he'd done that. He'd not allowed himself to doubt his decision. It was for her safety as well as his own peace of mind. For the most part, he'd succeeded in shoving away the images of her.

Yet one phrase replayed in his mind over and over. Milo's words. *It is not good that the man should be alone.*

Milo hadn't understood. He'd thought Isaac's choice stemmed only from his obligation to the ministry. That was only part of it. If Milo were here, he'd see the wisdom of Isaac's decision. He'd support him as he always had.

Isaac longed to believe that.

"Do you want to play with us, Parson?"

Mrs. Jay set out a board game called Parcheesi on the table. "We've got room for one more. It's quite a hoot."

"I want to play!" Tommy piped up from his spot next to Isaac.

Isaac shook his head. "I don't know how. I'd rather watch anyway." He ruffled the boy's hair, returning to his thoughts as the family members moved their pawns around the board.

After he'd left his sisters' ranch, Isaac had returned to his soddy for some rest, but at the first call of the magpie, he'd set out to return to his long-neglected circuit. He was more determined than ever to persist on the path he and Milo had charted—preaching, the school, even more orphan trains, and eventually a hospital. No more veering onto jackrabbit trails.

The school's supplies would arrive on the train in just three weeks, and he still didn't have a teacher. Of course, the idea of preparing for the classes sent his thoughts back to Julia. If only he could ask her to take the job. In his mind he viewed her explaining fractions and Shakespeare's *Henry V* to an enthralled classroom of Montana's youth. "Once more unto the breach, dear friends, once more. . . ." He could see her rousing the children's interest.

But how could he expect her to change plans and stay in Lonesome Prairie? He picked up his mug and took a swallow of the freshly boiled well water. A wave of shame, as tangible as the liquid flowing down his throat, overtook him. He recalled the disappointment on her face when he left that night, her effort to hold back tears—tears that he caused. How could he ask her to bury the anger and hurt she must possess toward him and take on a working relationship?

The truth was he didn't know if he could bear to be near her, either. Perhaps it was better that she return to New York. Julia had told him her plan to get a job in the home of Mrs. Gaffin. That sounded safer than trying to make it on the vast Montana prairie with its outlaws, hardships, and even the land and weather that seemed to fight against the hardworking homesteaders. Yet even as he thought this, a claw of anxiety pawed at him for her safety on the return trip. He knew the evil that resided in men's hearts, the dangers that could steal a beloved one away forever. . . .

His mind rolled and swayed. There had to be a way for him to get her safely home. He owed her that much. He'd do the same for any young woman under his influence.

"Coffee?" Mrs. Jay held up the tin coffeepot, waiting for Isaac's response to her offer.

He was just about to decline, thinking he needed to head out in order to make Fort Belknap by first candlelight, but his answer was forestalled by a pounding knock on the door.

"Lemme in!" a voice demanded. "I needs ta talk ta Parson Ike." More thumping hit the door. "Lemme in!"

The captain stood, marched to the door, and opened it. "What do you want, sir?"

Isaac followed the captain. "Horace?" He eyed the old prospector, whose face was contorted with worry. "What's wrong?"

"Oh, Parson Ike. I'm glad I found ya. Done hightailed it all the way from Old

Scraggy Hill." He shoved his palms to his thighs, catching his breath. "You gotta come. Them vigilantes are headin' up to Jim's cabin fer Mabelina." He grabbed Isaac's wrist. "We gotta go right now."

The tone in Horace's voice told Isaac that the situation was serious. He knew Jim would protect Mabelina from the vigilantes—at all costs. "All right, Horace. I'm comin'."

Isaac glanced around the room. "Forgive me."

Mrs. Jay thrust his Bible into his hand. "You go on. Those folks need you."

"Well, then, thank you." Without another word he hurried to the stable with Horace alongside him.

"All right, tell me what happened," Isaac said as they strode toward the stable.

"I were out on the Beaver River pannin' fer gold when I seen a posse take off toward Old Scraggy Hill. I overheard 'em say they were searchin' fer the woman who done shot Elder Godfrey. Heard 'em talkin' 'bout splittin' the bounty."

Isaac's gut squeezed tight.

"The thing is, I know'd them two newlyweds were out at that ol' cabin. Me and him used ta squat thar'. I saw 'em headin' up that way last week when I was pannin' out on the river. They all happy and married, an' I thought, gee, it's too bad she had ta use me to make 'im jealous when he done loved 'er all along."

They reached the stable, and Isaac mounted Virginia, her butterscotch coat muted in the cloud-coated light. "Thanks, Horace." Isaac reached down and touched his shoulder. "You did the right thing by finding me. I'm real proud of you."

Horace beamed up at him. "The Good Lord's workin' on me." He tipped his chin up. "I'll shoot up a prayer."

Isaac nodded then set off.

* * * *

Julia lost count of how many mornings she'd risen before the rooster's first crow this week. Sleep seemed to arrive late and depart early. Yet she plodded through her days, counting down until she'd return to New York. Despite the busyness of the household, the hours seemed to trickle by.

Finished with breakfast dishes, Julia wiped her hands on her apron and edged out of the kitchen. She passed Abe and Jefferson as they ambled through the sitting room on their way back outside to tend the sheep and, little by little, build a prosperous life for their families.

She'd been watching the two men. They were sheepherders, and while they did care about the animals, it was evident the men's priority was to provide for their wives and children. Julia stifled a twinge of shame at the jealousy creeping into her heart.

And yet it was easy to be envious of Elizabeth and Miriam. These women had husbands to create a home with. Where was Julia's home? She'd lost it years ago when her parents died. Now the closest thing to home was with Mrs. Gaffin. But she hadn't heard from her.

No matter. In a few weeks she'd return—if she could avoid becoming Mrs. Horace Whitbaum till then.

The prospector hadn't shown his face since that afternoon in the barn, but the threat of him always loomed over Julia. Why had Mrs. Gaffin accepted his money? If she hadn't, Horace would probably have forgotten all about her by now. And why had Mrs. Gaffin offered her to him—a stranger—in the first place? Julia slowly shook her head. Because her former headmistress saw the lovely ad in the paper and thought it'd be the perfect way to take care of Julia. It was her way of providing.

She did love the woman's kindness, but if only Mrs. Gaffin had more common sense! Julia had to admit, though, that doubts were starting to creep in, and the longer she didn't hear from Mrs. Gaffin, the more those doubts took root. What if when she finally reached New York, Mrs. Gaffin no longer had need of her— or worse, didn't want her around?

"Julia, honestly, you do too much." Miriam patted Julia's arm as she entered the house from outside, where they had eaten breakfast. "You already did all the dishes? I was just coming in to help." She rubbed her lower back and leaned against a kitchen chair, then plopped into it with a winded sigh. "I'm gettin' mighty ripe."

Julia squeezed her shoulder. "You poor thing. Just let Elizabeth and me do the dishes from now on."

At that moment, Elizabeth sauntered in and pinched her lips together. "Was Miriam trying to do the dishes again? I told her to come inside and rest."

Miriam laughed. "If you two had your way, I'd do nothing else."

Julia nodded, forcing herself to sound cheerful. "Yes, she was trying to boss me around again, but I didn't listen. With that baby coming any day now, she shouldn't be on her feet."

"No, no." Miriam dismissed their concerns. "I'm fine."

Elizabeth shook her head as she exited through the front door with a bucket in hand. "You still need to rest," she called over her shoulder.

A yawn pushed its way from Julia's mouth, and she stretched. "I think I might need to sit a spell myself. Do you mind if I go back to my room? I'd like to finish my sampler—if I don't fall asleep first."

Her eyes angling in a compassionate slant, Miriam patted the chair next to her. "Sit down here with me first. I'd love the company."

A twinge of anxiety hit Julia. She'd been avoiding discussing Miriam's brother with her all week, and she didn't want to have the conversation now. Isaac's intentions—or lack of intentions—had crystallized the night he left, and Julia had accepted that. She only wished she hadn't let her desires go as far as they had. She thought back, remembering the last smile he'd given her that night before she'd told him about the Bible. The smile of appreciation, admiration, even love. But it was the last smile.

What was the point of discussing it with Miriam, or anyone? "I really am quite tired." She inched her way to her room.

Miriam opened her mouth to speak but was interrupted by the sound of Shelby and Johannah padding through the house with Bea tagging along behind.

"Your students are ready." Shelby pointed through the window to the backyard table, where all six of Miriam's children—along with Julia's cluster of other pupils—sat with their hands folded.

Julia smiled and pulled Shelby into an embrace. "Did you put them up to that?"

Shelby and Johannah peered at each other and giggled. "We thought if we were really good, we could do school today."

Elizabeth re-entered, and Bea scurried over to her. As Elizabeth gathered the little one in her arms, a renewed sense of affirmation struck Julia about returning to Manhattan. The girls were in a good, safe home. They were loved and accepted. She wasn't needed as their caretaker anymore. They did need a teacher, but someone more qualified could do that.

Julia glanced at Shelby and Johannah. "I'm sorry, girls. Not today."

Both girls' shoulders drooped, and Julia noticed frowns on Miriam's and Elizabeth's faces, as well.

"Please, it's been a whole week." Johannah smiled sweetly, her voice persuasive.

Julia massaged the back of her neck, wishing she could rub away the knots. She hated to disappoint everyone, but with the lack of sleep—and the weariness in her heart—she just couldn't force herself to teach them anymore. What did it matter? She'd be gone and forgotten soon.

"Maybe tomorrow."

Elizabeth shooed the girls away. "Off you go. I'll come out in a few minutes. I'm no teacher like Miss Cavanaugh, but maybe we can do some reading and writing."

Shelby and Johannah moaned as they slogged through the door.

Now even more, Julia longed to avoid Miriam's conversation. She needed a respite from this place, these people. "You know, I think I'll go for a walk instead. Maybe that'll perk me up a bit."

Miriam remained silent as Julia shuffled through the room and reached the door. Opening it, she spied a teenaged boy with his hand raised as if ready to knock.

"Oh! Howdy, miss."

Julia stepped aside, and the boy strode in as if he owned the place.

"Homer, what're you doin' in these parts?" Miriam welcomed the boy inside. "Let me fetch you some water." She went into the kitchen.

Julia closed the door behind him, noticing a letter in his hand.

"I was just on an errand for my ma," he called to Miriam in the kitchen. "Seems this letter came in on this mornin's stage."

Miriam returned and exchanged the mug of water for the letter. Her eyes glanced over it, and then she gazed up at Julia.

Julia's heart raced. *Please let it be from Mrs. Gaffin.*

"And I'm supposed to tell folks that we got word 'bout the train."

"What about the train?" Julia asked eagerly.

"Well, seems like there was some kind of mudslide back in Minnesota. Real bad one, covered a huge section of tracks. They say it's gonna take a few weeks to get it uncovered. So the train'll be delayed."

"It'll be here for the Fourth, though, won't it?"

Homer nodded. "Oh yeah, sure, but the weekly arrivals won't be comin'. The next train won't be till that one on the Fourth."

Julia released a relieved sigh. "Well, those weekly ones weren't very reliable anyway."

"Just passin' along the information." Homer handed Miriam the glass, thanked her, and left.

"It's for you." Miriam held out the letter.

Julia grasped it and scanned the envelope. It was from Mrs. Gaffin. She closed her eyes and clutched it to her chest. *Finally.*

Chapter Twenty-Four

Isaac slowed Virginia's trot as he noticed more trees spilling onto the prairie ahead.

Almost there.

The rickety old cabin, he knew, was on the top of the tree-lined hill in the distance. It wasn't exactly what he considered the perfect honeymoon spot, but he supposed that to the newly married couple, it really didn't matter much. He just hoped that the vigilantes hadn't arrived yet.

A shootout's not exactly what I had in mind for today's agenda.

Isaac took off his hat and wiped his

brow with his red bandanna. He sat back in his seat, signaling to Virginia to slow. Then, before he even had a chance to step off, he heard a familiar voice filtering through the trees.

"Step back! I'm not afraid to take on all of ya." It was Jim's voice, backed by Mabelina's sobs.

Isaac stepped slowly, quietly up the hill. *Lord, help me know what to do. Protect those who belong to You. Bring peace.*

Isaac dropped Virginia's reins, knowing she would stay right where he left her, and raced up the evergreen-strewn hill. The front door to the cabin was open, and he saw the backs of four men. Three, he guessed, were paid lackeys. The fourth—a stocky man with a tan, wide-brimmed hat—must be their leader.

He jolted to a stop as he approached and realized the three lackeys aimed Colt .45 pistols at Giant Jim.

Isaac's heart pounded as he watched the stocky man approach Jim and shove a small, pearl-handled derringer against the newly redeemed man's temple. His back was turned, and Isaac couldn't see his face. It was like witnessing a raccoon holding a pistol to a bear. Isaac knew that in five seconds flat, Jim could overpower the stocky man. It was the other three he worried about.

"Jim! Let them take me," Mabelina, almost completely hidden by Giant Jim's mammoth frame, said between gulping cries. Seeing that her husband wasn't backing down, she turned her attention to the men. "Don't shoot him!"

"Just hand her over!" the stocky man in the front commanded.

"You'll hafta shoot me first." Jim closed his eyes. "God, take me home."

The man cocked his pistol, and Isaac sucked in a breath.

"Stop!" Isaac shouted. He raised his hands and stepped slowly onto the porch.

The three lackeys turned, guns now on him. Isaac looked upon each face. Their eyes were narrowed, their gazes hardened. No light reflected from their eyes, and he knew with one word from their boss they'd have no problem shooting him, too. Isaac's eyes moved to the barrel of the closest gun, and faces of those he loved flashed before him. *Dear Lord, help me.*

Isaac swallowed hard. "There is no need for violence," he said, voice raised.

Then, as if his feet had a mind of their own, he dashed forward and stood beside Giant Jim. "Men, put your guns down. We'll talk about this."

The three gunmen, seeing that Isaac was a parson, relaxed their stance. Isaac inspected the leader, whose iron was still shoved against Jim's head. The man turned, and Isaac suddenly wanted to vomit. "Warren?"

Milo's son was the leader threatening to shoot Jim. He smirked and cocked an eyebrow. "Hey there, Parson Ike. Fancy meetin' you here." He mocked Isaac's name but didn't lower his gun.

"Warren, what are you doing? Put Milo's gun down."

"Oh, I'll put it down when this here idiot turns over that lady who killed my father."

Isaac searched Warren's face. *Revenge? Is that why he's doing this?* Isaac doubted the man cared enough about Milo to fuel such a vengeance. There must be another reason. A bounty on Mabelina, perhaps.

"They gonna string 'er up, Parson," Jim

blurted out, his eyes wild. "It were an accident. I told 'im, but he won't listen."

Isaac forced a smile and stepped toward Warren. "Listen, I know you're a law-abiding man. Why don't you lower that fine pistol and send one of your boys to go fetch the judge? We'll let him decide. Then, if she's convicted, you'll get your bounty."

"Now there's a fine idea." Warren's brow furrowed over his scornful eyes, contradicting his appeasing words. "But you see, if we bring her in alive, some judge may let her go, and then I won't get my money."

"Don't ya mean 'we'?" one of the gunmen asked before spitting a stream of tobacco on the floor. "You aren't going to hold back on us, are you?" The man's gun turned slightly from Jim to Warren.

Warren glared back at him. "You'll get yours."

Isaac stepped closer to Jim. "Well, if you're not going for the judge, then you'd better shoot all three of us. Like Jim, I refuse to turn Mabelina over to you."

Warren's jaw dropped and his eyebrows furrowed—a splash of surprise mixed with fear as the ramifications of that option seemed to sink in.

"You may get off for shooting Mabelina, since she's got a price on her head, but another innocent man and a parson?" Isaac lowered his hands. "You interested in living like an outlaw—or getting hanged yourself?"

Warren hesitated and then finally uncocked the gun, lowered it, and replaced it in its holster. The other men did the same.

"Praise the Lord," Jim exclaimed, hands raised. "I was prayin' fer help and then you showed up, Parson Ike." He reached behind him and pulled Mabelina around front, wrapping her up in his beefy arms. "You all right, darlin'?"

"Buck." Warren pointed toward the man closest to him, obviously unmoved by the lovers' display. "You and Thad go on to Fort Benton and find out where Judge Booker is. Then go get him and bring him here."

The weak chin on Buck's too-long oval face tipped up. "But we ain't got supplies to go all the way to Fort Benton."

Warren leered, and then he reached in

his pocket and took out a leather coin sack. He threw it to Buck. "Now go on. When you find the judge, bring him on back."

Isaac held out his hand. "Hold on. Why don't we all go to Fort Benton? We can wait for Judge Booker there. He may be there already."

Warren's lips clamped together, and he shook his head. "No. That big man's too much of a risk—and that woman, too." He pointed toward Jim and Mabelina. "I ain't hightailing it all over the countryside with them." He lifted his head toward the door, indicating to Buck and Thad that they should go.

They slogged out the door, disappearing down the hill.

"This is how it's gonna work, parson. You and Lefty"—he eyed the third man—"and them two are gonna stay here till the judge comes. I got some business to take care of, but I'll be back. Then, after the judge convicts her, like I know he will, we'll all watch the hanging together." He leaned over and gazed out the door. "On that tree right there."

A sick pain hit Isaac's gut as he eyed

361

his best friend's son. He and Milo had prayed so many hours that this young man would follow the truth. Milo had given him every opportunity to lead a respectable life, yet he'd chosen to ride the path through the wild briars.

Isaac glanced at Jim and Mabelina. The woman moved in front of her husband and lifted her eyes to meet Warren's. "I done wrong shootin' your pa." Her eyes glistened, but her voice was strong. "I'm ready to have a judge hear it out. I'll accept what he says, no matter what it be."

Jim rubbed her arms. "And I will, too," he said, to her more than the others.

Isaac eyed Warren. "How do I know your men'll bring the judge back here?"

"Well, I guess you're jest gonna have to trust them. They're men of fine virtue." His sudden burst of laughter matched the sound of a crow cawing outside. "The question is, how do I know you won't try to overtake my man here and skedaddle?"

"We won't," Isaac answered simply. "But we aren't waiting for more than a week. If you can't find the judge by then, we'll head for Fort Benton."

"Fine." Warren abruptly stomped past Isaac toward the door. "You all settle in nice and cozy." He pointed at Lefty, who stood waiting with his thumbs in his belt loops. "Make sure they don't leave, or you'll pay."

"Don't worry, boss." Lefty crossed his arms and squared his shoulders.

Warren tramped out the front door. Isaac followed him. How could Warren have grown so cold, hardened, since Milo's death? Isaac had noticed uneasiness about him at Aponi's home a month ago, but he thought it was just the freshness of grief. He hated that Warren had decided to send Aponi to the reservation and the girls to boarding school, but for Milo's sake, Isaac had hoped Warren's actions were fueled by good intentions.

Now Isaac wasn't sure if Warren's character consisted of anything but selfishness. Yet, for Milo, he'd try one more time. Isaac had nothing to offer the young man, nothing but Christ.

"Hold up, Warren."

Warren swung around, irritated. "What? I told you I got business to take care of."

Isaac breathed out. "Business? I'm sure you do. Is it at the saloon?"

Warren grinned, but an unsettled look lay beneath the surface of the man's eyes.

"Maybe. What's it to you?"

Only God's transforming grace could reach him. Over the years, Isaac had seen many degenerate westerners—outlaws, prostitutes like Mabelina, and even the most difficult to persuade, the self-righteous—begin new journeys in Christ. No one was too far gone for Christ's love. Not even Warren.

"You have another option." Isaac spoke softly.

Warren leaned against the porch railing and tipped his hat back. "Oh really, and just what would that be?"

"Forgiveness."

Warren snorted and moved toward the path back to town, but Isaac reached out and grasped his shoulder.

"I ain't forgiving anyone, Parson. Forget it."

"That's not what I meant." He focused on Warren's eyes, seeking a spark of light to show that God was working in him.

Finding none, he continued anyway. "*You* can be forgiven."

"You don't even know what you're sayin'."

"Yes, I do. It doesn't matter what you've done. God forgives."

"Answer me this, Parson. How do you think the law found out about Mabelina shootin' my stepfather anyway?" Warren didn't wait for an answer. "I told them." He leaned in close to Isaac's face. "And you know why?"

Isaac waited.

"Because I told her if she didn't start turning her 'night work' again with those fine gentlemen callers at the saloon and giving me a cut, I'd turn her in. Mabelina said no. Dusty was willing to let her go, but I think she's too valuable. So here we are." He shrugged. "Business is business, after all."

Isaac closed his eyes as a rush of sorrow tumbled over him, not for himself or even for Milo anymore, but for the empty soul standing before him. He stepped back, releasing the man into God's sovereignty.

A deep scorn exuded from Warren's

face. "Oh, and that business I've got to do," he rasped in a low tone. "You're right. It does involve a saloon. A new one being built in a couple weeks. Finest in Chouteau County. Guess where I'm gettin' the supplies?" His dark eyes held Isaac's. "A railcar full of everything I'll need will be comin' on the Fourth of July train."

Isaac's mind worked, fitting bits of information together like a puzzle.

"C'mon, Parson, you know what I'm talking about—a special shipment, planned by my father, coming on the Fourth. . ."

Isaac sucked in air as if the man had physically punched him in the gut. "The school's?"

"You guessed it."

"But you can't," Isaac protested. "What do you want with a bunch of school supplies?"

He laughed. "No school supplies are coming. One telegram changed those slates and books into glasses and barstools."

"Your father was investing in the school—in the children's education, the future." Isaac clenched his fist. If he'd ever wanted to punch a man, it was now.

"*My* inheritance, Parson. Not yours." Warren turned his back on Isaac and left.

* * * *

Goosebumps, a result of the chilly morning, danced across Julia's arms as she slid onto the bench at the picnic table behind the ranch. Her hand trembled slightly as she held the letter from Mrs. Gaffin. The prairie breeze rustling through the tall grass, like the musical accompaniment of those who made their homes there, followed Julia into the gray afternoon. Too nervous to open the missive, she gazed at the vast prairie broken only by the lake, dingy in its reflection of the sky. She couldn't look at Lonesome Lake without remembering the night Isaac had guided her with a hand on her back and calmed her as they looked for Bea. What would it be like to walk through life protected by such tender attention? She'd never know.

No, please no. Everywhere she looked, reminders of Isaac pummeled her fragile heart, and she longed to be far from any place where he'd ever been. Soon she would. In fact, hopefully this letter held a quick and easy strategy for making it happen.

She glanced at the looped writing and couldn't help smiling at the familiarity of her headmistress's penmanship. The curlicue letters and sprinkled hearts bespoke Mrs. Gaffin's cheery demeanor. How Julia longed to hear her cackling laugh and feel her arms receive her in an uninhibited embrace.

She slit open the envelope and unfolded the letter. Clutching it tightly in her hand to withstand the gusts, she read.

Dearest Julia,

Oh my sweet girl, I have done it again, haven't I? You poor dear. I had no idea Mr. Whitbaum was a gold miner. When he said prospector I thought that meant he was a banker. Prospecting investments! Oh, you should've heard Mr. Gaffin when I told him. He feels terrible that you are in such a position, and he's come up with the perfect plan to fix everything.

368

"Thank goodness," Julia said out loud. She knew Mrs. Gaffin would want to help, but what a relief that Mr. Gaffin formulated the measures. Perhaps he'd provide the sense dear Mrs. Gaffin lacked. Julia continued to read.

> **And my darling Julia, of course you can stay with us when you return. I would've offered, but I thought you'd be married by now. You will live under our elegant roof as a family member, not as a servant. Dear Julia, how could you even think I'd want you as a servant? You are like a daughter to me. A wonderful, beautiful daughter, whom I love with all my heart. I wish I could embrace you.**

Julia smiled imagining Mrs. Gaffin dabbing her eyes with a handkerchief as the emotions flowed.

> **Finally, I want you to know that I feel so terrible about the awful predicament I've put you into that I have found you a wonderful place of employment! The Butterfly Academy for Young Ladies**

was looking to fill a position for an assistant to the headmistress. I had tea with the headmistress just last Tuesday, and I told her all about you. She said my word was good enough and offered you the position. Julia, you will be the English and history teacher, and you'll be in charge of the pupils' extracurricular activities. These are very wealthy families, my dear. It's the perfect opportunity for you to meet a nice young man.

I must finish so I can post this today, but please know that I love you, my dear, sweet, lovely girl. We will see you at the next train.

Yours,
Mrs. Gaffin

Julia set the paper on the table and placed her hand over it. *Thank you, Mrs. Gaffin.* A calm acceptance settled over Julia's heart for the first time in days. Mrs. Gaffin really did return the affection Julia felt for her. She'd reside under her protection as a daughter. She'd be part of—a family. And the employment was more than she could've asked for.

A deer leaped into Julia's vision followed by another and two fawns, their hooves crackling the dry grass.

Finally, Julia would be able to leave her past behind, like closing chapters in a book—her parents' death, life in the orphanage, the pain of leaving the girls. . .Isaac.

Her eyes moved to the firepit next to the table. The memory of Sarah Mack's song and the gaze she and Isaac had shared in the dancing firelight fluttered to her thoughts. And despite everything—all her striving to push it away—a part of her heart still longed for him to return to her. That's why she sat out here each day pretending to need rest or to work on her embroidery. She longed to see his butterscotch mare clopping over the field with him mounted atop. She longed for him to spy her sitting there. If he came to her, apologized and confessed his love, Julia would gladly accept him back. She knew she would, despite her attempts to convince herself otherwise.

The deer family frolicked away, and Julia scolded herself. She knew allowing those thoughts to fuel her imagination only brought pain. *O God, help me let him go.*

She glanced back at the letter, her salvation.

Reading it again, a bit of uncertainty niggled at her. She checked inside the envelope. It was empty. Something was missing. Mrs. Gaffin said they had a plan to "fix everything," but she didn't say what that plan was. If she'd just sent Horace's money—and perhaps a train ticket—Julia could pay him back and go home, but. . .

Oh, Mrs. Gaffin.

She groaned. It would take three more weeks to post another letter and wait for a reply. Three more weeks of worrying about being kidnapped by Horace. And then there was the question of whether she'd get an answer before the Fourth of July train arrived. Or the money to get on it.

Maybe she should pray that Horace would find a vein of gold up in those hills. *Yes, that would keep him occupied for a while. . . .*

Julia slumped on the hard wooden bench where she sat. Although Mrs. Gaffin's words brought comfort to her emotions, the letter had done nothing to provide relief from her situation. She realized she'd been fastening her plans on getting a letter from Mrs. Gaffin before the train arrived, assuming her former headmistress would include the money and ticket she needed. But now. . .

A stray, dry leaf from a distant box elder tree slapped against her face then whirled away in the murky day—just like her plans.

She glanced at her hands and decided to go back to her room. Perhaps she could finish the sampler. Even if the Home Sweet Home pattern held only ironic pleasure to her now, the repeated movement of the stitching would at least distract her thoughts.

Then, in a quick rush, an idea struck her. "That's it."

Chapter Twenty-Five

"Parson, you been staring out that
window fer the last week. Don't you think
you need to get your mind on somethin'
else?" Jim, who sat on a log, hollered to
Isaac inside, nudging him from his
thoughts.

Lounging on the cot, Isaac's gaze
swung lazily to Giant Jim playing cards
with their sentinel, Lefty, outside the
cabin—the makeshift jail for him,
Mabelina, and Jim.

"Can't you think of nothin' to pass the
time? You got yer Bible, why not work on
them sermons of yours?"

Lefty sucked on his ebony pipe then released the smoke from the side of his mouth. "Yeah, Parson. The way Giant Jim here's been preaching to me, a body'd think *he's* the minister, not you."

"Just can't help but talk 'bout the Lord. Plus, if we gotta spend a considerable 'mount o' a time stuck like two gophers on a spit, might as well make friends." Jim planted his cards for Lefty to see. "Full house. Read 'em and weep."

"Aw!" Their captor took off his hat and punched it against his knee. "You call that friendly?"

"The friendly part is the fact that we ain't bettin'." Jim's mustache arced up in a grin. "Parson, you wanna play a hand?"

"Nah, I'm just gonna rest a bit." Isaac leaned against the wall of the dark, dank cabin. A drab moth flew to the window. He moved his attention out the door to where Virginia was nibbling on grass under the shade of the tall pine, with Calamity napping at her side.

"Suit yerself. Mabelina's skinnin' up a coon she trapped. We'll cook it up fer dinner soon." Jim licked his lips.

Isaac didn't respond. Instead, he

shifted his gaze inside, scanning the wobbly shack. Last night a windstorm had blown in, causing the structure to shudder on its foundation. Any stronger blast surely would've sent its planks tumbling down the hill.

Isaac exhaled a weary sigh. For all the years he'd been in Montana, he and Milo had planned and prayed. Bit by bit, doing their own part to construct a foundation to build a far-reaching ministry. To tend the spiritual landscape of this untamed land.

Their first structure was to be the school. In Isaac's mind, its whitewashed walls, neat desks lined up in rows, blackboard, and schoolmarm's desk were already established. But most importantly, he envisioned the children. His sisters' brood, the Indian little ones who'd have no chance to learn without a school, the soldiers' children, the new homesteaders' tykes—they all depended on Isaac. And the orphans who came across the country on the train. He'd promised them an education. His stomach ached as failure's fist jabbed him anew.

He and Milo had dreamed that their one schoolhouse would lead to others and that eventually their ministry would impact not just Chouteau County—or even Montana—but the whole West. The whole country.

He laughed at his own hubris. Had he really thought the efforts of two countrymen—an elder and a preacher—could "civilize the West"?

Ripping off a bit of loose newsprint, previously stuck to the walls for insulation, he flicked it to the floor. Now, because of the death of one of those men—and the naïveté of the other—their plans had collapsed as easily as this shaky prospector's cabin might.

A long list of accusations wrangled through his mind. He should've urged Milo to put the school in his will. And in hindsight, Isaac realized how gullible he'd been about Warren's character. So much pain could've been avoided if he'd only heeded the warnings. *Maybe Aponi and her girls would still have their home. . . .*

More than that, Isaac had never found a teacher. One simple task. If he had, perhaps they could've started without a building. But he'd gotten sidetracked, and now the whole project would be delayed.

Isaac shook his head. He didn't know when, if ever, the school would be built.

The two men outside apparently finished their game, because Lefty's harmonica sent its melodic twangs to Isaac's ears. He moaned. If he heard "Oh! Susanna" one more time, he'd take that harmonica and chuck it into the fire. Is that the only song anybody knew around these parts?

He returned his gaze out the window and tried to tune out the annoying ditty. He'd made a decision sitting here this week. And his resolution made more sense with every moment that passed.

It was over.

All his plans, his big ideas to start a school, a hospital, even the orphan train—someone else could dedicate his life to such futile tasks. Six years of fruitless toil were enough for Isaac.

As soon as Mabelina's trial was over, he'd pack up and go back to St. Louis. He could be gone in a week. He'd talk to the dean of the seminary and apply for a teaching position. Isaac folded his hands behind his head and lay back on the scrawny pillow. It was the perfect plan.

He could train an army of future ministers—and never have to ride a circuit again.

"Suppertime!" Mabelina called from the firepit a couple yards beyond the house.

Isaac scooted off the cot and moseyed outdoors. He grabbed a tin plate hanging from a nail in the outer wall and brushed it off with his hand. Then, following the others, he took his share of raccoon stew and beans.

"You know," Isaac started, as they settled on logs and stumps by the cabin, "today marks a week since Warren left. I say if he doesn't come on the morrow, we pack up and head out to Fort Benton."

Isaac expected them all to agree. Nobody would want to stay in this dingy sty any longer than absolutely necessary. But Jim, Mabelina, and Lefty all gaped at him, chewing their meat silently.

Isaac sent a questioning grimace. "You mean you don't want to go?"

"Nope." Jim jumped in first. "I don't see why we'd hurry the trial when we don't know what's gonna happen to my sweet lady." He scooted closer to her.

"He's right." Mabelina's curly red hair

outlined her face like a starburst. "Why not just stay up here? I ain't never been so happy in my life." She tucked her head under Jim's neck as he wrapped his arm around her shoulder.

Isaac eyeballed Lefty, who was happily eating. "You agree, I suppose."

"Yup. I don't cherish seeing old Warren and them rascals again. Much rather bide my time with you folks."

Isaac stood and chucked his plate to the ground in a huff. "I'm going to the stream."

"That parson's a cantankerous fellow," Isaac heard Lefty say as he stalked off.

"Naw, he's a good man," Jim replied. "Just needs to figure a few things out."

Isaac ambled down the wooded trail to the stream. Parking himself on a rotting log, he listened to the water trickle over the stones and watched the fading sunlight's glimmering reflection.

Before long, Jim plodded down the trail and sat beside him.

"I don't want to talk." Isaac threw a pebble into the stream.

"I know ya don't, but I was jest discussin' with Mabelina, and if you want to go back to the fort tomorrow, we'll go. May as well git it over with, I s'pose." Jim's head angled toward Isaac, an intent look in his eyes.

Isaac's lips pursed, and he clenched his jaw, steeling himself as the significance of Jim's words seeped in. Jim would sacrifice his happiness to ease Isaac's discomfort? *How can I be so selfish*?

"No," Isaac said, hearing the shame thick in his own voice.

A tinge of relief flickered over the man's face. "All right, then, we'll jest wait."

"Yeah."

A brown-feathered swallow fluttered down and landed on a rock.

"You all right, Pastor Ike?" Jim faced the stream, apparently watching the bird.

Isaac's neck grew weak, and his head collapsed to his hands. The man's selfless generosity triggered the thoughts, options, plans, worries, and complaints he'd indulged in all week to swirl around him like a court of accusers. He rubbed his forehead. He still didn't know what to do next.

He picked up a stick from the dirt and, throwing it into the water, watched it swirl and jerk and finally get lodged against a fallen log.

He was that trapped stick. And he couldn't free himself. He'd tried all week to find a way. . . .

"I don't know what's got you so down," Jim said after a moment. "But I know you ain't behavin' like yerself. And from what I can tell, you ain't behavin' right." He picked at his fingernails. "I know I ain't one to judge—boy, I know that—but you done told me when I did wrong and, well, I oughta tell you, too. That's what friends do." He gingerly patted Isaac's back, then returned his hand to his lap.

Isaac searched Jim's face, not as a parson gazing at a sheep, but as a friend. A friend in Christ. "I don't know what to do."

"You have a problem trustin'." Jim shook his head. "A big one. You ain't trustin' the Good Lord with that school of yers. If He wants a school in these parts, there'll be one. I never knew why you were so worked up about it."

Isaac closed his eyes. Jim was right, but there was so much more at stake than just the school—not just his grandiose plans, but his entire purpose for being in the ministry. He wanted to be honest with Jim and with himself. He needed to finally exhume the truth he hated to face.

"If I don't have the school to plan, the hospital, the next orphan train," Isaac peered at the stick wedged in the stream, "I don't know what I'll do." He let out a slow breath.

Jim looked Isaac full in the face. "I already done told ya. Trust Him."

The sky's blue shade blended to pink and purple as the sun began its journey to rest. Isaac watched the light gray smudges of clouds sail across the sky, and felt, in their wake, raindrops landing on his hands and arms.

"Trust Him." He whispered Jim's words, and like the stream's waters dancing over stones, the truth began to cleanse. He'd been so set on his own plans to shepherd his flock, he'd forgotten to rest in the Good Shepherd. As splashes of truth revealed the dirt beneath, Isaac asked himself why he'd striven so hard to make his plans happen. *I wanted credit for myself.*

Perhaps that wasn't his only purpose, but it made up the part that wouldn't let go, that failed to trust. Isaac took in a long, deep breath of the freshly rain-cleansed air. "My failure wasn't about a school, or hospital, or anything else. You're right, my friend. I failed to trust."

Jim nodded slightly. "He'll forgive you."

Isaac bowed his head. "I guess that's what I told you once."

"Yup."

As a measure of relief rushed over Isaac, he glanced at Jim's face. It held a frown, a speck of doubt, as if he wondered whether he should continue. Then the faithful Goliath gripped his giant paws together and moved his thumb over the silver band on his left ring finger. His deep brown eyes pierced Isaac. "You say you'll trust God with yer ministry, but can you trust Him with a wife, Parson? Even that?"

At that, Jim stood. "I'm gonna let you be. I'll be back at the cabin if ya need me."

Jim disappeared into the woods, and Isaac sat in silence.

Jim's words replayed in his mind, and then Isaac shook his head. This week his aching mind had reeled over Warren, Aponi, Milo, and his own failed plans. But even more, Julia's pained expression as she watched him leave plagued his thoughts day and night. A thousand needles pricked his heart every time he thought of it.

Years of stubborn adherence to a promise, and the fear it represented, surrounded Isaac like the walls of a fortress. Losing his mother and Bethany had created so great a dread of being hurt that he'd refused to open his heart to love again. And hiding within the walls of a foolish vow kept him safe from that pain—or at least it had for a time. But the truth was, Jim was right. The promise had always been built not on faithfulness, but on *faithlessness*. He didn't trust that God could bring someone to work alongside him. More than that, he didn't trust that God could keep her safe.

Yet now, here—because of the words of a giant man with a giant-sized faith—the door to the fortress opened before him. Could he again refuse to step through? Did he want to?

True words from those who loved him

echoed through his thoughts. *It is not good that the man should be alone.* Milo had said it. But so had others in different ways. Miriam's hints, Aponi 's attempts to match him with her daughters, even Elizabeth's wordless looks.

Trust Him. Jim's simple words.

The wind picked up, bringing with it more raindrops. The rain began to pour, washing over Isaac as his stubborn fortress melted in a rush of repentance.

He lifted his face to the sky. "Forgive me for treating my fear as a vow of service to You." His voice cracked. "I pretended I was living the life You called me to—one of true devotion—but it was only a façade for the truth, the pain, the worries of my own heart." A teary cough emerged.

As the rain continued its cleansing flood, a light filled Isaac's heart. Joy seeped in, unexpected but appreciated, and Isaac embraced his freedom for the first time. Freedom to love. To be a husband. A father.

Then like a melody rising at just the right moment, the words from Ezekiel chapter 34 draped him. In his tortured darkness, when he'd clung to the Word for dear life, he'd replayed the words yet not received their truth: "'And I will make them and the places round about my hill a blessing; and I will cause the shower to come down in his season; there shall be showers of blessing.'"

Isaac lifted his face to the sky as the drops slid down his face. "Thank You, Lord," he whispered. "Thank You for forgiveness, grace, freedom."

The rain let up, and as Isaac sat basking in the reality of his new understanding of the Shepherd's love for him, a thought almost too good to consider inched its way in. Did this mean—? He dared not think it. So he said the name out loud instead.

"Julia."

All the suppressed affection that was born the day he met her and grew each time he talked to her inundated him. He loved her, and the joy of freeing that love was sweeter than he'd ever imagined.

But would she return his love? Julia—so strong, beautiful, kind, intelligent—he didn't deserve her, not after what he'd done. Not only had he acted frivolously with her affection, but his selfishness was so great he'd forced her to turn her back on the home she was building here. Why hadn't he seen that his disregard for her needs and wants sentenced her to an uncertain future?

But if she could forgive him—if she could accept his imperfect, yet wholehearted, devotion—he'd humbly seek to serve her all the days of his life. With God's grace he'd strive to be a godly husband. . .and he'd love her.

Always love her.

Chapter Twenty-Six

"You'll have to tell me what was in that letter sometime." Miriam hauled back on the reins, bringing the wagon to a stop inside the Pioneer Livery Stable in Big Sandy, and Julia gripped the buckboard to steady herself. "You've been staring off into the wild blue ever since we left home. Now, you can't be leavin' a pregnant lady waitin' so long. You know the smallest thing'll send me cryin' and carryin' on." Miriam cupped her hands around the ever-enlarging orb that occupied her middle and then perked her chin up.

"A foot!" She tugged Julia's hand to the spot on her belly.

A bulge of what had to be baby shifted under Julia's hand then rolled away. "That's incredible." Julia moved her palm, seeking another touch. "To have a little life inside you, it must feel. . .I don't know. How does it feel?"

Miriam looked up. "Well, having a baby in there means your back aches, you're always hungry but never have what you want, you can't sleep but you're always tired, you never feel comfortable, and you want to cry all the time—or snap at the people you love most."

Julia frowned. "I thought you were going to tell me how wonderful it was. You know, the gift of life growing inside you."

Julia swung her legs off the buckboard as Miriam labored down the other side. "I didn't finish. I was going to say that all of the holy suffering is worth it when you feel that little darlin' move inside. Even more glorious when you hold him or her." She rubbed her stomach again, searching for an appendage. "You're right. It's unlike any other experience."

Miriam handed the reins to the paid

hand at the livery, and Julia grabbed a crate of goods from the back—potatoes, corn, eggs, and two handkerchiefs, as well as the Home Sweet Home sampler she'd embroidered—to trade at the mercantile. She'd come up with the idea after she received the letter from Mrs. Gaffin that offered no practical help. She'd try to sell her embroidery to get the money she needed for the train. She prayed it would work; otherwise, she didn't know what she'd do.

The two ladies sauntered down Main Street, wide and overgrown with weeds. Up ahead Julia spotted the Broadwater and McCullah Store—the only general store in town.

Despite Julia's recent longing to somehow fly far away from Lonesome Prairie, she couldn't deny the kindness the family had shown. She suspected Miriam proposed this jaunt more for Julia's sake than for the needed supplies. Miriam deserved to know about the contents of the letter—and her plans.

The town was busier than it had been the last time Julia had walked these streets. She eyed the saloons and the interesting characters—cowboys, miners, Indians—moving in and out of the swinging doors. In the distance a group of soldiers was riding into town. Julia had heard about the frontier cavalry who protected the Canadian border, watched the Indians on their reservations, kept peace, and guarded the safety of the settlers. They rode by, and Julia felt their eyes on her. Some were young, possibly of good character, but it didn't matter; only one man would spark her interest. And she had no idea where he was. Who knew if she'd ever see him again?

"So you're wondering what Mrs. Gaffin said?" Julia shook the relentless thoughts away and determined to be cheerful—for Miriam's sake—as they ambled past The Spokane House.

"By the horn spoons!" Miriam threw up her hands, and Julia puzzled at what on earth that phrase meant. "You're finally going to tell me?"

A chuckle escaped Julia's lips, and with it came a surge of gratitude. She'd been too serious of late. She needed a laugh, and it seemed Miriam sensed it.

Arriving at the mercantile, Julia swept

open the door for Miriam and held her elbow. "Let me help you, ma'am," she teased. "You sure you can walk with that belly?"

Miriam jerked her elbow away and stomped inside with a hearty laugh. "I got a spell to go yet till the baby comes. You wait until it gets closer, and then you can coddle me all you want."

Julia followed, letting the door swing closed behind her. She looked around and noticed the store was empty except for the shopkeeper, who was on a ladder straightening high shelves.

Wandering through the musty but clean store, Julia sized up the goods stacked on shelves lining the walls. As she judged the bags of sugar, baskets of eggs, cans of ham and corned beef, beans of every shape and size, and other essentials, she recalled her strolls through the New York City marketplace. One could find just about any food from any culture in the world—she remembered the lutefisk at Mrs. Sorrenson's shop—and any smell.

Julia grasped a jar of pickles then swiveled to Miriam. "I think you need these. Don't all pregnant ladies?"

Vinegar glugged from a barrel as Miriam filled her clay jug with the pungent liquid. She peeked from the spigot to Julia. "Yeah, grab a jar. I tell ya, I crave those store pickles more than anything." She smiled. "Well, almost anything. I want lemonade even more. We better get some lemons while we're here."

Julia tapped her back and grinned. "Is that why you're always making lemonade 'for the youngsters'?"

Miriam winced. "Maybe." Finished filling the jug, she hoisted it into a wooden crate on the counter. After about an hour of intent picking and choosing, with little conversation, Miriam called Julia over to her. "You 'bout ready?"

"Yes," Julia answered, edging next to her. "Any time."

Miriam placed a final item on the counter—several yards of fashionable blue fabric with tiny light blue flowers and a faint touch of yellow.

Julia smoothed her hand over it. "It's beautiful. Are you sewing yourself a dress?"

Miriam pressed her palm over Julia's hand and smiled. "It's for you."

394

"For me? Why?" Julia felt her forehead crumple.

Miriam's dark hair wisped out of her bun and framed her face. "Elizabeth, Jefferson, Abe, the children, myself and—all of us." She paused. "We love you. And we want to say thank you for teaching the children and for all the other ways you've blessed us."

Julia objected. "It's you who've blessed me. I haven't done anything but impose on your generosity. Especially lately, with all my moping. Oh, I've been awful."

Miriam pushed back, still gripping Julia's arms. "No, dear. Far from it. You're a joy, a delight to have in our home." Her eyes brimmed with appreciation as she dropped her hands and leaned against the counter.

"For me," Miriam continued "it's more than just having a kind, sweet girl brightening up the place." Her brow knitted together and she shifted her weight. "You know, it's far from easy to be a mother of six out here on the frontier. I mean, the young'uns are a blessing, but," she sighed, "man alive, they're more work than a year's worth o' laundry. Especially

395

when the oldest is a rambunctious one, like my Christopher."

She eyed Julia and her voice softened. "I know the Lord wants me to be longsuffering and full of charity and kindness, but sometimes, especially before you came, I'd get so plumb tuckered out. I wasn't the kind of mother I knew the Lord wanted me to be. So, Julia, I'm not saying you've cured me of my misconduct, but seeing how you don't let things get to you and how you smile and laugh with the children, the way you listen so fixedly when they talk—well, it encourages me to do the same. Why even when those naughty youths were branding mice that day, you whipped them into shape without an unkind word. I know you're not a mother yet, but you make me want to be a better one." Her eyebrows slanted upward and her lips curled into a smile. "So there's my long way of saying that I'm grateful to have you in my life, and I hope, no matter what happens, that we can be friends, sisters."

"Oh, Miriam." Julia sent her friend a grateful smile. "That's so kind of you to say."

"Well, I don't know what that letter said, but I imagine your headmistress is longing to have you home. I know I would. But we all wanted to tell you that if you decide to stay here, you're welcome."

The shopkeeper set to work tallying up the order, and Julia sat on the chair beside the door, the impact of Miriam's words hitting her. She was welcome here. She wasn't a burden. They wanted her to stay.

Looking at this woman and envisioning the friendship she'd felt from each member of the family during her days at the ranch, she suddenly ached to hold onto it. Certainly, before the night Isaac left, she'd begun thinking of Lonesome Prairie as home. She'd even considered finding work and eventually staking her own claim, if perhaps Abe or Jefferson would help.

She hadn't considered staying only because of Isaac—although she had to admit the parson's character had drawn her from the first moment she met him—but because the whole community enticed her, from the Pretty Apron Brigade to the way Isaac's parishioners displayed their appreciation at his birthday party. Even teaching the children had been a joy. She could make a place for herself here. At least she thought she could.

Yet even though she appreciated her friends and had considered staying, returning to New York was still her plan. Julia rubbed the back of her neck as a tide of reality tensed her muscles. She could never be part of their family, or even the community—not without Isaac returning her feelings. It would be too painful. . .impossible.

If she stayed in Lonesome Prairie, or even Big Sandy, she was sure to run into him. Knowing Miriam and Elizabeth, they'd pull her into their family and make her one of them. She'd be invited to birthdays and holidays, and of course Isaac would be there, too. Not only could she not imagine hiding her feelings for him, she had to admit she felt a little foolish, too. Everyone at that party surely noticed how she cared for him. She hadn't been shy about catching his eye across the fire or clinging to him after they found Bea. She'd forever be known as the New York lady who set her bonnet for the preacher but was rejected. No, she couldn't be known as that person.

The door creaked as a burly cowhand walked into the shop, and Julia lifted her head, remembering she was supposed to help Miriam, not wallow in self-pity. She returned to the counter, where the shopkeeper still added up the total, and turned to face Miriam.

"I appreciate all you've done for me, and I'm thankful for your kind offer, too. . . but I'm sorry." Julia bowed her head. "I can't stay."

Miriam's lips puckered in a slight frown, and Julia could see tears pooling in her friend's eyes. The older woman squeezed Julia into another embrace, seeming to accept Julia's statement and choosing not to push. She let her go and then wiped a tear from her cheek as she lifted the fabric and placed it in Julia's arms. "We know your beautiful skirt got ruined on your train ride here. This fabric doesn't compare with your fancy New York styles, but we hope we can make one to replace it. Elizabeth and I thought the three of us could do it together."

"You're too kind. Thank you."

Miriam gave Julia a smile then surveyed the crate's contents. "Well, I think that's about it. I used to always stop at Aponi's house for a quick visit, but since that's not possible, I suppose we should just head home. Jefferson will appreciate a warm meal when he gets back from tending to the sheep."

"A warm meal?"

A man's gravelly voice rattled through the store, and Julia's stomach clenched at the sight of Horace Whitbaum. She hadn't even heard him come in.

"Is that my wife talkin' about a warm meal? Ain't nothin' I'd like more."

Chapter Twenty-Seven

"It's amazing how a change of attitude can make time go by faster." Isaac scraped the last bite of his oatmeal breakfast from his plate and swallowed it with a grin. "It's been another week. This one went by much faster than the first." He moseyed over and put the tin plate in the dishpan resting on the ground next to the cabin.

Jim threw a bit of dry oatmeal to a sparrow and swigged a sip of coffee—or the mixture he called coffee. Isaac wasn't sure what was actually in it. "Yeah, you're much easier to live with since you started trustin' the Lord."

Mabelina smiled, her red hair glimmering in the crisp sunlight. "But Parson, we need to think of something. You gotta tell that Julia how you feel or you're gonna burst. I was telling Jim on our walk that if you smile any bigger, your face is gonna split in two, and all types of sunshine is gonna spill out."

Isaac fingered the bill of his parson hat and then rubbed his cheeks. "I know. She is cramming the bull's portion of my thoughts these days."

"Not just your thoughts. Your words," Mabelina added with a teasing smile. "I feel downright tired of that girl, and I've spent less than a day with her my whole life."

"I'm sorry." Isaac's neck warmed. "Everything seems to remind me of her." He lowered his head then peeked up at Mabelina. "I'll try to hold back."

Mabelina moved from her spot beside the campfire and tapped Isaac on the head. "You better," she teased.

"Now, my little marmot." Jim scooped himself another serving of oatmeal. "You shoulda heard me talkin' 'bout you before I told ya how I felt." He took a bite, leaving a glob on his mustache.

"That's true!" Isaac pointed at Jim. "He barely saved a breath for breathing when it came to blathering on about you." Isaac eyed the couple. "I have to say, I was all for getting out of this place a week ago, but I'm glad for your and Mabelina's sake that Judge Booker doesn't seem to have turned up yet. I like watching you two doting newlyweds."

"They sure are dotin'." Lefty returned from getting a drink of water from the well spout, apparently unable to bear the bitter "coffee." "All that cooing and love talk, boy howdy, it makes me want to find a wife of my own."

Jim squinted. "Ain't no better way to make a man become his best than ta bring a good woman into his life." He winked at Mabelina, who batted her eyes.

"That true, Parson?" Lefty asked.

Isaac grinned. "I suppose one of the reasons the Good Lord made marriage was to help the male persuasion be what He called them to be. He did say it wasn't good that man be alone, remember?"

Lefty perked up as he plopped down on his stump. "Guess after we get outta this place, I'd better follow the Good Lord's instruction then. Find me a wife."

"Me and you both." Isaac laughed. "Well, I'm gonna head out for a walk. Be back in a bit."

"You and those walks, Parson. Every morning these days." Jim spooned himself yet another helping of oatmeal.

Isaac peered at Jim. "Not much better than a morning walk to clear the mind and—"

"I know," Jim interjected. "'O Lord; in the morning will I direct my prayer unto thee.' Psalm 5. Just read it this mornin'." He leaned an elbow on his knees.

Isaac tilted his head. "That's about it, Jim. See ya in a bit."

Isaac headed down the trail toward the stream, rays of sunlight deflecting mottled shadows on his arms and legs. He breathed in the fresh sap-scented air, and his thoughts started up in the spot they had finished the night before. Ever since that day in the rain when God opened his eyes to finally trust Him, possibilities he'd never explored played in his mind. The one that kept returning was the idea of pastoring one church instead of the whole circuit.

Isaac kicked a rock as he stepped down to the streambed. He'd heard of circuit preachers who planted churches, building parsonages and training up pastors along their route. He'd thought of doing that himself, sort of like the apostle Paul, but now the idea of being the one in the parsonage appealed to him like never before. Serving at one location, baptizing, performing marriages, praying with the sick, and rejoicing at new births—natural and spiritual. A rush of joy filled his chest as he pondered the idea.

He'd deliberated over the practical side, too. Could these emerging communities support a local pastor? And his conclusion—well, yes. It seemed each year more and more families came, seeking life away from the established towns in the real frontier. And with the cheap land where folks could stake claims, more were sure to come. Plus, he could get by on little and perhaps raise a small herd of sheep or cattle to supplement his own household. Nothing wrong with that.

Isaac paused, savoring a fresh sense of God's abundant goodness. Even though he now would gladly trust the Lord with a wife's safety—Julia's, he hoped—he wouldn't have to leave her for weeks at a time while he was on his circuit. Not if he ministered in a stationary pastorate. Isaac strolled along the stream watching the water clip over the rocks. *It's so like You, Lord, to give us our hearts' desires just when we least deserve it.*

And another thing about Isaac giving up the circuit was that Jim could take over. Isaac laughed out loud at God's strange providence. Whoever would've thought Giant Jim Newman, the rude, rowdy gold miner, would long to preach the treasure of God's Word more than seek earthly gold? Isaac knew it'd take a couple years for Jim to be ready to serve as shepherd of the Lord's flock, but Jim certainly had the heart to serve. Just look at how he'd shared his faith with Lefty. Perhaps a little overzealous, like one young in the faith, but he studied the Bible and longed to learn more.

Isaac followed his usual morning route down the stream to the tree line that formed the abrupt border between the oasis of Old Scraggy Hill—with its pine trees, streams, and wildflowers—and the low-lying, yellow fields of prairie. He hiked up to a boulder tucked into the hillside and gazed out at God's creation. "Thank You for this beautiful spot, Lord." Isaac spoke out loud, knowing no one would come around.

A cluster of pink flowers grew at the foot of the boulder, and Isaac imagined Julia picking them and placing them in her long brown hair. How beautiful that hair looked, glowing in the light of the fire that first night she'd cared for him in his soddy. Even then he'd felt a connection to her, a longing to know her, understand her, even protect her.

Yet, although he was sure of his feelings for Julia, he wasn't sure how she felt about him. And for some reason, that didn't bring him anxiety. Every idea about his future, every plan and dream involved her. But despite that, he knew she might still return to New York. Perhaps it was even likely. She seemed to care for him, but he hadn't been honest enough with his feelings. He'd failed to give her the opportunity to share her heart.

No matter what happened, he'd trust

the Lord. If he never married, never started a school—even if God closed every door for him to minister and called him to ride herd his whole life—he hoped he'd ride herd for God's glory alone, being content to serve the Boss with joy each day.

He pulled his Bible out of the small satchel he carried and took a moment to run his fingers over the leather cover, thinking again of Julia and how she'd stitched this for him with loving care. Then, taking Jim's suggestion, he read Psalm 5. After a while, having prayed and meditated, Isaac hopped off the boulder and ambled back up to the cabin.

As he approached, he heard a voice he didn't recognize.

"What? The parson's not here? Why'd you let him go? And where's the woman?" Isaac heard the sound of a hand smacking flesh, and then he set off at a run toward the sound.

As he viewed the cabin, he saw one of Warren's lackeys, the long-faced Buck, perched next to Lefty, who had his hand on his face and was crouched down in pain. Isaac sprinted to him.

Isaac glared up at Buck. "What are you doing? I'm right here."

"But where's the woman?" the man demanded.

"I don't know." Isaac's eyes raked the area. "Maybe they're off trapping."

"I told him that's where they were," Lefty said nervously. "They go off every morning and come back with some good game. Weasels, coons, foxes, squirrels—even a snake one time."

A spasm of irritation crossed Buck's face. "How do I know you didn't let them run off? They could be nigh to Canada by now." Buck's hand fingered his Colt .45.

Isaac wiped his hands on his pants, hoping he could talk the man down from his anger. "I told your boss that I'd make sure they stayed, plus you've got your guard here who's been with us the whole time. He wouldn't let them leave." Isaac tilted his head as a stomping sound floated to his ears. "There. I bet that's them."

Jim and Mabelina tromped out of the woods with a dead fox and big grins on their faces.

"They always have that grin when they

come back. I think they're doin' some smoochin' while they're out there." Lefty let out a nervous chuckle.

"Smoochin'?" Buck cursed under his breath. "This is not a fancy hotel, and you're not their butler. It's high time they realize the seriousness of the situation. A man is dead. Justice will be served."

Isaac wanted to chide the man. Who was he to talk about justice? He doubted Buck had ever met Milo and assumed the gruff vigilante was in it only for the bounty. But Isaac rubbed his jaw and kept his lips pressed tight. In these parts, knowing when to shut one's mouth was just as important as knowing what to say when the time was right.

He eyed Buck as Jim and Mabelina approached. Then he turned to his friends, hoping his calm demeanor would remind them to act the same.

Jim's and Mabelina's footsteps slowed as they realized another visitor had joined their camp. Jim placed a protective arm around Mabelina's shoulders, and she looked at him as if understanding that the next few minutes could change everything.

"So since you're here, I guess that means the judge is in town and ready for a trial?" Isaac asked.

Buck ogled the fox, and a rumble gurgled from his stomach. Then he returned his gaze to the group. "Nope, that's not it." He wound up his lips and let a long line of tobacco juice trail onto the dirt. "We got word that the judge was in Great Falls tending to some big trial over there. Well, the trial's going on for another week or so. Boss sent a telegram telling him about this here murderer, and so the judge'll take the train back soon as it's done—on the Fourth of July."

Jim and Mabelina looked at each other and grinned, seeming to accept their extended sentence as a prolonged honeymoon.

"That's fine with me," Lefty said, scratching his head underneath his hat. "I sorta wanted to get started on finding a good woman to be my wife—like the Good Lord commanded—but I s'pose that can wait a couple weeks. Maybe I could write a love poem. Y'know, the more I think about it, that there Petunia

Vincent, she's a mighty purdy one. Maybe I should set my hat for her—"

"What you talkin' about, boy?" Buck sneered at the hopeful youth. "You're not stayin' here. You let these weasels wander all over the countryside, they'll take off and the boss'll be scorchin' mad. Nope, you're going back to the boss, and I'm stayin' with these outlaws."

Lefty's shoulders drooped, but then he perked up. "All right. I'll do it. Then I can call on that Petunia."

"Wait a minute." Isaac gazed at the weak-chinned man. How could he wait another two weeks to talk to Julia? His heart pulsed faster. "Warren can't expect us to stay here that long. It's unreasonable. He should let us go about our business and we'll show up when Judge Booker arrives—where's he arriving anyway?"

"Lodge Pole."

"Fine. We've proven that we're trustworthy. We could've escaped a hundred times a day."

Buck let out a low breath and shook his head. "You can go, Parson. Tain't no reason you need to stay, and the man, too, I s'pose. But that lady's got a price on her head. She ain't goin' nowhere."

Jim edged in front of Mabelina. "If she's stayin', I'm stayin'."

Isaac knew he couldn't leave them. He spotted the flask gleaming from Buck's pocket and figured the lackey to be a drinking man. A drunk, an isolated cabin, a long waiting spell—the combination would most certainly lead to harm. Jim could handle any man who tried to confront him, but Isaac didn't want to risk it. The odds were better if another man was here.

Plus, he needed to be close at hand for the trial. If he left, Warren might figure out a way to change the trial date to exclude him. With a preacher at the proceedings vouching for Mabelina's character as well as testifying as a witness, she had a chance. Without him, the judge'd probably see nothing more than a lady of easy virtue who shot a man in a jealous rage.

Isaac nodded his agreement. "Well, I guess you have us. Two more weeks it is."

With that, Buck ordered Lefty to pack up and head out.

"I'll see ya, Parson, Missus, Jim," Lefty said, after grabbing his belongings. "Thanks for—well, just makin' this a pleasant occasion."

"Get outta here," Buck snarled, and Lefty trekked down the hill and out of sight.

Buck took a seat on Lefty's stump and leaned back, a brooding look on his face. "You gonna fix up that fox or let it rot?" he growled to Mabelina.

Isaac tried to take in the idea of two weeks with the man. But more than that, a twinge of anxiety hit him. The judge was coming on the train from Great Falls to Lodge Pole for the trial. The next stop after Lodge Pole was Big Sandy, and the last he'd heard, Julia was planning to depart Big Sandy on that train.

His heart raced. If he was stuck up here, how would he reach her before she boarded the train back to New York? He jolted to his feet and ran after Lefty. Catching up with him, he pulled him aside. "Please, Lefty, if you can, you've got to get a message to. . ." His shoulders slumped as a tinge of embarrassment grabbed him.

Lefty grinned knowingly. "To your little filly?"

Isaac chuckled. "Yeah. She lives at Lonesome Prairie. At the Lafuze Ranch. If you can, just tell her to please not leave town until I talk to her."

Lefty eyeballed Isaac skeptically. "You'd better tell her more than that."

"Well, I want to tell her the rest myself."

"All right then. But a girl needs to know when a man's in love."

"Believe me, I understand. I'll tell her. You just make sure she's not halfway to New York before I get the chance."

Chapter Twenty-Eight

Julia breathed in the sweet mid-June air as she, Miriam, Elizabeth, and the children trudged down the side of Lonesome Lake Coulee with a supply of picnic goodies. Elizabeth strolled in front of her with Bea in her arms. A ladybug landed on Bea's back, and Julia trotted closer to let the insect climb onto her hand. Then she placed it near Bea's hand and helped it to crawl onto the girl's chubby finger.

"Wadybug, Mama." She held it up for Elizabeth to see.

As they strode down the shrub-lined,

dusty coulee's walls, Julia pondered how glad she was to have another week behind her. Only two more weeks left of burying her feelings, forcing herself to be cheerful, and employing any activity she could think of to distract her thoughts. As much as she loved and appreciated Miriam and Elizabeth, she longed for the struggle to end. Longed to go home.

She glanced up at the rolls of clouds gliding across the sprawling sky, like lambs moving through a field of blue. Julia cracked a stick from a shrub along the path. Once she got established in her new life in New York, the ache would fade—she was sure it would.

"I don't think I ever saw a man look so surprised as Horace Whitbaum." Miriam laughed as she straggled at the end of the queue.

"You two have been giggling about that ever since you got back from your shopping trip to town a week ago." Elizabeth pursed her lips. "You better tell me and the youngsters what that's all about."

Shelby and Johannah sidled up on either side of Julia. Their share of the supplies swung from baskets on their arms as they clomped down the hard-packed trail.

"Yeah, what happened?" Shelby asked. "Did the old guy try to marry you again?"

Julia smiled teasingly, refreshed by the diversion from her gloomy thoughts. "Well, of course he tried. He always does that. The funny part is how we escaped him."

"What happened?" Johannah asked.

"First of all," Miriam started, as she walked a few steps behind, "that Sarah Mack helped with our getaway. She showed up just as we were leaving. Did you see the way she laughed at his odd humor?"

"Yes. When she stayed the night back when I was first here, she talked about all his virtues. I mean, did she honestly think she could talk me into falling in love with him?"

"That's not it." Miriam cocked an eyebrow. "She's not trying to talk you into anything. I think Sarah is honestly fond of Horace. I've watched closely, and I'm pretty sure I saw her blush when he leaned forward and took that twig out of her hair."

"You're saying Sarah has eyes for

Horace?" Julia mocked jealousy. "That her heart grows all aflutter over my husband?" Then her shoulders slumped. "I guess that's not really funny, is it?" Julia pouted. "Maybe I should just tell Horace to chase Sarah instead. Heaven knows I jump at the slightest noise. I'm just certain that one of these days he's going to grow tired of waiting and snatch me away to his lovely home—shack—in the hills." Julia shuddered. "I sure hope I'm wrong."

"Don't worry." Elizabeth ran her free hand over Julia's shoulder. "We'll get it worked out."

Bea touched Julia, too, mimicking her mother.

"I know," Julia answered as she gave Bea a smile. "If nothing else, I'll be gone soon. I don't think he's going to chase me all the way to New York."

"Anyway," Miriam continued, "I think it would be wonderful for both Sarah and Horace. She could clean him up a bit, and he'd keep her company, be a father to her boy."

Julia nodded, relief flooding over her. "I suppose stranger things have happened. And he does have a sweet heart."

Brushing a hair from her eyes as they reached the bottom of the trail, Julia found a level spot of dirt beside the stream and spread out a few blankets. Julia and Elizabeth sat on the blanket while top-heavy Miriam opened a chair that Jefferson had made for her, which folded in half.

"Hope you don't mind," she said as she fixed it in a sturdy spot in the gravelly dirt. "If I squatted down on the blanket like you girls, I'd never get back up."

Elizabeth laughed. "Oh sure you would. You'd just have to hoist yourself over to your knees like a stuck heifer."

Miriam whacked her sister on the back then plunked down into her chair. "I never."

Johannah and Shelby lounged with the women, and the other children soaked their feet in the water.

Bea, who'd been digging her hands in the dirt, bopped over to the ladies. "I swim?" she piped up, pulling her dress over her head.

"Well, the water's pretty low." Elizabeth helped with the last tug of her dress, revealing a miniature girl in bloomers. "So it should be fine. But just your feet for now, all right?"

"Yes, ma'am," she said and splashed into the knee-deep water.

As Bea played, an adoring smile dawned on Elizabeth's face.

Julia leaned back and eyed the young woman. "You're a wonderful mother. I couldn't have asked for a better place for my girls." Julia's heart tugged as she sensed the loss she'd feel when she said good-bye in a couple weeks, but not the cutting pain that she'd felt before. Knowing Elizabeth and Abe's characters and knowing they already loved Shelby and Bea lessened the ache.

Elizabeth tilted her head. "Thank you." Her eyes filled with gratitude. "When they first came, I didn't know how to be a mother. I still don't, of course!" She shook her head, and loose strands of her golden blond hair draped over her shoulder. "But I'm trying, and I really do love both of them." She rubbed Shelby's shoulder, tugging her into an embrace.

Shelby eyed her mother and smiled, and Julia said a silent prayer of gratitude.

"So do you still want to know what

happened with old Horace?" Julia sat up tall. "You can imagine my shock when he walked into the store. I thought he was going to take me away at that very moment."

"I thought so, too." Miriam leaned forward. "Especially when he said he would if we didn't invite him to dinner."

Elizabeth slapped Julia's leg playfully. "He said that?"

Julia nodded. "Yep. He did, and then he grabbed my arm." She gazed at Elizabeth, Shelby, and Johannah, who sat with their eyes glued to her.

"I don't think I told you," Miriam inserted, "but when I saw that grimy prospector's face all stern and serious, I thought you were done for. I thought, *I don't know where Isaac is, and he's the only one Horace'll listen to.* I started planning how I could get ahold of him and Jefferson and Abe to rescue you."

A slight sting of sorrow struck Julia at the mention of Isaac's name, but she continued. "So Horace had his hand on my arm, and then some young men came in, just a little older than Christopher. Teenaged, I think. Horace was standing directly in the doorway, preparing to haul me away, and the boys accidentally bumped him. I don't think they meant to. Do you, Miriam?"

"No, they were just trying to get by."

"Well, for some reason—"

"Probably because he was so worked up about taking you."

Julia laughed. "For some reason this set Horace off. He ripped into them with a holy anger. 'You hooligans don't know how to treat no one with no respek.'"

Shelby jumped up. "Oh, I can just see it." She spread her feet in a Horace-like stance and pointed a finger at Johannah, who also stood and pretended to be one of the boys. "You better watch yourself, or you'll be in a heap o' trouble before you turn sixteen." Shelby eyed Julia inquisitively. "Is that about right?"

Julia nodded. "Yeah, but he was much worse. He called them crow eaters and dirty varmints. They were pretty mad when they left."

Elizabeth leaned back and opened the picnic basket, set out a plate of berries, and popped one into her mouth. "So is that how you managed to get away? When he was distracted by the boys?"

Julia shook her head. "No. He kept a grip on me the whole time he was talking to them." Julia picked up the plate of berries and offered some to Miriam.

Taking a handful, she smiled. "But after the boys left, we tried everything we could to persuade him to give up and let Julia go."

"I even told him I'd repay his money, but he didn't believe me." Julia glanced at the girls. "I probably shouldn't have said that anyway, since I don't know how I could possibly pay him back." Julia remembered the letter from Mrs. Gaffin and shook her head. "Anyway," she continued, "as we were talking to him, we looked out the front door and there was his mule, you know, the one he calls Ladygirl. She was tied to one of the tent saloons. I tell you— "

"They're not going to believe it," Miriam popped in.

"I know!" Julia glanced from face to face. "Those teenaged boys pranced behind that mule, whipping her into a trot—and getting her to pull the whole entire tent saloon behind her! She dragged that saloon right down the middle of Main Street."

The girls and Elizabeth leaned back on their hands and laughed out loud.

"I can't imagine the sight," Elizabeth said. "A saloon just moseying down the street."

Miriam held her hand to her chest. "Well, Horace 'bout blew his top. He forgot all about Julia and went seekin' to save his Ladygirl from those boys. So Julia and I soft-footed it out the back of the mercantile and round behind the stable. With the hired man's help, we got hitched up real fast and put the whip on our horse. We were out of town before Horace even realized it."

Shelby shook her head. "I never saw anything like that in New York." She glanced at Johannah. "I did see a lot of other neat things there, though."

The two girls chattered as they walked to the water and stuck their feet in.

Julia opened the picnic basket and set out the food. "Next time I just don't know if I'll be so lucky with Horace. And if he shows up at the ranch again. . ."

A swift breeze fluttered through, and with it, a butterfly. Julia watched it fly and land on a flower. Elizabeth noticed it, too, and smiled. "You know, if he shows up at the ranch, you'll have nothing to worry about. Our men'll make sure of that."

Julia was grateful for Jefferson's and Abe's protection—she certainly needed it—but they weren't always home.

The children returned to the blanket from swimming and greedily ate up the cornbread and dried meat as well as the apples and cheese they'd brought. As Julia watched them, she felt a part of the family. Yet the sick feeling of loss—always under the surface, always waiting to crowd out her happiness—sprang up again.

Why couldn't she be a part of their lives? Others knew this type of love and just took it for granted.

She'd spent the last few days thinking about what was to come next—a new life in New York, the academy where she'd work, her own room in Mrs. Gaffin's home. Before, the knowledge of these opportunities would have been more than she could have hoped for. But now she'd found the prospect of those things sadly lacking. It seemed that no matter where her thoughts took her, she couldn't find the home her heart so desperately longed for.

A bird called overhead, and she lifted her face. As she watched, it circled once and then swooped down, landing in a high nest in the closest tree.

If only she could find such a place of her own.

From the position of the sun high in the sky, Julia knew it was close to noon. The day was warm—not too hot. And she was thankful. Thankful for the day, her friends, the laughter. If only her own troubled memories didn't keep pulling her back, the day would be perfect. *Almost* perfect.

"Well," Miriam said, the meal finished and the children rambling off, "we're almost done sewing that skirt of yours. It's looking mighty fine."

"Yes, it is looking fine," Julia said.

"Bea! Oh my, look at you!" Elizabeth stood and trotted over to Bea, who, having finished lunch, now decided to take a little mud bath.

Julia leaned back on her hands, watching Elizabeth dip a rag in the water and wash the grime from Bea's face.

Miriam cleared her throat. "Now that everyone else is occupied, there's something I've been wantin' to speak with you about."

Judging from the tone of Miriam's voice, Julia knew she had something serious to say. Miriam slanted her legs toward Julia. "I don't know what happened between you and my brother. The night of his birthday party I saw a look in his eyes that I'd been praying to see for years."

Julia's stomach grew taut. She'd maneuvered and sidestepped to avoid this conversation over the past weeks. Miriam had graciously given her the time she needed. Couldn't she let it go forever? Why did they need to talk about it? She didn't want to discuss that night. Couldn't bear to share how much it scarred her. If she could bottle up her feelings inside, maybe they wouldn't hurt as much. It's what she'd always done.

She realized that now. Realized how she'd learned to suppress her emotions deeper and deeper over the years. An orphanage, even one with a loving headmistress, wasn't a place for blabbering about your own heartbreak. Too many others also suffered, perhaps worse than you.

Julia had learned, for her own sake as well as for the girls, to put on a smile. And for the past two weeks, she'd determined not to prattle on about the stabbing ache of loss that accompanied her every movement. And the humiliation she felt for hurting over Isaac.

How foolish I was to think he'd choose me over his promise to God. How absurd to let my feelings take flight so rapidly.

Miriam's lips pursed together in a frown. "I love my brother, Julia. But he's got to work out the painful stain his past left on his heart. He wants to serve God—and others—and he's got the strange notion that marrying will keep him from that. I don't know how he can get over it." Miriam's eyes slanted in concern. "I want him to be happy. He's suffered a lot in his life."

Julia's throat grew raw as she remembered what Isaac had told her about his fiancée. "I'm so sorry. I didn't mean to remind him of his hurt—to bring it all back."

"Oh no, sweetie." Miriam's voice softened, like a breeze blowing through prairie grass. "You didn't, or if you did, it was time for him to face it. I just feel so awful that you got caught in the wake of his struggle. I've seen how much you hurt, and I fear he broke your heart." She closed her eyes. "I didn't want you to leave without talking about it."

Julia had been stifling the words that threatened to emerge ever since that night with Isaac. She thought talking about it would only make it hurt more, but now, hearing Miriam's empathy, she wished she'd shared earlier.

"I think I was falling in love with your brother." The words fell from her lips, stinging as they flowed. "I know it's silly, but I had hoped we could at least, you know, court—" She took in a breath, then gazed at Miriam. "No, that's not true. It was much more than that. I'd already built a whole world of hopes around him.

I know I shouldn't have, but I've never met someone as kind and intelligent and strong as he is. When I was with him, I no longer felt like an orphan without a place in the world. It felt right. Like I belonged, like I had found a safe haven. He trusts God so much, I even thought he could help me understand the Scriptures and grow in my faith. I imagined building a life together, making a home." She pressed her hand to her forehead. "A home. It's all I've ever wanted."

A butterfly skipped through the air between them, and then it danced to a poppy creeping from between two rocks and folded its wings.

"We all want a home," Miriam said.

"But it's not meant to be." Julia sighed deeply and folded her hands in her lap. "So you see, my only hope is to return to New York. Mrs. Gaffin will let me live with her. She's even found a place of employment for me."

Miriam caressed Julia's hair, and her face shone with a wisdom Julia had rarely seen before. "I understand that you want a home."

Something about Miriam's voice

brought back words she'd said a long time ago. Julia waited, expecting her to speak, but instead the woman sat silently. And with the sound of the wind shifting down the coulee, the words came back to Julia: *The one thing that helped this place feel like home was remembering that it's* not *my home.*

Julia hadn't known, back then, what Miriam meant. She still wasn't sure. Julia had thought the woman was talking about Lonesome Prairie not being her home, but maybe she meant something else.

She shifted her legs and rubbed her temples, trying to unravel Miriam's words. Maybe she meant that no matter where on this earth Julia would go, she'd never find a home. The pain of that truth whipped her like a quirt on a horse's back. She glanced up at Miriam. "I'm never going to find a home, am I?"

Miriam shook her head.

"Not in New York, not here." A surge of grief lunged through her chest when the next thought struck her. "Not even if my parents were still alive."

Miriam's eyes cradled her with compassion.

"There's only one home," Julia confessed. "I know what it is, but how do I find it, Miriam? I don't know how."

"Do you remember Sarah Mack's song?" And without waiting for Julia to answer, she began to sing, not in the strong, angelic tones of the Englishwoman, but in a gently embracing voice, full of heart and kindness.

"Rock of Ages, cleft for me, let me hide myself in Thee. . ."

She continued with the hymn, but Julia camped in these words as the Savior's love embraced her. All her life, since she lost her parents especially, she'd searched for a home. She'd chased it in people like Mrs. Gaffin, the girls, Miriam, Elizabeth, and especially Isaac. She'd crossed thousands of miles and planned to retrace those miles—all to find a place where she could rest her head and entrust her heart.

"Rock of Ages, cleft for me, let me hide myself in Thee. . ."

Yet all along, when she thought she was an abandoned orphan, God was there. He called her, knowing she'd come, but waiting for His perfect timing to draw her into the cleft where she could hide. Somehow, sitting here on this coulee in the middle of the Montana frontier, Julia finally grasped the truth. Christ Himself was her home.

"Christ is my home." She said it aloud. *I am not an orphan.* "God is my Father."

And He encompassed all the love, acceptance, compassion, honesty, and comfort that home represented to her. The embroidered sampler she'd left at the mercantile flashed to her mind: Home Sweet Home. Yes, home was sweet. Not a temporary home—in New York, Lonesome Prairie, or anywhere—but home with the Savior, hiding in His loving arms.

And now, for the first time in her life, when the Savior called, she came with no reserve, with no worries about not knowing enough about the Bible or understanding His ways. She just came, like a child running to her father.

Miriam finished the song and lumbered from her chair to sit on the blanket next to Julia. Once again, like the first day she arrived in Lonesome Prairie, Julia collapsed into the woman's arms. For so long she'd tried to be in control—to hold her emotions tightly—as if doing so would bring her acceptance. But she'd been wrong. It was releasing her feelings, honestly admitting them to Miriam, and especially to God, that brought acceptance.

After a moment, Julia drew in a breath and pulled back. The butterfly that had been dancing about them like an eavesdropper now alighted on Julia's hand.

"Oh, look." She giggled and showed Miriam as it fluttered away.

Miriam smiled. "Have you found your home, Julia?"

Julia gazed at her as peace rushed in. "It's not here." She waved her arm around. "Not anywhere. My home is in the cleft of the Rock. My Father is with me. . .always." She eyed Miriam with confidence. "And so that means that it doesn't matter if I go back to New York or stay here or move to Timbuktu."

"That's right, and when we find our refuge in Him, then even in the midst of the pain of this life, we feel at home."

Julia embraced Miriam's words, not

just assenting to their truth but claiming them as her own. No matter what pain found her—and she knew it would come—she'd hide in that cleft. For the rest of her days.

Elizabeth hiked up with a clean little Bea in her arms.

"I think I got all the mud off." Elizabeth cocked her head toward Julia and Miriam, perhaps noticing their red eyes and the glow of joy on their faces. "And we had a lovely time in the water, didn't we?"

"I all clean!" Bea piped up, pointing to her white bloomers and undershirt.

"You are all clean," Julia agreed, laughing.

Yes, all clean.

Chapter Twenty-Nine

The sun's position high in the afternoon sky told Isaac, leaning against a wall at the depot in Lodge Pole, that the train would be arriving soon. The normally quiet town bustled with motion, the festivities already starting.

Isaac watched the townsfolk, including many cowboys who'd stayed around for the Fourth of July celebrations. In addition, ladies from ranches and homesteads, wearing their best aprons and bonnets, bustled about with finishing touches—a banner, signs. All seemed to look over their shoulders toward the depot every so often, waiting for the train. On it, everyone knew, was Judge Booker coming to preside over Mabelina Newman's trial.

Isaac gazed into the distance. Once the train arrived, it would take an hour for the tanks on the steam engine to be refilled before the train could head to its next stop, Big Sandy. Isaac's hands sweat and a blast of anxiety clutched his heart. He knew Julia planned on taking that Fourth of July train—away from Lonesome Prairie and on to New York. He only hoped Judge Booker would hear the trial, listen to the jury, and make his verdict within an hour.

Isaac sighed. He'd seen much shorter trials than that. Without fancy lawyers, the judges usually took the side of the vigilantes. Isaac hadn't met the new Judge Booker though, so he could only speculate at the pace at which he ran his courtroom. Yet, if Isaac guessed correctly, the judge would want to get back on the train as well.

Jim and Mabelina sat holding hands on a bench next to the wall. Buck tilted his body against the doorjamb, his head tilted downward, his eyes skimming everything around him.

A rooster crowed, setting off two more, and Jim stomped his foot. "There must be more roosters in Lodge Pole than any other town in the West." He shuffled nervously and thrust his hands in his pockets as another crowed. "Don't they know it's not mornin'? Hush it."

Mabelina eyed her husband from a lowered head. Without a word, Jim received the rebuke. "I'm sorry, my little marmot. I jest want that train ta come and ta git this trial over with."

Patting his back, Mabelina sighed. "Not me. I wish we coulda stayed in that cabin all our days."

Isaac stepped across the wood-planked porch and searched the horizon for the train again. In the distance, he spotted a plume of smoke that didn't look like a cloud. "I think it's coming."

He eyed Jim and Mabelina then searched down the wide street, seeking Warren. If the judge arrived and there was no one to accuse her, this whole trial could be over before the roosters hustled to their coop to escape the heat.

Just then a stout, blond man stalked out of the Lodge Pole Saloon, next door to the depot, with a couple of other cowboys moseying beside him.

Warren. Isaac guessed he'd been in there all along, drinking to pass the time.

His best friend's stepson stumbled and then steadied himself on a pole and gazed up. His eyes connected with Isaac's. For a moment he scowled, but then his face became unreadable. "Howdy, Parson."

Isaac edged his way into the street, past the crowd gathering to watch the trial. "What do you want, Warren?" Isaac called from where he stood.

Warren inched closer, still on the saloon's porch, his two lackeys, Lefty and Joe, behind him. "I want to talk to you about the trial. I've been doing some thinking."

Isaac took a few steps toward him. "What about? You gonna drop the charges?" Isaac doubted it. He knew now Warren was no decent citizen.

Warren sauntered back to the saloon and leaned against the railing, staying on the dirt road.

The train's loudening rumble pulled Isaac's gaze. The eyes of the townsfolk turned, too, and many hurried to the platform to watch the train, still a good mile down the track. The large metal dragon snorted steam as it slowed.

"Now! Grab him!" The words filtered into Isaac's mind a moment too late.

Before Isaac could defend himself, he felt arms around him. Lefty and Joe yanked him around the back of the saloon and shoved him down onto the dusty ground. Isaac yelled, but Joe punched a handkerchief in his mouth with his grimy fist. Joe's knuckle smashed Isaac's gum against a tooth, causing a warm liquid to trickle down his chin.

With Warren towering over him, Isaac felt a piece of a rope being pulled around his mouth like a horse's bit. Then rough hands girded it tight around his face, cinching it in the back of his head. The handkerchief tasted like dirt and sweat, and the rope dug into his cheek.

Lefty, Isaac's old housemate from Old Scraggy Hill, approached, grabbing Isaac's hands. He eyed Isaac, a glimpse of an apology on his face, and then Isaac felt his arms being jerked behind him. His shoulder sockets burned, and he struggled for air. Lefty's knee dug into Isaac's back as he pulled the rope tighter. Isaac sucked in deep breaths through his nose, wincing as he tried to ignore the pain that was everywhere at once.

A low moan escaped his lips as they bound his feet, pulling the rope tight. Then, just when Isaac thought they were through with him, Joe approached and pummelled the side of his head. Isaac's ear smacked his shoulder and a hundred chimes sounded in his head.

He hunkered down in pain just as the point of Joe's steel-toed boot slammed into his gut. Isaac attempted to lift his head, but the ground around him swayed. Then the ground faded to gray before finally filling with color once again.

Isaac lifted his eyes and glared at Warren.

"Throw the parson in the wagon," Warren commanded.

Isaac felt Lefty's and Joe's arms wrap under his armpits. They hoisted him up into an old wagon that waited between the depot and the saloon. Joe covered him with a canvas tarp.

No! They can't do this.

Isaac pulled against the ropes. *Mabelina. . .who's gonna stand up for her?*

"Sorry, Parson." It was Warren's voice through the fabric. "I just didn't want to run the risk of a fool judge takin' your word for that tramp. Believe me, the bounty's worth more to me than that worthless piece of used-up garbage."

Isaac squirmed and kicked his legs, trying to work his way out of the ropes. Fingering them, he tested the knots. It was no use. These men were used to tying up steers. There was no way he was going to loosen the ropes.

His mind raced. More than anything, Isaac yearned to set aside his Christian demeanor and give Warren what he deserved. Perhaps it was a good thing his mouth and hands were gagged.

He slumped down, unable to move. His shoulders trembled as he urged himself to puzzle out what to do.

Over the sound of the men leaving,

Isaac heard the train's brakes screech and the voices of what he guessed were passengers spilling out.

Since the wagon was parked next to the saloon—and the saloon was situated beside the depot where the trial would take place—Isaac shimmied his way to the side, pushed the canvas off by wiggling his head, and looked through the open window. *Lord, I have to get in there.*

He struggled harder against the ropes as another thought shot to mind. The train. If he wanted to reach Julia in time, he had to be freed before the train left.

Isaac scooted to the other side of the wagon bed and watched a man in a black suit, Judge Booker, walk through the depot's doors into the sunlight gleaming through the front-paned windows. Beside him marched a uniformed man who loomed over the short judge.

Giant Jim and Mabelina meandered through the door, their eyes searching the faces in the room. Isaac's gut tightened. He was sure they were looking for him. He kept working the knot, hoping to somehow nudge it loose. *I'd be there if I could. Lord, they need Your help.*

After erecting the judge's ebony fold-up bench and setting his chair behind it, the bailiff motioned for the onlookers to sit down.

"You the accused?" The bailiff's strong voice drifted through the open window to Isaac's ears, and he saw him point at Mabelina.

She nodded, her face full of shame. As Isaac watched, the bailiff gripped her arm and walked her to a chair beside the judge's bench.

＊ ＊ ＊ ＊

The stallion's hooves kicked up dust as Julia rode on the wagon seat next to Elizabeth and Shelby on her last trip from Lonesome Prairie to Big Sandy. She tried to swallow down the emotion she felt after saying good-bye to the rest of the family, including little Bea, for the last time.

She brushed the dust from the new dress the ladies had made together. The sun beat down on her, warming her face. She thought about opening her parasol to block the sun's rays, but doing so seemed silly now. She actually enjoyed the heat on her cheeks, the wind caressing her skin, and the view of the expansive Montana sky.

Miriam sat in the back, trying to get comfortable in her almost-to-term state, and ten-year-old Christopher moseyed alongside, stating he was strong and could keep up. Every so often he'd jog off to check on a trap, sometimes returning with a jackrabbit or gopher. Julia chuckled. When she first came here, the sight of those dead critters would've made shivers crawl over her skin. Now, in her mind's eye, she flipped through Miriam's recipe book, trying to consider the best way to cook them.

"Can you not hit *every* pothole, Elizabeth?" Miriam moaned from the back as the wagon jerked over a wide divot.

"I'm not trying to, dear." Elizabeth yanked the horse to the left to avoid a bump in the rut. "Sorry!"

Julia felt her body tipping to the side, following the motion of the wagon, and then leveled herself. "You all right?" She twisted and eyed Miriam, whose face looked flushed from the Fourth of July heat. "Do you want to use my parasol to shield the sun?"

Miriam hugged her middle. "I'm fine. I need both hands just to steady myself." She sucked in a breath. "In these last weeks, a body does feel every movement of the wagon."

"Oh, dear." Julia ached for her. "You didn't have to come with us. We could've said good-bye at the house, you know."

Miriam smiled up at Julia. "I wanted to see you off the right way."

"I got a prairie dog this time!" Christopher ran and jumped onto the back of the wagon. He clambered to the front and leaned between Julia and Shelby. He shoved it in Shelby's face and then in Julia's. The dead creature smelled like Calamity when she was wet and sweaty, only worse.

"Oh!" Julia pushed his hand away. "Get that loathsome varmint out of my face."

Shelby screeched and thrust him back, landing him on his rear next to his ma in the back.

Christopher laughed at the girl's squeals. "What?" He mocked an innocent grin. "Ain't foul to me. Just a little head and body. Nothin' gets me squeamish."

"Boy!" Miriam scolded. "Get out of this wagon with that thing."

Christopher hopped out and hung the creature on a nail sticking out from the side of the wagon, next to two gophers.

"You're so disgusting!" Shelby accused as she craned her head around and glared at Christopher.

Elizabeth palmed Shelby's arm. "That'll only make him want to do it more. Believe me, the best strategy is to ignore him."

Shelby smiled at her mother. "Thanks. I'll have to remember that." Then Shelby put her arm around Julia's waist and leaned her head against her shoulder. "I can't believe this is really the last day."

Julia tilted her head toward the girl. "We'll write, you know. It's not like I'll forget about you and Bea. And you've got a wonderful home here. I need to make a life for myself, too, and Mrs. Gaffin's expecting me."

Shelby examined her hands, picking at her fingernails. "I know, and I promise not to throw a conniption fit like I did last time you tried to leave me." She tipped her head up and grinned. "But don't you think you could make a life here instead of so far away?"

Julia's eyes moved from Shelby's face to the snowcapped mountains far in the distance and then encircled the prairie. It was a desolate place out here, but it could be home, she knew that now. Part of her wanted to stay, but if home could be anywhere—and Julia believed it could with Christ—then she may as well go back to Manhattan and teach at a school. Maybe she'd even join the Children's Aid Society as her father had. She smoothed Shelby's hair. "I just think it's best, for—everyone."

"You mean for Uncle Ike." Shelby straightened and sat forward. "If it weren't for him, you'd stay."

"Shelby." Elizabeth's voice held a hint of scolding.

Julia patted the girl's arm. The mention of Isaac's name didn't bring the burning ache anymore. In fact, it brought a sense of gratitude for the privilege of knowing and befriending the man, even if just for a short time.

"Boy, it's hot out today," Christopher piped up as he bounded up on the board next to Shelby. "Scoot over, cousin Shel-*brain*, I'm gonna ride a spell."

"Christopher Lafuze!" Miriam scolded from the back. "That is not how you talk to a girl, cousin or no." She snapped her fingers. "Now get down. If you want to ride, you come back here with me and ask properly."

Christopher grinned at Shelby then hopped back to the road and continued walking.

"Are all boys so annoying?" Shelby shook a fly from her arm. "They're like buzzing insects."

"Yes!" All three women spoke in unison.

"But you still like Uncle Ike."

Julia gave a slight nod. "I do." She peeked at Elizabeth, who sent over a sympathetic smile. "But that's not why I'm leaving. I had hoped we could have a future together, but Shelby—" Julia closed her eyes and opened them. "My future is not with him or anyone else. It's with God, so it doesn't matter where I live."

"Yes, it does." Shelby shot a glance right back at Julia's eyes. "Don't you think I've learned a few things since we've been out here?" She tilted her chin up.

"Well, miss, tell me what you've learned." Julia twisted her head, bestowing a sidelong look.

Shelby played with her pale green cotton skirt. "Johannah and I were watching a butterfly the other day at the coulee. It fluttered around until it found a daisy to rest on. Then it took off and landed on an old, dry weed. But somehow, with the butterfly on it, the weed looked prettier." She curved her straight yellow blond hair behind her ear. "We decided that the butterfly was so beautiful that it didn't matter where it landed. It could go anywhere it *wanted*, because the butterfly's beauty comes with it wherever it goes." Her blue eyes gazed at Julia, and she frowned impatiently. "Don't you see? That means you can stay here."

Julia pursed her lips together. "I think I know what you mean. Because God's love makes me beautiful, my home can be anywhere?"

"Yeah, but don't you get the rest?" Shelby rolled her eyes. "The point is, the butterfly can land on whichever flower it *wants* to land on. It gets to choose." She sat up tall. "Where do you want to be? I think maybe you want to stay here, with us. Don't you, Miss Cavanaugh? Because if you want to stay, but you go back anyway, then you don't get to be a butterfly anymore."

Julia opened her mouth, unsure what to make of the young girl's reasoning, but before she could respond, she heard a moan from the back of the wagon. Looking behind her, Julia saw Miriam laying flat on her back, grasping her belly and breathing hard.

"Miriam!" Julia yelped. "What are you doing?"

"Well." Miriam let out a breath then sat up again as the struggle seemed to pass. "I think I'm having a baby."

Chapter Thirty

It was mostly curious cowboys and enlisted men who lined the long benches, waiting for the trial to begin. Isaac attempted to shift to get a better view, but he could only see the sides of the spectators' heads.

He tilted his chin and looked farther back in the room, and he spied a row of folks he recognized—members of the Lodge Pole church. Isaac's heart warmed with appreciation. He didn't know if the judge would consider what the fellow believers, his friends, had to say, since none were witnesses of the crime. At least they'd come to support a sister who was seeking the things of God.

The bailiff stepped through the rows and grabbed ten men to be the jury. These men moved to the front corner of the room and sat in two rows of benches.

Sitting near the front, closest to the judge's bench, was Mabelina. Jim sat beside her, and his large frame blocked most of her from Isaac's view. Isaac again worked to free himself from the ropes. It did little good. He tried to shout, but the sound was no louder than a muffled whisper.

The bailiff swore the participants in and then sauntered to the center of the room. "Come to order! The honorable Judge Whalen B. Booker presiding."

The judge walked from the corner where he'd been waiting and sat down in front of the shellacked bench. His glasses fell to the tip of his nose as his dark eyes gazed up above them.

Isaac longed to help Mabelina. Judge Booker couldn't have expected a woman shooting a man with a roomful of witnesses to be a tough case. And thanks to Warren, who now stepped forward to testify, it wouldn't be.

Dear Lord, if You can shut the mouths of lions, surely You can find a way to loosen these ropes.

The train still rumbled on the tracks as its water tank was refilled. And though Isaac couldn't hear all the words, he could tell by the expressions on Warren's face—anger and mock sadness—that he spewed lie-filled accusations. And when he was done, Buck and Joe took their turns standing before the judge, although Isaac knew they hadn't even been present at the shooting.

Then the judge gave Mabelina a chance to talk. Isaac strained to listen.

"Judge, I did shoot our dear Elder Godfrey. He was a good man." Isaac watched Mabelina's eyes flit to the pew where the church members sat. "And I'm so sorry." Her voice thickened. "I never should've pulled that gun out." She turned to the cool, ruminating judge. "But it was an accident. I didn't mean to kill him, Your Honor." She shifted her gaze to the jury. "I swear, I didn't."

Mabelina took a moment to compose

herself. "I loved a man and was jest tryin' to get his attention. I never meant to hurt a fly, let alone a good, godly man like Elder Godfrey."

"Thank you, ma'am." The judge showed no emotion. He excused her with a wave of his hand. Then he scanned the room. "Are there any other witnesses for the defense?"

Hands went up all over the room. The judge's eyes widened in disbelief, and he readjusted himself in his chair.

Isaac couldn't help but feel a hint of pleasure.

Jim was the first out of his seat. He stood without being called on.

"We know Mabelina's turned her life right 'round ta where she's doing good now." Jim peered directly at the judge. "And we want to speak on her behalf."

The tall, sturdy-looking officer waved the witnesses down.

The judge scanned the depot. "Any of you folks there on the day of the crime?"

Jim stood and told everything that happened in his own way. Isaac was proud of him for telling the truth, but he was the only other witness present who'd actually seen the shooting happen. And Warren had himself plus two others who swore they saw her shoot Milo in cold blood.

Isaac assumed it was all over, when another witness stood up. It was one of the women. Her hat was pulled down, shielding most of her face. Isaac had seen her earlier, sitting with his parishioners. She stood and took the hat off. "I say something."

Isaac squeezed his eyes tight and then looked again. It was Aponi.

Warren and his men jumped to their feet. "She can't be a witness. She's an Injun and a woman!"

Contrasting voices of protest and support blared through the small depot, and the judge pounded his gavel.

"Order! Calm yourselves down," the judge demanded. His eyebrows furrowed as he gazed at Warren. "Now, you listen to me." He spoke in a quiet yet firm tone. "The woman may speak."

Aponi walked to the front. "I not have much to say. Only truth. I was there that day. I saw Mabelina take out gun. She shoot up toward ceiling. Not trying to kill my husband. I saw." She faced the jury. "And I forgive her for the accident." She gazed at Mabelina, nodded, and then walked to Mabelina's side, sitting down and taking her hand.

After a brief silence, the room erupted again. Isaac heard one of the men sitting in the jury commenting, "I don't care what some Injun says."

"Me neither," another said. "Everyone knows how fool-headed they are. Can't believe a word they say."

Isaac peeked at Mabelina. Her hands covered her face, and her shoulders shook. Tears rolled down Jim's face, as well. Isaac knew Jim longed to hold her, sweep her away. He again tugged on the ropes with his thumb and forefinger. If only he could get inside that room.

The judge calmed the room down and turned to the jury. "It is your responsibility to seek justice, no matter who the witness may be. Do you understand?"

"Yes, sir," the men answered, nearly in unison.

"Well, I believe that's all the witnesses we have." He glanced around, searching for more hands, then returned his attention to the jury. "Take time to deliberate."

A tall man who sat at the foremost chair stood. "Give us a minute, please, Yer Honor."

Isaac's heart sank. Would Mabelina go to the gallows because he was stuck in this wagon? He struggled one more time with the knot. Twisting his head behind him, he noticed the end of the rope poking out at an awkward angle. His heart leapt. He knew that knot. It was how a cowhand tied an unbroken horse so it couldn't squirm itself loose, but the owner could easily untangle it.

Isaac remembered Lefty's apologetic look. *Why didn't I think of it earlier?*

He twisted his hand and gripped the loose bit of rope, freeing himself. *Thank you, Lefty.* A minute later he'd untied his feet, ripped the gag from his mouth, and lunged out of the wagon, sprinting around the building toward the depot's entrance.

* * * *

Without hesitating, Julia climbed over the wagon seat into the back beside Miriam. She felt the hem of her new skirt catch and tear, but in didn't matter. She knelt beside her friend, and her heart pounded.

Elizabeth pulled back the reins, slowing the stallion.

Julia settled Miriam's head on her lap, smoothing back her wavy brown hair. "Dear Heavenly Father," she prayed out loud, "please help Miriam deliver this baby safely."

"What should I do?" Elizabeth turned in the seat. The color had drained from her face. Here eyes were wide. "Go back to the ranch? We're almost at Big Sandy. What do you want me to do?"

"This baby won't wait till we get back home." Miriam winced as another contraction hit. "I think I can last till we get to Big Sandy. Maybe Margaret from the hotel will still be in town. I know she's delivered babies before. Everyone else is probably already at the lake for the picnic."

"Yes, all right. Hee-ya." Elizabeth flicked the reins, and the horses lunged forward. The wagon resumed its journey over the rocky, pitted road.

Rolling to her side, Miriam hugged her belly.

Julia stroked Miriam's moist forehead with the bit of fabric that had torn from her skirt. *So brave.* Yet bravery would not ensure a safe delivery. They needed to find someplace better, cleaner. A hawk flew overhead, circling the wagon, causing shivers to race up Julia's spine. "A wagon's no place to have a baby."

"Have you ever helped with birthin', Julia?" Miriam panted, her eyes pleading up at her as she lay in the back of the wagon.

Julia clenched her teeth uneasily. "Um—well, yes, actually."

"You have?" Shelby twitched her head toward Julia, who threw her a warning glance.

"I *did* help a new mother deliver her little ones."

Shelby leaned over from her seat in the front and moved her mouth close to Julia's ear. "Are you talkin' about when Sammy the dog had pups?" she whispered.

Julia lowered her voice. "I'm just trying to keep her from fretting. I'm sure we'll make it to Big Sandy in time. Now shh." Julia's heart kicked against her chest.

Dear Lord, please let us make it there in time.

"Oh! Here comes another one." Miriam moaned.

As Julia stroked Miriam's hair, she spied Christopher's head bobbing toward them. Reaching the wagon, he hoisted himself up on the side and jerked his floppy blond hair from his forehead. "What y'all doin' back here?" When he saw his ma's face strained and her hands holding her middle, his normally puckish face drooped.

"Ma?" He climbed inside and held her hand as it jostled from the wagon's motion. "You ain't birthin' that baby right here, are ya?"

The contraction passed, and Miriam drew in a breath. "No, dear. We're going to town, and Margaret will help." Miriam gazed at her son, obviously disturbed by his worry. "Why don't you head on back to the coulee and fetch some water?"

He hesitated, his forehead knitted with concern.

She patted his hand. "Go on now."

He again hurdled out of the moving wagon then grabbed a canteen hanging from the side.

"I'll go with you." Shelby vaulted out after him, and the two ran toward the coulee a quarter mile back.

Julia reached into her satchel, pulled out a handkerchief, and continued mopping Miriam's forehead.

"That looks like the one Isaac let you borrow." Miriam took in deep, long breaths, which seemed to help her through the episodes.

"Yes, well, I guess I won't be borrowing any more of anything from him."

"You still could." Despite her state, Miriam eyes held that now-familiar hint.

"Miriam Lafuze, you're relentless. Aren't you the one who told me to trust God?"

Miriam let out a laugh, which turned into a moan as another contraction started up. Julia held her hand, praying with Miriam as she breathed through the pain.

Beads of perspiration dotted her forehead. "That was a hard one—oh no."

Another contraction started only moments after the last one ended.

"I know," Miriam panted, "but I'm still hopin'."

Julia let the laboring woman clamp down on her hand. Her groan was more high pitched and louder than the others had been.

Once the intense moment eased up, Julia swiveled her shoulders toward Elizabeth, who still urged the horses toward Big Sandy.

"The contractions are coming every three minutes or so. Are we almost there?"

Elizabeth launched a quick glance toward Julia. "Yeah, about five more minutes. See the water tower over yonder. Do you think she can make it?"

"I don't know. They're growing more intense." The side of Julia's foot tapped fast like a woodpecker against the wagon's running board. "Have you helped her deliver in the past?"

"No, not really," Elizabeth responded, her voice heavy with concern. "I helped our midwife, Aponi, but she was the one who really did everything. I wish I'd insisted she teach me."

"Me, too!" Miriam exclaimed. "Julia, I need you."

Julia's pulse flew as she whipped around. "What is it?"

Miriam grabbed Julia's face and peered into her eyes. "I have broken my waters."

"Yes, but some women still have hours before the baby is born after their waters break," Elizabeth said from the front. "Or so I've heard."

"Not me. Not this time."

"Oh, for horn spoons!" Julia said. "Elizabeth, stop the horse."

The wagon eased to a halt under Elizabeth's skilled guidance, and Julia switched positions to Miriam's other end.

"I'm so glad you've done this before." Miriam's voice rose to a near scream. "Oh, dear Jesus, help me."

Julia squeezed out a smile. "I—well—I'm still going to need your help." She pulled the traveling skirt Mrs. Gaffin had given her from her bag and scooted it under Miriam. The woman's legs bent up, seemingly instinctively, and her hands gripped her knees. She let out a wail as she engaged in the first push.

"Miriam?" Julia asked when the push was done. "I need you to tell me what to do."

"Can you see the baby?"

Julia peeked, and she felt a smile spread over her face. "Yes! I can." She rubbed Miriam's knee and caught her eyes.

Miriam breathed in, taking advantage of the brief respite between surges. "All right, you need to—"

Before Miriam could finish, Christopher and Shelby's footsteps pounded as they raced to the wagon, their faces red from running.

"Ma!" Christopher panted, his green eyes panicky. "Here's the water." Before Julia could stop him, he bounded onto the back of the wagon to give it to her but then froze. "Oh, no."

Julia twisted toward him and watched the color drain from his face, leaving it a greenish hue. "I'm gonna go," he said in a low voice and then, dropping the canteen next to Julia, tipped backward in a dead faint. He landed in a curled-up heap on the back of the wagon.

"Pay attention to *me*!" Miriam screamed in the middle of a push. "I can feel the baby!"

Julia focused on Miriam, waiting for the head to appear as she howled through the contraction.

Shelby rushed over to Christopher and splashed water on his face, waking the boy from his fainting spell.

Elizabeth made sure Christopher was all right and then ordered Shelby to run to town for help. Then Elizabeth scurried next to Miriam.

"What do you see?" Miriam squealed as she finished another pushing bout. "Has the baby crowned yet?"

Julia checked, and what she saw made a pang of fear surge through her. She peered over Miriam's legs.

"Miriam." She focused on the woman's strained eyes. "It's not the head, it's the bottom." *O Lord, we need Your help.*

Chapter Thirty-One

A hot wind spurred up dust from the road as Isaac sprinted around the building into the depot. His side ached from where Warren's brutes throttled him, but he ignored the pain.

The foreman stood. "We the jury find the accused, Mabelina Newman—"

"Wait!" Isaac's boots clunked on the planked floor as he rushed to the front of the room, skidding to a stop just short of plunging into the judge's bench.

The judge bucked back as the bailiff bolted to Isaac and grabbed his arm. The bailiff shifted his other hand to his gun. "Hold up!" he growled.

Isaac relaxed his stance to show he wasn't a threat. "I'm sorry." He gulped air. "I'm Parson Isaac Shepherd. The woman's minister." He eyed the judge. "I was there when Elder Godfrey was shot."

Warren marched to the judge. "He can't come in here." He pounded his fist on the bench. "The jury already decided."

The bailiff let go of Isaac's arm and shoved Warren away from the judge.

Judge Booker sprang to his feet, his eyes sharpened at Warren. "I will find you in contempt! Sit down, sir!"

Warren's eyes narrowed as he turned his attention to Isaac. "What do you care about the worthless strumpet?"

Isaac's chest boiled with suppressed rage, and his eyes drilled into Warren's. He'd heard enough of the man's insults, seen enough treachery. He'd pilfered a school out of the hands of innocent children, stolen Aponi's home and possessions, and wrenched away her children. And his almighty greed was the basis for Mabelina's murder trial. Gratified by the bounty, Warren had no qualms about her impending death if he were to win. And perhaps more disturbing than the rest, Warren Boyle had betrayed his stepfather, Milo, after all the sacrifices, effort, and love the godly man had invested in raising him. In a way, Isaac was glad his friend wasn't here to see this.

In Isaac's mind, all Warren's wicked acts culminated in that last insult he'd spewed on Mabelina. Everything in him screamed to smash the scowl on Warren's face into the dirty floor.

"That's enough, Warren." He snagged the man's eyes with his own. "Or you'll be meeting my fist."

Warren sneered. "You really gonna hit me, Parson?" he asked with a pompous laugh. "That pile of dung ain't worth soiling your hand over."

Isaac steadied his stance. "Watch your tongue." His body felt hot all over, and his chest tightened. He knew there were others in the room, but they seemed to fade as his attention focused on Warren and the sneer spread across his face.

"What? Only thing she's good for is

lyin' on her back. That what you want, Parson?"

Lord, even a parson has his limit. Isaac clenched his fist and yanked his arm back, ready to launch. The bailiff reached out to block Isaac's hand but was too late.

Isaac's fist slammed into Warren's jaw, toppling him to the dusty floor. Gasps erupted around him, followed by cheers.

Isaac gripped his hand, aching from the impact, and glanced around the room. "Oh no," he muttered under his breath. Then a rush of satisfaction chased away the tinge of guilt. *Lord, I know it's better to handle things by the law, but sometimes a villain just needs a good throttling.*

Isaac waited for the bailiff to arrest him, but after a silent moment, the room erupted into more cheers and clapping.

"That scoundrel deserved it!" Grandpa Pete shouted, holding up his cane.

A rancher waved his Stetson hat. "He swindled me outta forty head o' cattle last year!"

"That a way, Parson! I—" Lefty hollered, but his words were halted when Buck squeezed his shoulder and pushed him back into his seat.

Warren lay like a lump on the floor, curses spewing from his mouth.

Isaac glowered at him. "I've spent many years praying for you, and I'll probably spend many more. But you will *not* speak of a lady that way ever again."

Warren spit on Isaac's boot before the bailiff yanked him to his feet.

Jim rushed forward and faced Warren, and the giant miner hulked over the stocky swindler. "That shoulda been me shovin' my fist in yer rat-faced head," Jim's booming voice warned. "And I'll take my turn, if you don't keep yer comments 'bout my wife to yerself." He leaned his face nose-to-nose with Warren. "When I'm done with you, you'll be nothin' but a greasy spot on the floor." He tipped his hat to Isaac and moseyed back to his seat.

The judge slammed his gavel. "Order!"

"I'm pressing charges, Your Honor," Warren stated as the bailiff slammed him into his seat. "Everyone in this room is witness. He assaulted me."

Isaac gaped at the brazen man. "Do you want to tell the judge why I was late? Why my head is bleeding and my ribs are bruised? I'm sure he'd be interested to know. Or maybe the judge would also like to hear how you've swindled your father's money and dream of building a school so that you can build a saloon? Or maybe he'd also like to hear how you broke up your father's family to satisfy your own greed."

Warren shook his head. "What do I know? I have no idea."

The judge slammed his gavel again, and the spectators finally simmered down, returning to their seats.

"This conduct is unacceptable! You will all sit quietly—in silence!—or you will all be asked to leave." Judge Booker's gaze slowly moved over the courtroom, stopping on Warren. "That includes you, sir."

Warren frowned and crossed his arms.

The judge cleared his throat. "And you, too, Parson."

Isaac turned to face the judge. "I'm sorry, Your Honor."

The judge peered over his glasses. "In the interest of time, we'll save the explanation about the assault till later. For now why don't you tell me what it is you're doing here, Parson Shepherd."

Isaac gazed at Mabelina, who was unmoved by the scuttle with Warren. Her head still drooped, her hands were clenched in her lap. *She's why I'm here. Lord, let my words be honest and persuasive. Preserve justice today, and save this woman's life so she can serve You. Your will be done.*

He took in a breath. "Thank you, Judge Booker." He eyed the man respectfully. "I am here to not only vouch for this woman's changed character." He pointed at Mabelina then glanced at the men in the jury. "But to tell you that I was there that day." He shook his head slowly. "She did not intend to kill Milo—" Isaac paused, the sound of his friend's name bringing a rush of grief. "I mean, Elder Godfrey."

Light slanting in from the window from which he'd watched the proceedings heated his neck. Grateful for the chance to speak, he continued.

"It's like Aponi said. I saw the gun in her hand and watched her as she pointed the gun at the ceiling. The bullet must've ricocheted, because the next thing I heard was Milo hitting the floor. Mabelina was as shocked as the rest of us." He glanced at the judge. "There's not much more to tell. Except. . ."

Isaac's voice softened. "I know this woman. I knew her when she had nothing in this life but the men who frequented her bed. And I've seen how the Lord used the love of one man, Giant Jim Newman, to change her. She's married now, and her husband has great hopes to be a parson some day—a calling I support with my prayers and guidance. I believe Mabelina will make a fine parson's wife. Please don't let her past destroy their future."

Isaac shifted to face the twelve frontiersmen who sat on a bench at the side of the room. He perused each man's eyes. A few of the men were elderly, but most were young to middle-aged ranchers or cowhands. He knew they came from untamed backgrounds and probably held to the Code of the West above any biblical ethic. How could he convince a group of crude cowboys to set free a former prostitute who'd kill a man? He hoped the truth would persuade them. It was his only opportunity to touch their consciences.

He strode to the judge's bench, picked up the Bible, and then rotated, standing before the room as if in front of a congregation. "There's a woman told of in this book who was caught in the act of adultery. The vigilantes of the time hauled her to the Lord Jesus, proclaiming her sentence—death by stoning. And according to the law, they were right. When Jesus bent down to draw in the dirt, I suspect the woman feared He searched for a stone. She knew the law, knew she'd broken it, knew the punishment.

"But Christ stood up, empty handed. He ordered those without sin to cast the first stone, knowing He Himself was the only one who met that criterion. But despite the fact that the woman deserved His stones to pummel her sin-ridden body, Jesus forgave her. And what's more, *He* took the judgment she deserved." Isaac paused, in awe of God's grace. "He allowed godless men to judge Him, the perfect Son of God. And He carried the weight of that woman's sin in His flesh as He died on the cross."

Isaac moved closer to the spectators. "And because He later took the woman's place, I believe His words, 'Go, and sin no more,' changed her. His words always bring newness and light to those who trust in Him and not in their own ways."

Pacing across the room, Isaac noticed that not even Warren turned his gaze away, and he shot up a quick prayer for God to breathe life into the depraved man's heart. "We've all turned away from God," he continued. "Prostituted ourselves—maybe not in the same way as Mabelina. But every time we lie, or cheat, or steal—placing our trust in earthly gain—we give our souls away, just as Mabelina did."

He paced to the woman who now sat upright in her chair, her eyes still fearful but lit with a flicker of hope. He touched her shoulder.

"Christ will take the most wretched sinner's dead, black heart," he raised his voice, "and create a new heart, changing a prostitute to a daughter of God, a cheater to a son, a liar to a child of the King. That's what he did for Mabelina."

He searched each face in the crowd. "Will you heed His call? Will you?"

Isaac paused, letting the words of the gospel sink in. "This woman did not murder Milo Godfrey." Isaac lowered his head, thanked the jury and the judge, and took his seat.

"Thank you, Reverend." The corner of Judge Booker's mouth twitched up. "Probably not the best place for a sermon, but it was a good one nonetheless."

Isaac grinned. "I've preached in much stranger places than this, sir."

Judge Booker shifted to the jury. "Gentlemen, do you need some time to make a decision?"

Isaac gazed at Jim and Mabelina clutching each other's hands. Their eyes were closed, and Isaac was sure they prayed. He prayed, too.

The men in the jury whispered among themselves, and then the foreman stood.

All in the room was silent, and Isaac noticed the sound of a clock ticking. His eyes flitted around the room, and he saw the clock on the wall above the door. 2:55. A surge of worry filled his chest as he wondered whether both he and the judge would miss the train that would be leaving in fifteen minutes. He returned his attention to the jury.

"We the jury find the accused, Mabelina Newman. . .not guilty of murder."

Isaac raised his fists in triumph and faced the twelve men. "Thank you!" He rushed to Mabelina, whose head was buried in Jim's chest. "Congratulations! This is wonderful." As Isaac spoke, the train's whistle echoed through the room.

Isaac's heart dove into his stomach. *Julia. I've got to stop her.*

Jim's head shot up, his eyes wide with realization of what that whistle meant. "You've got a train to catch, Parson Ike!"

"I know!" A rush of joyous excitement combined with anxiety moved his body toward the door.

"You get her, Parson," Mabelina called. "Tell her you love 'er. And thanks for all you done for me."

"You're welcome!" he called as he sprinted outside where the train waited.

With two long steps he crossed the platform, and with one long jump he hurled himself onto the train and rushed through the narrow aisles toward the front.

The conductor stopped Isaac as he accidentally stepped in the first-class cabin. "Where ya headed so fast?"

Isaac halted. "I'm sorry." He smiled apologetically to the only two passengers, an older, distinguished-looking man with a generous smile and a plump lady. "I didn't mean to come in here."

"You'll have to go back to the lower-class cabins. Where's your destination?"

"The next stop, sir. Big Sandy." Isaac reached into his pocket and pulled out his payment, joy surging through him at the thought of finally being able to talk to Julia.

The youthful conductor grinned. "You must be off to fetch a lady."

"I was thinking the same thing!" The plump woman's round belly rolled as she chortled.

Isaac blinked. "How'd you know?"

"A smile like that can only mean a feller's got a girl in his sights."

The older man agreed.

Waving his hand in front of him, the conductor winked. "No charge for you."

"Thank you. That's so kind." The excitement growing in his heart was laced with nervousness. "But I'm not sure she'll accept me."

"Well, if she doesn't, come back and pay the two bits," the conductor teased.

Isaac thanked him again and headed to the passenger cars.

"No, no!" The woman objected on a giggle. "Why don't you stay in here with us? We were getting antsy anyway. Nice to have some company, right, my dear?"

"Yes, yes." The older man nodded.

The train's wheels rumbled on the rails, and it slowly began to move.

Isaac slid into a seat and gazed out the window. In moments he'd be at the Big Sandy depot, just in time to stop Julia from boarding. He closed his eyes. He could only hope she'd forgive him, accept him, and love him as he loved her.

Chapter Thirty-Two

Miriam howled in pain, and Julia saw the fear in her eyes.

Julia sat up tall, her hands on the woman's knees. "Tell me what to do," she said firmly. "How do I turn the baby around?"

Miriam closed her eyes and sucked in a breath. Tears rolled down her cheeks as another round of stabbing pain surged through her. She gingerly rolled to her side, and Elizabeth massaged her back.

"This happened with Johannah," Miriam said, her voice screeching with pain, but not panic. "We're going to have to deliver the baby rear first."

After what seemed like an hour of Miriam pushing, Elizabeth massaging, and Julia gently guiding the baby, Miriam told Julia to check again.

Julia dipped her head down. An elated sob rose to her throat. "It's almost out! You did it, Miriam! You are an amazing woman."

Miriam carefully twisted to her back. "I know!" she breathed. "I'm amazing!"

"Now push!"

A scream, which seemed to explode from the deep regions of Miriam's very soul, echoed across the prairie as she squeezed her knees and hurled her body forward. The baby slid out into Julia's waiting hands.

A sob exploded from Julia as she held the wet child in her hands. "Oh, Miriam. It's a beautiful boy." She wiped him off with Elizabeth's apron and placed the bald, screeching child in the arms of his mother. "Thank You, Lord," Julia sighed.

Elizabeth helped Miriam finish the delivery process and then cut the baby's cord with a sharp knife. Then she cleaned both baby and mother as best she could with the water Christopher and Shelby had brought.

As Julia watched them, the trembling began. It started in her shoulders and moved down her arms. *I can't believe I delivered a baby.* The reality of what had happened hit her. She looked around, at the back of the wagon, at the sky above, at the expanse of prairie, and her legs suddenly felt as if they were made out of water. She sank lower, sitting hard on her bottom on the wagon's box.

"Yes, thank You." Miriam closed her eyes, snuggling the baby to her chest. She kissed the top of his head. "Someone needs to go tell Jefferson that he has another son."

"Yes, we will. Let us catch our breath." Elizabeth touched Julia's hand. Julia felt Elizabeth's hand trembling, too. "Our Lord helped us, didn't He?"

"He did." Julia gazed at the sweet baby, now comforted by his mother's touch. "He does."

"Liberty." Miriam's face glowed. "We'll call you Liberty for Independence Day.

Lib for short." She touched her newborn son's cheek. "Christopher, come see your brother."

Christopher stood up from where he sat beside the wagon, but he didn't peer at the women. "Is it safe?"

"It's safe," Julia said.

He turned around and peeked at his little brother. "He's sort of ugly."

Elizabeth tugged on Christopher's ear. "You don't say that!"

Miriam glanced at Julia. "Thank you. I'm so glad you were here. And I'm so glad you've done this before."

Julia grinned. "Just with dogs."

Elizabeth and Miriam both gawked. "Dogs?" Elizabeth fanned her face.

Julia nodded apologetically. "Yes, our adopted pet at the orphanage had puppies. Sweet Sammy. The poor little pups had trouble coming out, so I had to help. I didn't say what kind of little ones I helped deliver, remember." She pinched her lips playfully. "I didn't want you to worry."

As the ladies giggled, the sound of a train whistle floated along the warm breeze.

Elizabeth gripped Julia's arm. "The train."

Julia shifted her head in the direction of the town about a mile off. Nestled into the horizon, beneath the sparkling blue sky, stood the windmill, the buildings lined up at attention along Main Street, the rickety old water tower. She smiled reflectively, remembering how Isaac had teased her that the water tower outshone the Statue of Liberty.

Her mind and heart had been set on boarding. She eyed the horse, and in her mind's eye pictured herself mounting and racing to town.

Christopher can share the saddle and return the horse after he drops me off. Yes, that could work.

If she did that, she would make the steam engine, and within thirty minutes she'd be rumbling out of town, her Western adventure near an end. Julia untucked her skirt around her and prepared to stand. But then she hesitated. . .

She thought of New York. Mrs. Gaffin's smiling face and her position at the school. How rewarding it would be to work there with a group of girls again. She thought of the people and the pulse of the city. It had its own schedule and pace. And for the first time, the idea of walking down the street and passing one hundred people she didn't know made her sad. Her face felt flush, and it was more than just the warmth of the sun overhead.

Miriam held the baby's head to her chest and leaned back against Elizabeth, closing her eyes.

Julia bit her lip as she thought about the rich, fulfilling life that would be waiting at the end of a train ride. But somehow the prospect of returning didn't inspire her. The truth was, in the weeks since she'd received Mrs. Gaffin's letter, she'd tried to conjure excitement but couldn't. That world, New York, seemed far away, and her life there a distant memory. Like the memory of a dream.

A butterfly, yellow with charcoal lines, caught a gust of wind and landed on Miriam's shoulder then skittered away. Julia gazed at the two women, Miriam reclining against her sister's chest as they cherished baby Liberty. And as sure as butterflies fluttering on the prairie, Julia's path was clear. She didn't want to leave Montana. Shelby was right. Julia desired to dig her feet into the dry, dusty, prairie life and embrace whatever difficult, toilsome, and sometimes lonely life it offered. She wanted to remain with these people and teach their children. She wanted to serve the Lord here.

"Julia, are you all right?" It was Elizabeth's voice. "Maybe you need a drink of water. Christopher, can you please—"

"I'm fine." Julia held up her hand. "I just need a moment to think."

She took a deep breath and thought about encouraging Shelby as a mentor through her young adulthood. She considered watching Bea grow into a beautiful girl.

As clear as anything, she knew staying here was the right answer. Maybe not in Lonesome Prairie, but close by. Perhaps she'd find employment as a schoolmarm in a neighboring town. And as the thought grew, excitement expanded with every flicker of her imagination.

Smiling at the two women who'd become like sisters to her, she touched their hands. "I'm not going. I want to be a butterfly."

Elizabeth squealed with delight. Miriam reached over and brushed Julia's hair from her forehead. "I'm so glad. I've been praying!"

Julia chuckled. "Well, your prayers must have worked. This morning my plans were completely different."

Elizabeth scooted over and pulled Julia tightly into an embrace. Then, as she pulled back, Julia heard another voice.

"What?" It was Shelby. Sarah Mack followed behind, fanning herself and breathing hard. "You're staying? Is that what I heard?" Shelby jumped onto the wagon and embraced Julia. "I knew you would."

Shelby pulled back and gestured to the woman behind her. "I couldn't find Margaret, but I found Mrs. Mack on her way to the party." Julia accepted Shelby's tight squeeze, and when she looked up, she saw a scowl on Sarah Mack's face.

"I'm dashed, I say, simply dashed!" Her normally pasty white face was flushed red as a huckleberry pie. "I've been waiting and waiting for you to go back to your precious New York, so fancy and fine, as you say—though not nearly as refined as

London—but I've held my tongue. Yes, I have. But now you—out of pure disregard for my feelings—have decided to stay." She took off her bonnet and put it back on, her hands restless. "It's not that I don't like you, dearie, but for heaven's sake, how will I ever win my Horace if you don't take your leave?"

Julia hurried out of the wagon to her and spoke gently. "Sarah, I'm not staying to marry Horace. I have no plans to do so."

Sarah staggered, wiped her brow, and then plopped down on the end of the wagon. "I—I'm sorry, Julia. I suppose I have always pictured that I would be the one to marry him." She shook her head and rocked like a child. "There, I said it. I've waited, knowing that once you were gone, that sweet, kindhearted man would come to his senses and see that I'd make a much better wife to him than some skinny New Yorker. No offense, dearie." She swung her head and pouted. "Maybe we'd already be married by now if you weren't here." She fanned herself. "It's so dreadfully hot." She let herself fall backwards onto the wagon bed next to Miriam.

Her eyes apparently landed on the newborn. "Oh yes, the reason Shelby came for me. Well, I see everything is fine. What a beautiful baby." Her voice held a suppressed sob. "How happy you must be."

Miriam patted the Englishwoman's head. "Oh, Sarah."

Not knowing what to say, Julia moved to the front of the wagon, returning with her frilly blue and tan parasol. Then she held it open over Sarah where she lay. "Here, Sarah. This is for you. I don't need it anymore."

"Thank you." Sarah stilled for a moment, and then Julia watched as the fret seemed to start again in her hands—tightening into fists—and move up her pinched face to her knotted forehead. "Why must you ruin my last hope of happiness?" she finally burst out. Then Sarah thrust herself upright, and Julia yanked the parasol to keep it from poking the woman's eye.

Sarah peered at her son, who was shyly inching backwards as if longing to disappear into the horizon. "And my poor William. You're stealing his happiness, too. Horace has been like a father to him already. He even showed him how to pan for gold and—"

"Sarah!" Julia crouched in front of her and attempted to hold her gaze as Sarah continued her tirade. "Listen to me."

Finally Sarah paused to wheeze in a breath.

Julia gazed directly into the woman's pale blue eyes. "I don't want to marry Horace," she stated slowly, firmly. "I've told you that. I will not marry him. If I have to, I'll work to repay him, but I will not marry Horace Whitbaum. Never."

Sarah started to shake her head as if not believing, and Julia grasped the woman's shaky hands.

"I promise you, Sarah Mack. I will lay my hand on a Bible if you want. I have no intentions toward that man." She tilted her head in a sympathetic smile. "As kindhearted as he is."

The tightly constricted lines on Sarah's face loosened. "You promise?"

Julia sighed in relief. "I promise. But if you want Mr. Whitbaum to start courting you, there's something you need to do."

Sarah's thick eyebrows knit together, questioning.

"Have you told Horace how you feel?"

Sarah shook her head.

"You need to be honest with him. Tell him you care for him."

"But it's not proper. How could I?"

A blaring *boom* reverberated from the direction of the ranch, and Christopher leaped to his feet. "The fireworks up at the lake! They're getting ready." Another boom sounded followed by a series of crackles. "We need to get back there, or we're going to miss the picnic!"

"That's right. The Fourth of July picnic. I almost forgot." Shelby scampered around the wagon near Elizabeth. "Folks must be arriving soon."

Elizabeth glanced at Miriam and Julia. "The young'uns are right." She tilted her head to peek over Julia's shoulder. "In fact, I see a troop of ladies heading out of Big Sandy now."

Julia touched Miriam's ankle. "Guess we didn't expect your little Lib to be arriving so soon, did we? A Fourth of July baby."

Miriam scooted up to a seated position,

taking on her leadership position despite the baby rocking in her arms. "Here's what we'll do. We'll go on back home and get me and Liberty situated in my bed. Elizabeth, if you don't mind missing a bit of the festivities, you, along with that husband of mine, can stay and take care of me."

Elizabeth stood and climbed to the buckboard, grabbing the reins.

"And you, Julia." Miriam threw her a smile. "You'll take the children to the picnic—to give me time to rest."

Julia smiled, grateful to be part of the scheme, the family. "Perfect. But if you don't mind, I'm also doing one more thing." She stood tall before Sarah, her hands bunched on her hips. "I'm taking you by the hand and putting you in front of Horace Whitbaum. I'm sure I'll run into him—he always seems to show up wherever I go. Then it's up to you to share your heart. Will you do that?"

Sarah shook her head, her hands covering her mouth and her eyes fearful. "No, I can't possibly. He's got his mind set on marrying you."

Redheaded William slunk next to her

on the wagon and held her hand. "You can do it, Mama. I think he loves you, too. He asks about you all the time. He'll change his mind about Miss Cavanaugh, you'll see."

A blush deepened Sarah's already pink face, and she nodded. "For you, William." She wrapped her arm around her son. "I'll tell him." Then she shrugged. "I suppose it's worth a go."

Julia swiveled around, headed for the buckboard. She climbed on, and as she stood, she realized she could see the town. In the distance, her eyes snagged on the train parked at the depot that created a black line across the golden fields. She imagined the newcomers trickling off, entering Big Sandy. As she settled into her seat, she pictured the departing passengers climbing the big steps.

Thank You, Lord, that I'm not climbing those steps. There's no place I'd rather be than right here.

Chapter Thirty-Three

The steam engine slowed, and Isaac clasped the handrail on the train's iron exterior. Before it completely stopped, he vaulted off the big step. *I've got to find Julia.*

A hot July breeze shifted his parson hat as he rushed the few steps to the railcar depot. Isaac's hands went clammy in a cold sweat, and he wiped them on his trousers. His cheeks stretched into a smile as he peered inside, expecting to see Julia's traveling clothes and sparkling brown eyes. She wasn't in there.

"Young man?" The woman from the train

tapped Isaac's shoulder. "I'm sorry to be a bother, but my dear husband, well . . ." She let out a loud guffaw. "He has only so many hands, and I have such a large amount of luggage. . ." She turned and pointed back to the train.

Isaac barely heard the woman's words. Instead, he gazed over the mile-long road leading to the town, remembering the last time Julia had missed the train. He pressed his lips together in a smile as he remembered how she'd walked toward the depot with quickened steps. But at this moment, no young woman traipsed the dusty walk. No wagon rumbled closer, either. His heart raced. Was she already aboard?

"Sir?" The woman tapped his shoulder again. "Would you be so kind as to help us with our luggage?"

Isaac faced the chubby, rosy-cheeked matron, her elegant purple city dress gathering dust that was carried in the breeze. His shoulders slumped. "Of course." Even though he wished to search the passenger cars, just to make sure, he couldn't refuse to help this woman.

"Oh dear," the woman commented, more to herself than to him. "What is this place? Is this the depot? Where is the town? It is quite—primitive."

Isaac walked to the conductor, who was helping the older man unload numerous trunks and valises onto the dirt.

"Sir." Isaac grabbed a valise and shoved it under his arm. "Has anyone boarded here? A young woman?" Isaac grasped two more parcels in his hands.

"Well, now." The woman's husband twisted his curlicue mustache. "That's just what we'd like to know. We're looking for a Julia Cavanaugh. Have you seen her, my good man?"

Isaac gaped at the man, who was dressed in a black suit and white shirt with a beaver skin top hat as he'd seen in pictures of Abraham Lincoln. "You know Julia Cavanaugh?" He dropped the valises.

The woman jiggled over to him and thwacked his arm with the hooked handle of a purple and gray parasol. "I told you on the train. We came here to save her from a terrible *gold miner*." She shuddered. "Weren't you listening? Oh!" Her hand flew to her puffed red lips. "You're not the gold miner, are you? I'm always getting myself into trouble with my blabbering words." She eyed her husband, who gazed at her adoringly. "Though I don't know why she wouldn't want to marry you. My, but you're a handsome one."

Despite his anxiety over finding Julia, a laugh escaped Isaac's lips. "I'm not the gold miner. I'm Parson Isaac Shepherd." He removed his hat and offered his hand to shake.

"Mrs. Gaffin." She took his hand in her flimsy one. "It's nice to make your acquaintance. And this is my husband, Henry Gaffin."

"Very well."

Isaac ran his fingers through his hair, and suddenly it struck him who these people were. This was the woman who took Julia in after her parents died—something he should thank her for. She was also the woman who promised Julia to Horace as his bride—something he didn't understand yet didn't have the time to figure out.

"I've heard so much about you, Mrs. Gaffin. Julia expressed her gratitude for your care on several occasions."

A huge grin spread across the woman's face. "So you know Julia that well, do you?"

Isaac didn't bother hiding his feelings. "Yes, I'm very fond of her." He grinned at his cool understatement, so inadequate for the deep emotion he felt. "In fact, I came here to try to stop her from returning to New York."

Mrs. Gaffin squeaked with joy. "So my Julia's going to get married, after all! Oh, I just knew the West was the place for her." Her eyes fluttered to her husband, and she clapped her gloved hands together.

"You did well, my love." Mr. Gaffin stroked her cheek with his finger. "Very well."

A hawk circled overhead, and Mrs. Gaffin lifted her head. A wagon with a team of horses trotted up, and a scraggly cowboy lifted his hat at a woman with her three children who'd also disembarked from the train.

"Oh my, but this is a wild place, isn't it?"

Isaac raised his eyebrows and returned to the conversation about Julia. "There is a problem, ma'am. I don't know if Julia shares my feelings. That's why I had to hurry here. To find out."

"Oh, don't be silly. I'm sure she does. She has good taste and is quite smart, too." Mrs. Gaffin beamed. "Now the only problem is to get you two love puppies together."

"Yes. Very well." Mr. Gaffin slipped a pocket watch from his black overcoat, checked the time, and then replaced it. "Four o'clock," he said randomly. "Do you know where the young lady might be?"

The train began rumbling, its smoke shooting high into the sky.

Isaac shook his head. "I don't know. I thought she'd be here. I'd be happy to take you to my family's ranch out in Lonesome Prairie. There's a Fourth of July picnic. I can't imagine where else she'd be, and if she's not there, perhaps my sisters know her whereabouts."

Even as he said the words, the muscles in his stomach tightened. He'd been gone for weeks and hadn't heard a thing. What if she'd found a way to leave earlier?

"Wonderful." Mrs. Gaffin clapped her hands. "I'm so thankful you know where to take us. Heaven knows I'd have had no idea where to look. I'd never thought of that. It's a big place, you know."

They managed to heave the luggage into the small depot, and then Isaac tramped off to the livery stable to rent a wagon since no hired drivers waited at the depot today. After getting the two city folks checked into The Spokane House, the three of them headed out to the ranch.

Lord, please let Julia be there, Isaac prayed. *Help me find her, and when I do, give me the words to show my love. And whatever happens, help me to trust You.*

* * * *

"All right, Joshua," Julia called to the five-year-old towhead. "Your turn."

On the makeshift pitcher's mound in the field below the ranch, Julia waited for Miriam's second-youngest son to take the plate.

Upon arriving home, they'd settled

Miriam and the baby into the house. After that, Julia had joined the other homesteaders as they gathered for the day's festivities at Lonesome Lake. The first order of business had been for her and Sarah to search for Horace. Not finding him, Sarah had wandered down to the lake to listen to the brass band assembled for the occasion.

Although the music was wonderful, Julia instead rounded up the children for a game of baseball. She couldn't help but smile as she taught them the basics of the game. *I'll be here to see them grow up. I'm not leaving them. This is my community now.*

People from the ranches all around Lonesome Prairie and the neighboring townships had gathered near the lake. Now they milled about eating fried chicken, roast quail on sticks, pies, and cakes. One family even donated a fruitcake saved all the way from Pittsburgh. In about an hour the bronco riding would begin. Julia grinned. Finally she'd see a real live Wild West rodeo.

With the tune of "The Old Folks at

Home" playing in the background, Josh pressed the bat on his shoulder and squirmed his bum, ready for the pitch. Julia lobbed it toward him. To her surprise, the youngster made contact, and the leather-stitched ball popped over her head.

"Run, Josh!"

The boy let out a whoop then set off toward first.

Shelby, perched at second base, fumbled, letting the ball drop to the ground.

Reaching the base, which was an old scrap of leather, the boy raised his hands in triumph.

Julia's jaw dropped at Shelby's uncharacteristic error, and she placed a hand on her hip as she turned to the girl. Shelby winked, letting Julia know she'd done it on purpose so that her cousin could make a single.

"Nice one, Josh." Shelby picked up the ball and tossed it to Julia.

"Who's next to bat?" she asked, swiveling around.

"I am." It was a man's voice. A voice that sent Julia's heart straight to her toes.

She froze and eyed Shelby, who covered her mouth and giggled. Julia gaped at the young girl, longing for help, but she didn't know what type of help she needed. *Maybe some way to protect my heart. . .*

"It's him. Look, Julia!" Shelby called, to Julia's utter embarrassment.

Julia slowly rotated toward the plate, and there, holding the bat over his shoulder, stood Isaac. Seeing his sturdy build, his mouth curved in a smile, and his kind dark-brown eyes made her chest constrict, as if it were trying to hold in the flurry of emotions she felt for him.

She bit her lip, realizing that would be impossible. It was as if no time had passed since that night they'd found Bea together. Despite the hurt of the last weeks, she longed to be near him, to support and encourage him. . .to love him.

She sighed, knowing this was not to be. She jutted out her chin and squared her shoulders. "Hello, Isaac." As hard as it was to keep her legs from running to him, she shuffled her feet and smiled warmly. "Welcome back."

Isaac winked at her, and a chill sent goosebumps to her arms. "Pitch me a fast one."

She stood up tall, holding the ball to her chest. "You sure you're ready?"

Isaac's face brightened with a smile, making the lines in his cheeks form long creases. "Oh yeah." He brushed his boot against the dirt. "Go ahead."

Julia lifted her chin. "I should warn you. I've pitched ball in the streets of New York City since I was eight."

Isaac's brow wrinkled. "You think I'm afraid?"

In place of an answer, Julia hurled the ball as hard as she could. Isaac swung but missed, the thrust of his swing making him stumble and lose the bat. The team lacked a catcher, so the ball sailed into the field behind him.

The children chortled as Isaac regained his stance. And Julia treasured the humble way he laughed along with them. "Y'all like to see your parson make a right fool of himself, don't you?"

Joshua abandoned first base and scurried to Isaac. "You almost fell right down on your rump, Uncle Ike." He poked Isaac in his mid-section.

Isaac stumbled then purposely plopped down in the dirt.

Joshua held his tummy and giggled.

"You've got a mighty powerful finger there. Let me see it."

Joshua showed him his finger, which Isaac perused with awe.

"You be careful with that thing. You'll be knocking folks down all over the country."

Joshua's eyes opened wide. "Aw, Uncle Ike."

Isaac stood and brushed off the dust. "All right. You young ones better fetch the ball." He spoke with his gaze fixed on Julia, his mouth holding an awkward smile.

A handful of the players scampered past him, but Isaac paced toward Julia.

"That's one fast pitch." He reached her and stopped, his eyes locking with hers.

Julia's heart pounded as he drew closer. She brushed her hair from her eyes. "I warned you." She folded her arms.

"You did."

A quiet moment passed between them,

and Isaac's gaze held Julia's. She wanted to ask him what he was doing. Why he was paying attention to her. But the children circled around them, their voices rising like a cawing of a dozen crows.

"Is it my turn to bat?"

"No. You already had a turn."

"Miss Cavanaugh, can you show me how you threw that so fast?"

"I think the parson needs to try again. It's three strikes before you're out."

"C'mon, Miss Cavanaugh." Christopher grabbed the bat as he twitched his hair back. "I'll hit it all the way to the lake."

Johannah ran up from behind the others, ball in hand, and tossed it to Julia.

Isaac gently removed it from her hand. "Shelby?" He stepped toward the girl. "You know how to pitch? I have something I need to show Miss Cavanaugh."

Shelby snickered and walked to the mound. Taking the ball from Julia, she gave her a knowing smile.

Unable to contain herself, Julia stuck out her tongue. Then she held in a chuckle as she noticed Isaac's eyes on her. Her face warmed at his laughter.

"You ready?" Isaac offered his arm, and his eyes softened. "If you don't mind." His voice suddenly sounded thick, earnest.

Julia looked into his face, searching for meaning. She longed to know his thoughts, his feelings. Hers were so strong, she was sure they were plain on her face. He must be able to notice her awkward movements and quick breaths.

She cautiously looped her hand around his muscular arm, and she felt his body relax. He escorted her toward the house.

"Isaac." She slanted her head toward him as they walked. "What is this about?"

Isaac kept his eyes focused in front of him, but Julia saw the corner of his mouth tweak upward. "You'll see."

They approached the house, where several food tables were set up out back as they'd been on the night of Isaac's birthday party. The firepit was lit, and the smoky scent of roasting buffalo meat made Julia's stomach stir in hunger.

A group of people lingered around the tables, talking as they nibbled, and above the clamor Julia heard her name.

"Miss Cav'naw!" Bea's voice hailed.

Julia's eyes searched low for a toddler scrambling toward her, but she didn't find the gold-haired bundle of joy.

Isaac raised Julia's chin with his thumb, and his touch sent a gush of warmth through her. Glancing ahead, she spied Bea—her arms stretched out and a big smile on her face—in the arms of Mrs. Gaffin.

Julia's heart danced at the sight of the one person who knew her better than any other.

"My dear girl!" Mrs. Gaffin wrapped her thick arms around Julia, squishing the little girl between them. Bea wiggled down and clasped Isaac's leg. Julia felt her body relax as she breathed in Mrs. Gaffin's familiar scent of rosewater, and she relished the comfort of her headmistress's embrace.

Julia stepped back and gazed at the woman, taking in the sight of her cheery eyes, her plump cheeks, her wayward brown hair.

"My dear, sweet Julia." Mrs. Gaffin dabbed tears from her eyes. "It's so good to see you. How I've missed you. And my sweet girl, I'm so sorry for putting you in such a predicament. What was I thinking?"

Julia patted the woman's shoulder, knowing she always meant well. "What are you doing here?"

Mr. Gaffin tweaked his mustache. "My dear wife has the most outrageous ideas, you see," he interjected. "Well, you tell her, my dear."

Julia watched Isaac scoop Bea into his arms. He raked his fingers through her curls as he stood next to Julia.

Mrs. Gaffin's excited laugh exploded from her lips, and a surge of joy spread through Julia at the remembrance of that happy sound. But it was quickly followed by a blow of anxiety. "Mrs. Gaffin." Julia lowered her head. "What do you have planned?"

Mrs. Gaffin touched Julia's face. "You're worried, dear, aren't you?" She glanced at Isaac. "No need. I told you in the letter about your new work opportunity? Well, I was thinking that before you came back, you, Mr. Gaffin, and I could go on an adventure out West. I've heard the parks out here are breathtaking. All my friends have already seen Yellowstone." She slipped a gaze at Julia. "But none have gone so far as Puget Sound." She grabbed Mr. Gaffin's arm and yanked him toward her. "So you see, my dear, if you want to come with us, you are welcome." Julia's headmistress glanced at Isaac again, and this time she added a wink.

Julia eyed her suspiciously. *Why the attention to Isaac?*

As the sounds of the community she loved echoed in her ears, Julia gazed at Mrs. Gaffin. A month ago she'd have jumped at the chance to be invited on such a trip, but as much as she loved Mrs. Gaffin, everything had changed in the last month. She'd changed.

Julia gripped Mrs. Gaffin's hands in hers, her heart heavy to have to disappoint the woman she so adored. "I'm sorry, Mrs. Gaffin. You know I love you very much, and I truly appreciate your coming all this way, but I can't go with you, not on your adventure—or back to New York." She glanced at Bea in Isaac's arms. "This is my home now."

To Julia's surprise, Mrs. Gaffin

laughed and threw her arms around Isaac in a tight embrace. "Congratulations, my boy!" She took Bea back into her arms.

Then Mr. Gaffin shook his hand. "Very well, my good man."

Julia's mind tangled in confusion. "What's going on?" She grabbed Mrs. Gaffin's arm. "What aren't you telling me?"

Mrs. Gaffin patted Julia's hand. "Don't ask *me*, sweetie." She dipped her head toward Isaac.

Julia glanced at him. Isaac's face glowed with an endearing smile as he slowly stepped toward her. The Gaffins and everyone else seemed to disappear into a haze as his gaze intertwined with hers. Julia's chest throbbed as her heart hammered its speeding beat.

"Julia, I—well, I have so much to say to you." Isaac took in a breath. His gaze left hers momentarily as he skimmed over the prairie, landing down by the lake. "Will you go on a walk with me?"

Joyful expectation brimmed in Julia's heart, but she tried to push it away. This man, this incredible man—he couldn't be planning to say the words she longed to

513

hear. Words of affection, admiration, love. But if those feelings did brew in him. . .

A thrill of hope rushed over her like the prairie wind. She slowly studied his eyes and then nodded. "Yes, I'll go on a walk with you."

And for the second time that day, Julia accepted the arm he offered to her.

Chapter Thirty-Four

The warmth of Julia's hand on Isaac's arm was like a deposit of hope. Hope that he'd escort her to many picnics, country fairs, hoedowns, and weddings throughout the span of years he prayed they would share together. His heartbeat paced expectantly as he reveled in her strong yet feminine frame ambling beside him, her wavy, sun-dappled hair twisted in a bun, her brown eyes holding questions he longed to answer.

"You look beautiful today." He gazed at her as they passed alongside the baseball field and headed down toward the lake. Isaac spotted a hint of pink flush Julia's cheeks.

"Thank you." Her eyebrows scrunched in perplexed lines, but her lips formed a smile.

He glanced toward the rodeo arena set up for the day, where a crowd was gathering for the greased swine competition.

"Are you going to try that?" Julia asked.

Isaac enjoyed her mischievous grin. "Maybe. I won last year, you know."

Julia twisted her head, her eyes narrowed in rebuke. "You're not fooling me again. I don't believe you for a minute."

Isaac grinned. "You got me. I did try it once, though, over in St. Louis when I was about ten years old."

Julia chuckled. "I can just imagine. Did the pig survive?"

"Well, yeah, he survived my attempt at him, at least. The question is, how did *I* survive."

They reached the lake, and the band's music grew louder. Isaac raised his voice as he led her toward the west side, where a wood-planked white bridge had been set up as a station to award prizes at the end of the day.

"Well?" Julia prodded.

"It took me a good five minutes to even get my hands on the slimy rascal, and when I finally did, I somehow found a spot without much grease. I held on, and that old girl yanked me at least twenty feet across the dirt. Thing is, I'd just gotten some hand-me-down trousers from my cousin Tim, and they were a bit too big around my girth."

Julia touched her hand to her lips and smiled sympathetically. "Oh, no."

Isaac nodded. "Oh yeah. By the time that sow got done yanking me, my new trousers had traveled 'bout down to my ankles."

A laugh burst from Julia's mouth.

Isaac mocked a hurt look. "It was terribly embarrassing for a young boy."

Julia shook her head. "I'm sorry."

They reached the little bridge, and Isaac led her up the white planks. The sun smiled down, and a gentle breeze waltzed about the lake's waters. His hands gripping the railing, bedecked with red, white, and blue ribbons, he gazed out over the mass of people—most whose homes he'd helped raise, whose weddings he'd performed, or whom he'd prayed with after a tragedy.

Julia stood next to him, and Isaac remembered the last time they'd walked along the lake. The moon's, not the sun's, rays had lit their path, and a night overwrought with fear led to her collapsing into his eager arms. He'd longed to hold her, protect her all his days. How that moment of closeness had affected him, changed the course of his life.

He rotated to face her, and the sight of her eyes peering up at him made his knees feel feeble.

The corner of her lip turned in a grin. "Well, Parson, are you going to keep telling me embarrassing stories from your youth, or will you explain what this is all about? What on earth were Mr. and Mrs. Gaffin talking about?"

Isaac suddenly didn't know where to start. Should he explain about the vow? The peace he'd made with God? His plans to start a church and stop riding the circuit? The school?

His gaze moved over her face, and he

paused, stilled by the beauty that flowed from her remarkable heart and shone through the features he cherished—her bright eyes, smooth skin, slender waist, tender hands.

"You are so beautiful." The words breathed out in a whisper, almost before he realized they'd left his mind and moved to his tongue. He longed to touch her, to grasp her hand, to caress her cheek, but he knew he must wait to discover if she returned his feelings. His stomach churned with anxiety. "I just . . ." A thick gravel seemed to bury the words in his throat. "I want to—*need* to—tell you something."

A hint of fear, like waves in a brewing storm, spread in Julia's eyes—perhaps fear of being hurt or else simple uncertainty—and Isaac longed to still her worries, to calm the waves.

The lively band music slowed to a waltz, and Isaac paused, reaching for calmness from the slow tune. A draft of wind shifted a strand of hair to Julia's forehead, and Isaac tucked it behind her ear. The music came to an end, and all seemed to suspend in motionless silence.

Isaac's horse Virginia whinnied, as if asking for an encore, and then dipped her head again to drink from the lake.

"I love you," Isaac finally said, and in saying the words, his nervousness released and a downpour of contentment breezed over him. *Lord, whatever happens now, I trust You.*

A smile hinted on Julia's face, but her forehead still furrowed with confusion.

"I was wrong," he explained. "That vow I made was a result of my own fear. I wasn't trusting God, and so I held back from, well, loving you. But I've had some time lately to think, and pray, and read the Word, and I've learned that my 'stupid' vow—as Milo called it—was *my* idea, not God's." He smiled, unabashedly relinquishing the love in his gaze.

Julia leaned toward him, her eyes fixed on him as he spoke.

Isaac tilted his head. His voice softened. "I'm free to love, Julia. To marry, to serve a wife the rest of my days—if one will forgive me." He held her hand, which trembled under his touch. "If you will have me."

Julia's chin quivered. Her eyes

shimmered. "Isaac." She squeezed his hand, and Isaac's heart thumped against his chest.

"That night when we rescued Bea," he trailed the backs of his fingers over Julia's cheek and down her jawline, "my feelings for you were so strong. I never should've let you go. I love you, Julia. It started the moment you drenched my handkerchief at the hotel."

Julia chuckled.

"And it grew as I witnessed your tender care of me on the night of the storm, your kindness to the children, your bravery with the buffalo. I'd be honored—humbled—if you'd accept my love."

Julia smiled into his eyes, relief and joy filling her face. "Isaac, I—"

But before she could finish, a grimy hand grabbed her arm, smudging the ivory fabric. The hand's owner peeked around as he yanked Julia to him. *Horace.* Isaac had been so caught up in Julia's nearness that he hadn't even heard the miner approach.

"Parson Ike?" The all-too-familiar gruff voice blasted Isaac's ears. "What you doin' with my wife?" The hope that had been cresting in Isaac's chest came crashing like a horse with a broken leg. *What now?*

Horace didn't wait for an answer. And before Isaac could comprehend what was happening, the old miner tugged at Julia and stomped off the bridge, lugging her with him.

"No, stop! Let go of me," Julia squealed. She reached for Isaac. "Stop him!"

Isaac hurried after them, but he'd taken only three steps when his foot caught on a loose plank in the bridge. He felt his body flying forward. His right knee hit first, then his elbow and his cheek. His head seemed to bounce off the ground, and his eyes lost focus. *Julia.* Pushing away thoughts of the pain, he jumped to his feet and grabbed the rail, trying to regain his footing once again.

"I done waited long enough! I paid fer her. I been real nice—writin' letters, comin' to call."

Horace moved with remarkable speed to the horse and hoisted Julia onto the saddle. Issac hurried after. "Horace, no, wait!"

Horace acted like he hadn't heard. "Comes a time when a man's got to collect his claim," he called as he hurled himself behind Julia. "I'm jest borrowin' this here horse. I'll bring 'er back. Don't worry 'bout that."

"Horace! Wait!"

"Next time you see me, I'll be a married man!" Horace reached around Julia, grabbed the reins, hollered, and then jabbed his heels into Virginia. The horse and her passengers took off in a gallop.

* * * *

"Isaac!" Julia screamed as she twisted toward him. He ran after her, yelling at Horace to stop, but Horace didn't hesitate.

Sitting on the back of the saddle behind her, Horace steered the horse past the bandstand, and Julia spied Sarah Mack. First shock, then anger, then disappointment flashed on the woman's face. Julia's heart sank with pity for the poor woman. The last thing Julia wanted to do was steal Sarah's man—she had her own now. Well, almost. If she could just get the opportunity to give him an answer.

"Horace." She leaned back and spoke above the galloping hoofbeats.

"No point in tryin' to talk me out o' it."

"Listen to me." She knew her words needed to be quick and to the point. "Sarah loves you, Horace. And I think you love her. Why don't you let me go? You can be with her. She would make a wonderful wife."

Julia glanced back and saw Isaac racing after them on foot. He paused as he approached the group of picnickers, most likely asking them for help. Soon a posse of country folks, all dressed in their Sunday best, hurried behind him.

"Horace, look! Look behind us!" Julia turned around. Even the band members had put down their instruments and rushed down the road. Sarah skulked behind, her head lowered beneath Julia's parasol.

Horace slowed the horse but only slightly. "You say Sarah loves me?"

"Yes! She told me so. We were looking for you earlier today so she could tell you herself."

"Nah! You're jest sayin' that so I'll let you go."

Julia spied Christopher sprinting ahead of them, calling to the group of people near the sheep arena. A throng of cowboys, ranchers, and soldiers, as well as a brigade of prairie women, their unbridled protectiveness showing in their fierce stamps, formed a wall in front of Horace.

"You stop right there, Horace Whitbaum!" one of the cowboys hollered.

"Hold up, you nasty old gold miner!"

With nowhere to go, Horace angled the mare around and attempted to head back the way he came, but the posse of musicians and partygoers halted him from that direction. Finally Isaac raced forward and grabbed Virginia's bridle.

Julia slid off and raced to him. "Thank you, thank you." She clutched his arm, not wanting to let go.

Isaac winked. "I couldn't let you marry a prospector before I got an answer out of you."

Despite the chaos with Horace, Julia's heart overflowed with unexpected joy. A week ago—an hour ago—she wouldn't have dared hope for Isaac to gaze at her with those loving eyes. Her heart longed for him—for his affection, companionship, and love—and now here he was offering those cherished gifts to her. *Lord, You have blessed me beyond what I deserve.*

But before she could share her heart with Isaac, there was a lonely gold miner who needed her help. Glancing up at Horace, she spied his lower lip poke out and in and a tear trickle down his cheek. Julia stepped next to him and patted his hand. "Get down, Horace. It'll be fine."

Horace labored out of the saddle and plopped to the dusty grass. "I jest wanted a wife, Parson Ike." He jutted his chin toward Isaac.

"You can't have her!" a child's voice piped out of the crowd, and Julia spotted Joshua. "She's marryin' my uncle Ike."

A laugh rolled through the crowd, and Julia tossed Isaac a smile.

Mr. and Mrs. Gaffin edged forward from the wall of people. "We're here to help, Julia," Mrs. Gaffin called. "Whatever you need, dear."

Julia nodded to her then turned her attention back to Horace, aiming her gaze into his eyes. "Do you love Sarah Mack?" she asked quietly.

Horace's eyes grew large. "Yes, o' course I do. What red-blooded man wouldn't? But she's too fine a lady fer me. That's why I picked a skinny city girl, like you." His voice was taut with sincerity, not insult. "But it seems you love our parson. Guess he's a good pick, even though I doubt he would treat you as good as old Horace, though."

Julia tilted her head. "I've got some good news, Horace." She glanced up, searching the crowd for Sarah. Finding her hiding underneath the parasol, Julia walked to her and clutched her hands. "Come on." Behind Sarah, Julia spotted Elizabeth ambling toward the crowd, probably investigating what all the commotion was about. Miriam sat in a rocking chair by the firepit, watching as she held little Liberty.

Sarah shook her head. "No, I just can't."

Julia finally placed the two reluctant sweethearts in front of each other. "Horace, go ahead. Tell her how you feel."

Horace peered at Isaac.

"Go on, Horace. You can do it." Isaac motioned for him to remove his hat.

Horace obeyed then glanced at Sarah Mack, who peeked from under the parasol. "Well, Sarah. I'm guessin' you already know what I'm wantin' ta tell ya." He dipped down, trying to catch her gaze. "Will you move that blasted umbrella?"

Sarah thrust it in front of her and closed it. Her face beamed, and her cheeks glowed like cherries.

"Well, I love ya dearly, Sarah." Horace moseyed to her and held her hands. "I always have. I know yer too fine fer me, but if you want me, you can have me."

Sarah burst into a torrent of sobs. "Oh, Horace. Of course. I love you, too."

A broad, toothless grin spread over Horace's face, and he took the woman into his thick prospector's arms.

The crowd clapped and a few hats flew up in the air.

"Isn't that the sweetest thing." Mrs. Gaffin fanned herself. "Even the gold miner found someone."

After a moment of embracing and taking in the cheers, Horace bolted upright. "Hold up!" He glared at Julia. "I done paid fer you. Where's my money?"

Sarah tapped his arm. "Oh, Horace, dear, does it really matter?"

"It's the principle. A man's gotta get somethin' when he pays out."

Mr. Gaffin ambled up. "I'm sorry, my good man." He pulled out his black leather wallet and removed several bills. "This was all a misunderstanding, and I'd be happy to repay you. Plus a little extra for your trouble." He handed the money to Horace, who accepted it and showed Sarah. "Now alls we've got to do is get us hitched."

Sarah raised her chin. "Anytime."

"Well, why not now?" He shifted toward Isaac. "Parson Ike, you up fer a wedding on this Independence Day?"

"Yeah, Parson Ike, let's have a wedding!" a woman in the crowd called.

Isaac's gaze met the two would-be newlyweds, and he nodded. "I would be happy to marry you tonight, but. . ." He sauntered to Julia and clasped her hands in his. "I'm going to collapse if I don't get an answer from this woman." His eyes locked with hers, and he touched her face. Julia's heart skipped and bounced.

"What's the question, Parson?" a voice from the crowd blared.

Undaunted, Isaac held Julia's gaze. "Julia, I love you. Will you be a parson's wife—my wife?"

All her fears and expectations, all her longings for a home, all her worrying about the future disappeared in the showers of blessing this moment contained.

"Yes, of course I will marry you."

Isaac's arms encased her and lifted her feet from the ground in a burst of happiness.

"Julia." He set her back down. "Finally, *my* Julia." He gently ran his hands down her neck and to her shoulders. "You've made me so happy."

Julia's hands smoothed over his chest and behind his neck.

"I love you, Isaac Shepherd."

Isaac's strong hands gently enclosed her face, his fingers edging into her hair. He gazed at her with a look that spoke not only of love, but also commitment, protection, and gratitude. He slowly leaned close. Julia closed her eyes as his soft lips pressed against hers, and she was lost in the bliss of the long-awaited moment. And in that kiss, Julia felt herself promise to love, serve, and stand by this man for the rest of her life.

"Miss Cavanaugh!" Two tiny arms clasped Julia's legs, breaking the moment, and Julia looked down to see Bea. "You kiss Uncle Ike on the lips?"

Isaac's arm still clutched Julia to his side as the spectators to the "event" cheered.

Shelby and Elizabeth joined them. "I know." Shelby scooped Bea into her arms. "Isn't that silly? Big people do that sometimes." Shelby gave Julia a one-armed embrace. "I knew he was the one."

"Congratulations, Julia." Elizabeth gave Julia a smile then glanced up toward the ranch.

Julia followed her gaze and saw Miriam wiping her cheeks.

Mrs. Gaffin also rushed to Julia. "I'm so happy for you, my dear, dear girl!" She squeezed her so tight, Julia thought she'd never breathe again.

"Make it a double wedding, tonight," a voice hollered.

Julia glanced up at Isaac, who caressed her shoulder. "I think a fine church wedding will suit us. Am I right?" he asked.

Julia rested her head against his chest, relishing his scent and the security of his embrace. "I don't care. As long as I'm with you."

"Well, Parson Ike?" Horace piped in. "What about us?"

Julia pulled back, and Isaac faced the couple. "Horace, Sarah, let's get you two hitched. And then," he added with a wink, "fireworks."

Epilogue

The smell of freshly cut lumber greeted Isaac as he walked into the small building that would be used for both a school and a church. Julia stood by the paned window, the light from the spring sunshine bringing out touches of gold in her brown hair. Isaac felt the return of a smile that had frequented his face since last Fourth of July, and he hurried next to her. Wrapping an arm around her waist, he peered over her shoulder to see what she was looking at.

"I don't believe I've ever seen a prettier

sight." She leaned back against him, resting her head against his shoulder.

Isaac took in the view of Lonesome Lake and the small house not far from its shore. "Within a few weeks we'll be living there as husband and wife."

Julia stepped forward and turned around, her small hands resting in his gentle grip. "Speaking of which, I need to head over to Aponi's house. I hear everyone's there, including Mrs. Gaffin. I still can't believe she and Mr. Gaffin made the trip for our wedding, but I'm so glad she did. It wouldn't be right without her."

Isaac fingered her cheek, soaking in the joy in her eyes. "It'll be a perfect wedding." He sent her a smile. "Because you will be the most beautiful bride. My most beautiful bride."

Julia nuzzled her head against his chest. "All our friends will be there, too. That also makes it perfect."

"Yes, very true." He kissed her forehead. "I only hope Jim and Mabelina will make it back from Fort Benton in time."

"I'm sure they will. Parson Jim wouldn't miss his first time officiating a marriage, would he?" Julia glanced at a clock on the wall. "Anyway, the ladies are working on my dre . . ." Julia pressed her lips together and swatted his arm. "Never mind I said anything. It's supposed to be a surprise."

"What is?" He winked.

"Perfect. Thank you for forgetting so quickly. It'll keep me out of trouble with the ladies."

He placed her hands around his waist and moved his hands up her back to her shoulders.

She beamed up at him. "Can you believe school will start a week after the wedding? This has to be the best May I've ever had."

"Better than last May when you first met a handsome but rude parson?"

Julia chuckled. "Just slightly." She gave him a kiss on the cheek and then wiggled out of his hold and hurried to the door. "You going to be staying in here long?" she called back over her shoulder.

"Not too long. I promised Elizabeth we'd make it to dinner. I guess she was teaching Shelby how to make chicken pot pie today and we're the first victims—er, I mean, tasters."

Julia's laughter followed her outside into the bright May morning. "I love you, Parson," she called.

"And I love you, Julia." She was already gone when he added, "with all my heart."

Isaac strolled to the front of the room and sat on the first wooden pew, amazed things had come together as quickly as they had—even after he thought the idea of a school was gone forever.

The first step to making this building possible was Warren Boyle's arrest in Big Sandy. Isaac heard it had happened not a week after Mabelina's July fourth trial. Turned out that although he hadn't mentioned it, Judge Booker had an inkling he'd seen Warren's face before. After sorting through a stack of Wanted posters, he'd finally found it: Warren *James* wanted for bank robbery in Texas.

Isaac stood and walked to the pulpit, tracing his finger over the expertly carved wood. His brother-in-law Jefferson had labored on it for a month, wanting Isaac's first real pulpit to have a "God-honoring beauty."

Isaac knew the love of family was a huge part of the happiness he felt. He only wished Warren would've accepted the love his own family offered. Instead, he sought worldly gain and had tried his best to secure it any way he could—first by stealing money in Texas, then by stealing Milo's house from Aponi and her daughters.

But within days of Mabelina's trail, Warren was sentenced to ten years in some hot Texas prison. Isaac mourned the loss of his best friend's son and continued to write letters to him, always sharing the gospel. He hadn't heard back from Warren, but he continued to pray for the man's soul.

After Warren was taken away, the responsibility for the care of Aponi and the girls had fallen to Isaac, a position he was glad to assume. And his first task was to reunite the girls with their mother. The look of utter joy on Aponi's face when the girls came running toward her after their months away at the boarding school—well, Isaac wouldn't soon forget it.

"Parson Ike," Aponi had told him later, "I need no house in town. I wish for one by the lake, close to my friends."

Aponi's new house had been completed by September.

The next order of business was for Isaac to cancel Warren's order for a new tavern and transfer the shipment to its original order for school supplies. When the supplies arrived some weeks later, Isaac was shocked to discover that his good friend Milo had ordered not only supplies for the school, but also plans for a small parsonage for Isaac.

"A home," Julia had told him the first time she looked over the plans. "A home for us, Isaac. What did we ever do to deserve it?"

"Nothing." He shook his head. "That's what grace is all about—getting what you don't deserve."

And now it was all reality—the school, Isaac's position as permanent parson, Aponi's house, and the parsonage, which he would soon share with Julia, close to the lake.

He leaned forward against the pulpit and bowed his head, again humbled by the showers of blessings. "Thank You, Lord."

Isaac strode to the door. His family was

waiting. He wouldn't be late for dinner, and as much as he wanted to tease her, he'd refrain from sneaking in to catch a glimpse of Julia's dress. He'd wait and see it next Sunday as she stood across from him here in this room, as two once-lonely souls were united as one.

Isaac again glanced out the window at the lake and beyond to the vast prairie. *You know*, he thought to himself, *perhaps Lonesome Prairie's not the best name for this place anymore.* He smiled to himself. *No, I don't think it is.*